Autumn Falling

Written by Nikki Norman

Autumn Falling

Nikki Norman

Published by Nikki Norman, 2023.

AUTUMN FALLING

First edition. May 6, 2023.

Copyright © 2023 Nikki Norman.

ISBN: 979-8988186700

Written by Nikki Norman.

Chapter 1:

So, here I am, waiting for my life to begin. Actually, I'm waiting for my flight to depart, but you can see why it's sort of the same thing. I've been living this life for twenty-five years, but it feels like my life is just starting now. I'm on my way to start on a career that I've always wanted in a city that I've never been to, and I've never been more excited. I couldn't even sleep last night; I was so anxious. After graduating in December and moving back to a place that I hadn't lived in seven years, things were looking bleak. It's amazing how life can change with one phone call and an interview via video conference.

Perhaps I should introduce myself since we're becoming friends. My name is Autumn Blaire. So about now you're picturing a white girl, right? Well, don't. I am 5'5". At least that's what my license says. I'm really 5'3". I weigh one hundred and twenty-three pounds. I used to have black hair, but th8anks to Garnier Nutrisse, it's sangria now. I have slanted eyes, which would make you think there was a hint of Asian ancestry somewhere, but no dice. Anyway, on to my complexion. By that I mean skin tone. I am what now would be described as chocolate. When I was little, and light skin was in, I was called a tar baby. But since black is back, I'm suddenly gorgeous to the very same people that tried to make me self-conscious about my melanin levels when I was a child.

Now on to deeper things, since self-description makes me uncomfortable. I have two sisters, a very strong mother and grandmother, a grandfather that remembers the days when men were men, and a father who is trying to be a man.

My mother made sure that we went to church every Sunday with my father's mother, even though she never went herself. "Do as I say, not as I do" was a very popular philosophy. My grandmother is a God-fearing, hard-working, and stubborn woman. She has never forgotten when someone has owed her money, but she'll lose her glasses while they're sitting on her face. Don't get me wrong, she is generous. She also believes that God will always make a way. That's where her strength comes from.

My mother has been taking care of others since she was thirteen. This woman would literally give you the food out of her refrigerator. She is also one of the most cynical people I know. An odd mix if I do say so myself. See, I think that she's been taking care of other people for so long that she doesn't know how to stop. She needs to be needed. She also sees the bad in everyone. She sees it, and she accepts it, because she knows that no matter how much bad there is in someone else, you should still show them the good in you. She taught me that I should8 never let others dictate my actions. My mother is the strongest person I know, because love her or hate her, she doesn't make excuses for being who she is

My grandfather never went beyond the third grade in school and believes that education is the most important thing in the world. When I was seven, he came home with a fox skin. I asked him where foxes live, and he got an encyclopedia, and made me copy every word from the section on the red fox. I never asked him another question. He also believes that a man is a provider, but not a nurturer. So, he isn't very sentimental, and while we all know that he loves us, I have never heard him say it. But I have felt his love for me every day of my life. My grandfather is the reason that I trust actions more than words.

My father is still trying to figure out who he is. It wouldn't be a problem if he weren't fifty-five. He is a good person, but he is a weak man, and a terrible father. Contradictory, right? He's mostly just selfish, but only when it comes to his wife and children. He's very generous to his nieces, 8nephews, friends, and hell, even strangers. My father doesn't work, but then, he doesn't have to. When he was seventeen, he lost the pinkie and part of his ring finger on his right hand in an accident at a factory he was working at. He also did permanent damage to the nerves in that hand. He was awarded a settlement for what I assume was a large chunk of money, and he collects disability.

My parents are what I refer to as ghetto separated. You will find this situation in any number of homes in America. There is no divorce, no formal separation of any kind, the wife simply bags up the husband's belongings, changes the locks, and informs him that he no longer lives in the previously inhabited home. They've been this way since I was ten. My sisters and I are what these people have made us. Prideful, strong, conscious, sympathetic, and a little crazy. Not the: you so crazy, ha ha funny crazy either. The: need to be on a couch telling Dr. Phil about our dreams of dancing soap, crazy.

Now, for the reason I'm in this airport. Better yet, the destination. I am on my way, to Peachtree City, Georgia. Yes, that is the actual name of a town. I recently got a job in Atlanta. Well, I didn't so much as get this job, as it was handed to me. You will be disgusted to know that nepotism is alive and well. I will leave the name of my new employer out of this, but I will tell you that I will be working in advertising. My aunt, great aunt actually, has worked her magic, and pulled a career out of her Coach bag for me. She is retired from this company, but still has enough pull there that her suggestions carry a lot of weight. She and my mother are only three years apart in age, and when my mother moved from my great grandmother's home into my grandmother's home, they lost touch. Apparently, my grandmother wasn't that close to her little sister. They have since reconnected, five years ago in fact, and are once again, very close. This works out well for me.

I have found and rented a town house in a gated community called Melody Villas with my aunt's help. She had to scout it for me since I was living on Long Island. This should be interesting considering all I could afford was a full-sized bed, a nightstand, television, futon, and coffee table to start out. Thank God this place comes with a refrigerator. If it didn't, I'd starve. Not that I can cook. I am however the microwave gourmet.

It's funny that I can't cook, since I think I have a four-hundred-pound sumo wrestler living in my stomach. Maybe I'll buy a Foreman Grill, do the cooking made easy thing. Learning to cook never appealed to me. Then again, neither did any of the other things that most women loved to do when they were little girls in body not just in heart. I spent most of my time reading and writing when I was a kid. I can't cook, I rarely clean (since you'll probably come over to visit, I thought that I should tell you), I can corn braid, but I have no interest in doing hair. I generally settle for a blowout and a wrap; I am also a ponytail princess. My sisters, however, are really good in the kitchen. Those talents apparently skip certain members in a family. But that's okay, as long as Chinese restaurants deliver, and there are pre-made meals, I will survive.

Okay, so they're calling for my flight to board. Don't take this the wrong way, I mean as much as I love talking about me, given that you aren't the best conversationalist, I think I'll sleep on the flight. See you when we land at Hartsfield-Jackson.

Chapter Two:

This airport has a Disney Store. Personally, I find that to be a little strange, but hey, look who's talking, right?

The thing that I hate about airports is this, it feels like the plane that I'm on always lands and goes to the gate farthest from the baggage claim, and then I'm stuck with the carry-on bag that, when I packed it, seemed to be relatively light weight, but becomes like a cement block with a strap on it as I make my way to the rest of my belongings that are conveniently located four miles away.

As I'm making my way through the airport, attempting not to fall over from the weight of my bag, I spot a sign that says: 'to baggage claim'. As I'm turning toward the escalator, I see the most beautiful man I've ever laid my eyes on, and he's white. I am not one of those women that get angry when she sees a black man with a white woman, or vice versa. I've just never been as attracted to anyone as I am to this particular man, and I'm not usually attracted to white guys.

When I say that he's white, I mean like straight-up white. He is about 6'2", I give him a solid one hundred and eighty pounds, he has black hair, and it's cut in that marine boot camp kind of way. He has a neatly shaped up goatee that reminds me of the baseball players I went to college with, smooth skin, and c2lear green eyes. Right about now, I'm realizing that while I'm staring at him, he's walking toward me. Awkward. I should look away, but I don't; what the hell, I'm already embarrassed right?

I notice his clothes, and there's something about this guy that screams geek. He is wearing a shirt that should be illegal. The thing is black, button-up, and actually has multi-colored bowling pins and flames on it. His jeans look comfortably worn in and on his feet are what have to be the oldest Vans in the history of the walking man. But then his lips move, and everything superficially offensive about him fades away.

"Hello."

It's said with this southern drawl and is accompanied by a half smirk that makes me almost forget to breathe.

"Yeah, hi. So, I was just wondering if you could tell me of a shorter way to get to the baggage claim, 'cause my shoulder is about to fall off." Not exactly true, but apparently when embarrassed, I lie with ease. *Scary isn't it?*

"Oh," he sounds a bit disappointed, "you could take the train."

"I'm sorry, what?"

"The train." He's looking at me like I'm off in the head, and I'd be offended, but I'm still trying to understand why we felt the need to build an airport that is so large that it needs a train. I don't respond, and he's clearly becoming impatient, so he continues. "If you want, I'll show you to the train, I'm going that way so it's no trouble."

"Thank you." I'm about to tell him how much I appreciate his help, when he takes my bag off my shoulder, takes my arm, and starts leading the way.

I now realize that chivalry is rude.

I appreciate the fact that he took the boulder off my shoulder, but could I have gotten a warning first? Not from around here and where I'm from if somebody takes the bag off your shoulder, they usually run with it. But okay, I can be very forgiving if the man is good looking enough, and he so is. We get to the bottom of the escalator, and the digital sign over the door to the train says that the next train will arrive in thirty seconds. When it arrives, and the doors open, he takes my arm again, and leads me to a bench like seat at the back of the train. I feel the need to introduce myself to him, possibly because it should have been done already, but since he's the one with all the southern hospitality, I was expecting him to start the introductions. Since he's not, I will.

"Autumn", I say it with as much courtesy as I can muster considering the fact that despite this man being gorgeous, he's still a little too rude for my liking. I extend my hand and wait for him to shake it like a normal human being. He doesn't shake it. He doesn't even look in my direction, he just answers with a grunt. Not a mumble, or an intelligible name, but a grunt.

"Yeah, so can I get my bag back please? I really appreciate all your help, but I think I can manage from here." I have had just about all I can stand from tall, rude, and gorgeous.

"No problem. Anytime."

He's still not deigning to look at me, but at least he didn't speak Wookiee this time, and now I am in possession of the heaviest carry-on known to man again.

The rest of the train ride passes without incident, and now I'm just waiting for my baggage to come circling around the carousel. And waiting. And waiting. And it's been about a half hour and I realize that due to the beauty of air travel and computer-generated tags, my luggage is not coming. It is in fact doubtful that my luggage is even in this state. I make my way over to the customer service counter for Delta Airways and wait behind three irate people. While the man in front of the line is banging on the counter and demanding that someone pull a Houdini and make his luggage appear from Jamaica, I decide that maybe I should call my aunt and tell her what happened since she's picking me up.

"Hello?"

"Hello, Aunt Mae. This is Autumn. I'm at the customer service desk for Delta. My luggage never came out, and I didn't want you to worry that I missed my flight or anything."

"Well that's no problem. Let me call Daniel and tell him where you are. I wasn't feeling well so I asked him to pick you up for me. Do you remember what he looks like?"

I have not seen my cousin Daniel since I was about three and we went to Alabama to visit my great-grandparents for Christmas. But I don't want to tell the aunt that just got me a job that I can't remember what her only son looks like.

"I sure do. Could you have him meet me where I am if that's not a problem?" small lie, I hope.

"I don't see why that would be a problem. Let me call him, and I'll give you a call back."

"Thank you, Aunt Mae." I hang up the phone, and pray that he'll recognize me, because I know damn well I won't recognize him.

While I'm waiting for my aunt to call me back, my attention is drawn again to the insane man banging on the counter. He is actually holding up a tape recorder and demanding that the woman behind the counter speak clearly. *A tape recorder!* He looks very unassuming, but those are always the ones you see on the news that go ballistic.

He's maybe 5'9", wearing wire rimmed glasses and a sweater vest. He's got on some Docker's and construction boots that have seen better days. There's something about him that reminds me of a character from a Dean Koontz novel, and now I'm freaking myself out. He's getting really pissed about his missing luggage, and the fact that he fits the profile of a serial killer has me wondering if my clothing is really that important. The other thing that has me freaked out is that the other people in the line aren't freaked out, while the woman behind the counter clearly is. Southern hospitality? I don't think so. And they say that New Yorkers are hostile? Like I said before, I'm from Long Island, and if I were there right now there would at least be a man or another woman putting that jackass in his place.

I suck my teeth as loud as I can and mutter "asshole" in a less than conservative whisper. That got his attention, but now that I have it, I don't think I want it. I, however, never did know when to shut up, so I put my hand on my hip, turn up my nose, and wait for the argument that I know is coming to begin.

"Look little girl, this doesn't concern you. You best just mind your business." He has this smooth southern accent, and he's actually being condescending.

"Considering the fact that your insanity is holding up the line, and you're not the only one with lost luggage, it does concern me. Your bag is in Milwaukee, she told you that. You will have it back at the latest tomorrow morning, she told you that. It will be delivered to you, she told you that. You have to file an insurance claim if anything is missing, she told you that. The fact that you are being a raving lunatic is not helping your situation, and the tape recorder is just creepy, 'cause unless you work for the Daily Planet, there's no reason for you to have that. Stop your bitching and take the claim ticket that she's handing you so that this line can move, and I can find out where the rest of my shit is, because unlike you, standing in a customer service line, and making an issue out of something that I can't control is not the high point of my day. I have other things to do, and you are keeping me from doing them. Suck it up you freaking whiner." I finally stop talking because the need to breathe was becoming overbearing.

I think I managed to upset the psycho. He's got this expression on his face like he's in church listening to the preacher curse from the pulpit. It's almost funny, except he's still just standing there holding up the line and staring at me. I watch this idiot compose himself, and then I listen as he starts talking to me as though I'm a small child.

"Little girl, I'm sure that you're probably just tired, and so I'll excuse your rude behavior. Now if you don't mind, I'm trying to resolve an issue with the woman behind the counter."

I know he is not talking to me as though I were a small child in the middle of a temper tantrum. *Now I'm offended.*

"Are you serious right now? Listen you ass puppet—"

"Autumn?"

Whatever I am about to say is cut short by the male voice that calls my name from the doorway. I turn around to see, who I assume is, my cousin Daniel looking very amused.

"Are you responsible for this rude young lady, sir?" this, again, from the jackass at the counter.

"I'm sorry sir, you'll have to excuse my cousin, she's from New York." My cousin has the gall to look embarrassed.

I have recently been promoted from offended, to pissed off.

"First of all, don't ever apologize for me. Second of all, I was not being rude. I was being impatient. He was being rude." As defenses go, it was a weak one. Kind of a, well he hit me first, kindergarten defense.

"Look, I just feel that an airport is not the proper place to start a conflict. In the interest of everyone involved, perhaps we should just let this matter, whatever it is, go." Daniel looks sincere enough."

"Fine." I say it with a twist in my neck, just making sure he knows I'm aggravated. The rest of the time in the customer service office is spent in silence.

So, here's the story of my cousin Daniel: he's thirty-five, technically single, and good-looking. He's my complexion and stands just under six feet tall with sculpted cheekbones and warm brown eyes. He graduated in the top of his class from St. Johns University where he majored in business law, and he passed the bar on his first try after attending Harvard Law. He worked for some large corporation for a while, and for all intents and purposes was doing very well, until the stress of it got to him and he quit. He's a dog-groomer now. Less money, less stress, new semi-girlfriend that happens to be a stripper named Delightful.

You are probably wondering how I can know all of this, but I couldn't remember what the man looked like, right? Simple, I come from a large family. Meaning that the only way we communicate is through inside gossip. You should also know that my aunt is completely heartbroken by my cousin's recent activities, but she's pretending to be unaffected because she doesn't want to push away her only child.

In case you were wondering about the luggage situation, they say I should be receiving my luggage at my home in a few hours, tomorrow at the latest. For some reason it was put on a later flight from JFK. I'm glad that I don't start work until next week. It would be awkward to walk in naked on my first day. I gave myself a week so that I could adjust to the ride to work, buy some food, unpack my menial belongings, and get a car. Yeah, I don't have a car yet. I have money for a car, or at least for car payments. My uncle has agreed to take me car shopping the day after tomorrow. I can't wait.

We're sitting in the car, riding to my townhouse, in non-companionable silence. He keeps shifting his eyes from the road to me and back again. I can't stand it anymore.

"What?" I hear myself, and I'm surprised that I don't sound annoyed.

"Huh? Nothing. I just wanted to know if you were still upset by what happened at the airport. My mother really wants you to feel comfortable with us, since we're the only family you have here, and I was just hoping you wouldn't tell her that I offended you."

His sincerity is starting to look a little practiced, but he is right. They are the only family that I have here. They're the only people that I know in this entire state, and what's scary is that I really don't know them. But since I don't want my mother getting upset over anything happening between Daniel and myself, I'll be nice.

"Don't worry about it. I don't hold grudges; besides, you were only trying to help." I am now mentally patting myself on the back for making my tone so light and convincing.

I totally hold grudges.

"Good, I'm glad you understand that I was only doing what was best. You're very mature." He says this while not taking his eyes off the road, but he looks (at least from a side perspective) to be surprised.

That: "you're very mature", comment has me gritting my teeth. Do I look like a five-year-old? Okay, let me calm down. He doesn't know me, so he can't know what will offend me, right?

With visible effort, I smile and say, "thank you."

"Oh, and I can't take you home yet. My mother asked me to bring you to the house so that y'all could talk."

"I can't, I need to be at my apartment when the airport sends my things, and I need to straighten out my apartment and buy food." I'm genuinely flustered. I wasn't expecting this. Maybe I would have been expecting it if my aunt had picked me up, but the fact that I clearly heard her say that she didn't feel well put that to rest.

"The airport will call before they come, your furniture is already put away, and my mother went food shopping for you. She talked to your mother to find out what kinda food you like." He says all of this as if it's the most natural thing in the world.

I guess to them, it is.

"Okay then." Really, what else could I say?

Chapter Three:

This house is bananas. I mean, from the outside it looks like every other house on the street. For all I know, they may all look the same from the inside too... but damn. You can see the houses from the street, but only because they're sitting so high up. They look like they belong in the Hamptons. When we walked into the house, our footsteps echoed. I looked up at the vaulted foyer ceiling and saw the most beautiful fifteen light chandelier I had ever seen. Don't get me wrong, I'm not a complete stranger to expensive possessions or large homes, but this is still amazing. To think of where my aunt came from, this tiny town in Alabama, and to see where she is now, it's awesome.

"Mom, we're here," Daniel shouts, and I can hear that footsteps aren't the only thing in this house that echo.

I'm not trying to throw dirt, but why do two people need this much space?

My aunt walks into the room... and she's all smiles. She is a very beautiful woman, who looks to be in her late thirties. If anyone told me that she was fifty-two, I wouldn't believe it. She has my mother's eyes, with that Asian slant. Those eyes that are so dark brown that they seem black. And she has dimples. She's healthy-thick, not too fat or too skinny. About an inch taller than me, and about a hundred and fifty pounds. She's wearing black cotton Capri pants, a sleeveless black blouse with gold embroidery along the neckline, and black and gold sandals. Minolo Blahnik sandals.

I should probably tell you that I have a thing for shoes. Expensive shoes that I can barely walk in.

"Hi, Aunt Mae. I was surprised that you wanted me to come over after you said that you weren't feeling well," I hug her as I say it. I don't want her to think that this is a complaint.

"Of course, I wanted to see you. It probably could have waited until tomorrow, but I have something for you."

Good she's still smiling. Not offended.

"Daniel said that you all unpacked the things in my apartment for me, thank you so much, I really appreciate that, but you didn't need to go to all of that trouble. You've already done more than enough for me." I really do appreciate everything that she's done. Even if one of those things was to raise a jackass and release him on the world.

"Baby, this is what you do for family. Anyway, I wanted you to be able to spend a lot of time here before you go to work next week, and you couldn't do that if you were unpacking. Now stop with that and come on into the den."

I'm following her through the house and trying to assess everything around me without being too obvious. It's difficult to say the least.

We arrive at the den, and I find myself in what has always been referred to as the living room in my household. There is a couch, a loveseat, several end tables and comfortable looking chairs complete with footstools. They have a fireplace, and above the mantle, is one of those mounted singing fish that were popular well over a decade ago. And that one thing makes me feel at home.

"Please have a seat," she gestures to the love seat, "are you hungry? We can barbecue. Earnest bought steaks from the grocery store earlier, and there's chicken. But first, open this." She hands me a small, gift-wrapped box.

Should I have gotten them gifts? Maybe this is why their airport resembles a mall. Now I feel like the girl in elementary school that didn't bring in a secret Santa gift, and hopes that no one, not even the person that is supposed to get the gift, notices.

"The box isn't going to bite. And don't worry; I wasn't expecting anything in return. This is a house-warming gift." She's still smiling and waiting for me to open the gift. There is a gold crucifix on an eighteen-inch chain in the box. The crucifix looks like interlocking hearts. I love it.

"Thank you. This is a wonderful house-warming gift."

"I'm glad you like it." And I can see by the look on her face that she is genuinely pleased.

There aren't many things that I know about my mother's side of the family. Like I said, my mother moved in with her mother as a teenager, and they went to Long Island. The rest of the family lived in the south, and so being separated from them by about a thousand miles; there weren't any Sunday dinner opportunities. The weird thing is my sisters and I grew up very close to my father's family. That being weird because my father wasn't exactly prevalent in our lives.

My aunt's husband enters the room at that moment, and lord, he's a bigun'. This man literally fills the doorway. He has a very military looking flat-topped haircut; he is wearing a polo shirt with tan slacks, and no shoes. His eyes are warm, reminding me of spiced rum. He has a pleasant smile and lifts me into a bear hug before I can get to my feet.

"Baby girl! It is so good to see you. My god you got so big. I haven't seen you since you were about three years old." His smile is so wide that I can count his teeth. It is a smile-inducing smile that pulls me in. These people seem to know what family is all about. The rest of the evening passes in anecdotes and peach cobbler. Before I know it, I am putting on my jacket and making my way to the door.

"Now, baby girl, I'll be 'round your house at nine to go looking for that car. If you want, I'll come earlier, and we can come back here for breakfast before we go." The offer is made by my uncle Earnest.

"Breakfast sounds great. What time should I be ready?" Like I said, I don't cook, so I'm not about to turn down a meal that's not microwaved.

"Eight o'clock then." He says this while nodding his head as if in confirmation to himself.

"I'll see you both then. Thank you for that wonderful dinner." I hug my uncle again and make my way out to my cousin's car.

Daniel is already in the driver's seat waiting for me. He looks upset. I think to ask him what's wrong, but it occurs to me that I don't care. The moment that his parents and I seemed to be enjoying each other's company, his mood became increasingly worse. Let him pout. You would think by the set of his jaw that he was a six-year-old pissed about having to share a toy that he didn't play with but denied others out of spite. The pouting is punctuated by glances in my direction and exaggerated huffing and puffing. Daniel is waiting for me to speak. I stare out of the window and watch scenery go by. Once at my apartment, Daniel hands me the keys that my aunt gave to him earlier for me and continues to pout. Thanking him for the ride, I get out, and make my way to my humble abode.

Upon entering the town house, I think I have the wrong place. There's furniture here. Nice furniture. It isn't new, but it doesn't seem very used either. Making my way through the rest of the house, I see a dining room set, a small kitchen set, several floor lamps, the living room furniture (couch, loveseat, armchair, coffee table, end table, ottoman, floor vase), and in the bedroom, besides the bed that is made and folded down, there is a vanity. Either this is the work of an extremely ass backward burglar, or my overly hospitable aunt has donated me furniture. I'm going to go with the aunt assumption. I don't think a burglar would bother to make sure that the living room furniture matched the strategically placed area rug in the dining room. In case you're wondering, my color theme is apparently hunter green and wine. Nice. I really should get her a card, or a punch bowl or something.

I am now thankful for the carry-on that could anchor the titanic. I take out an oversized t-shirt, underwear, and my headscarf. Get a comb and a brush and make my way to the shower. She even bought towels. My aunt should open up a bed and breakfast.

After my shower, the exhaustion overtakes me, and I am asleep before my head hits the pillow. I am awakened by the ringing of my phone. It's the airport. Or more specifically, a man that works for the airport. My luggage is at the gate; security won't let him through without a security access code. Thanks to the clock, ideally located at my bedside on a nightstand that I am unsure as to how I acquired, I can see that it is two-thirty in the morning. Son of a bitch. The problem is I don't know the damn security code for deliveries.

Shit.

I ask to speak to the guard, and after answering enough questions to be given clearance to the pentagon, the guard is satisfied that I am me, and I'm allowed to give approval for my delivery. I hope this day isn't an instance of foreshadowing, cause if it is, I should go back to Long Island now. But I'm no quitter. A gift and a curse.

The thing is, I'm a Capricorn, and I do believe in all that astrology crap. The thing about Capricorns is they will stick with a losing situation longer than any other sign, because they honestly believe that if they work hard enough, they can make it work. I looked all of this up during my last relationship. It was toward the end of it, and I was running out of reasons as to why we were just naturally butting heads on everything. The answer given by astrology was that since he was an Aries, the relationship was impossible romantically. I wish I had known that three years sooner. I was very angry by the end of the romance, because of the way it ended. We'll get into that later. Right now, I need to throw on some jeans, because my doorbell is ringing.

The delivery guy from the airport reeks of southern charm. I have always been put off by men that come on too strongly. My theory is that they are this way with all women, looking for as many screws as possible without having to work at getting to know any of their conquests beyond the answer to the question, "are you allergic to latex?" This guy is no different than the men that I've just described; he's just wrapped in a package that has a drawl. Don't get me wrong, he's attractive, but there's just that thing about him. You know, when you meet someone, and they seem perfectly nice, but you take an instant disliking to them anyway? Yeah... that's where I am with this guy right now. So, it's no wonder that I got him out of my house as soon as possible.

Do I seem a little uptight? I hope not. I wouldn't want you to get the wrong impression of me. I don't exactly have a padlock on my coochie or anything. I'm just selective. The delivery guy was making me feel like I had fallen into a porno from the seventies or something. The man actually looked me up and down, licked his lips, and smiled. Like I was supposed to open my door to some strange man, bat my eyes, and say, "here's my pussy, please take it as a tip", yeah right. I don't give a damn how many heavy suitcases his ass had to carry. I've never been so happy to see a person leave. I actually put the chain on my door after I closed it.

The problem with me is that I attract crazy people. Right before I left Long Island, a man waited for me outside of a bathroom at Target and told me I was beautiful and reminded him of his grandmother. When I told him that I was in a relationship, which we know isn't true but there's no rule saying I have to be honest with crazy people, this fool actually tried to follow me home. What the hell? So, I'm a little cautious. Wouldn't you be?

Now that all of my clothes are here, I guess I should put them away. If I leave it to do later, it won't get done. Guess I'll be a little tired at breakfast. I'm going to let you get some sleep though. No point in both of us being tired.

Chapter Four:

Well hello there. Good to know you haven't fallen off of the planet. It's been about three months since we last spoke; I have a lot to tell you. Work is going well. To a degree. We work in teams. Teams are good if everyone pulls their own weight. Not everyone on my team does. The teams each consist of ten people. There is the team leader, the team supervisor, the stat person, and everyone else. On my team, the supervisor is sleeping with the head of finance, and so he only does the bare minimum.

You were thinking I was talking about a woman, weren't you?

Nope, he's a man. A very worthless, very gay man. He is also so far in the closet that he may as well be a part of the wood grain in the back. The reason that I know he's gay isn't that I have some magnificent gay-dar. I know because he told me. One day, he notices my Jimmy Choo's, then comes up to me during my lunch, and after a few minutes of conversation, begins to vomit information to me. He has become my best friend here, in spite of the fact that, work wise, he's as useless as a knife in a gunfight. His name is Mark. His father is a Baptist minister, and his mother is a homemaker. As far as looks go, he's very all-American Gap ad. Blonde hair, blue eyes, roughly 6'1" tall, and very muscular. He even played football in high school and college. When he's with his parents, he watches football with his father while drinking Bud light. When he's with me, we watch project runway and drink apple martinis. Talk about a double life. Mark is twenty-seven; the guy he's seeing is almost fifty. This cradle robber is also married to a woman and has three children. Their situation gives me migraines.

My team leader is a forty-five-year old woman named Chelsea. She is happily widowed and never had children. She is a bit of a bitch, and I think that she Dr. Kevorkianed her husband. According to everyone, she was really miserable while he was alive. Then, he has an unexpected stroke at the ripe old age of forty-seven, and she is rejuvenated. Starts injecting more color into her wardrobe, changes her hair color, and makes it from team player to team leader within eighteen months. She also feels that Mark is worthless, but she can't do anything about him without screwing herself over. She hates me. I'm the stat player, which is actually a title on the team. The reason for my elevated status is not the nepotism that got me in the door; it's actually earned. I've had the position for six weeks now. She feels like I didn't deserve the position. Didn't pay enough dues so to speak, so she holds me responsible for everything from late reports to bad weather. I bite my tongue and do my job for two reasons. One: even though she is a possibly murderous hyena, she's also good at her job. Two: she has horrible taste in shoes, and so I could care less about her opinion of me. I recognize that the second reason may sound shallow, but the woman comes to work in black penny loafers.

The rest of the people on my team are pretty cool. Ages range from the youngest being twenty-three to the oldest being fifty-two. They are a very eclectic mix of people, most of them hard-working. Being there some days is tantamount to being on a soap opera.

There is one more person you should know about. Its name is Keyana Gray, and it is the most conniving bitch on the planet. At an unknown age, she is the most miserable person I've ever met. She is a team leader that I had the misfortune of working with on a project that my agency deemed too important for one team. She is a person that shouldn't be around other people. She speaks to everyone as if they were a particularly slow child, with whom she's run out of patience. That's enough to piss me off right there, but she goes further. She demands that everyone bend to her will at the immediate second she commands it, and if you're a person that refuses, straight to the vice-president of our division she goes.

I suspect that Keyana wasn't always bitter and evil. She has a long history in this business and has been with this company for at least five years. In those five years, she's pulled more ads than any other team. The problem is, she thinks she's doing it all by herself. She takes total credit, verbally, for each landed account, acting as if the people on her team are lucky that she's so good at her job. In the time that I've been here, five people have resigned from her team, or transferred to other teams. And get this; she refers to her team members as "the subordinates".

So that looks like everyone. Everyone at work anyway. On the personal front, there really isn't much to tell. That could be because most of my personal time is spent with a gay man. Speaking of which, I gotta get ready to go. I told Mark that I'd go with him to his friend's birthday party. It's at some club in Metro Atlanta that I've never been to. I bought this red jersey dress a few weeks ago that I'll finally get a chance to wear tonight. Wide neck, loose sleeves, loose on the top and open backed, but tight on the bottom. It stops mid-thigh, and it has a metal belt with interlocking disks that rests on my hips. I will be completing the look with a pair of silver Dolce and Gabana peep toes. The hair will be worn down with spiral curls. I've learned that if you do the spiral curl look when going to a club, where the atmosphere will undoubtedly be humid from all the sweat and smoke in the air, when your hair begins to frizz, it looks more contrived. Now, as I said, I've never been to this club before, so I can't predict the weather, but better safe than sorry. If you'll excuse me, I need to take a shower.

Chapter Five:

Why can't straight men look like gay men? I don't mean appear gay or anything like that...I mean the personal awareness that gay men have? I realize that not all gay men are svelte and well put together, but really. The gay men that I know take a certain pride in their appearance. These men are groomed and bathing suit ready. Don't believe me? Pay a visit to Fire Island. Straight men don't realize, most of them anyway, that the beer belly affects the way your shirt rises from behind. Those that exercise, don't realize when enough muscle mass is enough. Those that do take pride in their appearance are often vain and childish.

This is why I haven't had sex in ten months. Yeah, count 'em. Ten Months. Luckily, I have a rabbit, or I'd have gone insane eight months ago.

You're probably wondering where the gay men/straight men talk came from? This party. Not all the men are gay here. The club is full of straight men that dressed appropriately to gain entrance. But the men that are here for this party, most of them are a little on the feminine side. Okay...a lot on the feminine side. While this doesn't bode well for breaking my sexual dry spell, on the bright side, these are some of the nicest, funniest people I've met since coming here. The party is for Mark's friend Joshua. It's kind of a birthday slash coming out party. Apparently, he told his parents that he was gay a week ago, and they took it very well. His mother wasn't surprised, according to him; she said that she always knew. His father got drunk and made him promise not to bring his boyfriend to the house until he was dead. Joshua's father, not Joshua himself, because if he were dead, there'd be no way for him to bring his boyfriend over anyway. I don't see that as a win, but okay.

Mark looks uneasy. I think I'm the only person here that knows he hasn't come out to his family yet. I feel for him. He is possibly one of the best friends I've ever had, and I love him as a person, but I'm disgusted by his choices. I'm not talking about his being gay. I think for the majority of homosexuals there is no choice involved. I say the majority, because I know a good number of straight women, who after too many failed relationships with men, have turned to women trying to find that compassion and understanding that is sometimes so elusive with men. When I talk about Mark's choices, I'm speaking mainly about his relationships. The married man is current, but from what he's told me, there have been a lot of bad decisions in his personal life. There was a professor when he was in college, an intern at work, and when he was in high school and still trying to be straight, there was a married woman. His friend's mother in fact. He was sixteen; she got pregnant, terminated the pregnancy, and stopped seeing him. He told me that the reason she didn't keep it was because her husband was away on business a lot, and the date of her conception was about a month shy of when he would've been home to knock her up. Mark's life is like a Lifetime Original Movie.

The person to the right of me looks up to greet someone, and she's smiling so hard I can count her teeth. Since I'm nosy, I look to the left to see this miracle of perfection that she must be staring at, (because why else would she look like that?) and when I see his face, I choke on my drink. It's Mr. Tall, Rude, and Gorgeous. The guy from the airport who speaks fluent yakkastanesian. Any of this ringing a bell for you? Good. Once the pear mojito that I'm drinking safely makes its way into my lung, I stand and try to find Mark. He's not standing where I last saw him. Shit!

"Excuse me?"

I turn around and standing there is the gorgeous beast that I was trying to avoid. Plastering a smile on my face, I prepare to pretend as if I don't recognize this man.

"Yes?" Okay, doing good...

"You're not gonna pretend that you don't recognize me, are you? From the airport?"

Shit, shit, shit! And he's wearing that goddamned smirk, and I have just enough liquor in my system to think that it's sexy. *Where the fuck is Mark?*

"Actually, I was. But then again, I wasn't even aware that you had any intentions on speaking to me in a language that I could understand."

"What do you mean?" He looks amused.

This is in no way funny.

"The last words you spoke to me were in Wookiee or maybe Ewok." I say this while nodding my head slightly as if trying to recall the exact language choice.

He's laughing.

"Why are you laughing?" I'm really confused. I wasn't trying to be funny; I was going more for rude.

"I'm sorry. I was nervous. Not now I wasn't, at the airport I was." He's stammering, and it's the cutest thing I've seen in a while.

Definitely had too much to drink.

"Why were you nervous?"

"Because you're hot, and you were sitting right next to me, and I didn't know what to say to you, and you started getting pissed off that I wasn't saying anything, and that makes it harder to think of something to say, and by the time I thought of something you were walking off the train, and I wanted to follow you, but I would've missed my plane."

That was a lot.

"Wow. Um...wow. I don't really know what to say, which is odd...for me." Now I'm stammering.

"She's speechless. Well then, may I take advantage of this temporary break in judgment, and buy you a drink?"

I really shouldn't let him, right? I don't even know anything about this guy.

"Sure, I'll have a Corona."

"A woman that drinks beer?"

"Liquor before beer, never fear. And I've already had a little liquor."

"Okay, you wanna come to the bar with me?"

"Yeah, sounds good." After all, he could try to put something in the drink if I let him go alone.

About halfway to the bar, I spot Mark. He's talking into his phone, more like screaming into it. It's his boyfriend. He does this every time Mark goes out. He's afraid he'll meet a younger man that's actually available and leave his down low ass. So, he calls with some bullshit issue, or starts an argument, or gives the: "I really need you tonight", speech. I tell my drink buyer to hold on a minute so that I can tell Mark that I'm going to the bar. He just nods and waits.

The problem with expensive shoes is... that you can rarely walk in them. I'm not exactly drunk, but I am *nice*. Therefore, I must take special care not to fall on my ass. Especially since there is a very attractive man watching me. I safely reach Mark, and I mentally give myself a perfect score in the tipsy balance Olympics.

"Mark. Sweetie—"

"Autumn, honey, are you ready to go? I need to get out of here. Papa needs me. He's been calling for something like an hour now, I can't hear anything he's saying because of the noise in this damn club...you ready or what, girl?" He's looking at me very expectantly, and I glance back, and there my guy is, waiting.

First rule: you come together, you leave together. Damn, damn, damn!

"Yeah, sure. Just... I need to tell someone I'm leaving. I'll meet you back at the table in like three minutes and we'll leave okay?" I can see him relaxing.

"Okay, baby, meet you at the table. But hurry up okay, 'cause I really don't wanna keep him waiting."

"Sure." I stop myself from rolling my eyes. I need to rush so that a married man doesn't have to wait. And what's with the papa thing? If your lover is old enough to be your father, and you call him papa, you need professional help. Can you say daddy issues? Fuck!

I slowly make my way over to the not so rude one. Slowly, as to maintain balance. He smiles when I approach, and notices my expression, because the smile falls. He's about to think that Mark is my boyfriend or something. I'm never getting laid.

"So. No Corona?"

"I'm really sorry. Really. I came here with my friend Mark, and he's having a relationship emergency and has to go, so I've gotta go, but I'd really like to get that drink with you sometime." I bite my lip and wait for his response.

"Okay. I guess I can understand that. Do you know when you're gonna want that drink?"

"Give me your phone." I put my hand out, palm up, and wait. He looks at me for a second, then hands me his Samsung, and I program my number into it. "There, now you have my number, and you can call me when you want."

He smiles at me. "I'll be calling you soon."

"I'm sure you say that often. By the way, what's your name?" I almost forgot to ask.

"I'm Jonah. Nice to meet you." He holds out his hand.

Placing my hand inside of his, I give him my name again. "Autumn, nice to meet you too, Jonah."

He kisses my palm, and an army of butterflies erupts in my stomach. *Wow. I really hope he calls me.*

We walk back to the party table together where Mark is actually tapping his foot in annoyance. I give him my best "I'm sorry" look, grab my coat, and follow him out the door. As soon as we get in the car, I take off my shoes, and listen as Mark frantically dials the cradle robber. I have nothing against dating older people, but when they let you call them Papa... I'm still a little skeeved out. I look out the window and listen as Mark reassures him that he's left the club and is on his way. I close my eyes, and when I open them, we're pulling up to the gate of my complex.

Home sweet home. Maybe I should buy a cat. The only thing worse than being sexually frustrated, is not having anyone or anything to come home to. The problem with pets is that you need to care for them, and I work sixty hours a week. Not counting my lunch break. I killed a cactus for Christ's sake. But I hear that beta fish are extremely resilient.

I make my way to my bathroom and begin the before bed ritual. You know, wrap the hair, wash the face, brush the teeth, and take a shower. I blame Zane for my sexual frustration. I should have never read "The Sex Chronicles." The woman is a very talented writer, very descriptive, and her books should come with a warning. "Do not read unless immediate sexual gratification is to follow." Though, I suppose a warning like that would have been a little presumptuous. Even tacky. I still would have appreciated it.

Chapter Six:

I wake up to my phone blaring. House, not cell. Looking at my clock, it's five in the morning. On a Saturday. Who the shit calls someone at five in the morning on a Saturday? This better be an emergency. Someone had better be on fire.

"Hello?" I sound like a man.

"Hey cuz. How are you?" It's Daniel. He still doesn't like me, so I have no idea why he's calling.

"How am I? I'd be better if I was still asleep. What are you doing calling my house at five in the morning? Is God even up yet? What do you want?" Seriously! He must be on something.

"Look, I know we don't always see eye to eye, but we're family."

Here we go with the family shit. He needs something that he knows I don't want to give.

"You want us to see eye to eye? Why don't you call me when my eyes are open?" I suggest. Jackass. Just a simple jackass.

"Listen, I really need you. My girl had to leave her apartment, and you know I'm staying with my parents right now. They won't let her stay here 'cause we aren't married, and I was wondering if she could stay with you?" He's talking like this is an absolutely normal thing to call someone and ask at five in the morning.

"Have you lost your mind? You want me to let a woman I met one time, almost three months ago, stay in my apartment?" Unbelievable.

"Why are you being like this? Is this because of her job? It's just a job. Get off your high horse. I mean, your parents are drug addicts."

And now I'm mad.

"My parents are drug addicts, and I work in advertising. Her daddy is a doctor, and she works a pole. Don't you dare call me, asking for a fuckin' favor, and then get indignant because you think somebody's trying to insult the hooker you wanna turn into a housewife. Why don't y'all just get a place together? From what I understand from my HBO watching, good strippers make great money. Don't call me for another favor, not ever." I slam the phone down so hard after ending the call that I think I broke the damn thing.

The fucked-up thing is, now I'm mad, I can't fall back asleep. I hate people. Favor seeking motherfuckers. Meanwhile, this selfish bastard wouldn't throw piss on me if I was on fire. And he has the nerve to bring up family in one breath, and my parents' drug addiction in another.

A lot of shit happened in my house while I was growing up. I saw things that I shouldn't have seen. Often. I have a mother that suffers from Bipolar disorder. Before she was diagnosed, she was using. She was just looking for something to take the darkness away. When I was a kid, I didn't understand. That's not to say that I understand as an adult either. I've never had an addiction, so I can only see it through the eyes of a person that had drug-addicted parents. Through my own eyes. I still have issues with my parents because of that. More with my father.

My mother was battling drug addiction, and a chemical imbalance, yet she helped me with my homework every night. I had a bedtime. I ate healthy dinners, and breakfasts. We ate when my mother didn't. When she could only afford to buy so much, and so she went without. I never felt unsafe, or unloved. And so, when the mistakes of my mother—especially my mother, are used as an attack... I come out swinging. I don't think I'll be at my aunt's Sunday dinner. If I see this spoiled bastard, I may catch a charge.

I need a bubble bath.

I have a great bathtub. My bathroom was built for comfort, with a bathtub and separate shower. There is a mirror that runs the length of one wall and a vanity with an oval mirror on the opposite wall. It gives that endless image effect. It sounds really nice, but it can be disorienting if you're drunk. In all actuality, the only thing I like about this bathroom is the tub, which I don't use enough anyway. Ten-minute showers being a staple of life. But when I can use my tub...sweet Jesus. It's a bathtub built for two. If I ever fell asleep in the thing, I'd probably drown. And it has a whirlpool/Jacuzzi mode! I turn on the water, add my bubble bath, dim my lights, and prepare to immerse myself in the stress relief. However, I must admit that having someone to share the bath with would relieve the stress a little quicker. Hell, in that case, I may not have even needed the bath. But I'll be thankful for what I have.

Anyway, not that I don't love you and all, but it's a little too early to be sharing all the details of bathing. I'll talk to you at a decent hour.

Again, I wake up to my phone hitting a high note. Looking at the clock, it's nine in the morning. Better, but I personally feel that if you call someone's house for anything before eleven on a Saturday, your parentage should be called into question. You're obviously a bastard. Since my life is filled with an impossible number of dramatic people, I apparently have to deal with two bastards before breakfast.

"Hello?" There's the man-voice again.

"What in the hell is the matter with your voice? Are you just waking up when I'm having an emergency?" It's Mark. He sounds like he's crying.

Great, just great.

"Yes, I'm just waking up. What's wrong? Do you need to come over?"

This is going to sound really selfish, but I'm hoping his answer is no. Saturdays are mine. They are the only day I have for me. And sometimes I choose to spend them with my favorite he-girl, but sometimes I don't. To be honest, I can only take so much of the drama in my personal life. I have work and Project Runway for that.

"Come over? I really shouldn't, but if you insist, I could really use you right now. I need a friend."

Shit. Here we go.

"Alright, just um...call me when you get here." I need to get dressed. And make coffee. And take an aspirin. It's a preventative measure for the headache that I know is coming.

"Okay, well can you give me the gate code, 'cause I'm here and I don't remember it."

Whoa what the fuck!

"You're here?"

"Yeah."

"At the gate, here?"

"Yeah."

"Are you joking, Mark?" I rub my forehead and squeeze my eyes shut.

"You know I wouldn't have just come all the way out here if it wasn't important, Autumn." He sounds nearly hysterical.

"Okay," I say and give him the gate code.

Mark lives in Atlanta. In Dunwoody, actually. Peachtree City is nearly an hour away from him. I give him the gate code and say a silent prayer. I should start putting rum in my coffee. It would make mornings like this so much easier. As a child of addicts however, I try not to form any habits that may be a problem later on. I prefer to be addicted to shoes and Chick-fil-a.

Climbing out of bed, I throw on a pair of sweatpants and a wife beater. A girl's gotta have something comfortable on when drama's imminent. When I get to the door, Mark's a little pissed off. He always is when it takes me longer than the speed of light to answer the door. I live in a townhouse, not a studio apartment. My bedroom is on the second floor to the rear. And if he thought that I was going to answer the door in the towel I fell asleep in, yes, the towel, then he must be smoking something.

"What, did you need to walk from Alabama to answer the door?"

I am so not in the mood for this.

"No, Guam. Come in or stay out." Note: if you're going to come to someone to unburden the quagmire of antics that is your life, you may want to do it nicely.

Mark walks by me and into the kitchen. He's still wearing what he had on last night. That alone is reason for alarm. The man will only repeat an outfit every four to six weeks. Four weeks if he receives more than six compliments about it. To say that I'm worried is an understatement. Following him into the kitchen, I see him making coffee. He walks over to the fridge and takes out eggs, milk, and bacon.

Don't seem so surprised, I can make breakfast food.

"Autopilot, where's the bread? I'm thinking French toast. I need to eat right now. Something really high in cholesterol." His hands are shaking. I don't think people with shaky limbs should be around open flames, and I have a gas stove.

"Sweetie, I was gonna buy bread later today. Why don't we go to the Waffle House?" *Good suggestion, right? Wrong.*

"No, no, no! I can't be around too many people right now!" He's getting agitated. It looks like he's about three seconds off of hysterical crying.

"Okay. Alright. I'll go and pick it up. Let me comb my hair, and brush my teeth, cause my mouth is rank, and I'll go. While I'm gone, take a shower. I have a pair of men's sweatpants, and a big shirt you can wear until you get home. Okay?"

At first, I don't think he'll agree, but then he nods his head and starts towards the stairs. I follow him up and grab the clothes out of my closet. Grabbing a towel out of the closet in the hall, I put everything on the sink in the hall bathroom. I never knew that I could comb my hair and brush my teeth at the same time, but you do what you gotta do sometimes. Snatching my keys off the hook by the door, I'm out of my house and into my car in two seconds flat.

I drive a sky blue 2015 Lexus RC F. Breaking several rules of driving, I manage to get to the Waffle House, order and receive two all star breakfasts, and make it home in a time frame that should be recorded in the Guinness Book of World Records.

Entering my house, I notice two things. One: it smells like burnt coffee. Two: the radio is turned up loud enough for me to get evicted. My own fault. No one told me to leave an emotionally distraught gay man in my house with my Best of Sade CD. "Is It a Crime?" is playing so loudly that my ears hurt. Never again. Walking over to the stereo on the kitchen counter, I turn it down and then off. I don't want my heart to jump out of my chest the next time I turn it on. Now to find the culprit.

"Mark, sweetheart, where are you?"

"Living room."

Well alright. I arrive at my living room to see my very best he-girl lying face down on my couch in a pair of too big sweatpants sans shirt. The sweatpants belong to the ex-boyfriend. I have no idea why I still have them. I mutilated a good portion of his clothing at the end of the relationship. That's a story for another time. Today is about Mark.

"I got food. Now if I can figure out what you did to my coffee-maker we'll have caffeine." I say this with a perkiness in my voice that I do not feel.

I'm not a person that handles the soft emotions well. You know the heart broken sadness. The tearful depression. When these emotions affect me personally, I react in anger. My childhood taught me that. I have too much pride to go to therapy, and so it's something that I deal with. I do have a large capacity for empathy. Perhaps this comes from rocking my depressed mother to sleep from the age of eight. Listening to her sobs, punctuated with: "why doesn't anyone love me?" Mark looks like he's approaching this point, and I need to know why so that I can fix the problem. With humor, or alcohol, or shopping, or a shoulder to cry on.

"Do me a favor?"

He raises his head and gives me a look. The, are you kidding me, look.

"Set the food out while I make coffee? There are lots of calories to be discovered." I wait for him to get up before I leave the room.

My coffee maker looks horrible. I don't know what he did but there are coffee grains everywhere and the coffee smells burnt. I wouldn't be angry, but it came from William-Sonoma. This is a twenty-two-hundred-dollar coffee pot. I don't even use it unless my aunt is here. She bought it. All of the lights are flashing on the thing and I don't even know what that means, so I just unplug it. I'm gonna have to buy another one. With my own money. I make good money for a single person, but I've got rent, utilities, a car note, car insurance, credit card bills, student loans, and various other expenditures. Now I gotta replace a twenty-two-hundred-dollar coffee pot. I should make Mark do it. That would be wrong though, considering his present issue. Whatever the hell it is since I still don't know!

Twenty-two hundred fuckin' dollars!

Taking out my target brand coffee maker, I brew my French vanilla nectar of life. Making two cups of the blessing that is coffee, I go back to the den to see Mark devouring his grits.

"Couldn't wait huh?" It really is funny. Here is a man that looks like he stepped out of an Abercrombie ad, on his knees, in front of my coffee table, shirtless and in a pair of borrowed sweatpants, shoveling grits into his mouth.

"Gimme my coffee, please." He says it while laughing at himself with me.

"I give you coffee, you tell me what happened. Deal?" I feel bad for the sobering effect that the question has on him. Holding out the mug, I wait.

"Deal." He takes the mug from me and blows on the coffee to cool it off before taking a sip. "Henry's wife walked in on us at six this morning."

I choke. There is coffee in my nose, my eyes are watering, and I can't stop coughing. Mark hands me a tissue and waits for me to settle down.

"I'm sorry. What? What do you mean she walked in on you? Not, in on you, in on you, right? How did she find you? I thought she was in North Carolina or something visiting family?"

Now do you see what I mean about the drama?

"We were at this motel near his house when it happened." He leans back and rests against my couch.

"What happened Mark?" I need all the details now. It's like seeing a horrific accident happening. You see it coming, you know that there isn't anything you can do about it, so you watch and pray that everyone makes it out alive.

"We meet at this motel sometimes. Not often, 'cause it's near his house, and he's afraid of getting caught. Usually he just comes to my place. Well, last night he asked me to meet him there. I got there, and we pretty much started arguing right away. You know, the same controlling shit he always tries to pull? He was at it again. Well, we ended up just falling asleep in the room. He wakes me up at a little past five all apologetic, and we start with the making up.

"Apparently, his wife was on her way back from her trip and was driving past the motel when his daughter saw his car—he's got that custom license plate and everything. Well, his wife thought he was with another woman, so she pulled into the parking lot. She left the kids in the car and went to the manager's office. I don't know what she told them, but they gave her a spare key, and she walked in on us in the middle of the making up." He looks at me like he's waiting for something.

I hate to disappoint. "When you say making up, are we talking kissing or what?"

"He was giving me a blowjob." He cringes. Mark doesn't give oral. He says that he wore braces for too long to have all that orthodontic work flushed down the tube for the sake of some rocking hips. But he'll accept it happily.

"You're telling me that this poor woman walked in on her husband with another man's dick in his mouth, and you think you're having a bad day?" This shit is unreal. "What did she do?" I would've stabbed someone.

"What do you think? She started screaming at us and crying. Then she got all violent—with him, not me. Called us a couple of faggots, among other things. Stormed out. Henry tried to follow her, but I guess he changed his mind, 'cause he came back and started blaming me. He said that he was gonna lose his family and it was my fault. Started calling me selfish. Said that he was disgusted with himself for not realizing what a depraved thing I was sooner..." he looks lost and I just want to hug him.

Is he selfish? Yes. But everyone can be a little—okay—a lot selfish when it comes to certain things. He didn't create this situation alone. And even though I feel for Henry's wife and kids, they're not my friends. Mark is. Right now, I just want to comfort him, but I can't let him get lost in this. I continue the conversation instead.

"What did you do?"

"I punched him. I think I broke his jaw. Then I left too. I drove around on 285 for a while; you know how that thing is like a big circle anyway. I looked up, and I was closer to your house than mine, and I knew that if I went home, I would just call you anyway, so I came here." Closing his eyes, he rests his head on the seat of my couch. Getting up, I walk over and sit next to him. He looks at me and then rests his head in my lap. I rub his head for lack of something to say and wait.

"Why couldn't I have been born straight? Then we could've ended up together." He sounds almost wistful.

"We wouldn't have ended up together if you were straight. You woulda been married to some white girl named Becky Lou right outta college, and worse, you woulda been a republican. I think the only reason you're a democrat is to piss your father off," I joke.

"I'd have been better off married to a Becky Lou. Her name alone implies that at least she can cook." He's laughing now. Good.

"I don't need to cook, I'm gonna hire a chef as soon as I get to the seven-figure range that I'm destined for. You know what we should do? We should have a Blu-ray day. Family Guy, Boondocks, and Sex and the City." It's exactly what we need. Stereotypes and girl talk.

"Hell yeah. Where's the ice cream?" Mark gets up, and clearing the breakfast trash, he heads to the kitchen, the freezer, and the New York Chocolate Fudge Chunk. Looking at the clock, it's only ten forty-five. How can so many lives be altered before lunch?

Like I already said, I feel sorry for Henry's wife. Even more so for the kids. They are going to need a really expensive shrink. Walking over to the movie cabinet, I take out the required line-up. I can't believe that man would lay all the blame at someone else's feet. He'll either go back to his wife on his knees or try to blame her, too. I can't really believe that he feels guilty. The fact that he didn't immediately follow her shows that much. Instead, he went back to attack his boyfriend.

Don't get me wrong, Mark is an opportunist. He started dating Henry because of his position. He knew the man was married, had kids...he just didn't care. He isn't blameless in this, and I'm not trying to paint it that way. I just feel that you have a greater responsibility to your family and yourself that anyone else. Meaning, though Mark isn't blameless, the greater blame is at Henry's feet. He betrayed his wife and children. He broke vows, told lies, and when Mark tried to leave him, which he has done, he has manipulated and schemed to keep the situation going.

Despite the way their relationship started, Mark really does love this man. The fact that he hit him blows my mind. Mark isn't violent. During his free time, he's either at the gym, or with his kickboxing instructor. The kickboxing is a way for him to work out his frustrations, but he's never actually hit a person outside of sparring. He has a good amount of free time too. Think about it. He does the bare minimum at work; he clocks maybe thirty-eight hours, including lunch. His boyfriend, or should I say ex-boyfriend is married. He gets scraps of time with this man. Outside of holidays and birthdays he doesn't see his parents often. Unlimited free time.

Mark re-enters the room and we begin the marathon. About halfway through the second episode of Family Guy his phone starts to ring. He looks at it, shuts it off, and turns back to the television. Obviously, that was Henry. Maybe he didn't break his jaw after all. Then again, it's amazing what painkillers will do for you. I reach down and squeeze his hand while taking a spoonful of the ice cream.

Who needs reality TV?

Chapter Seven:

Putting in the third season of Sex and the City, I realize that my life is entirely too uneventful. Taking into account the events of this morning you may disagree. May I point out, that was not my life unfolding; that was Mark's life. My life consists of work, shoes, the rabbit, and trying to help Mark stabilize his life. I don't need all the rah-rah of Mark's life to be happy or anything, but I need something. I just haven't figured out what.

"You want Chinese?" Mark is planning our dinner.

I am sitting on the couch with a Carol's Daughter facial mask on. That's right. I slathered mud on my face to feel beautiful. Do you ever feel as women, that our view of skin and beauty maintenance is a bit warped? I once heard a famous actress in an interview saying that she put urine on her face to try and cure her acne. Urine? Are people aware that other than the gross factor, urine contains ammonia? But don't get me started on the various bodily fluids that contain ammonia. Hell, if I did, you would probably never swallow again if you know what I mean. But I've gone off on a tangent.

"Shrimp and broccoli with brown rice?" I love shrimp and broccoli.

"I was thinking we could get a happy family." Mark's voice is full of hope.

Of course, he was. I don't want no damned happy family.

"Too much food. Okay, I know. We'll order both. I'll have whatever we don't finish for dinner tomorrow."

Mark starts to laugh at me and dials the restaurant.

As I'm trying to get back into the show, my cell rings. Who's calling me? My aunt calls the house phone, my best-friend in New York calls on Sunday, and my mother doesn't call me. I have to call her. She doesn't have long distance. Reaching for the electronic leash, I don't recognize the number.

"Hello?"

"Hi, Autumn?" A man's voice. A sexy voice.

I sit up a little straighter, and Mark stares at me with a raised eyebrow. "Yes...who's this?"

"It's Jonah. From the party...last night...you promised me a drink."

I'm smiling so hard that my face hurts. "Were you hoping to collect on that drink tonight? Because it's very ungentlemanly of you to give me such short notice."

Mark chokes at the flirtatiousness in my voice, and I start making exaggerated shushing motions with my hand.

"Who said I was a gentleman? I could be completely nefarious."

I giggle. *Giggle, for Christ's sake. When did I become thirteen again?* "You must be a gentleman. A shifty character wouldn't use a word like nefarious."

Mark is rolling his eyes and pretending to gag. I kick him. Hard.

"Not true. I actually use a pocket thesaurus during phone conversations to be disarming and seem innocent. But about that drink...what *are* you doing tonight?"

I'm going to have sex with him. Not tonight or tomorrow. Nothing that immediate. But it's definitely going to happen, and I hope he lives up to my expectations.

"Actually, I'm helping a friend with something tonight—" before I can finish Mark snatches my phone. He stiff-arms me, and

I can't get the thing back. I stare at him like he's crazy when he starts talking into it.

"Hello? This is Autumn's friend. She would love to have that drink tonight."

What? Is he serious right now?!

"What the hell are you doing?" I'm more surprised than annoyed. He holds up his finger in a motion for me to wait and starts giving this man directions to my house.

"Hello? What are you doing?" *Good old anger, creeping on up.* I watch as he hangs up the phone.

"Look, I love you. But you need to get laid." He states it like it's a fact. In a way it is, but still. The man just...

"Did you stop to think what kind of a man calls a woman at eight at night to ask her out?" I'm going to die. He just gave some murderer directions to my house.

"Okay, stop with the Susan Lucci looks, and get it together. Wash the mud off the face, and put on something else, 'cause he'll be here in like twenty minutes. And don't worry, I'll stay until he comes and have a really good look at him. I'll even take down his license plate number. That way, if you end up on a missing persons' flyer, I'll be able to give the police a good description, and a way to track him down." He's walking me up the stairs while he's talking. Annoyance is turning into excitement. I'm going on a date. I should be afraid. I'm not. Maybe lack of sex is dulling my brain.

Going into my bathroom, I wash my face, trying to remove all traces of forest life. I start brushing my teeth, and Mark comes in holding a bubble dress. I shake my head at it, and he walks away huffing and puffing. While I'm rinsing my mouth, Mark comes in with an above the knee, caftan dress. Peasant sleeves, ruffled hem, and its sage with pink embroidery. Is he kidding? The dress is cute, but it's made to cover a bathing suit, not for an impromptu date.

"Are you serious?" *Gay men have fashion sense?*

"It shows your quirky side." He's serious.

"Men do not want to know your quirky side on the first date. You are supposed to hide the quirky side until, like, date six. The representative needs to be firmly in place on the first five dates. The real you is only supposed to peak in and out," I tell him. He's trying to sabotage me, I know it.

"First of all, you only have a quirky side. And as far as a representative goes, you don't have enough free time to practice perfecting a personality for one. And you can't cook." I start to speak, but he cuts me off. "Breakfast food doesn't count." He's got this grin on his face as if he's just won an unprecedented victory in front of the Supreme Court. Bastard.

"I'm not wearing that dress in the middle of September." I'm not losing this argument.

"Autumn, just wear the goddamned dress!"

Fine, I'll concede since he's having a bad day. He's taking this dress thing way too seriously.

"Fine. Don't be such a brat." I take the dress from him and start changing into it. I've got a pair of pink Manolo's that'll work with it. The things I do for friendship.

I'm finishing up with my lip gloss when I hear the intercom. Mark buzzes him in, and I start making my way down the stairs. Carrying the shoes of course. The nervousness is starting to come back, and I'm scared that I'll trip and fall down the steps. That's an attractive picture. Sounds like something out of a romantic comedy.

I get to the front hall in time to see Mark opening the door for Jonah. Oh my damn. He's wearing a vintage Captain America t-shirt and some Diesel jeans. The boy does casual well. He seems taller than I remember, and then it occurs to me that I'm not wearing shoes.

"Hi. Just let me put these on and grab my purse." I raise the shoes as I say it so that he knows what I'm talking about.

"Okay, no problem." He and Mark are standing awkwardly in the small foyer. I try to hurry.

I finish putting on the shoes that were obviously not made for comfort, grab my purse, and head back to the boys. I had to put the shoes on in the living room, because there's nowhere to sit in the foyer. I'm glad to be getting out, but I feel like a horrible friend. I know that Mark pushed me to do this, but I could've objected a little more. I don't want him to be alone. Would it be too weird for me to invite him to come along? It would. Okay, maybe I just shouldn't go. Entering the foyer, that thought quickly leaves my mind. There is no way that I'm not going out with this man.

Jonah looks up at me when I come in; he's bent over the table writing something. Mark is leaning over his shoulder nodding. The hell?

"Hey, what did I miss?" I say it laughingly. Hopefully this is all innocent.

"According to your friend here, I look too honest. So, he asked me to write down my address in case you pop up missing." Jonah's laughing a little, so I hope this is a joke.

"Mark?" *This had better be a joke.*

"I'm just taking precautionary measures," he defends himself.

I can't believe this man is defending himself. This has got to stop before he asks my date for a urine sample.

"Mark, can I speak to you in the living room please?" If he says no, I'll grab him by the neck and drag him in there, I swear to God.

"Yeah. Of course, you can." Smiling like an idiot, he follows me into the living room. As soon as we're safely in there and out of sight, I slap him in the back of the head.

"Ow! You hit me."

He has the nerve to be surprised? I should hit him again.

"What the shit are you doing? You made the man give you his address? Are you trying to seem insane? 'Cause you do. And what's worse, I seem insane for being associated with a person as obviously touched as you no doubt are!" I'm saying this in a raging whisper. I don't want the date to think I'm crazy. *Ironic isn't it?*

"I'm just trying to look out for you. I would do the same for my sister, if I had one." He's dead serious. I can't believe it.

"Mark, I cannot believe you." I don't even know how to deal with this.

"Autumn come on. Don't be angry at me. He looks too honest. They're always the ones." He thinks he's being rational.

"What ones? What the hell are you talking about?" Now I'm confused. *Great, just great.*

"You know what ones. The ones with the neighbors that think he's such a great guy, meanwhile he has like thirty women buried in his basement."

I laugh. I can't help it. The man is nothing if not priceless. The weird thing is, our roles were reversed about twenty minutes ago. What happened to, *you need to get laid*?

I hear a sound behind me. Turning around, I see Jonah laughing. I really hope he wasn't there the whole time. Because one: it would have been rude of him to listen. And two: I think I've been embarrassed enough already.

"Have you been there the whole time?" Please say no. Don't make me dislike you for doing something I would have done.

"No. Actually I came in on the, 'thirty something women buried in his basement', part."

Thank you. This is one of the innumerable reasons why I know that God loves me.

"You think it's funny that my friend thinks you're a serial killer?"

"I really do. Besides, I can almost understand where he's coming from. I have a sister. And I do fit the profile somewhat."

Is he defending my psycho friend?

"So, do you think I'll end up on a missing person's flyer?"

Mark looks at me like *I'm* crazy now.

"Not a chance." Jonah doesn't even hesitate in his response.

Quick answer. I don't really like those.

"Why not?" I ask. If he says, just because, I'm kneeing him in the groin and calling the police.

"Because even though I fit the profile, you don't. So, if I were going to fulfill my bloodlust tonight, I'd choose another victim."

Is he saying he wouldn't kill me because I'm black? Should I be offended?

"Dahmer killed black men." I really need to learn when to shut up.

"Dahmer practiced cannibalism. That's different. He was also homosexual. Different type of killer, different type of victim. I don't eat people. And I'm very heterosexual." He emphasizes the 'very'.

"I guess it's a good thing that affirmative action doesn't open every door. You ready to go?"

He takes my arm and leads the way to the front door. I look back at Mark to see him shaking his head at me.

"Lock the door on your way out if you leave before I get back." With that, I'm out the door, and on my way to a margarita.

We agreed to just going out for Mexican food. There's this restaurant close to my house that has really good nachos. Fact of Georgia life: there are more Mexican restaurants here than any other place I've ever been to in my life. I have nothing against Mexican food, you know, yo quiero Taco Bell. But I'm from Amityville. Not many Mexican restaurants there. Oh well, when in Rome.

Pulling into the restaurant parking lot, I groan. There is a line going out the door. My internal magic eight ball is flashing a huge, *outlook not good*. I look to my left—we took his car—and see that he isn't too sure about this either. Wonderful. The getting-laid-o-meter is steadily dropping.

Do I sound like a slut? Funny, a few months ago I was afraid you would think I was prudish. Okay, look...I'm not exactly Samantha Jones a la Sex in the City or anything, but I'm an adult. Who hasn't had sex in a really long time. And I do usually want to know more than a person's first name before granting them the keys to the kingdom, so I'm not exactly talking about sex tonight. I would however like to lay the groundwork for sex in the near future. In about two weeks or so. Very do-able. My body is going to explode if I don't get some very adult physical contact soon. If something would go right. Anything, anything at all, I would be grateful.

And then something does. I have a light bulb moment.

"Ooh! So, we ordered Chinese food before you called, and it's probably there right now. We could eat at my house." *I'm so proud of me.*

"Okay, but there were only two of you, how much food could there be?" he asks doubtfully.

Silly man.

"There will be plenty of food. Enough to feed an entire Chinese family," I assure him. God bless Mark and his happy family loving self.

"You sure your friend won't mind? I mean, is he going to be comfortable third wheeling?"

He has a point. I remember nixing the idea of asking him to come along. Shit!

"Possibly?" I should have said definitely.

"I don't know..."

Fine. No Chinese food.

"Well we could just do this another time." *Rabbit here I come.*

"NO! I mean...you know... I always wanted to eat enough food to feed a Chinese family."

I knew I liked this man. He starts to pull out of the parking lot, and I laugh. I wonder what Mark's going say when we come back.

Two rum and cokes, a corona, and a shrimp and broccoli combination later, I have this to report: Jonah has a very good sense of humor. He is a graphic artist and website developer with his own business. He is the oldest of four children, three boys and one girl. His mother is Samoan, and his father is from Ireland. His father moved to the U.S. when he was five, he and his mother came alone. Jonah's mother was raised in Hawaii and met his father when she was seventeen. She married him there, without telling her parents, and they moved to Connecticut. Jonah was born there, they lived there until he was eight, and then moved to Fairburn, Georgia. His father is a contractor, and his mother ran a daycare until about three years ago. His last name is McInerney. He is also a little drunk right now. Mark is asleep in my guest bedroom; he doesn't handle hard liquor well.

"So, your friend Mark, he's...special."

"Special how?" I need to figure out if I should be insulted on my friend's behalf.

"He just seems really...um...excitable."

Excitable?

"He's coming off of a really bad break-up right now. He's usually very low key with people he doesn't know. How is it that the two of you have never met?" I don't know why this is just occurring to me. He was at the party for Mark's friend. They should know each other, right?

"Why would we have met before?" He leans back against the couch and looks confused.

Wait...what?

"Well, it was his friend's party that I was at when we bumped into each other." Was I hallucinating that night? The woman beside me knew him.

His expression clears, and he nods to himself. "You were at the party; I was at the club."

What? "You weren't there for the party?" He's shaking his head as I'm talking. "But the woman next to me knew you, and you came over to our table." I'm too tipsy for this.

"I went out with some friends, saw you across the room, and came over."

This is the problem with going to a party at a club.

"So, you just happened to be there." This is not a question. I'm pretty much thinking out loud.

Jonah leans forward and takes my hand. He plays with my fingers for a second, then he kisses my hand. There go those butterflies.

"Autumn, I don't know if I just happened to be there, or if I was supposed to be there. I do know that I've been thinking about you since the airport. I know that when I saw you again, all that I could see was you. I know that you're smart, and funny, and beautiful. So, does it matter why I was there?"

Wow. I'm not sure if I kiss him, or if he kisses me, but all I feel are his lips on mine. I feel one of his hands on my hip, and the other on the small of my back. My heart is hammering, I'm feeling warmth spread throughout my body, and I'm afraid. I'm afraid he'll keep going, and I'm even more afraid he'll stop. He pulls back and looks at me. I need to say something.

"Do you want to see the rest of the house?" *Where did that come from?*

"The rest of the house?" he sounds confused.

"Yeah, you know...kitchen, dining room...bedroom." *Did I just say that?* My voice doesn't sound like mine, and I'm breathing a little heavily.

"Oh! Of course, I would. Lead the way."

I'm really nervous. It's a good thing I took off my shoes when we came back to my house.

I know that I said the sex would happen in a week or two, but screw that. I'm gone already. As I'm leading him to the kitchen, he moves in closer behind me, wrapping his arms around my waist. We don't really need to see the kitchen. I'm never really in there anyway. I go straight to the stairs. To make climbing easier, he lets go of my waist and takes my hand.

Going to the end of the hall, we enter my bedroom, and I turn on the lights. Turning him so that his back is to the bed, I push him onto it. I straddle his lap on my knees, and he looks up at me smiling while sliding his hands up my thighs. I kiss him again. I'm pretty sure now that I started it the first time too. After a few minutes, the clothes melt away, and his skin touches mine. Hot, literally. It feels like we're on fire, and there isn't a better feeling in the world.

Laying me back on my bed, he begins kissing and nipping me from my neck to my breast. One of his hands slides up from my hip to my breast and his thumb circles my nipple before he pinches it. My gasp is swallowed by his kiss. Fuck, this feels good. Really good. Like it should come with a nutritional breakdown that includes trans fats.

"God, Jonah. Don't stop." My hands slide into his short hair and I pull him closer.

"Stop? Why the fuck would I do something that stupid?" he whispers the words against my mouth.

I'm legitimately afraid that I'm about to burst into flames. I can feel my legs start to tremble as he moves his head down and takes my breast into his mouth as his hand slides up my leg until his fingers are teasing my pussy. His thumb is circling my clit and I'm biting my lip to keep from making too much noise, but that goes all the way out the window when his fingers thrust into me.

"Ah! Fuck, Jonah!"

"You like that, baby? God damn, you're tight."

Moving back to my mouth, he kisses me again while he moves his fingers in and out of me in a rhythm that's slow and deep.

"You ready to come for me, baby?"

If I had the capacity for actual speech, I'd say something sarcastic. I have never come from anyone's fingers but my own. Don't get me wrong, I've had guys that think that they're good with their hands attempt to get me off this way. Mostly when I was in high school, and then there was the ex. He would mostly just touch my pussy to make sure that I was wet right before we had sex. But Jonah is taking me to a place that I've only been to when accompanied by my handy dandy rabbit. I feel his fingers curl slightly inside of me, and he's hitting that spot. That magic fucking spot that mother nature hid so unfairly in a place that is unreachable by any dick on the planet. I feel dizzy from the sensations flooding my brain. I feel like I'm floating, and then the sky shatters and light explodes with my orgasm. Jonah's tongue is stroking mine, and I'm holding on for dear life.

"Do you have a condom?" He's looking at me, waiting for an answer.

It takes my brain a second to register the question. "No. You don't have a condom?" This cannot be happening.

"No. I don't. I wasn't planning on this." He motions his hand between us.

Like I was?!

"I wasn't exactly planning on it either." Not immediately anyway.

"But it's your house. How do you not have condoms?" he looks baffled.

He's joking right?

"My house isn't exactly a hotbed of sexual activity." I'm not offended. I sound it though.

"Sorry. I didn't mean it like that. It's just...you're an adult."

He has a point.

"I know, but I'm not exactly sexually active right now, so there was no hurry on the condom situation. You don't have one in your wallet?"

He shakes his head. I raise my eyebrow.

"Wallets are obsolete. I have a card case. No condom compartment." He's smiling.

"This is funny to you?" How can he be smiling right now?

"No. No it isn't funny. You're just really cute when you're mad."

I'm going to keep him.

"So, what do you want to do?" I really shouldn't give him a choice in this situation. But I do.

Looking down at me, he rolls onto his side and rests his hand on his head. I didn't get a chance to look at his body before. Okay, hell yeah. He is very well defined. Lean and muscular with abs on top of abs. I didn't know people really looked like this. I really wish I had a condom. The man is hung, too. Definitely a Magnum man. Damn it! He reaches for the blanket at the foot of my bed and covers us a little. Pulling me into him so that my back is against his front, he kisses my shoulder.

"Tell me something about you," he whispers it in my ear.

Sighing I lean into him.

"I once broke a boy's arm in three places with a baseball bat." I have no idea why I thought of that. It just popped into my head, and then flew out of my mouth. Maybe Mark is right. I don't have a representative.

"Are you kidding?" He sounds very surprised.

"No." I lace my fingers through his where they're lying on my stomach.

"Tell me the story." He's amused. Good.

Jonah and I spend the rest of the night talking about the things we did as children. I learn more about his siblings, and I tell him about mine. We fall asleep together, and I wake up to my phone ringing.

Chapter Eight:

What the hell is the deal with people calling me early in the shittin' morning? My life has turned into a made for TV movie. I feel the arm resting on my waist tighten as Jonah wakes up behind me. The ringer on my house phone is set ridiculously loud. Then I realize that's not my phone. It's his cell phone. The thing sounds like an old school rotary phone. He sits up and starts looking for his jeans. They're on my side of the bed, so reaching over the side I swing them up to him. He needs to answer that thing before I break it.

I'm a little aggravated. Not that the touching and storytelling weren't good or anything. The man has a very talented mouth if you catch my drift, but since when is oral a substitute for sex? It's like being trapped in the desert, thirsty and starving for weeks, and then being rescued by a person that owns a cattle ranch with a clear stream behind it, and when you get there, they offer you tofu and Guinness stout for dinner. And as an answer to your unasked question of: "why not steak and fresh cold water?", they tell you that there's been a revolution in dining, and at this ranch they offer vegetarian food only because the cows need to be protected from the savage meat eaters, and they need the water for the cows to be strong and give good milk. So, excuse me if I'm a little upset at being awakened from my wild and crazy sex free night by a phone that doesn't belong to me. I'm not a morning person anyway.

He's answering his phone, naked I might add, when I hear Mark in the doorway.

"Well good morning, Mr. Jonah. Early morning wood?"

Shit! I roll over and tell Mark to get out, as I hear Jonah telling the person on the phone that he'll be there soon. *Really?*

"Mark, get out." I'm calm.

"Get out? Of the house, or the room? 'Cause technically, I haven't come into the room yet." He has the balls to be smirking at me.

"Pick one and then do it!" I really only raise my voice a little.

Jonah is still on the other side of the bed, holding his jeans in front of his "wood". This is becoming a dramedy.

"Then I choose out of the house. I need to get home. I haven't been there since Friday afternoon."

We cannot have this conversation right now. There is a naked man in my bedroom. Not that I'm about to get any, but still. "Okay, I love you, bye-bye. Sort of busy right now. Call me later?" *Get out, get out, get out!*

"See you tomorrow." He wiggles his fingers at me.

I release the breath that I didn't know I was holding when Mark leaves the doorway, closing the door.

Turning to Jonah, I try to apologize. "I'm really sorry about that."

He's wearing underwear now. Boxer briefs, black. I get up with the blanket wrapped around myself and go over to my dresser. Pulling out a huge New York Giants jersey, I put it on.

"What's up with the coverage?" Jonah's staring at me with his brow furrowed.

What's the problem? Is he not standing here getting dressed?

"I have body issues. And didn't you say you were leaving?" I'm fine with being naked in the dark or in passionate situations, but it's morning, and this room has really good lighting, and unless you're Halle Berry, who through an obvious pact with the devil, has remained eighteen for the past thirty something years, you are a little self-conscious if you're standing nude in front of a near stranger without the added liquid courage that alcohol provides.

"Seriously, *you* have body issues?" He's looking at me like I'm crazy.

"Yes. I'm a woman. I have a plethora of issues that I really don't want to discuss." Didn't he say he was leaving? It's way too early in this possible relationship for us to be having this conversation.

"Everyone has issues. But body issues? You? You've got to be joking." He takes me in from head to toe and squints.

Autumn Blaire, discomfort is on line one for you. Should I tell it that you're in a meeting with self-consciousness and to call you back?

"I'm not joking. Why would I be joking about that?" I need some caffeine.

"Because...have you seen yourself naked?"

The hell kind of question is that? And before you ask, he's serious.

"Of course, I have. What was with the phone call?" *Subject change anyone?*

"Don't change the subject. So, is this the whole, pretty girl that doesn't know she's pretty, kind of thing?"

"I didn't say I have face issues. I said I have body issues."

"Well excuse me. If it helps, I think you're hot." He grins at me. *Okay.*

"Thank you, but you were looking through beer goggles." *When did I become this person? Why am I trying to talk this man into thinking I'm ugly? My voice needs to be taken away.*

"Look, I really have to leave, but I'd love to see you naked without beer goggles, and I promise that if it gets heavy again, I will have a handy dandy condom." He's putting on his shirt, his shoes are in my livingoom. "Walk me to the door?" he holds out his hand.

I take it and lead the way out. That was too much conversation this early in the morning. The wall clock in the foyer reads seven thirty. I am definitely going back to bed. No church today. When Jonah is wearing proper foot attire, I walk him to the door. Opening it, he bends down and gives me a kiss goodbye. Light and sweet.

"I'll call you later?"

"Okay." Closing the door behind him, I lock it. I haven't failed to realize that he never answered my question about the phone call.

Chapter Nine:

I'm running very late. I actually combed my hair while I was driving. It was either comb my hair, or put on my make-up, and I cannot apply make-up while driving. The lip gloss, yes. The eyeliner, shadow, concealer, and mascara...no. I have seen women attempt this in early morning traffic however, and I wholeheartedly believe that it is the reason that there are so many accidents on the interstate. When I see this modern marvel occurring, I usually pray that this idiot that couldn't either, a: be a little late by doing this at home, or b: wait to get to work to look human, will crash into another idiot, and while riding away in the ambulance together, they can exchange beauty tips. Or die.

I'm a little cranky today. I spent my day yesterday avoiding my aunt's phone calls. I didn't feel up to getting the lecture about not showing up for church for the second week in a row. Besides, I was busy pondering the mystery of the phone call. Suffice it to say, I haven't heard from Jonah. It's been a week. A long week. I didn't really expect to hear from him this soon, if at all, but I still want to know what the deal was with the quick escape. Do not remind me that toward the end I was pushing him to leave. I already remember.

When I get to work, I'm a half an hour late. As soon as I sit down, the team leader from the depths magically appears. She was probably waiting behind something or was cloaked in dark magic that rendered her invisible.

"Thank you for finally joining us, Autumn. I was starting to wonder if you would grace us with your presence, and now that you have, I'll need the new numbers for the Chambers' pitch in about five minutes."

That, right there, is one of the many reasons I can't stand this bitch. The good thing is, that since I already know that this tramp has it in for me, in addition to pondering the mystery call all week, I also worked on the numbers for this account. I usually try not to take this home, but I wasn't expecting my life to be interrupted last weekend, and I knew she was going to want this today. She only wants it because it isn't necessary. I've done this over four times, and the differences are marginal at best. I hope a house falls on her.

"Actually Chelsea, I have that for you right here. How was your weekend? Good, I hope. Now if you'll excuse me, I need to run the numbers for the Phelps account. They could look better, don't you think?" The secret to pissing Chelsea off is to kill her rude ass with kindness. Ask a lot of questions without giving her a chance to answer, then dismiss her by engaging yourself in something else before she has a chance to leave. After I finish my very loaded sentence, I reach into my oversized Dooney & Burke bag, and hand her the report. As soon as she takes it, I turn my back and begin to put away my things. I smile when I hear her hoof away.

When I sit up, a cup of coffee appears. It's attached to an arm; the arm belongs to Mark. He looks better. Last week was very up and down.

"To what do I owe the free beverage?" I ask the question with a raised eyebrow. He better read between the lines. He likes to think that no one here knows he's gay.

"You looked like you needed it. And I want you to come to lunch with me. Sushi at Tomo?" The invitation is a sham. We eat lunch together every day.

"Absolutely. I'll see you at one." Mark walks away, and I fall into my day.

So, here's the bad thing about my job, the day to day. I'm good with numbers. I always have been, and that's the problem. Just because you're good at something, that doesn't mean you find it stimulating. I love the adrenaline that my job gives. From the moment we're given an account, to the brainstorming, first number quotes, first pitch, and finally the green light. But that isn't my every day. My daily job is to get the very best initial budget that I can for the pitch. Sounds easy, right? Wrong. The budget for any account can be revised up to five or six times before the pitch is approved by the client. After the pitch is approved, the budget is given to our finance department, and they determine how feasible it is. If I want to keep my job, my numbers need to be very on. A little variation is expected, but if the actual cost shoots over my projected budget by more than five percent, my job becomes an endangered species. If it happens more than three times, my job is officially extinct. I'm working on budgets for five accounts. The problem is, that when I get the budget to something that I think everyone can agree on, the idea for the ad changes, or the client wants to change their perspective, or the hell beast (Chelsea) decides that the numbers can "look better". So, if you'll excuse me, I really need to work.

When we get to Tomo for lunch, it's a bit busy. Mark leads us to the sushi bar, and I sit next to him and wait.

"I love those shoes, Autumn. Ferragamo?" He's looking down at the four-inch metallic blue torture devices that I've chosen to punish myself with today.

"Choo."

"God bless you."

"No, you idiot, they're Jimmy Choo. Why are we here, with you pretending to care about my shoes?" What the hell? He's acting like I don't know that he either wants something, or he's done something. I'm drinking a green tea with ginseng and orange. His reply makes me choke.

"I'm going to come out to my parents this weekend."

He's waiting for my reaction, but I think that I'm dying.

I'm going to die at a sushi bar, because my idiot friend waited until I was swallowing tea to tell me something that was supposed to surprise me. And then, the tea comes up. I'm fine now, in case you were worried.

"What?" *Maybe my hearing is acting up.*

"I'm gonna tell them the truth this weekend."

Nope. Hearing is still the last thing to go. "I thought your father's birthday was Saturday? You cannot be that selfish. It isn't possible. And, not to be a bitch, but you've been in the closet for over twenty years. It isn't going to kill you to stay your ass in there another week."

Should he come out? Hell yes! But there's a time and a place. His father's sixtieth birthday isn't it.

"Can you be more supportive please? You're the one always saying how I need to be more honest with myself about the situations that I find myself in." He takes a drink of his coke.

You would think, that after the weekend that this man recently had, he wouldn't need any more drama for like a month.

"Yes, be more honest with yourself. Key word, YOURSELF! Don't do this, this weekend." *Am I speaking Ancient Egyptian?*

"Autumn, I need to do this while I have the nerve. I already know that my father's never gonna talk to me again when he finds out, so don't make it seem like I'm being a selfish prick this time. I'm not." He's speaking earnestly. Not even acknowledging his food.

Maybe he's right. He isn't. But I'll concede that maybe somewhere, in some distant parallel universe, he could be in the right.

"Okay, just...why now?" I hope he has a good reason.

"Henry called me"

"What?!" Apparently, I'm getting loud, because people are looking at us.

"Ssh! Just listen. I talked to him this time. We're going to move in together. We're going to work things out. The man lost his family because of me, and I think we need to be on an even keel." He plays with his straw for a second.

"One: he lost his family because he pretended to be straight from day one, when he shouldn't have. Two: did you think that maybe he's trying to work things out with you because his wife dropped him on his ass? Three: you alienating your family by coming out on your father's birthday does not put you on an even keel. It just proves that you are a selfish prick."

My California roll has been sitting in front of me for ten minutes. I'm starving, but I can't eat it. Every time I reach for my food, he moves it.

"She didn't throw him out. She wants them to go to counseling. He says that he's tired of living the lie. I am too."

He looks so pitiful.

"If you want this relationship, then fine. I'll cheer you on from the proverbial sidelines, but I still think you should wait to tell your parents. Just another week."

"If I wait, will you come with me?"

And the trap springs. I walked right into that one.

"Please, Autumn. For moral support. I really can't do this alone."

Bastard.

"Fine. I'll go. But if the rednecks get violent, I will leave you there. As a matter of fact, I'll drive. I'll need the keys to the getaway car."

He hugs me when I tell him he's a prick. So dysfunctional. The rest of our lunch hour passes with me avoiding talk of my date.

This avoidance thing is getting a little old. Mark keeps asking me questions about the incredible disappearing Jonah. I think he's trying to avoid the head on collision that is his life, by distracting himself with mine. The fact that I haven't given him any direct answers has him a tad bit pissed off. He tells me about every aspect of his life, and when something finally happens in mine, I shut up about it. It probably feels a little like betrayal. I'm not really trying to keep him on the outside of this situation, it's just that my pride is a little hurt by the fact that Grunting-man hasn't called me. I know that I made it sound earlier like I didn't expect the phone call so soon...okay, so I actually said that I didn't expect the phone call so soon but fuck that shit! You knew I was lying! At least, you should have known I was lying. The man was about to get the drawers, and the only reason he didn't was because of the absence of a little piece of latex, and he can't pick up the phone? So disrespectful.

I'm on my way to my car, silently thanking the good Lord for the end of this hellish Monday, when my cell phone rings. Looking down at it, I'm surprised to see my uncle's number. My mom's baby brother. I don't think I've ever told you about him. He's forty, unhappily married, and has an eighteen-year old daughter. My mother is ten years older than him. She met him when he was four, because up until that point, she was being raised by her grandparents. I think I mentioned something about that a while back. Anyway, seeing his name on the screen of my phone is a huge shock. He never calls me. Probably because I usually don't have anything that he needs. He's that uncle. You know, the one that you only hear from if he needs money, or a place to stay, or a kidney?

There's a note of suspicion in my voice when I answer the phone. "Hello?"

"Hey, Reign what's going on? This is your uncle Donovan." He's cheerful.

Maybe I should explain the Reign thing? Middle name. Yes, my mother gave me a name that sounds like an air freshener when you say it. Just use Autumn Reign to rid your house of those pet smells.

"Hi, Uncle Donovan. How's everything on your end?"

"Everything is wonderful here, sweetheart. Just taking care of the family, you know. Speaking of the family, Angel is gonna be starting college near you in January, she's waiting a semester..." wait for it, wait for it... "and I thought it would be a good idea if she came down there in October, and stayed with you until then."

There are just traps springing up all over the place today, I see. He cannot really think that I'll be okay with his eighteen-year old daughter staying with me. I haven't seen this child in something like seven years.

"Uncle Don, I don't know if that's such a good idea. I'm really busy with work, and I'm just getting to know the area myself." I do not have time for this. This man has barely spoken to me over the past seven years, and now I'm supposed to jump at the opportunity to baby-sit his nearly adult daughter? How about, no.

"I see where you're coming from Reign, but the truth is I really want her to be around a positive female right now. And, I don't want her going down there, acting all wild, just because she thinks no one's watching. I'm not asking you to baby-sit her or nothing like that. The girl has enough sense to know right from wrong, but I do think that you'll be a good person to guide her through this transition."

Convincing argument, but I don't want a roommate.

"Okay...does she really need to come in October?" Did he not say she was starting school in January?

"Actually, that was your mother's idea. She said you sounded lonely when she spoke to you yesterday, and she also said that Angel coming this early would give you two a chance to bond."

My mother is such a fucking Judas.

"October what?" I'm not getting my way on this. This is the second time in two weeks that a family member has tried to move someone in with me. The difference is if I say no this time, I'll have to deal with my mother. I can already hear the speech about how I'm becoming a selfish bitch.

"We were thinking we could drop her off on the thirteenth. We're driving down that way for my father's retirement party, and we could drop her off on the way."

"Okay, just call me to let me know what time you'll be here. Do you need directions?" I wonder if he can hear the obvious irritation in my voice.

"Your mother gave me the address, so I can get directions from google maps, thank you for this. You don't know how much it means to me."

Apparently not.

It may be necessary for me to explain that my mother and her brother don't have the same father. My mother never knew her biological father, and as far as I've ever been able to tell, she hasn't wanted to. My great-grandfather played the role when she was growing up, and that has always been enough. Besides, she was living in the town that her mother got pregnant in until she was fourteen. Her father never came to her, so maybe he wasn't worth knowing. Anyhoo, hopefully this situation with my cousin works out, I really don't have time to be any body's babysitter. On the other hand, it's only for two months. Only so much can go wrong. Right?

Letting myself into my humble abode, I kick off my shoes, and make my way to the kitchen. I need coffee. My nerves are shot. I really should put some rum in it. I'm trying not to call my mother. At the moment, I'm very much pissed off at her, and being in any way disrespectful, verbally or by voice intonation, is in no way acceptable. Due to her recent actions however, I'm not in a very respectful mood. How do you volunteer someone else's home as the, Do Drop Inn? The thing that kills me is that if I call her pissed off, she'll get mad at me. I'll be the bad guy. The most offensive part is that she thinks that my uncle is a leech. She's been saying it for years, and now she put me into the user circle. Damnit!

I stop my mental rant at the sound of my phone ringing. I should not answer that. The last time I did, my home became the headquarters for the babysitters' club. I answer it anyway. I don't look at the Caller I.D. this time, so I'm surprised by the voice on the other end.

"Hello?"

"Hey, Autumn...this is Jonah. How are you?"

Well, this is unexpected. I thought he fell off of the planet. The surprises just keep coming today. "Hi. Long time no speak, I'm okay. How have you been?" I'm making coffee. I'm desperately in need of coffee.

"I've been good. Um...so, I wanted to know if you wanted to get together and do something tonight?"

Whoa! Am I a jump-off?! Oh my God, oh my God!

"A little last minute don't you think? I could be busy." I sound calm. I'm proud of me.

"You could be. Are you?" He's flirting.

He treats me like a jump-off, and now he's flirting?

"No, but that doesn't mean I want to go out tonight." So, there!

"Okay, how about we stay in?"

Excuse me?

"I'm sorry, what?" Again, with the calling me a jump-off.

"I didn't mean like that. I meant have dinner together, at your house if you'd like."

What to do, what to do?

"You know I don't cook, right?" Might as well put that out there.

"I do. Or we could order something?"

He cooks? We'll see about that.

"I'm kinda liking this, you cooking, thing. What will you be making exactly?"

"How about steak and potatoes?"

I could eat some steak.

"Okay. What time should I come over?" Simple choice, hot pocket, or steak. I'll take the steak for three hundred, Alex.

"Why don't I come over there?"

Time to pump the breaks. "How about, no?"

"What? Why not?"

Is he offended? Sounds like it.

"My mother told me never to trust a man that won't let you come to his house; he could be hiding a whole life." She really did tell me that.

"Okay, fair enough. But two things. One: my house is not exactly spotless right now. Two: it's gonna be a long drive, and you may not feel like taking the drive home later."

"Thanks for the warnings; I'll keep both in mind. Now what is your address, please?" I grab an envelope off of the counter and write down the address. Now, I just need to shower and get dressed. I hang up after telling him that I'll be there in an hour or so. I'm leaning more toward the, or so.

Okay, so now that I've showered, I can't find anything to wear. I probably should have chosen the outfit first, but that's why hindsight is 20/20. What does one wear to dispel the idea that one is a jump-off? Should I wear jeans to kill the whole easy access assumption, or a pencil skirt and blouse to appear classy and sophisticated? After standing there for fifteen minutes, I come to the conclusion that clothing is highly overrated. That being said, I'm going with the skirt. I leave the house, finally dressed in a pinstriped pencil skirt that has a slight ruffle at the hem, a sheer silk blouse, white, tapered at the waist, and a pair of black Chanel sling backs. I figure I might as well look good. Because after I establish the whole, "I'm not a jump-off", thing, I'm having some sex. You may feel that this is counterproductive. As a friend, I must express how little your feelings mean right now when weighed against the fact that I'm horny, and the rabbit is out of batteries. Besides, if it doesn't work out, I'll get over it. Now, let's just pray that I don't get lost.

It takes me over an hour to get to his apartment. I got a little lost. So, the downside to Georgia, every apartment complex is a gated community. You have to be swiped or buzzed into everywhere unless you have the gate code. He buzzes me into the parking lot (insanity), and I park in front of his building. Before getting out of the car, I call Mark.

"Hello, Automobile. What do you need?"

Isn't he precious?

"I'm at Jonah's, he's making me dinner, I hadn't heard from him in a week, he called today, if I die, tell the cops he killed me." So, I'm a little dramatic. Bases need to be covered.

"Yeah, so what're you wearing?"

Relevance?

"Pencil skirt, sheer blouse, Chanel shoes."

"At least you'll die looking fabulous. I'll make sure your missing person flyers only get posted in the trendiest restaurants and store fronts."

"Thank you." Hanging up the phone, I get out of the car and make my way to the door. If he does kill me, I hope he spares my shoes. I've only worn them twice. It would be a shame to see them buried.

When I get to the door, I raise my hand to knock, but it opens before I can pull my hand back. I actually hit him. In the nose. Hard.

"Fuck!" He's holding his face, so it came out sounding muffled.

My hand is covering my mouth, which is hanging open, and if it wasn't for the narrow slant of my eyes, they'd be as wide as saucers. "I am sooo sorry! Are you bleeding? I'm sorry...maybe we should put ice on it. Do you have ice?"

This is going to sound really bad, but I'm trying not to laugh. I don't know if it's because I'm embarrassed that I hit him, or if this is just a funny situation. Very confusing. I'm going to go with the: this is a funny situation, reasoning.

"This is funny to you? You punched me in the face, and now you're laughing at me?" It's still muffled because he's holding his face, and he sounds like a muppet. This time, I can't stop the laughter, and my eyes start watering. Hot pocket, here I come.

"Come inside. I'd rather my neighbors not see that a woman that's a foot shorter than me almost knocked me out. I can't believe you're laughing at me after I made you a steak dinner." He moves aside, and I enter the apartment. I'm still laughing.

Okay, nice digs. The front door opens into the living room, a very large open space. Twenty-foot ceiling, looking up, I can see a loft. There is a breakfast bar that separates the kitchen from the living room. It's another large area. He has a waffle iron. I think I'm in love. There are two steps leading to a doorway on the other side of the kitchen. This is the dining room. A modest table, wood with a dark finish, seating for four, no centerpiece, are the basics.

There are movie posters on the walls. In every room. In the dining room there are posters from *Speed* and *Terminator 2.* These are movies to eat by? Walking back into the kitchen, I open the freezer, and look for something that can be used as an icepack. I spot a bag of frozen curly fries, that'll do.

"Come here." I walk over to the living room and sit down on the sofa. It's a brown leather sectional. Patting the spot next to me, I am pleased when he sits down, and I reach for his head. Holding his face between my hands, I inspect my handiwork. A little red, but not broken. No bleeding. What a wuss.

"You're fine. Stop being a baby. It's not broken, no swelling, no bruising either. Want me to kiss it better?" I'm smiling when I say it, and then he kisses me. The kiss starts off very innocent, a hello. It turns into something very mature as his hand finds its way into my hair, I'm mentally patting myself on the back for wearing it down. My body is reclined against the arm of the sofa and he's pasted to the front of me when I hear a loud beeping noise. Jonah doesn't seem to notice it, and I almost resolve to ignore it, but it's annoying the hell out of me, and I can't. So, I push against him until he gives a little. When he leans back to look at me, he's a little out of breath.

"What's wrong?" His voice is deeper than it was, and I feel his words more than I hear them.

"What's that beeping noise?"

He's looking at me like I'm touched in the head. "What beeping noise?"

"There is a very annoying beeping noise. How can you not hear that?" Maybe he's partially deaf. Either that or I suddenly became part canine and am hearing at a decibel that is imperceptible to human ears.

"Beeping noise?" He sits up, and then his face clears, and he looks around the room. "Oh shit!" And off he goes, running for the kitchen. Please lord, don't tell me he burned the food.

You'll be happy to know that the food was fine. The boy can actually cook. Though, since I can't cook, I have no idea how hard it is to make steak and potatoes. Still, the dinner was very good. We made some polite conversation as we ate, but now for the real. I'm on the couch once again. This time, I'm drinking a corona from the bottle (so classy) with my feet tucked under me. *Face/Off* is playing on the television. It's a 55" smart tv, and that's a lot of

John Travolta. This is my second corona; I had my first with dinner. Gotta admit, I'm feeling a little buzzed.

"So, what was with the mystery phone call?" He was in the middle of telling me about a design he's working on when that flies out of my mouth.

"What?"

I now realize that I asked that question out loud. This is the problem with feeling buzzed. You're loose enough to speak your mind, but coherent enough to feel embarrassed. Well, in for a penny.

"The mystery phone call." I'm looking at him trying to gauge his reaction.

"What phone call?"

He knows what I'm talking about. I know he does. The hell, man? "The one that came when you were in my bed a week ago. The one that had you rushing off."

"A friend of mine needed help with something."

Was that an answer?

"Do me a favor? Be a little vaguer in your answer, 'cause that was way too direct for my feeble mind to decipher." That sentence just redefined the word, bitch.

"My ex-girlfriend. We're still friends, she's engaged, there was a relationship issue the other day, she called me to pick her up, the end." He makes it sound like a normal occurrence. Interrogation time.

"How long have you two been broken up?" This is important. There needs to be closure in that relationship, or we won't be having a relationship.

"Three years." He's nodding as though he wants to have no mistake in my perception.

"How long were you together?" another important question.

"Four years."

Long time. Very long time. Wow.

"Well okay. What's your favorite movie?" Like I said, I'm a little buzzed. Random questions are a side effect.

"*Little Shop of Horrors*." He looks serious. "What's yours?"

"The mature answer is, *Imitation of Life*. The actual answer is, *The Princess Bride*."

He's laughing at me.

"What? Wesley and Buttercup found true love!" I sound so indignant.

"How can you possibly take a movie seriously when one of the main characters is named, Buttercup?" he sips his beer and laughs.

This from a man whose favorite movie is about a man-eating plant?

"Have you ever seen it?"

"No."

"Did you know that it's got everything from comedy to suspense?"

"No."

"We're watching it. I'll bring it over next Friday."

"Okay."

"You wanna show me the rest of your place?"

"Let's go." He gets up so fast that it makes me a little dizzy. Perhaps I'm behaving a little jump-off-ish. But the man cooked for me, I punched him in the face, and his kisses give me butterflies.

I un-tuck my legs from beneath me and give him my hand so that he can help me up. On our way up to the loft, we pass a bathroom, a bedroom, and another room with a closed door. The loft is huge. It covers half of the apartment, has a private bathroom, and a floor to ceiling window. There are movie posters in here also. A lot of *Star Wars*, and a poster from the Disney movie, *Hercules*.

"*Hercules*?" I point to the poster. No judgment.

"I'm very in touch with my inner child," he deadpans, and I laugh.

There isn't a television in this room. There is, however, an office like area with a laptop. There is a leather recliner in the corner, with a brass floor lamp to the left of it, and an end table to the right with a book lying on it. There are a couple of boxes in another corner, like he's moving out, or still moving in. I walk over to the half wall at the end of the room and look out on the room below. Far. Very far. I decide to sit on the bed instead of looking down on the fall that could be.

"You have a very comfortable bed. It's almost making me tired."

"I really didn't plan on us falling asleep at this point," he reaches for my beer as he says this and sits it on the bedside table. "Actually, I didn't plan on sleeping for a while." He sits next to me on the bed and angles his body toward mine.

"I said, almost making me tired. What exactly were you planning? You fed me, gave me alcohol, let me punch you. What could be missing? We could have sex, but the last time we tried that, you were extremely under prepared." I'm playing with the hair at the nape of his neck as I'm talking.

"I excel at second chances. Let me prove it to you?"

I kiss him in answer.

Grabbing the front of his shirt, I lean back, bringing him with me. I would've played the top, but the skirt won't accommodate. I pull his shirt over his head. It's another t-shirt, a black one, with a Decepticon logo on it. The kiss breaks off for a split second before taking off again. I feel his hand on my breast and realize that my blouse is open. I can feel his hand traveling downward, and my heart is hammering in anticipation. The words, "don't stop", are playing on continuous loop in my head. Reaching the waist band, his hand attempts, unsuccessfully, to slide further down. I can feel him trying to find the buttons, and he finally breaks the kiss and looks at me.

"Is this like, the tightest skirt known to man? How the hell did you get this thing on? Did you really drive in this?"

Pushing him back, I stand up. Reaching behind myself, I unfasten the skirt and push it down. I climb back onto the bed and straddle his hips. I was intending to kiss him again, but he places his hands on my hips and kisses the top of my right breast. Burying my hands in his hair, I give myself away to the sensations that he's creating. He pulls down the cups of my bra before groaning and leaning his head forward and burying it between my breasts. His reaction makes me laugh a little. My breasts are a 32C. It isn't like they're huge, but he's acting like they are.

"You have beautiful breasts. Fucking beautiful."

Before I can say anything, his tongue makes an appearance and strokes against my nipple. His hands slide up my back and press me closer to his mouth. I feel like he's consuming me. Reaching between us, I unfasten his belt and work open the button of his jeans. Don't ask me how we manage to do it, but his jeans are removed along with his boxers and my panties, all while I'm sitting on top of him and he's licking and sucking and fondling my breasts. Jonah is blindly reaching for the bedside table and I look over noticing the box of condoms that he's attempting to get to. Magnum man. I knew it. I reach over and grab the box, sitting it beside us on the bed.

Jonah releases my breast and smiles at me before kissing me and turning us so that I'm under him. Sitting up on his knees, he slides his fingers up along my abdomen, between my breasts, and up to my mouth. When he presses his thumb to my lips, I open my mouth and suck it in. When he removes it, its glistening and he wastes no time pressing it to my clit and moving it in small circles. Before long, I'm panting and reaching for him. I stroke my hand along his cock, and he slaps me between my legs. Not hard, but enough to make me jump. Then he removes my hand and shakes his head at me.

No one has ever done something like that to me before, and I don't know if it's supposed to feel good, but it does. Then he's opening the condom and sliding it on, and for a second, I'm worried that he might be too big. Leaning down, he kisses me again and I feel his hand between us, and then he's sliding into me an inch at a time. There is a feeling of being over filled and needing more.

When he's buried all the way in me, he gives me a few seconds to adjust to him. And, fuck, I really need it, because he's so big that it hurts. He raises my left thigh higher on his hip and goes even deeper until the pain sharpens and morphs into pleasure. How the hell is that even possible?

My thoughts scatter when he starts to move, and I follow along, moving to the pace he's set. I can feel that tingling pressure begin to build, our pace is increasing, and my nails are biting into his back. His mouth closing over the place where my neck meets my shoulder shatters the sun while my body seems to explode and implode all at once. My orgasm excites him, and he moves harder and faster into me. He's pounding me into the mattress and my nails are biting so deeply into him that I'm sure that I've drawn blood. The rest of the night is filled with the sounds of mutual pleasure. I'll definitely be hoarse tomorrow.

Chapter Ten:

A week and a half has passed since we last spoke, and it definitely seems longer. I've seen Jonah four times since, "the night of many orgasms", as I have affectionately dubbed it. I talk to him at least once a day, and we aren't tired of each other yet. But it's still early. Right now, I'm sitting in Mark's parents' living room, waiting for him to pop on out of the closet. I've chosen a spot near the door. His parents live in Byron, Georgia. No offense to the people of this town, but outward appearances do not give the impression that these people are gay friendly.

We made sure that there was enough gas to keep us from stopping anywhere near here to refuel. According to Mark, he didn't want me to feel uncomfortable. This isn't the first time I've met his parents. The surroundings are usually different though. They come into Atlanta for dinners with Mark occasionally. His mother is the picture of southern hospitality, and his father would be just another good ole boy, if it weren't for the white collar around his neck that never gets taken off.

Mark looks just like his mother, only he has his father's size. To his father's credit, he's sixty years old, without a gray hair on his head. That may change today. I really feel bad for these people. Not because their son is gay, but because I'm sure that they aren't going to know how to take it. And that never makes situations easy. They really are nice people.

"So, Momma, Daddy...Mom and Dad, I've got something very important to tell you." He looks like he's going to throw up, and I give his hand a supportive squeeze.

His mother gives me this *look*, and before Mark can say anything else, she has an outburst. "Please don't tell me she's pregnant. There is enough turmoil in this world without people creating children that are going to be lost and confused from birth. What am I supposed to say to the ladies on the Missionary Board?"

Whoa! Did I think that these were nice people? Closed-minded bitch!

"Mom, what are you talking about? Stop it! Autumn is my friend...we are not seeing each other." He squeezes my hand back, but I'm a little too shocked to give him a signal that I'm alright with his mother's outburst.

His father decides to chime in, and the atmosphere becomes a little explosive. "You're not dating her?"

The speculation is obvious. Mark just shakes his head. He wants to come out to these people? When he shakes his head, his mother actually puts her hand over her heart and begins to thank God. This would be funny if it weren't so pathetic.

Looking at me, she feels the need to "explain". "I don't have anything against you people. I think y'all are great. We had a colored lady that used to help around the church when Mark was a little boy— a lovely voice. It's just...well...you know."

That was supposed to make me feel better? Right.

"You're telling me that she's not pregnant?" This comes from his father. He's still not a believer.

"Dad, I'm gay!" He throws that out there in this, "so, there", tone. His father becomes really still, and his face is turning red. His mother gets up and leaves the room.

When his father speaks again, his voice is a roar. "My son is not a FAGGOT! And if you're telling me that that's what you are, then you are not my son! Leave this house and pray that the Lord forgives you for going so far against his word! You leave this house!

How could you come in this house with this vileness inside of you?! Leave, I said!"

I'm too stunned to move, and I feel Mark pulling me with him as he moves toward the door. I knew that they wouldn't react well, but I didn't expect this. I don't think anyone could've expected this.

The next thing I know, we're in the car and on the road. I look over at Mark in the driver's seat of my car, and there are tears coursing down his cheeks. He pulls the car over to the side of the road and rests his head against his hands. He's trembling. Unhooking my seat belt, I pull him over to me. He lays his head upon my breast and cries. Deep, wrenching sobs that make me hurt for him more than I can ever remember hurting for myself. One of my hands cradles his head, as my other hand runs up and down his back. I am lost. Trying to soothe a pain that is beyond my comprehension...knowing that I am failing in this...I have never wanted to succeed so badly. I, who have always had a "suck it up" mentality, cannot find the words to push him out of this trench.

We sit in the front seat for what seems like hours before I make him switch seats with me so that I can drive us home. This place is better left as a memory that we can bury, but never fully forget. As we leave this town, I take a moment to take in the peacefulness of it. It's a Norman Rockwell painting come to life. A town that decides your worth, by where you grew up. Some small towns always house the worst parts of human nature. I am so happy that he got out of this town, and if left up to me, he'll never come back.

When we arrive at my house, I have to prompt Mark out of the car. Inside of the apartment, I lead him into the spare bedroom. He lies down on the bed, and I lie beside him and hold his hand.

"Do you want me to call Henry?" My voice is a whisper, and I'm not sure that he hears me until he responds.

"No." His whisper is as silent as mine, but it somehow manages to be bleak.

"He'll be worried when you don't come home." I don't know if I'm telling the truth. I need him to feel like he's loved. He needs to see that, even though his parents have opted out, there are people that know who he is, and love him because of it.

"Don't tell him about today? Promise?" He's looking at me now, and I can't help but to agree. It isn't my story to tell anyway. Nodding, I kiss him on the forehead and go to make the call.

Henry answers on the third ring. "Hello?"

"Hi, Henry. It's Autumn. Listen, Mark wanted me to call you so that you wouldn't worry. He's gonna stay here tonight, and he'll be home in the morning." Please don't ask.

"Okay...but why didn't he call me himself?"

"The battery on his cell died. He went to pick us up something to eat, and I told him that I'd call while he was gone." That just sounds like a lie.

"Oh. Okay. Thanks for calling. Tell him I love him, please?"

"Okay, no problem. Bye, Henry." Hanging up the phone, I lean my back against the wall for a moment and rest. After taking several deep breaths, I move away from the wall and make my way back to the bedroom. He's asleep. Its seven p.m. and I'm exhausted. Walking into the living room, I lie down on the couch and turn on the television. I fall asleep before I even know what I'm watching.

I wake up from a dead sleep at eleven p.m., the house is too quiet. I turn on the lamp on the table and listen. Nothing. Getting up, I pick up the cordless phone, and begin making my way to the spare bedroom. I'm flipping on lights as I go. I have an unsettled feeling, like something is crawling on me. Entering the bedroom, the first thing I notice is that the bed is empty. Leaving the bedroom, I continue down the hall. I'm reaching for the next switch when I trip over something. It's Mark. He's unconscious on my bathroom floor. There's an empty bottle of tub and tile cleaner on the floor next to him, and I can hear the wheezing sound of his breath being expelled.

God, please no. Not this.

My hands are shaking so badly that I almost drop the phone as I'm dialing 911.

"911 emergency." The voice on the phone sounds bored. Like this call is just one in a series of many and saving lives has somehow become redundant. When I speak there's a tremor in my voice. I didn't know that I was crying until that moment.

"Hello, please send someone. My friend, he's unconscious, he's...I think he drank bathroom cleaner. I know he did! Please help me! Please, he's gonna die!" The crying is in earnest now. I don't recognize my own voice. There's a note of hysteria to it, and I'm praying that I'll wake up on my couch, and this will have all been a nightmare. Even as I'm praying for it, I know that it won't happen.

"Ma'am, I need you to calm down, and give me your name and address." She sounds slightly interested now. That knowledge gives me a sense of relief. She'll send someone.

"Autumn Blaire. I'm at 3547 Peachtree Station Way, Melody Villas, unit 114. The front door will be unlocked." I'm running to the front door as I'm talking to her. I disengage the lock and run back to the bathroom. He's still breathing but he's sweating. His face is red. Sitting on the floor, I place his head in my lap.

"Ma'am, how old is your friend?" I forgot there was a person on the phone.

"His name is Mark. He's twenty-seven. He's twenty-seven, and his favorite food is pancakes, and he watches Family Guy, and he wants to buy a Toy Poodle and name it Butch. So, he can't die like this. He can't die! You need to send someone! Please send someone! The front door is unlocked, and I don't know what to do, so please help! Please!" That hysteria is back. It never left. I hear it in my voice, but it's like I'm standing outside of myself.

"Hello? Peachtree City Police!" They're here. Thank God.

"Hello? We're upstairs. Hello?" I hear their footsteps getting closer. Finally, there's a man in a police uniform standing in the doorway to the bathroom. More people enter, and soon I'm ushered out of the way while Mark is loaded onto a stretcher and then into an ambulance. They tell me that I can't ride with him, but that I can meet him at the hospital. The officers, after seeing the shakiness in my hands, offer me a ride. They also remind me to get my keys and purse. I remember my cell. I'll need to call Henry.

The last thing that I want to do is call him. A part of me knows that this isn't his fault, but that part of me is riding shotgun to the rest of me. And, the rest of me cannot abide his presence right now. I need to blame someone. The correct shoulders to carry that blame are stewing in their own ignorance in Byron, Georgia. I know that, but they aren't here. I don't have a phone number for them. Mark has a brother. I should call him. I don't know what I'll say. I know that if I call Henry, then I can't call Mark's brother. I choose Henry. Mark would want that.

There's no answer when I call Henry. I leave a message. Something to the effect of, "it's very important that you call me back". What am I supposed to say to him? They won't tell me anything. People are coming in and out of the doors to the emergency room, some in white coats, some pushing machines...there was a woman running like her life depended on it five minutes ago. I don't know if any of these people have anything to do with Mark, because no one will tell me anything.

The officers that brought me here are walking toward me. They had gone to the desk and spoken to the rude woman that told me to sit down and wait. Bitch! I try to give them all of my attention when they come to stand in front of me. It's hard.

"Autumn, we need to ask you some questions." The officer talking to me is trying to be gentle. He's tall. Way over six feet with black hair. He has warm brown eyes. He told me his name, but I can't remember it. It doesn't occur to me to read his badge. He looks too young. Like he's fresh out of high school, except for his eyes. There are creases around them that give a better view of his actual age. His skin is a shade lighter than mine, and his hands are worker's hands.

"Okay." My voice has a tremble to it.

"Can you recall the events that led up to you finding your friend in the bathroom?"

"His name is Mark. Is he alright? Can you find out? They won't tell me." I know that I'm not really answering his questions, but I can't really focus.

"The doctors are doing all they can for Mark. No one can answer your questions right now, because there aren't any answers yet. We brought in the bottle from the cleaner that he drank so that the doctors would know where to start. We need you to answer some questions so that they can help him."

I must look stupid to these people. I am not stupid! I am emotionally distraught! Why do people always insist on speaking to me like I'm stupid?

"Fine. He came to my house at 9 a.m. and we had breakfast. We drove to his parents' house in Byron. His mother made a late lunch. We ate. There was an argument an hour or so after lunch, and we were asked to leave. We got to my apartment at around 7p.m. and we talked for a few minutes before he fell asleep. I fell asleep in my living room. I woke up at 11 p.m. and found him on the bathroom floor." I know that my details are a bit vague, leaving out the whole: coming out to his parents, situation. The officers know it, too.

"Autumn, we need to know what the argument was about."

Why? What is the point of that?

"His parents didn't approve of his romantic life. His father disowned him. He was very upset." I'm trying not to be angry. I don't handle emotional pain well. I usually respond with anger. I think I mentioned that during Mark's last crisis. It's pissing me off that no one wants to tell me anything, but they're asking me a million fucking questions. Perhaps I'm being unreasonable. I can't help it.

"They were upset that the two of you were dating?"

What's with the past tense?

"They *are* upset that he *is* gay." I hope that Mark isn't angry when I tell him about this.

"Okay. Was Mark drinking tonight?"

Did I say he was drinking tonight?

"No." I shake my head when I say it.

"Does he use any drugs recreationally?"

Recreationally?

"No. Never."

"The cleaner that he swallowed, do you know approximately how much was in that bottle?"

Finally. A question that's relevant. "The bottle was almost full. I just bought the cleaner last week."

Before the top investigators can ask any more questions, we are approached by what I'll assume is a doctor.

She's a forty-something woman of medium build with sandy-brown hair, put back in a ponytail at the nape of her neck. She has a caramel skin tone, and very serious eyes. Her scrubs are a light blue and she has a stethoscope around her neck. She clears her throat when she comes to stand in front of us, and without sparing the officers a glance, she proceeds to speak to me.

"Hello, I was told that you are the young woman that came in with our poison victim?" she has a warm voice.

Victim? I don't like that word. It seems wrong. The word, victim, implies that there was an accident, and this wasn't an accident.

"Yes, my name is Autumn. How is he?" She has to tell me something or I'm going to lose it.

"He's stable. Are you a family member?"

Is she blind? What the fuck kind of doctor is she?

"No, I'm his friend. He isn't on good terms with his family right now." Everyone here has questions, and no one has any answers. Typical.

"I'm sorry, but I can't give you any information on this patient without his consent, and he isn't in a position to give that consent right now. Do you have any contact information for his family? Maybe a relative that he is on good terms with?"

Oh My God. I can't believe this.

"He has a brother. An older brother. I can call him. Give me a moment please?" Nodding her head, she walks away. The police are still standing there when I pull out my cell phone to make the call. Looking up, I see the "no cell phones" sign on the wall and I walk outside. Everything feels surreal, like I'm floating. I don't remember dialing the number for Mark's brother, but I must have because he's answering now. I woke him up.

"Hello?" He sounds groggy. I can hear his wife in the background asking who's on the phone.

"Hello, Patrick. This is Autumn. Mark's friend? I'm sorry to call so late, but there was an incident with Mark." Hopefully he hasn't spoken to his parents. And if he has, hopefully he doesn't share their opinion.

"Autumn? What kind of incident? Is he okay?"

"I don't know if he's okay. They said he's stable. They won't tell me anything else because I'm not family. We're at Emory in Peachtree City."

"I'm on my way." He hangs up the phone, and I can breathe. Really breathe. I know that I'll find out what's wrong now. I'm not sure if the coming knowledge makes me feel better or worse.

Running to the bushes near the entryway, I throw up. My hands are shaking again. Going back inside, I don't see the officers. Locating a bathroom, I rinse out my mouth and throw cold water on my face. I look like someone kicked my ass. Swollen eyes, splotchy skin, messy hair. I've looked worse. Going back to the waiting room, I sit until Patrick gets there.

I must look like a junkie. I can't keep still, and I'm looking at the entrance every five seconds. I want to call Jonah. Is that weak? The feeling of needing to be held? I want to, but I'm not going to. This relationship is a little more than a week old, and this situation is too intense for a relationship that's still young. The problem is that I do need to be held right now. I know that it's selfish of me to be thinking of what I need, but that's the reality. I need someone to hug me and tell me that everything is going to be alright, even if it isn't. My family is huge, and close. With the exception of a small few. I have never had to deal with anything alone. From minor to major, someone has always been there for me to lean on if I needed to. This is unfamiliar territory for me. The truth is, since I've been in Georgia, Mark's been my go-to guy. His life is full of drama, but he is one of the strongest people...how did this happen?

I'm so lost in my thoughts, that I almost don't see Patrick at the desk. I stand up as soon as I see him. I watch him talk to the lady at the desk for a moment before I approach him. She hands him some papers and a pen before she goes back to the business of being useless. I tap him on the shoulder, and he turns toward me. Patrick looks like he could be the milkman's kid. Mark swears that he looks like their grandfather. He's about 5'7" with jet black hair and grey eyes. He and Mark barely look related. He's wearing pajama bottoms and a Georgia Tech t-shirt. At least he had a chance to put on sneakers.

"Hi, Patrick. I'm...thank you for hurrying."

"It's fine. He's my brother. Now, what happened?"

Maybe he hasn't spoken to their parents. "Mark swallowed some tub and tile cleaner."

"No...? No. He wouldn't do that." Patrick is shaking his head and looking at me like I'm the biggest liar on the planet. I wish I was.

"I thought so too. He's been going through a lot lately, and today was really rough. I found him on my bathroom floor. I'm not sure how long he was there before I found him. I dialed 911 and they came really fast. All they would tell me is that he's stable. You need to speak to the doctor." I feel like I'm floating just outside myself. My voice is too calm. It's probably because of Patrick. I need to maintain my calm. I don't want to panic him. One of us needs to be reasonable. I need to appear reasonable, so that he'll be reasonable. A convoluted way of thinking, but I'm operating on very little sleep after having found my friend in the midst of his very own transition into the afterlife.

"Today was really rough? What the hell does that mean?" he demands.

Shit.

"We went to your parents' house, and there was an argument." I have never told so much of someone else's business in my life.

"He told them? The gay thing?" He looks up at the ceiling and curses under his breath.

Wow.

"I didn't know that he told you already. But, yeah. They didn't take it well." Understatement.

"He told me last night. Well, I guess it was the night before last now. Anyway, he came to my house and said he needed to speak to me. He told me that he's gay. That he has a boyfriend, and that they're moving in together. I told him that he couldn't come around my kids anymore." Patrick starts to cry and I'm not sure what to do. Comforting him seems wrong. He has two children. A little girl named Kayla, and a two-year old boy, named after Mark. Mark loves those kids to death. He doesn't think he'll ever be in a position to have his own, so he sees them as being his in a way. He's god-father to his nephew. I can't believe that his brother would take that away from him.

"What did my parents do?" We're still standing near the desk, and the human statue behind the desk is suddenly very animated. And very nosy. Taking Patrick's arm, I lead him away from the desk.

"Your mother walked out of the room. Your father went full hate speech and kicked us out of the house. He told Mark that he isn't welcome there anymore." I'm waiting for him to say something. Instead, he turns back to the desk.

He's speaking to the woman behind the desk when I reach it. "...a doctor. Preferably the one that's working on my brother. His name is Mark Donnerly. He tried to kill himself, but this hospital has, so far, saved his life. I need to know exactly how successfully."

"Sir, if you could just fill out the paperwork—"

He cuts her off before she can finish. "Listen, I'm happy for whatever union you're in that allows you to be worthless, but if you don't get me a doctor that can give me some information on my brother, I'm gonna use this paperwork to set your desk on fire!"

I watch as she picks up the phone beside her and pages the doctor overhead. Why didn't I think of that?

We sit together until the doctor comes. Neither of us speaks. I think it's because we don't know what to say. If Mark makes it out of this alive, I'm going to kill him.

The doctor is the same one from earlier.

Chapter Eleven:

It's been four days since Mark almost died in my bathroom. That night is still fresh in my mind. I haven't been able to sleep. The doctor told us that he ingested a large amount of the fluid, and that it caused his lack of consciousness. They did everything they could do to flush his system, but they didn't know if he suffered brain damage, because there was no telling how long he was unconscious. His brother called me about an hour ago to tell me that Mark was awake. I don't know what to do. What to expect.

Patrick called their parents and told them what happened. Their father said that it was God's will that Mark pay for his sins. I hope he has a heart attack. I know that that's a horrible thing to want, but I can't help it.

Henry came to the hospital while I was there yesterday. He looked like he'd been crying. I didn't know what to say to him, so I left him alone.

On a personal note, I've called Jonah twice. No answer. No return calls. So much for the being held thing. I'm on my way to the hospital now. I've been at work all day, pretending not to hear people talk about Mark. No one knows what happened, but people speculate until fiction becomes fact. Patrick called our H.R. department and told them that Mark was in the hospital, but he didn't give many details. My co-workers have said everything from, Mark was fired, to, he had a nervous breakdown. The meanest thing that I've heard was that he's in jail for assaulting a random woman. What is wrong with people?

Walking up to Mark's room at the hospital, I see his brother talking to the doctor. He notices me, and waves me in. He's a good guy. He took time off from work to be here every day. Patrick's an engineer and a really good dad. He leaves here every night in time to read his kids a bedtime story and then comes back once they fall asleep. His wife is upset about his decision to be at Mark's bedside. She agrees with her in-laws' way of thinking.

Patrick keeps telling me things about his personal life. He and his wife were high school sweethearts. She's trying to make him choose between her and his brother. He's shocked. He says that he understands where she's coming from, after all, he did try to throw his brother out of his life less than a week ago. But, with Mark in the hospital he thought she'd see things differently. Patrick realized how much he loved his brother when he almost died. He says that he abandoned him too many times already, and he can't do it again. I figure that the only reason he's told me all of this is that we're here together every night with nothing but a few channels on a television with very poor audio.

The window is open. It's not exactly freezing in Georgia in October, but it's chilly enough that the window shouldn't be open. I walk over to close it, and I hear Mark's voice.

"Leave it open." He doesn't say it loudly. I stand there with my back to him for a few seconds. I'm avoiding looking at him. It was easy to look when he couldn't look back. Easy to hold his hand when his wasn't gripping mine. This is different. I don't want to talk about what could've happened. But, Mark will. I know him; he'll want to discuss it.

"Mark, you could get sick if we leave the window open for too long."

"I'm in the right place for it. Come here."

I drag myself over to the bed and force my eyes to his face.

"So, the good news? I don't have any brain damage. I did do some damage to my kidneys though." He makes a face.

I wasn't expecting this. I was expecting him to be weak. Confused. In and out of consciousness. Like a made for TV movie. He's not. He's awake, strong, and very clear minded.

"How much damage?" I'm steady.

"One is at a hundred percent, but the other is at like fifty." He's being very off-handed.

"So, you're gonna be alright?" I'm very doubtful.

"Physically? Yeah. But they think I'm crazy 'cause I tried to off myself." He rolls his eyes as if the thought is ridiculous.

He did not just say that.

"You scared me to death."

"I wasn't trying to scare you, baby. It's just...you ever feel like you're drownin'? Like you can see the surface of the water, but no matter how hard you kick, you can't break through? I was drownin', I couldn't kick anymore, so I went with the tide." He's looking at me like I have to understand. Only, I don't understand. I can't.

"You owe me a bottle of tub and tile cleaner. Preferably, some non-toxic, all natural, tub and tile cleaner."

He smiles at me. "I love you, Autobot."

I squeeze his hand. "I love you, too."

"So, I was out for four days?"

"Four long days." I nod while I say it.

"I'll bet Chelsea is pissed." He laughs, and it's the best sound I've ever heard.

"She's been trying to get me to give her all my Mark info," I tell him.

"Tell her that I looked at her shoes on Friday, and my brain, unable to process that level of ugly, was shocked into a coma."

I love this man.

"Will you give me a hug? I know this sounds selfish, but I really need one." I do.

"Come to daddy." He reaches out for me.

Kicking off my shoes, I climb into his narrow hospital bed, and being as careful as I can not to disturb the tubes and wires that I'm pretending not to see, I let him wrap his arms around me.

"It's such a waste that you're gay."

"Maybe you should have been born a man."

"I'd have been too masculine for you. You love those two steps from drag queen bitches."

He starts laughing again, and that's how Patrick finds us.

Mark and I will deal with the heavy stuff later. Especially since now, there will actually be a later. He's going through enough right now without me being all over protective. It'll be a long time until I can open that bathroom door again. I've also been having nightmares. Nightmares where the ambulance doesn't get there in time, or where the bathroom becomes a cemetery and a casket is being lowered into the ground. These aren't things that I'll tell Mark when we talk about this. I'll tell him about the 911 operator and her bored voice. I'll tell him about the dragnet police officers. I'll definitely tell him about Patrick threatening to burn down the receptionist's desk. But I won't tell him about the dreams. The reality is it doesn't really matter how this situation affected me. He's still here. He has enough guilt and pessimism in his life already, and I will not add to it. Mark is, sometimes, the most blinding ray of sunlight in my world. It terrifies me to know that he was almost gone. He is selfish, egotistical, obnoxious, and corporately useless. And yet, as a person, he is utterly beautiful.

I leave the hospital an hour after visiting hours end feeling lighter than I ever have. Mark will need to stay in the hospital for a few more days. They want to run some more tests to determine if he'll require dialysis or surgery to remove the now damaged kidney. He'll also need to see a psychiatrist. I would imagine that Mark's personal saga can keep even the most jaded of shrinks interested.

I haven't had anything substantial to eat in days. Kind of hard to get good food in a hospital. It's like being back in high school and eating in the cafeteria. Chicken strips saturated in grease, soggy fries, cardboard pizza, and wilted lettuce salads. It's amazing that we all graduated without getting food poisoning.

I walk in my front door balancing my oversized Chanel bag that is over-stuffed enough to challenge the shoulder straps, and my take-out dinner. My small purse, the one that contains my wallet and make-up, is hanging from my mouth by the straps. Ah, to be a career woman.

My phone is ringing. Great.

Dropping my shoulder bag, I release the lassie hold I have on my purse, let it drop to the floor and hurriedly dig around trying to find my phone before my voicemail picks up.

"Hello?" I'm out of breath. For some reason, I put my cell in the overstuffed bag instead of the small one.

"Hey, you. What's going on? I've been calling you all day." The incredible vanishing Jonah.

Kicking off my shoes, I keep the phone to my ear, and sit down for my dinner.

"Have you? What occasioned the phone call? Did you just land back on the planet?" It's Wednesday. I haven't even had a, *thanks for the last screw*, text message from this dude in a week. We're still supposed to be in the honeymoon phase of this relationship. All that sickening together time, and saying things like, *No, you hang up*, not dropping off the planet. Bastard.

"Yeah, I have. I missed you. I haven't spoken to you all week. Why do you sound mad at me?"

Like he doesn't know? Didn't he just mention not speaking to me for a week?

"I'm not mad at you." I'm such a liar! "I've been having a crazy few days, I'm stressed." Well, at least that part is true.

"Liar." He states it as fact, not saying it maliciously, or even laughingly, and it makes me defensive.

"Now, I'm mad at you. Don't call me a liar." I want to argue with him. I need to argue with someone. There's too much tension in my body right now.

"You were already mad at me. Maybe it has been a rough few days for you, so that part was probably true, but you were mad at me from the beginning of this conversation. Probably before I even called you, which if you had turned on your phone, you would've seen I've been doing for the past four hours. So, why don't we drop the bullshit, and you can tell me what I did." Firm, yet inoffensive.

"Okay, fine. Perhaps I was already a little angry. It could have had something to do with the fact that you disappeared, again."

"What are you talking about?" He sounds frustrated and confused.

Jackass.

"I haven't spoken to you in a week. I call you, I text you, and nothing. For a week." I do sound mad.

"I was in Chicago."

Like this was common knowledge?

"Why were you in Chicago? What could you possibly have been doing in Chicago?" My voice is registering disbelief.

"Business meeting. I do have those occasionally with clients, you know." He's getting annoyed.

"Why didn't you say anything?" Who goes out of town without telling their girlfriend that they'll be gone for a week? Am I his girlfriend?

"Since when do I have to apprise you of my every move?"

Oooh! It's like that?

"Since a few of those moves took your ass to another state." My hand is on my hip and I'm scowling. Men are unbelievable.

"Okay, so now I'm lost. The first night I go out with you, ends with you all but pushing me out the door the next morning. Then for two weeks, you are like the coolest chick I've ever dated, though you really have no time for me, and now you suddenly need my undivided attention at all times? Autumn, what the fuck?"

Valid points. All valid points, but I'm not wrong this time. "First of all, before I was pushing you out the door, you were already getting dressed for a hasty retreat. And, I make time for you; you should try to do the same. Finally, I do not NEED your undivided attention, but there was a really bad situation and a hug would have been appreciated. But you were across the country it seems. Jonah, what the fuck!"

Rebut that shit.

"Point taken. Now you need to realize something. I cannot, no matter how badly you need a hug, be there at all times, in every negative situation, because I have shit on my plate the same way you do. You work sixty hours a week and I deal. You love what you do, and I respect that. I love what I do, too, and you need to respect that. The difference is, what I do sometimes takes me to a different state, or country, so I can't always be here, but that doesn't mean that I don't want to be your man."

Reassuring. But did he have to be such a dick about it?

"That was a very rude, fucked-up, yet oddly sweet thing to say. And, how the shit do I know that you wanna be my anything, when you disappear more than a Vegas magician's assistant?"

"Autumn, I know you. Biblically. You need a little jerk in your man, otherwise you'd walk all over me. And, if I didn't wanna be with you, I wouldn't have ever called you back after the first night we slept together."

I can't stand know-it-alls.

"Then you would have screwed yourself over, 'cause I'm awesome in bed." And, just like that, I'm not as angry anymore.

"This is very true. So, you wanna tell me about your bad days that I missed?"

I really do, but this isn't a topic for telephone conversation. "Not tonight."

"Well then, how about this weekend? We could spend it together. I'll let you beat me at Soul Calibur IV?" He is so adorable.

"Your place or mine?" Seems too easy, right? Don't worry, I'm not over the disappearing acts.

"That simple? Never in the history of the world has an argument between a man and a woman ended so quickly. Not that I'm not grateful, but you aren't planning on braining me with a skillet this weekend or anything are you?"

Actually, I'm more of a poison person. Did you know that too much potassium in your system can kill you? That's traceable with an autopsy though.

"I try not to touch cooking tools if I can help it." Why pretend? He already knows I can't cook.

"Tell me what happened with you while I was gone?"

No thank you.

"Does your phone not work from Chicago?" See, I told you I didn't forget.

"Nice subject change. Yes, it was working. I called you on Sunday, house phone, check your messages. I didn't call the cell, because I thought you'd be at Church with your aunt, and I didn't want to offend God. I figured you were busy when you didn't call back. I got home at three o'clock this morning. Should I have called you then?"

"Yes. You should have. And I can't remember the code for my voicemail." I try not to let my embarrassment show through my voice at that admission.

He's laughing at me. How is this a funny circumstance?

"Didn't you write it down somewhere?" It's hard to understand him, since he's still laughing.

"Obviously I didn't. If I had, I'd be able to check my messages."

"Okay, sorry. Just reset the code."

"I don't know how to do that." I pick my food up and head for my kitchen. Why would I know how to do that?

"There should be directions in the manual."

"What manual?"

"The one that you got when they connected your phone."

"I threw that away." Do people actually keep that?

"Why would you throw it away?"

I guess they do.

"I didn't think I'd need it again."

"Who's your provider?"

"Comcast."

"You can borrow mine."

"My hero."

"My smart ass."

"I do try."

"You succeed rather well. Now, why did you need a hug while I was out of town?"

"Mark is in the hospital, he had an accident. I was worried." I don't really want him to know all the details about Mark. Jonah already thinks that Mark is extra; this wouldn't exactly change his opinion.

"I'm sorry, baby. Is he okay?" he sounds genuinely concerned.

"He's doing better. He'll be home in a few days."

"What kind of accident was it?"

Curiosity killed the cat.

"A personal one." I state it simply, and exactly. There will be no details given unless Mark greenlights them.

"Okay. What time will you be coming over on Friday?"

I silently thank him for not pushing the issue, and we continue to make plans for our weekend. It's amazing how things go from overly complicated to agonizingly simple in minutes. I could have asked him why he didn't call me back on Monday or Tuesday, but that feels like dragging out an argument for argument's sake. I've been seeing him for two weeks; how much does he really owe me in regard to his whereabouts?

Chapter Twelve:

I am exhausted. Jonah and I were on the phone for hours last night planning for our weekend. Considering that I didn't get home until after ten last night, and the fact that we were on the phone until one this morning, I'm glad that I was even on time for work. I have had three lattes in three hours. Crunching numbers is not exactly conducive to staying awake. I am working on the report that Chelsea, the sea witch, has given back to me for the third time, when the other wicked witch comes over to my desk.

"Autumn, how are you? I love those shoes." Keyana Grey should have background music. Maybe the theme from *Halloween*. I sincerely believe that she is that evil. Though she does show good taste occasionally. My shoes are black suede ankle boots. Gucci. This is why my savings account is on life support.

"Keyana, always a pleasure. What can I do for you?" The annoyance is heavy. I don't even have the energy to summon false politeness.

"Well, I know that you usually go to lunch with your friend Mark, but since he's fallen ill, I thought that the two of us could have something together. Maybe talk about this and that?" Keyana Grey is a pear-shaped woman, about 5'9" tall, walnut complexion, hazel eyes, and a sinister demeanor. When she talks, you can almost see her plotting.

"That is very nice of you. Really, but I haven't been taking lunches this week. I'm trying to get this report just right for Chelsea, and there is a plethora of other things on my plate. So, I'm going to have to decline." I put a tight smile on my face, and wait for her to leave, which she doesn't do. Instead, she continues this sham of a conversation.

"Please, Autumn. Like anything could ever be good enough for Chelsea. She's too anal for her own good. Besides, you really should eat. Just a quick bite."

Here's the gas: No one likes Keyana, and no one likes Chelsea, and these two bitches hate each other. It's like some weird office bitch *Highlander.* There can be only one. Mark and I always joke that one day they'll come in with swords, and one of them will cut the other's head off. My money would be on Keyana. Chelsea's feet are too swollen for her to move quickly.

Before I can refuse her again, over schlumps Chelsea.

"Keyana, please remove yourself from Autumn's work area. She's too busy to pretend to enjoy your company right now. My team is currently down one member, and we all take our jobs seriously."

Ouch. Chelsea seems annoyed, to say the least.

"Chelsea, careful, your jealousy is showing. I'm just trying to extend the hand of friendship to a coworker. If Mark has truly fallen ill, as is the rumor, well then Autumn must be devastated. They are quite close."

What the hell? Am I still sitting here? Remember when you were a child, and adults would talk about you like you weren't there? This is so very déjà vu.

"Listen you little piranha, we don't gossip about our teammates, unlike some others here, and I know that your stat person just gave his notice, so don't come over here trying to steal mine. Wiggle your trouble making self back over to your team section before I file a complaint with H.R. about you stirring the pot." Chelsea is steaming. I can practically see smoke coming out of her ears.

"We'll speak later Autumn, give Mark my best." With that, Keyana takes herself off to her own team.

"I'm sorry about that, Autumn. Keyana wants you for her team, and she thinks I don't know. She is such a ... anyway, I don't condone gossip either, and she's been trying to find out about Mark. She only wants to know so that she can try to use it to steal one of our accounts. There must be some rungs missing on her slut ladder, can't sleep your way to the top when some of the executives are straight women. Anyway, I'll let you get back to work."

The claws have come out and I now work at *As the Office Turns*. I'm still a little in shock as I see Chelsea walk away.

There is a saying about always expecting the unexpected, but really! I realize that I work in a nut house, but the nuts are usually well behaved. I've only been here for four months, and so I don't really know the Chelsea/Keyana back story. I've seen them civil with one another and that's all. Granted, it's usually ice princess meets frost queen civil, but it's still civil. I have never seen Chelsea that close to losing it, nor have I ever heard her speak ill of anyone directly. She usually makes sweeping disparages. The slut comment is what shocks me. See, we lower level team mates have been whispering about Keyana's whoredom for a while. It was being spoken about in hushed undertones before I was a blip on this company's radar, but never has a team leader even mentioned it. Chelsea must not have taken her Midol this morning.

Everyone knows that Keyana has slept with half the men in the company. Just like everyone knows that Mark is sleeping with an executive in the company. With Mark, they're not sure who he's sleeping with. Most people think it has to be a woman, because all the men are married, so they're obviously straight. Riiight!

This day has become so interesting. Mark is going to be so pissed that he missed it.

I have managed to avoid Satan's harpy for the majority of the day. I am ashamed to say that when it was time for me to take my lunch, I hid in the women's rest room for fifteen minutes to ensure that Keyana would be gone. I really don't have it in me to pretend to like her today. After my fifteen minutes of shame, I returned to my work area, and finished one of the reports I had been working on. When I saw her returning from lunch, I pretended to be on a phone call so that she wouldn't stop to talk.

I need Mark. Don't get me wrong, he's not the only person at work that I talk to, but he's the only genuine friend that I have here. The rest of the people that I associate with will no doubt try to pump me for info on my bestie. I wish another scandal would hurry up and break out, so that I can stop avoiding people. Every time someone asks me what happened, I get inexplicably angry. They don't care if he's alright. They don't care if they never see him again. But everyone wants to pretend to be concerned; a little compassion goes a long way. We work in advertising; we know how to use words to get what we want better than anyone else. Well, this consumer ain't buyin.

It's the end of the day, thank God. I have survived another day at the office, and I have avoided the Grey skank. As I enter the elevator, I breathe a sigh of relief. Very short-lived relief, Keyana just stepped on. The elevator is crowded, though, and she doesn't say anything to me. I realize it's only because there are others present, and her highness cannot be seen after work speaking to the peasants, but I'm thankful for it. Now if I can just keep this crowd thing going until I get to my car, everything will be fine. Stepping off the elevator, there are about three people heading in the same direction as me, I can hear the Hallelujah Chorus playing in my head. I hit the automatic unlock button on my key ring, and just as I'm about to get into my car, someone taps my shoulder. I turn around, silently praying to myself that the hellhound didn't follow me, but I must have forgotten my, "in the name of Jesus", stamp. Because, it's standing in front of me.

Smiling.

That's disturbing.

"Autumn, I looked for you around lunch time. I'm so sorry that I missed you. What do you say we do something tomorrow?" she has an expectant look on her face. Her eyebrows are raised, and her head is tilted to the right a little. It's creepy.

"Listen, Keyana, I'm really sorry, but I'm working through my lunches this week. I have a lot of work that I need to make some headway on." I even smiled when I said that. As close to a genuine smile as I could muster, and my voice was pleasant.

"It's really unfair of Chelsea to have you work through your lunches. If she has a sick subordinate, then she really should be the one picking up the slack. It's what I would do. It's what any good team leader would do. Maybe you're on the wrong team." The wind up and the pitch.

"I'm happy on my team. I have no problem helping when help is required, especially when I have a sick team mate. And, for all of Chelsea's faults, she doesn't refer to her team mates as subordinates. Now, please move. You're blocking my door." Keeping the same smile on my face, I get into my car and back out of my space, leaving Keyana staring after me. Unfortunately, I didn't run over her feet.

Chapter Thirteen:

Friday arrives with me leaving work early (shocking) and running home for my overnight stuff. I forgot it this morning. It's two o'clock. If I can make it home in a half an hour, I can beat the rush hour traffic, and be at Jonah's before four. Keyana the wonder dog hasn't tried to sniff a conversation out of me since Wednesday. I am eternally grateful to the powers that be for that one.

Mark gets to leave the hospital next Tuesday, if nothing changes with his condition. He has to set up an appointment with a psychiatrist before he's discharged. I didn't know that hospitals could do that, but apparently, they can.

Patrick and his wife are having a few issues regarding Mark. They involve whether or not the children will be allowed around him. His psycho sister-in-law thinks that being homosexual automatically means that you're a pedophile, and she doesn't feel that her son would be safe around his uncle. It amazes me how a person that small minded can even pronounce the word, pedophile. The man is gay, he isn't a sexual predator. As the drama that is Mark's life continues to unfold, and the hurtles continue to grow, I find myself praying more often. I pray for Mark's well-being more often, and harder than I have ever prayed for anything.

It's three hours later and I am officially sitting in rush hour traffic. I decided to change before heading to Jonah's, and it was all down-hill from there. The traffic isn't really as bad going north, thankfully, but it's still not great. I'm hungry. I haven't eaten since breakfast, and all I had in my kitchen was moldy bagels. I would pull over and get something to eat, but I'm supposed to be having dinner with the man. He's cooking. Something ala something else, and if I eat before I get there, he'll probably be a little upset. The good news is that I'm almost there.

I hear my phone ringing, and I'm tempted not to answer it. I do anyway.

"Yellow?"

"Blue. Where are you woman?"

Ah, there he is. My prince charming.

"I'm on 285, passing exit sixteen right now. I'll be there in a few minutes."

"I thought you were getting off early."

Who is the woman in this relationship?

"I did, but I forgot my clothes at home. I had to go pick them up. Then I decided to change, and by the time I left home it was five." This questioning is curiously coming from a man that disappeared to a whole other state last week.

"You didn't have to get clothes on my account. It would have been difficult, but I could have tolerated you being naked this weekend."

"You are so sweet. How did I ever land a man like you?" My voice is full of mock awe. Men are such pigs.

"Just lucky, I guess. I even cooked for you. Again. When are you gonna learn to cook and return the favor?"

"Are you asking me to give you salmonella? Why don't I just order something when it's my turn? Or we could just eat dessert?" He's a pig, but I don't want to kill him.

"Dessert? I'm thinking whipped cream and chocolate syrup. Are you opposed to getting sticky?"

"Is sex all men think about?" Seriously.

"No, I also think about video games, football, and food. In between thinking about sex."

"Am I an extended booty call?"

"No. I wouldn't be offering to lick things off of your body if you were. Now back to the sticky question. Light or dark chocolate syrup?"

He really is cute.

"Dark chocolate is healthier for you," I say helpfully.

"A woman that takes care of my health as well as my body. You are such a treasure. You wanna skip dinner and go straight for dessert?"

"Jonah, I haven't eaten since breakfast." I'll kill him if he doesn't feed me.

"That's a no, right? Can we do the dessert thing later?"

"Do you even have chocolate syrup and whipped cream?"

"There's a Publix around the corner from my apartment."

"I'm pulling into your parking lot."

"Does that mean no dessert?"

"I'll make it up to you."

"Promises, promises."

"Open the front door." I close my phone and get out of my car. Grabbing the overnight bag from my back seat, I make my way to Jonah's door. He opens it before I reach it and takes the bag from me. Grabbing my hand, he pulls me inside.

I love the amount of open space in this apartment. It looks like something you'd find in Manhattan. The entire apartment smells like food. He must have cooked with the windows closed. I smell garlic, and sausage. I think I might be part bloodhound. My personal chef is leading me into the living room, and I tug on his hand to stop the forward motion.

"I need to put my bag somewhere." I motion to his hand since he's still holding it.

"Speaking of your bag, what the hell do you have in this thing? It feels like there's bowling balls in here."

Is he kidding me?

"Stuff."

"Stuff? What kind of stuff? Like, edible underwear, or a dead body? 'Cause I gotta tell you, one of those is really hot, and the other...not so much."

This man goes from adorably geeky and shy, to hormone driven pig in three seconds flat. At least he's attractive with and without his clothing, and he knows more than two words containing three syllables or more.

"How was your day? Mine was great! What's for dinner? Are you detecting the sarcasm?"

"What kind of stuff?" He's like a dog with a bone.

"Clothes, shoes, make-up, hair stuff, bath stuff, tooth brush, lingerie." Had to add that last. He is a man, after all.

"I got you a present." He gives me this sweet, uncertain smile.

He did, did he? I love presents. They celebrate the wonder that is me.

"Is it shiny?" I can live with jewelry. Or shoes. Ooh, I hope it's shoes. Maybe it's a gift card for shoes.

"Actually, it's something smelly."

I look confused. I know this, because I can feel my confused expression. It feels like my eyebrows are meeting in the middle of my forehead, my nose is crinkled up, and my mouth is half open.

"That is a very interesting face you're making. I didn't know eyebrows could get that close together. Is that painful? That looks painful."

I manage to relax my face, with some difficulty, and formulate the question that needs asking. "When you say that you got me something smelly...what does that mean?" I am struggling to keep my face relaxed. I never knew how difficult it could be to do that. It's like the muscles in my face are fighting to do something that my mind really doesn't want them to do. This actually is painful.

"Not, bad smelly. Good, smelly. I went to one of those stores that men should never actually go into, and I got some bath stuff."

That doesn't sound bad. But this is Jonah...so you never know.

"You bought bubble bath? From a store in the mall?" I need to clarify.

"I just said that. It's upstairs in the bathroom. And, by the way, there was an overtly feminine man there and he tried to give me his phone number. Aren't gay men supposed to recognize other gay men?"

I'm trying not to laugh. But my face is so tired from fighting back the confused expression that I'm pretty sure I won't be able to control this one.

"Maybe his gaydar was broken. Ooh, or maybe he thought you were open to experimentation!" I'm full on laughing now.

Why do people think that gay men have this magical ability to tell other gay men? I know gay men in New York that are some of the most thuggish looking hooligans that you will ever meet. All gay men aren't impeccably groomed and metrosexual. Though, some are. Case in point, the club where I bumped into Jonah. The gay men that were at that party were all things of well put together beauty. Hell, look at Mark. He is a very attractive, very well coifed man. But when he goes to football games with his brother, he's all loose-fitting faded jeans, football jersey, fitted cap, and old sneakers.

"You're not funny. And, you could show a little appreciation. I braved various different fragrances, some not so pleasant, just so that we could take this romantic bath together, and talk about our hopes and dreams, and the rest of that shit. At least a modicum of gratitude is due." He looks and sounds genuinely offended.

I really can't stop laughing. There are tears and everything. "Thank you so much. I know how vicious and deadly some of those body lotions and bath gels can be. Add in the obvious sexual overtures of a clearly desperate gay man, and I'm sure you had a trying day." *I can't breathe.*

"Keep it up, and I'm not feeding you," he grumbles.

He is so cute.

"Poor baby, did I hurt your feelings? I'll tell you what. Feed me, and then take a sickeningly romantic bath with me, and I'll wear something from the pages of Victoria's Secret's new catalog for you, and I'll kiss those pesky feelings all better." Priorities people.

"Well, when you put it that way...dinner is right this way." He pulls me toward the dining room and dinner. Men are so easy.

Dinner was delicious. Jonah made ratatouille. This was the first time I had it, but hopefully not the last. It isn't something that I would ever bother learning to make for myself, though. It seems too involved. All the vegetable cutting and timing things...if I decide to learn to cook, I'm sticking to deserts.

I'm clearing the table, and loading the dishwasher while Jonah is starting the bath. It's still early, barely eight o'clock, but I think he wants to get to the whole, kissing it better, part of the night. I love spending time with him. It's this whole, drama free, relaxing environment. He's sweet, pig-ish-ness aside, and he makes me laugh. He's not traditionally funny. He'll never be Dave Chapelle or anything, but he's cluelessly funny. He doesn't always think before he speaks, and you would think that it would be offensive, but it's hilarious instead.

After I'm done in the kitchen, I make my way to the upper loft. Once in his bedroom, I see my bag on the bed, I need to take out a hairclip to put my hair up. No getting the hair wet until Sunday night when I wash it. I only go to salons for haircuts. Otherwise, I wash it, blow it out, and fake wrap it myself. You know, use a ceramic flat iron to give myself some curls, then wrap it, and put on the head scarf. I'll have to talk to Jonah about the head scarf. I doubt that his ex-girlfriend slept in one, and I would forgo it, but we're going out tomorrow. I don't want to surprise him by looking all sex-kitten one moment, and old school Aunt Jemima the next.

I just manage to find my hairclip, when all of a sudden, I hear Jonah in the bathroom cursing. Being the nosy person that I am, I must investigate. The sight before me, when I enter the bathroom, is priceless. It's like a sitcom in here. There is a mountain of suds and bubbles reaching far above the brim of the tub. My boyfriend, spaz that he is, is trying to scoop bubbles out of the tub and deposit them into the sink. Cursing at the bubbles, or himself, the whole time.

"Fuck, oh fuck, oh son of a bitch!"

The confused expression is on my face again. "Babe, what did you do?"

He stops midway to the sink, finally noting my presence, and looks at me like I'm crazy. *Yeah, cause I'm the one standing here with a hand full of bubbles.*

"I didn't do it. The evil bubbles are attacking. There's only like three inches of water in the tub, the rest is bubbles. The feminine man at the store was trying to sabotage me by selling me nuclear bubble bath."

He is insane. Hilarious, but completely insane. While I'm still staring at him, he decides that I'm apparently going to be of little to no help and continues bailing the bubbles. Looking around the bathroom, I see the culprit. A sixteen-ounce bottle of cherry blossom bubble bath and half of the bottle is gone.

"Jonah, did you use all of this just now?" I know he said that he bought it today, but I have to be sure before I call him an idiot.

He stops bailing for a moment to look at me. "Yeah. Why?" *Seriously?*

"Because, you only need to use a capful of this at a time. The bubbles aren't attacking, you're an idiot." I said that very diplomatically believe it or not. There was no mocking inflection in my voice. Amazing really.

"Why doesn't it say that on the bottle?"

What am I, the manufacturer?

"I don't know, what does it say?" I've never read the instructions on a bottle of bubble bath. I never knew it was necessary.

"It says use a generous amount. Generous! A capful is not exactly a generous amount. And what the hell kind of measurement is that anyway? Generous? What ruler can I pick up anywhere on the damn planet that measures something as generous? One inch, two inches, a generous amount of inches. Is this crap intentionally written in a language that only women can understand?"

While he's ranting, I walk over to the bathtub, pull the plug on the drain, and turn on the cold water to reduce the amount of bubbles. Grabbing the handheld shower head, I switch the shower on, and continue to rinse the evil bubbles away as Jonah warms to his topic. He finally stops flipping out long enough to notice what I'm doing.

"How did you do that?"

"Oh, didn't you know? Women are taught as little girls how to combat evil nuclear bubbles bent on destroying the world." I say this in earnest, and then after a beat, Jonah responds.

"My hero." The sarcasm is so thick you couldn't cut it with a chainsaw. Once the bubbles have met their doom, I stop up the drain once again, and after adjusting the water temperature, I add a capful of bubble bath, and show Jonah how to properly create a soothing and romantic environment.

Chapter Fourteen:

Jonah and I are lying in bed, discussing movies. We are at the cuddle phase of this evening. I'm taking advantage of it while I can, because once the newness of this relationship wears off, I'm pretty sure he'll start falling asleep immediately after sex. The bubble bath, once I took control of the mechanics, was very nice. The man is spastic, but he has talented hands. He was very enthusiastic about my choice in lingerie, and he's taking the head scarf in stride.

I love buying sexy little scraps of silk and lace, but only getting to wear them for a few minutes at a time can make them seem pointless. Another reason to appreciate Jonah. He spends a large amount of time kissing, and teasing my body, and so, the nightie that I was wearing stayed on for quite a while. We're both naked now. Well, except for the head scarf. Looking at the clock, it's well after midnight. The entire apartment is silent, the only sounds being our voices as we argue which movie was better, *Star Wars* or *The Matrix*. Jonah calls my assertions about *Star Wars* blasphemous.

"What was that noise?" I heard something downstairs. Like a buzzing.

"That was the sound of you being ridiculous by saying that Luke Skywalker was a pussy," he says with a frown. He is so offended.

"He was a pussy, and I heard something downstairs." Seriously, Princess Leia had bigger balls than Luke.

"No, you didn't. And Luke cut off Darth Vader's hand! How can you possibly call him a pussy?!" he is nearly vibrating with indignation. My boyfriend is such a geek.

"Because, in the end, he was whining like a little bitch, and big bad Vader had to save his ass. Now, Han Solo, there was a real man. Not as good as Morpheus...but not many men can be that strong in their beliefs."

I think there may actually be steam coming from his ears at my words.

"Morpheus? The guy was a religious zealot! *The Matrix* is in no way comparable to *Star Wars*. How are you my girlfriend? Do we need to spend this weekend watching episodes four through six? 'Cause I have them!"

I am about to offer a rebuttal when the phone on his bedside table starts ringing. He looks at me like he can't imagine who would be calling him, and then answers the phone with a puzzled expression in place.

"Hello?"

I can hear a woman's voice on the other end, but I can't make out what she's saying.

"This isn't really the best time...I'm sure you wouldn't, but I'm really in the middle of something right now...fine...okay, I said fine...see you in a few."

What the flip was that?

"Did you just refer to me as 'something'?" It's the first thing that comes out of my mouth.

"No. Well...kinda. Technically, I'm not in the middle of you, so, no. I didn't," he tries to joke.

I think he's trying to piss me off.

"You want to tell me who was on the phone?" I'm trying to maintain.

"My friend, Kaylin. She's coming over."

Is he joking? It's two in the morning, and we are very naked. No person on the planet is this clueless.

"Your friend, Kaylin? Ex-girlfriend Kaylin? Is coming over here? Now?"

I think he's cluing into my aggravation.

"It's not like that. She's just my friend. I promise."

Riiiiight.

"Do you have a lot of friends that ask to come over to your apartment at one in the morning while you're naked with your girlfriend?" Some people need things to be spelled out for them.

"Baby, come on. She's just my friend. She had a fight with her boyfriend, asked if she could use my spare room for tonight, that's all. Why would I lie about that? If something was going on with me and her, I would not let her come over while you were here."

He has a small, invalid point.

"Did she know I would be here?" Women are devious. They will try to put a man in a difficult position to force his hand. It's like that movie, *Sliding Doors*—if you haven't seen it, you should. This is why I have very few female friends. Not because of the movie, that's mostly the other woman trying to force the two-timing boyfriend's hand. No, the reason that I don't have many female friends is because everything with women has more than one meaning. Things are always implied, or alluded to, but never stated until teeth are pulled. Figuratively, of course. The female friends that I do have, I have had since I was about seven years old. A few have been cut loose. The backstabbing liars and boyfriend stealers were weeded out for the most part in high school.

"Yeah, she did know that you'd be here. Which is why I know that she's upset, 'cause she wouldn't interrupt otherwise."

Jonah is getting out of the bed now, pulling on sweats and a t-shirt, in preparation for our coming guest. I use that word loosely. I don't care about his friend's relationship issues. She's not my friend. From my understanding, she's from Georgia. Why the hell can't she ever call someone in her own damn family? This is the second time that things between us have been interrupted for this chick. I mean really, Mark was in the middle of having his lover's wife catch them in the act, and having himself held responsible, and he still gave us space. If her boyfriend is not kicking her ass, or psychologically abusing her to the point that she's contemplating suicide, she needs to stay her ass at home. You cannot resolve relationship issues by running to your friends every time there's an argument. And, in case you're wondering, I am absolutely taking this stance because her preferred shoulder belongs to my recently acquired boyfriend.

Drama-free weekend my ass!

"Baby, you getting up?" he's standing by his dresser awaiting my answer.

"The pajamas I brought with me aren't really conducive to entertaining company." Unless she's interested in my lingerie. Somehow, I doubt it.

"So, wear one of my shirts or something. Please. You guys are gonna have to meet anyway. Now's as good a time as any."

I beg to differ. But, instead of continuing this topic of conversation, I get up, and grab a big Mr. Potato Head t-shirt out of the drawer. Going into the bathroom, I take off the headscarf and comb my hair out. Jonah is looking at me with a raised eyebrow.

"What?"

"I thought that you said the bandana was necessary." He looks puzzled.

"It is not a bandana, and it is necessary, but I'm not about to meet someone for the first time wearing it!" That should have been self-explanatory.

"Okay, Autumn. Cease fire. I know that this is inconvenient, but can you just be a little less ball-busting?" He's holding his arms up, palms out.

It is possible that I could be a little more accommodating. Whatever. The sound of the doorbell stops me from commenting further.

I make my way downstairs with Jonah and sit in the living room as he goes to answer the front door. The doorbell was rung three more times before we got downstairs. Someone is obviously impatient. This chick had better be the sweetest person on the planet, cause after the week I've had with the termagants at work, I can't deal with another bitch. I'm channeling my inner Zen master and trying to feel at peace with the universe. It isn't working. Possibly because I'm a Methodist.

I look up from the *Wired* magazine that I'm pretending to read when Jonah walks into the room with the infamous Kaylin. She has a bag with her. Not a pocketbook, but a small suitcase. Jonah has this helpless expression on his face, so I try to appear unaffected. Fighting those facial muscles again, I stand up from the couch and wait for the introductions to begin. Where I'm from, when you intrude on a situation, you begin the greeting. Apparently, her parents never taught her that lesson.

Jonah breaks the silence for us. "Baby, this is my good friend, Kaylin. Kaylin, this is my girlfriend, Autumn."

He must have bought a clue on his way to the door. He's standing facing the both of us. I'd bet if someone were to find a ruler, we would discover that he was directly in the middle. I take pity on him and extend an olive branch by putting out my hand.

"It's very nice to meet you, Kaylin, I've heard wonderful things about you." I'm a very talented actress. I should have gone to Hollywood and tried my hand, but the whole starving actress thing never appealed to me.

She looks at me, and gives me the fakest smile I've ever seen, it looks like she belongs in one of those Nerf commercials from the 90's when all the facial expressions were overdone to drive home the message of how unbelievably awesome this toy was. She's obviously not as good of an actress as I am.

Kaylin is a good four inches taller than me. She has pale blonde hair, a thin, straight nose, grey eyes and eyebrows that have been plucked to death, and full lips that shape a mouth that's a bit too wide for her face. She's thin for her height, but maybe she's one of those women that believe that emaciation equals beauty. If she were a healthy weight, she'd look the way I imagine the Vikings of old did. Men have strange tastes.

"Autumn, hello. It's nice to meet you. I wish the circumstances were better." She lets out this little squeak and drops my hand. Looking at Jonah, she lets these Scarlett O'Hara crocodile tears fall. She's going all out here. Shoulders are shaking and everything.

And the Razzie goes to...

"Oh God, Kaylin! What happened?" This, of course, from Jonah who rushes to her side and gives her a hug.

Fact of masculinity: men cannot help but try to lend comfort to a crying woman. This is a trick that I never use, I abhor weakness. The only time I've seen my mother, or my grandmother cry was at my aunt's funeral. I feel that it would be disrespecting them in some way if I were to cry just to try to win a man.

"Jimmy is being such an unreasonable jerk. He doesn't even care about my feelings at all. I'm under so much pressure with this wedding, and it's like he doesn't even care."

I need to remove myself from this scene. "Jonah," he looks in my direction when I address him and pauses in rubbing the back of the damsel in distress, "I'm going to get us all something to drink. What would you like?"

"Oh, um...just some water, I guess. Kaylin, you want anything?"

I seriously consider spitting in whatever beverage she requests before I curb that disgusting and childish urge. Maybe I'm just tired.

"Do you have tea? I think I put some in the cabinet. If you haven't finished it, I'll take that." She pats his chest and allows her hand to linger for a second too long.

I love the way she stuck that in there. Like, she's such a fixture in his apartment that she stocks her own groceries here. The thing that I don't get is, if she's planning her wedding, why is she trying to claim Jonah. She might as well pee on him.

I go into the kitchen to make us all something to drink and try to harness my chi. I put the kettle that I find in one of the cabinets on the stove to boil, and keeping my back to them, I try to do some deep breathing. It doesn't work. I count to twenty, that doesn't work either. Taking a moment, I begin to recite the Apostles' Creed. Aloud, but keeping my voice low. Once I finish, I take a few more deep breaths, and I feel calm. It has been a long time since I felt the need to do that. It puts things into perspective for me. Kind of reminds me of who I am. Finishing the drinks, I head back into the living room with a glass of water for Jonah, a tea for the brood mare, and a soda for myself.

Reaching them, I see that Kaylin has taken up residence on the couch while Jonah is in the armchair. I half expected to see her sitting in his lap. They pause in their conversation long enough for me to hand off the drinks. I get a "thank-you" from Jonah, and Kaylin just nods. I'm convinced that she was raised by wolves. Jonah tugs my arm and pulls me into his lap on the chair. When I sit, he continues the conversation.

"I'm sure he didn't mean anything by it. You read too much into things." He's stroking my arm while he's talking to her, and it's going a long way toward renewing my cool.

"Why can't he be more like you? When we were engaged you didn't behave this way." She shoots a quick look at me after she throws that out there.

My jaw clenches so hard that I think I cracked a tooth and I feel my whole body tense up. She's waiting for my reaction. I'm pretty sure she knows that I wasn't aware of the engagement. I'm praying silently in my head for strength when I hear Jonah's response.

"If he were more like me, you would've broken up already. I mean, our relationship wasn't exactly smooth sailing. I just look better now, 'cause he has an opinion about things that I don't care about."

I can feel the hesitation in the hand that's rubbing my arm. I'm not really up for mental and verbal warfare at almost two in the morning. I'm going to bed. I lean into Jonah a little before speaking. "You know what, I'm really tired. And I'm sure that Kaylin doesn't want to discuss her relationship malfunctions with a complete stranger, so I'm going to go to bed." I give Jonah a kiss, more for Kaylin's benefit than anything.

I'm a little annoyed that he didn't tell me more about their relationship, but I can't really do anything about that right now. Pushing myself off of his lap, I head toward his bedroom. I would say goodnight to the chick on the couch, but I'm at my limit.

Once I reach the bedroom, any calm I could have restored has wisely headed for the hills. I head to the bathroom to take a shower. The warm water is exactly what I need to relax, and I desperately need to relax. I'm not used to biting my tongue and this is difficult for me to say the least. I'm trying to put myself in Jonah's shoes by imagining that Kaylin is Mark. It isn't working. I was never engaged to Mark. Yes, he did tell me that they dated three years ago. But dating someone, and nearly marrying someone are vastly different circumstances. If he admitted to dating her, why would he not admit to asking her to marry him? I have about a million questions running through my mind right now, but I will not have a conversation—let's be real here, an argument, with him about a relationship that occurred before he knew me while that anorexic Viking is in this apartment. He has vaulted ceilings, and our voices would carry. After wrapping my hair, and once again donning my headscarf, I step into the shower to wash my stress away.

When I re-enter the bedroom, Jonah is sitting on the side of the bed waiting for me. I really hadn't expected that. I thought he'd still be comforting Sally sob story in the living room. I don't really think I want to talk to him right now, but I doubt that I'll be able to fall asleep either way. So, here I am, in a towel, contemplating whether I should just put the spud shirt back on and pretend that I'm too exhausted for a conversation, or leave him and his ex to each other and go home.

Jonah is evidently not in the mood to pretend, and so he kicks off the conversation before I have the opportunity to avoid it. "You're pissed at me. I get that. And, I'm sorry, but...what do you want me to do?"

That question is so loaded that is should come with a caliber.

"I would have liked to have known that the woman that popped up in the middle of the night and currently stores her beverages in your pantry was almost your wife. It's a little too late for that now." My voice is very controlled, but my arms are crossed under my breasts and my hip is cocked out to the side.

"Autumn, that was three years ago. A lot can change in three years." He looks as tired as I feel.

Sucks to be him.

"Yeah, and a lot can stay the same." I hate when people try to make it seem like things are clean cut when they aren't.

"She's just my friend. I don't give you a hard time about Mark."

Excuse me? He must be delusional.

"Mark likes dick! And, so does Kaylin. Are you her only friend or something? Why are you the go-to guy whenever she's having relationship trouble? Does it occur to her that part of the problem could be that she runs to her ex-fiancé with everything? What the hell are the problems anyway?" It is safe to say that my voice is no longer controlled.

"I'm not her only friend, but I am probably her closest friend, and her fiancé does not have a problem with our friendship, because that's all it is." He stands up while he's talking and gestures defensively. He's making it seem like I'm being unreasonable.

"Who ended your relationship?" If he says that she did, I'm going home.

"I did."

"Why?" This is an important question, and since I'm already on such a roll...

"Because, I wasn't ready to get married. I'm still not ready to get married."

Do I appear to be proposing?

"That's good to know, 'cause the way things are going, if I ever decided to get married, I wouldn't want to marry you. Why didn't you tell me?"

He scrubs his hands across his face before crossing is arms. I've learned that he does that when he's frustrated. "I didn't think it was gonna to be that big a deal. The engagement lasted for about four months before I called it a day. You want a list of all my past relationships?"

I'm going to punch him in the face. I actually feel my hands ball into fists. I need to leave. Walking to my bag, I pull out some underwear and start getting dressed. I am so over this situation.

"Autumn, what are you doing?" He uncrosses his arms and looks a little alarmed.

He's a little slow on the uptake, isn't he?

"I'm leaving. This apartment has become very crowded." I start pulling on a pair of jeans.

He moves in front of me and puts a hand on my wrist. "Autumn...baby, please...what do you want me to do? Just tell me what to do. I don't wanna fight with you, and I don't want you to leave. We have an entire weekend planned, and I'm sorry that she's here. I can't throw her out, so...what am I supposed to do? I asked her to marry me a long time ago, but I ended it and I don't regret that! We stayed friends, and that's all we are. I should have told you. I realize that, but I can't go back and change everything now. Please don't leave."

I'm tired and pissed off, and I don't want to deal with this. I was looking forward to a nice drama free weekend with a guy that I really like, but it's already going wrong. I shake my head and keep pulling my jeans up.

Jonah bends down so that he's looking me in the face. "Baby, please don't leave. I'll get her out of here in the morning. I swear."

Even as I'm making the decision to stay, I can hear that little voice in the back of my head telling me to keep it moving. Just walk away. The problem is that I like him in a way that I've never liked anyone else I've ever dated. I haven't had butterflies in my stomach since the seventh grade, but he gives me butterflies. I really want to believe him. Putting on the potato head t-shirt and pulling off my jeans, I climb in the bed. I hear Jonah let out a sigh as he visibly relaxes. He pulls off his shirt and climbs into bed pulling me toward him.

"No more omissions."

"I promise." He kisses my shoulder after he says it. It takes a while, but I eventually fall asleep.

Chapter Fifteen:

When I wake up, I smell bacon. Jonah isn't next to me, so I can only assume that he's making breakfast. Getting out of bed, I head to the bathroom to get ready to face the day. After I brush my teeth and comb my hair, I put on my clothes, a pair of light blue skinny jeans and a white sleeveless mohair sweater and apply some light make-up.

Making my way to the kitchen, I steel myself for my next encounter with the bride of Chucky. Jonah is making waffles. From scratch. I think I'm in love. I need coffee. I'm obviously suffering from caffeine deprivation.

"Good morning, sleepy head. How many waffles can you eat?" He gives me a kiss and wraps his arm around my waist.

"I love a man that knows how to work a waffle iron. I can eat two waffles without too many problems, and if there's coffee, I may be able to have a reasonably intelligent conversation."

Jonah smiles at me. It's almost like the late-night visitor never came. "Aww, but baby...I love you stupid."

I push him away from me and get a coffee mug from the counter. Just as I'm beginning to relax, here's Kaylin.

"Good morning. How is everything today?"

Jonah greets her with a "good morning". I just nod in her direction. She must feel like flexing her non-existent acting muscles again, because she approaches me with a false look of regret on her face. Here we go.

"Autumn, I just want to apologize for interrupting last night. It couldn't have been easy on you having another woman ruin your evening like that. I may have also said some things that were out of line, and so I apologize."

Jonah looks like he thinks she's sincere. I don't. But I'll play along.

"There's nothing to apologize for. Really. Will you be having breakfast with us before you go home?" I manage to appear sympathetic. *Watch a master at work, bitch.*

"Well, actually I thought I'd stick around for a little bit. I don't want to intrude, but I'm not really up to a confrontation with Jimmy right now."

There go those crocodile tears again, but before I can press further, Jonah actually speaks up. "Kaylin, is it possible for you to go to your parents' place? Autumn and I are going out later, and you probably don't want to be alone."

Nicely played.

"I don't really want them to know about the problems. I mean...after what happened with you, I just know that they'll blame me for anything and everything that's going wrong with Jimmy." She's pressing her fingers to her forehead like she can't handle much more.

I hope Jonah packed enough luggage for this guilt trip.

"Why don't we eat?" I feel the need to interrupt this conversation before he pledges our weekend to her.

We all sit around the table in the dining room. The one in the kitchen only seats two. Breakfast is eaten in relative silence. The waffles are good. They aren't good enough to distract from the tension in the room, but then again, I don't think anything would be.

Kaylin once again decides that there isn't enough discomfort at the table, and so decides to inject more.

"I think that you should talk to Jimmy about the wedding." This statement is of course directed at Jonah, and he looks confused.

"What for?" He asks around a mouthful of bacon.

My pig is so sexy, isn't he?

"I think that maybe he's having second thoughts. Men talk to other men about that stuff, right? We can all have dinner together tonight." She bites her lip and nods as if by doing so we'll automatically agree to her suggestion.

She's commandeering my night? I look at Jonah through narrowed eyes, and I know that he can feel the hole that I'm burning through his head.

"Autumn and I have plans for dinner already."

Come on baby, stay strong.

"Okay. That's alright. I understand. I'll just stay here while you guys go out." Her voice trembles and she sniffles. She has become a squatter.

"You know what? I can call the restaurant and add two more people to the reservation. I'm sure it won't be a problem. Why don't you call Jim?"

She leaves the room with a smile on her face and I throw my bacon at him as soon as she's out of sight.

"If we don't let them come to dinner with us, she's bound to stay here for the entire week. This way, we all go out, and at the end of the night, she'll go home with Jim and we can be alone." He's speaking in hushed tones and leaning toward me.

"I thought you were trying to send her to her parents' house?" I whisper furiously.

"Did you not witness the guilt trip? She'll do the same thing if I suggest her sister's house. We'll still do mini golf, just you and me, it's only dinner. If she tries to come back here with us after that, I'll tell her no." He rubs my forearm as he's talking.

"Fine. But you'd better let me win."

Jonah smiles, and kisses me. "Thank you."

After we're finished eating, I help him load the dishwasher. I really wish I hadn't thrown my bacon at him. It smelled really good.

Jonah and I spend another two hours with the ex from hell. I really don't like her, but I'm doing my best to be cordial since she is his friend. I don't know if I'll survive this dinner.

Here's the low down on Kaylin: she's twenty-seven, lives with her fiancé, never had a job, and her father pays her credit card bill. She does not have a trust-fund, and really wants a husband. I personally feel that the reason for this is because she knows that she's useless, and she's trying to bag a man, or an alimony settlement, before her paltry looks become even paltrier.

It confuses me how Jonah was engaged to this woman. Aside from the physical differences between us, and they are huge differences, I've been working since I was eight. I was raking leaves and washing cars, bagging groceries and baby-sitting, you name it. From what he's told me about the women in his family, they're pretty hard working as well, so his relationship with Kaylin is a little puzzling. After listening to the nails on the chalkboard for longer than necessary, we escorted the princess to her car, and headed to play mini-golf.

I love miniature golf. I haven't played since I was in college, so it was a truly inspired idea. I also like bowling, but Jonah claims that he sucks at it. We are having an amazing time, Jonah is letting me win. Mostly, by pretending not to see me drop my ball in the hole when I fail to hit it in after three tries. There are two courses here and we've decided to play through them both. I'm not sure how long it's supposed to take to play one course, but we've been on the same course for two hours. It isn't our fault. There is an elderly couple that has decided that actual golf is too straining, and they've taken the course hostage. They're playing in front of us, and Jonah feels that it would be rude to play around them. I feel that if we excuse ourselves and make our intentions known that it would be perfectly acceptable. But, what do I know? It isn't really that big a deal anyway. Jonah is keeping me entertained by giving a play by play of the couples' game in his best golf commentator voice.

The funny thing is that they're dressed as though they're really golfing. As if they're at a country club or something. The man is wearing these orange and green plaid knickers, with knee socks, and white loafers. They have a little green ball on the top of them and everything. The woman is dressed in a plaid skirt and knee-high plaid socks. I can't comment on the shirts, because they're wearing jackets even though it's warm out.

We're approaching the last hole when my cell phone rings. We should just dub this the weekend of many interruptions. I'm tempted not to answer the phone, but it could be important. Giving Jonah a very put-upon look, I answer the leash.

"Yeah?" A little rude, but whoever called obviously knows me.

"Reigney? Is that you?" It's my mom. I'm a little confused as to how she's calling me. Her phone doesn't have long-distance.

"Hi, Mommy." I am suddenly nine years old again.

"Why are you answering your phone like that? You make somebody think that you don't have any home training." She makes me sound like a puppy. Home training? I hate that expression.

"Sorry. I'm just really busy right now and I don't recognize this number." The old people are finished, and I'm trying to putt while holding my phone to my ear. I really should have brought my Bluetooth, but I have no idea where it is. Or I should've left my phone.2

"This is your father's phone. He's pretending to be young."

I doubt that I've mentioned this, but my parents have a very on again/off again relationship. Growing up, there were a few times that she let him live with us, but it never lasted more than four months before he was locked out again. They must be on again. I prefer the off periods. I love my father from a distance, and when they're pretending to have a functional relationship, it makes keeping the distance that much harder.

"Mommy, you're not looking through his phone to start craziness, are you?" I ask tiredly. I know the answer before she gives it.

"This is my husband's phone. If I feel like it, I'll call every number in this motherfucker. These bitches know damn well he's married. Amityville ain't but an inch wide."

Today she claims him; tomorrow she'll be giving him away.

"Ma, is there a reason you're calling me? I'm on a date right now." This may hurry her off of the phone.

"A date? You have a boyfriend now?"

She's killing me.

"Yes, I do."

"Put him on the phone."

She cannot be serious.

"I don't think that it's really necessary to do that, Ma."

"You better give that boy the phone, or I will come through this phone like an electric shock on your ass."

"Yes, Ma'am." I hand the phone to Jonah, and he looks at me like I'm out of my mind.

I'm mouthing to him and gesturing that he needs to say hello. This day can't possibly get worse. I watch him as he looks at the phone like it's about to attack him, and finally he puts it to his ear.

"Uh, hello? ... Jonah... Yes, it is... Yes, I do. I'm a web developer... Yes ma'am... I went to Georgia Tech... No, I don't do drugs... McInerney... No, I don't... Not to excess... I'm thirty... Nope, never married... I don't have any children... You too. Okay, here's Autumn." He hands me my phone back like it's on fire.

I give him the most apologetic look I can when he hands me the phone. She has never done that before.

"Mommy. Is there a reason that you called me? I mean, you didn't do this just to interrogate Jonah."

He's pulling me off of the course while I'm talking, and I see that he's leading us toward the café.

"He seems nice. You should bring him for a visit. I called you to let you know that your uncle says that they'll be bringing Angel down on Wednesday. It's a little earlier than they were supposed to come, but hey."

I would complain, but it really is only a few days before she was supposed to come anyway, and my mother doesn't care about my complaints. I finally get her to hang up the phone and I turn to Jonah.

"I'm really sorry about that." That was very embarrassing.

"It's okay. Don't worry about it. What did she want anyway?"

My sanity.

"She was letting me know that the cousin that will be taking advantage of my hospitality is coming a little earlier than expected."

"How much earlier?"

"Wednesday. Not too bad."

We order lunch, and afterward head back out for another round. An hour later we head back to Jonah's to relax before the battle.

Chapter Sixteen:

Jonah and I are dressed and ready to go out. I am wearing a black jersey Henley tunic dress by Clu with a pair of red peep toes by Velvet Angel. I love bluefly.com. If it weren't for them, I'd have to declare bankruptcy. I was always into shoes, but since moving here I'm a clothes horse too. Jonah is wearing black slacks with a long sleeved blue button-down shirt that's cuffed to just below the elbow, and a black and blue striped skinny tie. We're going to Eight Sushi Lounge in Atlanta. I've been there once before with Mark, and we fell in love with the cocktails and lobster rolls. The restaurant is smart casual dress. But this is a date. Jonah helps me into my black and white corset back trench coat, and we're off. It takes us less than twenty minutes to get to the restaurant, which is good, because our reservations are for seven-thirty, and we left the apartment at five after.

When we arrive, Kaylin is already waiting for us with a man that I can only assume is Jim. They're smoking off to the side of the entrance.

So, classy.

I'm not a smoker. Both of my parents are. So is my oldest sister. I've never even tried it. I did know the chief for a while in high school, but he and I parted ways by my freshman year in college. The smell of cigarettes always makes my throat feel dry. And I hate the way that the smoke clings to everything. When we're close enough to them, Jonah begins a conversation.

"Hey, I hope you guys weren't waiting too long?"

I like the way he phrases it. A statement meets a question.

The man standing with Kaylin responds. She just looks bored. "Naw, not at all. We been here maybe five minutes."

He's a little shorter than Jonah, maybe 5'11", and very wide. I can't tell if its muscle or fat, because he's wearing a heavy, dark blue, cable knit sweater with these sharply creased tan slacks that are giving me a high school guidance counselor vibe, and an opened winter coat. It's cooled down considerably since earlier and is in the low sixties, but it isn't really winter coat weather. Jim has light brown hair, and brown eyes, I think. His nose is very straight, and a little large. His top lip is a little fuller than the bottom, and he has a cleft in his chin.

"Five long minutes. It's freezing out here." Leave it to Kaylin. She's also wearing a heavy coat. And here I thought that Vikings were impervious to the cold.

Before she can continue, her fiancé extends his hand to me. "It's nice to meet you. I'm Jim."

Taking his hand, I give him a polite smile. "Autumn. Nice to meet you, too. Do you guys want to go inside?"

It seems like no one wants to move. I'm hungry and I need a drink. If these people don't get mobile, I'm going to leave their asses on this sidewalk. I look at Jonah with a raised brow and he takes my hand, pulling me toward the door.

"Behave, sumo. I'm gonna feed you." He pinches my waist.

"Did you just call me fat?" Aren't sumo wrestlers like five hundred pounds? Rude bastard.

"Baby, you aren't fat, your appetite is. It's actually confusing how you don't weigh more."

He may be right. I like to eat. Food is your friend.

"Tapeworm."

"I was thinking high metabolism." He's laughing now.

"That may be it too."

"I'm realizing that you're kind of a hypochondriac."

"No, I'm just dramatic," I assure him. My tone is less than convincing.

"Daytime soap dramatic, or Oscar speech dramatic?" he narrows his eyes at me.

"Definitely daytime soap," I laugh.

"So, I'm gonna be listening to the same storyline for the next twenty-five years?"

"You probably won't last that long. But if you do, it will be different twists on the same story line." 8

Didn't he talk about marriage like it was unnatural? Twenty-five years? Pfft, he needs to last thirty days first.

"What makes you think I won't last that long? You breaking up with me?" And there's that smirk.

"Why don't you focus on making it through dinner?"

"Just dinner, no dessert?"

Men are perverts. That had a definite sexual bend to it.

"If you're good, we'll discuss possible dessert." I also like sex. Food and sex. I should have been born a man. Living without sex for as long as I was, almost killed me.

"We're getting whipped cream and chocolate syrup." He looks so excited.

"Down boy." I realize that we're in the restaurant now, and the hostess is ready to seat us.

Kaylin and Jim have been listening to us closely it seems. Jim is grinning, but Kaylin looks annoyed. We're shown to a table for four and after we're given our menus, we're assured that our waiter will be right with us. Jonah helps me out of my coat, and I place it on the back of my chair, getting comfortable. I need all the comfort I can get right now.

"So, how long y'all been datin'?" Jim has a very heavy deep southern accent.

Jonah answers him before I can. "A month."

What? More like two weeks. Have I been losing time? Maybe I have a tumor. Or, I could be a very delusional hypochondriac. Or, he's lying. Before I can call him on it, a waiter appears.

"Good evening. My name is Peter, I'll be your waiter this evening. May I start you off with some drinks?" Peter is a very pleasant looking, young Asian-American man. He's smiling, and he has dimples. Jonah gestures for me to begin.

"I'll take a Devil Wears Prada, please."

"No problem, ma'am. May I ask to see your ID?"

This is the problem with having a young face. I'll be thankful for it when I'm fifty, but at twenty- five, it's A PAIN IN THE ASS. Opening my purse, I produce my license. The waiter takes it and looks at it very closely. I definitely need a drink.

"Thank you." He smiles again and hands it back to me.

Jonah is beside me trying not to laugh. I shoot him a glare, and he composes himself to continue the orders. "I'll take a Sweetwater. Thanks."

The waiter turns to the other couple, and not surprisingly, Kaylin orders for the both of them.

"I'll have a Big Fire Pinot Gris and a Sweetwater for the gentleman. Thank you."

Peter thanks us for our drink orders and tells us that he'll be back shortly with our drinks.

Kaylin picks the conversation back up as if it were never interrupted. "Wow. Has it really been a month already? Time flies, I guess. I thought it had only been a few weeks."

You don't get paid for thinking, bitch.

"Yeah, it's been a month," Jonah says.

"How'd you two meet?" This is from Jim. The way he says meet, sounds like he's saying mate.

"The first time was at the airport when I first moved here, Jonah was exceptionally rude." I bump his shoulder.

"I was not rude. I was shy. And I carried your bag for you. What is with you and heavy bags anyway?" He brushes some hair away from my face.

"You took my bag and walked away. And it wasn't heavy." I half expect lightening to strike me for that lie.

"I almost dislocated my shoulder carrying that anvil with a strap."

The way he's looking at me makes me laugh.

"Anyway, the second time we met was at a club."

Jonah is reading the menu while I talk to Jim. I'm only looking at him, not his other half. She's probably studying the menu as well. I already know what I want.

"So, y'all met twice 'fore you went out? How long did it take 'im to call?" he folds his hands in front of him and looks at me like he's really interested in the details.

Jimbo is asking very female questions, and I wonder if his future wife didn't tell him what to ask.

"He called the next day." In my peripheral vision, I see Kaylin look up at Jonah like she wants to say something, but the waiter appears with our drinks.

"Have you had a chance to look at the menu, or would you like a few more moments?"

Kaylin has apparently elected herself to speak for the table.

"I believe we're ready." She looks at us waiting for an objection, and I take a sip of my drink.

"Would you like to start with appetizers?"

I would. I wonder if the table nazi will have a problem with it.

"No, that's all right." She waves off the suggestion.

Oh hell no.

"Actually, I would like an appetizer." I look at her, and she narrows her eyes at me. Here we go. "I'll have the calamari ringlets."

Jonah smirks at me. "You know that's listed under the 'to share' portion of the menu, right?"

"And...?" I raise my eyebrows and look at him like he's crazy. I know he doesn't think I'm giving him any of my calamari.

He laughs and takes my hand in his and gives it an affectionate squeeze. "Let me get the gyoza, please."

The waiter looks at Jim next. The man looks torn. After a moment, he risks a quick look at Kaylin before jumping off the bridge. "I think I want some of that shrimp saku-saku."

Kaylin looks annoyed but decides to get on board, nonetheless. "I'll just have a green salad."

"All right. Would you like to place the orders for your entrees now, or do you need a moment?" he's looking between myself and Kaylin almost nervously.

Before anyone can try to subvert her, Kaylin orders for herself and Jim. "I'll take the Chicken Teriyaki, and he will have the same."

The chicken must be punishment for ordering an appetizer. This place has great steak. I don't know a man on the planet that would choose chicken over steak. The waiter looks at me, and I place my order.

"The Miso Sea bass, please."

After writing down my order, the waiter looks at Jonah.

"I'll have the American sizzling Wagyu, medium. Thanks."

"Of course, sir. Thank you." Peter takes our menus after telling us that he'll return with our appetizers.

I'll need to order another drink when he comes back. As soon as the waiter is out of hearing range the questions start again.

"So, Autumn. How old are you?" Jim asks me.

How is that his business? I guess Jonah didn't give Kaylin vital statistics. How remiss of him.

"I'm twenty-five and you?" Since we're information gathering, I'll join in.

"Oh, I'm thirty-one. D'you get the ID thang a lot?" He looks genuinely curious.

I'm finding the longer I stay here that it's very easy for southerners to look genuine. It's all in the manner with which they present themselves. It's not always the case. The nature of being genuine. Perhaps I'm just meeting inaccurate depictions of Georgians. I take another sip of my drink before answering.

"Unfortunately. Lucky for me, I never forget my license." I say it with a smile. I'm trying to keep the mood light.

The other woman at the table has other plans, again.

"Wow! I don't think I've ever had to prove my age. You do look very young, almost like a child." She says it with false sweetness.8

This shit is going to get real.

"Some of us age slower than others I suppose. It must be wonderful to always look your age or even older. People can be so condescending when you have a young face. You're blessed to have no idea how irritating it can be." I apply the same sweetness to my response, but I keep a smile on my face the whole time and bat my eyelashes at her. *The benefit of this young face is that I always look innocent. Effing hag!*

Jonah clears his throat before changing the subject. "So, Jim, how's the team this season?"

Team? What team?

"They're lookin' real good. It's still kinda early, but I got some All-Staters for sure."

I am so very lost. Kaylin is nodding her head like there aren't any muscles in her neck. She looks like a dash ornament.

"I'm sorry, what do you do? I'm really out of the loop here," I say.

Before he can answer me, Kaylin swoops in. "Jimmy is the best high school football coach in Georgia."

This time I think she's being honest. She's holding his hand and staring at him adoringly. It's a very Hallmark Channel moment.

"Cool. How long have you been coaching?"

"Six years, but I got my first head coach position two years ago. What do you do?"

Back on track.

"I'm in advertising."

He has this blank look on his face. I've never met a person that didn't understand that statement. Would it be insulting for me to elaborate?

"She helps to create marketing campaigns for companies. You know, commercials and billboards, stuff like that."

Thank you, Jonah.

"Oh! Okay. I thought you said something else."

Aren't we supposed to be talking about their wedding?

"I hear that you're getting married. How's the planning going?" I ask.

Kaylin actually gives me a grateful look for that one. Wonders never cease.

"I don't know, alright I s'pose. The little lady don't want me to wear the tux that I picked. And we're battlin' over the menu."

The little lady? What the fuck is that?

"He wants to wear a light grey suit. It's not a tux, and it doesn't go with the color scheme." She seems to be getting upset. I need my appetizer. Food usually stops conversation.

"I don't remember agreein' to no pink and yellow colors. It's not just your day you know. I'm gettin' married too," James says.

He said that so calmly. I don't think I would've been able to do that. Bra-flippin-vo.

"Everyone knows that weddings are about the bride." Kaylin pouts after throwing that out there. Her voice is becoming a little whiny.

I see the waiter coming with the appetizers and almost feel the holy spirit. Thank you, Jesus! When he begins depositing the food, I motion that I'll be needing another drink. He gives me an understanding nod. He doesn't really understand. It's like those MTV documentaries, "you think you know, but you have no idea." When he leaves the table, I begin to eat my appetizer. If my mouth is full, hopefully, no one will ask me anything. I catch Jonah's eye and he nods slightly. He has the same idea I do.

"Baby, you wanna taste this? It's really good." He holds up a bite of his appetizer for me. Such a wonderful man. Really.

"Thank you." I let him feed me some of his food and pretend to get mad when he takes some of my calamari.

Kaylin and Jim are not ready to let their argument go, and we are pulled into the fray.

"Autumn, haven't you dreamed about your wedding since you were a little girl," Kaylin states more than asks.

Nope. I can honestly say that I've never even considered getting married.

"Most of my friends have." There, a nice neutral answer.

"He wants to serve pigs in a blanket at my wedding! He thinks that the reception should be filled with Van Halen songs!" She seems outraged. It's kind of surreal.

"It's not your weddin'. Dammit! It's our weddin'! Technically it's my weddin', 'cause I asked you to marry me!"

Good point Jim.

"My parents are paying for it!" Kaylin says the words like they justify all of her behavior. This is getting loud.

"Guys, we're in a restaurant. There are other people trying to eat." Jonah to the rescue, again.

If they get any louder, they'll be serving our food to us in doggie bags. And here comes the waiter with my drink. Not a moment too soon. A drink is definitely needed, and I already finished the first DWP.

"Sorry. It's just frustrating." Kaylin made the statement, but it's clear that Jim agrees with the sentiment. "I mean, really! Who wants to hear Van Halen at a wedding?" She's looking at me again.

Now we're allies?

"Hot for Teacher was a good song." It's the first thing that pops into my mind and I can see Jonah trying to cover his mouth to keep from laughing.

"Hot for Teacher is a fanfuckingtastic song!" This enthusiastic claim is of course from Jim. He's so precious.

"Would you play that song at your wedding, Autumn." She's giving me a really accusatory look.

I respond without thinking. "I'm not getting married. But I have been hot for a teacher once or twice. In college, of course."

These cocktails are really good.

"You don't ever want to get married?" Kaylin is looking at me like I have three heads or something.

Every woman does not dream of a husband.

"I've never considered it. I don't think it's for me." You'd think I just said that I spend my weekends kicking unicorns with the way she's looking at me.

Jonah looks amazed. Then he speaks. "You are the most beautiful woman I've ever seen. I think I love you."

He is such a weirdo.

"Flattery will get you everywhere." I wink at him when I say it.

"Except to the altar?"

"Tell me when you plan on getting married, and I'll be sure to send a gift."

"You don't want to be there?"

"Depends on whether or not our split is amicable."

"I'm a very amicable guy."

"We'll see. In the meantime, keep the compliments coming."

"Nah. I wouldn't want to give you an over inflated ego."

"My ego never over inflates; I make sure to release some of the pressure off it every three months."

"Or three thousand miles?"

"A traveling ego?"

"It's the latest in self-esteem."

"Cute."

"I try."

Our dinner companions have stopped their argument to listen to our conversation. People should learn when to go away. But, since Jonah did invite them, I can't exactly blame them for intruding. Where the hell is the dinner?

"You two are gettin' married." This off base statement is again from Jim.

I honestly do not plan on getting married. Ever. I cannot stress that point enough. I don't believe in divorce, and I don't think that the person that can hold my interest until death do us part has been invented.

"Jonah isn't the marrying kind." Kaylin just scored ten points for spite. She must not be over it.

"A man after my own heart." I lean in and give him a kiss. *So there.*

"I think that marriage is beautiful. It's the weddin' that's evil and unholy," Jim chimes in.

You go Jimmy boy! That beer must have some red kryptonite in it or something.

"Weddings are wonderful! Our wedding is going to be amazing. People are going to be talking about it for years!" Kaylin crows.

Yup, she is a psycho.

There is a muscle on the side of Jim's neck that keeps moving, it's doing a ripple thing. Fascinating. And here comes the waiter with the food. And he must be clairvoyant, because he brought me another drink. I'm going to tip the fuck out of him. This time, the two soon-to-be-married people continue their argument throughout the meal placement.

"Why do we need people to be talkin' about our weddin' for years? An over the top weddin' does not guarantee somebody a wonderful marriage. My parents got married at a courthouse, and they celebrate forty years in March!" Jim thumps the table with his hand.

He is racking up the cool points with me.

"It's not just about the wedding. You are being impossible with everything. The rehearsal dinner, the stag party, everything. Why do you need to have a stag party? The things are completely immature, and it's like begging for trouble." She flops back against their seat in a huff.

Isn't the last hurrah the best part? I give Jonah a confused look and he decides to explain.

"Kaylin thinks that bachelor and bachelorette parties are out dated and childish. She wants them to have a joint party at a hall or something."

She's daffy. Totally certifiable.

"Isn't it supposed to be a last night of freedom thing? I mean, if it was going to be a full-on party with exotic dancers and a bar, then okay. Otherwise, how is that different from the rehearsal dinner and wedding reception?" I should stop talking. But I drank too much, and I can't really taste my food.

"That's my point exactly. If the weddin' is gonna be all about her, why can't I have one night? I'm not about to sleep with a stripper or pull a run-away groom. What's the problem?" Jim waves his arm around wildly in annoyance.

I clink my glass against his in commiseration. *I am so very tipsy.* "Jonah didn't have all of these complaints when we were engaged," she snarks.

That was low.

"And look how well that turned out. Last I checked, he was dating me." I just said that. Fuck! I just had a through the mind, out of the mouth moment. I should have just ordered a glass of wine. It's the fruity drinks that sneak up on you. Oh well. It's out there now. I decide not to apologize for telling the truth. Raising my eyebrow at her, I take another sip of my drink, and go back to my dinner.

"Thank you! Do you have any idea how much that pisses me off?" Jim turns to Jonah, palm up, "No offense, man."

"None taken," Jonah assures him and just keeps eating his steak. Turning to me, he offers me a bite.

Even though my taste buds aren't quite functional, I accept. Mostly to irritate Kaylin. I am not above being petty.

"You got 'bout one more time to compare me to Jonah. I get that he's a good guy and all, but enough is a damn nough. You all decided that you're better off as friends. Were you a party to that decision or not, 'cause he clearly was. Before we walk down that aisle, you need to realize who you're marryin'. I'm wearin' my gray tuxedo, I'm eatin' my pigs in a blanket, and there will be at least three Van Halen songs at the reception! I'll even let you choose which ones!" He slaps his palm against the table and looks around the room. "I need another beer!"

Wow! That was epic. I'm so glad that we all came to dinner together. Kaylin looks contrite. Like a small child that was caught stealing out of the collection plate at church.

"I'm sorry. I know who I'm marrying. I love you. You know that I love you. I just want this day to be perfect."

Here come the crocodile tears.

"I love you, too, but we need to figure out what's perfect for us. Not just what's perfect for you." He wraps his arm around her and pulls her into his side.

It's like an episode of *7th Heaven*. Do people really act like this? The moral of the story is...what exactly? Stop being such a bitch, or you'll lose another fiancé? I'm just waiting for the credits to roll signaling the end of this dinner.

"You know what, guys? This is probably not the best place to have this conversation. Why don't the two of you continue it when you get home? I feel like we're intruding," Jonah says diplomatically.

We're not intruding. They are intruding. Damned wedding drama. We are so obviously the wrong two people to be having this conversation with them. Rocket science?

"We're sorry. This is inappropriate. Let's just try to enjoy the rest of this evening, shall we?" Kaylin is once again the well-mannered hostess, taking this wayward dinner by the reins.

I realize now that my plate is nearly empty. Yes!!! I'm doing my internal happy dance. We can leave soon. I nudge Jonah under the table and motion to my plate with my eyes. He nods, and then shovels the remainder of his food into his mouth.

"Ew, Jonah. Etiquette! You aren't at home alone you know." Kaylin twists her mouth up in disgust.

He was going to marry that woman? Who wants to be treated like a child for their entire adult life? I have my answer when Kaylin actually wipes Jim's mouth, and he grins at her. Ugh! Who does that? The waiter approaches the table to do the mandatory, "how's your meal", check-up.

Before he can ask, Jonah starts to talk. "Dinner was great, really. May we have the check please?"

Peter, that little psychic, already has it with him.

"Wait, I think I'd like dessert," Kaylin says before Peter can hand over the check.

She is really cock blocking right now.

I have just enough fire in my system to snap.

Jonah puts his hand on my leg to restrain the coming tide and speaks to Kaylin. "I couldn't eat another bite. And, I'm sure that the two of you have a whole range of things to discuss. Best not to postpone it."

If I were to briefly consider marriage, his name would possibly be on my short list of few. He hands the waiter his credit card and smiles when he takes it and leaves the table.

"Y'all don't want no dessert?" Jim is practically pleading. It's clear that he is fine with letting their discussion wait a while longer as well.

"We'll be stopping for whipped cream and chocolate syrup on the way back to Jonah's." I really shouldn't drink and talk. Kaylin looks scandalized.

"So, Jonah...thanks for paying man. You really didn't have to." Jim talks while trying to suppress his grin.

"No problem. You can leave the tip if you want. I figured that I invited you guys, so I should pay."

Under duress. They were invited under duress. At least she won't be spending the night with us again.

Finally, we're all leaving. We walk them to their car and exchange the customary phrases. 'I'll call you.' 'See you soon.' 'It was wonderful meeting you.' 'I hope we can do it again soon.' At least two of those are lies. It was nice meeting Jim. I'm sure that I'll see Kaylin again sooner than I'd like to. I hope to never have a meal in a restaurant with these people again in life. I'm not calling anyone but Jonah. And Mark. But I don't think he counts toward this conversation.

As soon as we're in Jonah's truck, I can hear myself talking again. "I can't believe you almost married that woman."

"I didn't almost marry her, we were briefly engaged." He starts the truck.

My face is doing that painfully confused thing again. Did he just say that? "You are aware that it's the same thing, right?"

"No, it's not."

"Are you mental?"

"It's not the same." He sounds exasperated.

I'm the one not making sense? "What's the difference?"
"Almost marrying someone is when you get to the altar and change your mind.

Being briefly engaged is when you ask someone to marry you, and then change your mind a few months later."

I don't even know how to respond to that. He has a way of being logically illogical that makes arguing with him difficult. And I'm drunk. "Jonah, that makes no sense."

"It makes perfect sense. It's all in the definitions. Clinton proved that when he debated the use of the word, are."

"That was different. The man was the president, and his wife was privy to everything that was being said. What man is going to admit to getting a blowjob from someone other than his wife, with her in the room?"

"Then it is very much the same. You are not my wife, you are my girlfriend, that puts me in a more difficult position." He says it like his reasoning makes perfect sense.

"How so?" Now I really am confused.

"Hillary Clinton had her own political agenda, so even if she wanted to leave his cheating ass, she had more motivation to work it out. You don't actually need me, so if I play my cards incorrectly, I lose out on great sex and conversations with a woman that has no intention of ever attaching a ball and chain to my ankle. Why would I do that?"

"So, what, I'm the perfect girlfriend?" I'm seriously flattered.

"No. You can't cook."

Cute. Just callously burst my bubble.

"If I could cook, you wouldn't appeal to me as much as you do now."

"But I'd still appeal." He smirks.

"Cocky?"

"Self-assured. It's the only way to be around you. If I let the nervousness shine through, you'll chew me up and spit me out."

"You know me so well. Are you implying that I've created the monster that you've become?"

"Absolutely."

"You know, the nervousness was very cute. When it wasn't coming across as rudeness. What happened to it?"

"Initially, talking to you was intimidating, because you're gorgeous and can be a bit of a ballbuster. But now, I'm dating you. It changes things."

"So, I went from unattainable, to an ornament?"

"Not an ornament. You're too outspoken and opinionated for that. Look, it's one thing to want the girl, and another thing to get the girl. It does wonders for a person's self-esteem."

"You are such a catch." I roll my eyes at him.

"You know what I mean. Autumn, there will never be a time in this relationship that I take you for granted. It isn't because you're a beautiful woman, because I've dated beautiful women, it's because you're an amazing person. You're smart and funny, and sexy, and confident, and a whole list of things that I can't even name right now."

Yeah, I'll keep him. I wonder if he practices saying these things in front of a mirror.

"I just can't cook."

"Depends on the room."

"You are such a perv."

He laughs and kisses the back of my hand. Our weekend is back on track.

Chapter Seventeen:

The horrible thing about weekdays is that you always have more tasks than time. My cousin that I haven't seen since God was a boy is coming today. They should be here at around eight tonight. My uncle will be dropping her off and continuing along on his useless way.

I was forced to do something this week that I have never done. I went grocery shopping. I usually just hit the freezer section at Target for all the frozen dinners and pastries, but I received a phone call on Monday from my mother reminding me that when people come to your home, you should feed them. I reminded her that I don't cook. She informed me that Angel does cook, and that I should buy things that she could make herself. After all, not every woman wants to be alone for the rest of their lives. Some of them learn valuable lessons, like cooking and cleaning. Things that really make men happy. I attempted to remind her that this is the twenty first century, and there are women that have corporate jobs now. I also mentioned that I have a boyfriend, to which she responded, "You usually have a boyfriend, when are you going to have a husband? Or do women with corporate jobs not get married?". I refrained from telling her that she and my father are part of the reason that I don't plan on getting married. Some things just shouldn't be said.

Grocery stores are terrible places. They are confusing and tedious. I spent forever looking for soy milk (apparently the little cherub is lactose intolerant), only to find out that it was located on the opposite side of the store with the organic food. There are eggs in the dairy section, and eggs in the organic section. The same goes for bread, and crackers, and vegetables. If it was organically grown, without hormones or pesticides, you have to walk to Kenya to get it. It's as if someone said, "let's make this grocery buying thing more interesting. Let's add an entire section on the other side of the store and fill it with overpriced food that should cost less seeing as how there were no expensive chemicals used during its production. And, let's put the word organic at the front of the aisle, on a sign that's being blocked by a balloon display, because if we use an SAT word, people will think they're getting something spectacular, and they won't question the price".

Newsflash, if you cover your organically grown asparagus in melted butter, or deep-fry your un-enhanced chicken, you just negated the whole healthy purpose of your over expenditure. And will someone explain to me why there are aisles of dog food, cleaning products, and personal hygiene products dividing the aisles of actual food? I'm never going back.

Right now, I'm at work. If I get out of here at six, I can be home by a quarter to seven and take a shower. I usually don't leave work until eight. Well, on days that I take a lunch I don't, but I haven't been taking lunches since Mark's been out. The good news is that Mark was out of the hospital yesterday, and Henry took him home. He's coming back to work next week. I didn't expect that from him. I think he just needs something to do. He and Patrick are still working out their issues. Not really their issues, I shouldn't say that. Patrick's wife's issues. Patrick is having her take tolerance classes. Can you believe that? Tolerance classes are necessary now for people to treat other people with respect? Especially family members? Who does that?

Thankfully, they've hired a new person for Keyana's team. She keeps sending me death glares. I must have pissed her off when I didn't jump at the opportunity to be a subordinate. Every princess needs subjects.

Chelsea has been unusually chipper this week. It is severely frightening. She's like a serial killer with a secret stash of zip ties and chloroform. She's been humming and smiling since Monday morning. If she were a human, I'd think it was from really good sex, but given that she's a husband killing android, the machines are obviously closer to subverting us. I should build a bomb shelter. I'd probably need to use tools for that though, and I can't tell a nail gun from a hack saw. I should have paid closer attention in wood shop.

Looking at the clock on my computer, I see that it's nearing six. I begin logging out of my systems and preparing to leave. I should stop on my way home for a burger. If the world is about to end, I should at least get a bacon double cheeseburger before it does.

An hour and a half later, I enter my house to the sound of my phone ringing. I should have it disconnected. It very seldom is heralding the call of a person that I want to speak to. I pick it up, mentally preparing myself for more aggravation.

"Hello?" It comes out sounding tired.

"Hi sweetie, it's Aunt Mae. How are you?"

She's fishing. I can hear it. The interrogation is about to begin. I should make her mirandize me first. I would love the right to remain silent.

"I'm great, just a little busy. How have you been?" I haven't been to church in three weeks. She's probably planning a prayer intervention.

"Everything is wonderful. I spoke to your mother." Here we go, buckle up. "I didn't know you were seeing someone. Is he saved? That is very important you realize?"

I have a headache. More of an eye-ache, really. It feels as if I'm being stabbed in my right eye.

"He's catholic. I don't think they get saved."

She's Baptist. I was raised Methodist. There are too many different names for Christianity. It's not like there are gonna be different entrances in heaven for the different factions. I can just picture it now, Catholics in the front door, Protestants in the back. Baptists and Methodists, please use the opposing side doors. All of those that fall in between, we would ask that you kindly use the handicapped entrance with the ramp. The Jehovah's Witnesses will show you the way.

"He's catholic? White catholic?" She's being cautious.

"At least fifty percent of him is white, yes."

"Well, that is just wonderful," she says with fake enthusiasm. "Why don't you bring him by for dinner on Saturday? We'd all love to meet him. And, make sure you bring Donovan's daughter too, she needs to know that she has family here. In case she needs anything, and you aren't around. We'll see you all at seven. I have to go now, that's my other line beeping in. Bye." Just like that, she's off the phone.

If the people in my family continue to ambush me, I'm going to start treating them like bill collectors and not answer the phone. I hang up the offending instrument and my cell phone rings.

What the hell?!

Looking at it, I recognize my uncle's number. I should ignore it. Maybe if I do that, they won't show up at my door. I say a silent prayer and answer the phone.

"Hello, Uncle Don."

"Hey, I just wanted you to know that we'll be there in about five minutes. Traffic was real good, so we're a little early. You home?"

I'm rubbing my forehead. The headache is spreading. "Yeah. I'm here. Just come on by. The gate code is twenty-seven fifteen."

"Okay. Good. We'll see you in a few." He hangs up, and I take a moment to ponder this situation.

How did I get here? Six months ago, I was sleeping in my sister's spare room listening to her complain about her boyfriend. I had been finished with graduate school for five months, and my biggest problem was worrying about getting a job that would allow me to pay back my student loans, and still afford the latest from Balenciaga. Well, not the latest. More like the clearance. Beggars can't be choosers, and classic never goes out of style. I feel like banging my head against a wall, but something tells me that it'll only make my headache worse. See, I can be smart. I guess my shower will have to wait.

My uncle is the size of a Buick. Truly a happy meal away from a heart attack. It's confusing. My mother weighs about a hundred and eleven pounds. Her other brother is in the one forty range. If he didn't resemble them, I'd think he was adopted. Here he is, taking up all of the space in my living room and eating a sandwich. He actually went straight to my refrigerator when he came in the house. He's wearing a pair of jeans that are hanging off of his super rotund ass, a wife-beater, and he has a polo shirt draped around his shoulders like a towel. He's sweating. Not from any physical exertion since Angel carried in her own bags, but from the chore of simply being. I wonder if he's a diabetic. We have several of them in our family. If he isn't one already, he will be soon. His wife didn't come with them. He says that she wasn't able to get any vacation time at work, and so she stayed home. He'll be going to see his family alone. He has also informed me that he'll need to spend the night here, because after driving all the way from New Jersey, he is exhausted.

He wouldn't be exhausted if he would have convinced his daughter to go to Rutgers.

Speaking of his daughter. Angel does look innocent, but those are always the ones. She's about three inches taller than me, my complexion, no hips, huge breasts, and two pony tails. She's wearing skinny jeans and a cardigan sweater. She hasn't really spoken other than to thank me for letting her stay here and asking where to put her things.

"You doing alright, huh niece?" My uncle is talking around a mouth full of food as he takes in his surroundings. Lord, help me.

"I'm doing okay. Apartments are a little cheaper down here." I hate small talk.

"I like the furniture in here."

This is a pathetic conversation.

"Yeah, Aunt Mae gave me most of it; except for the dishes, the stuff in Angel's bedroom, and the electronics."

"Yeah, that was definitely peace. Hopefully she can bless my baby girl's dorm room. Maybe take her school shopping for some new clothes."

Does he realize that adults don't go school shopping? The girl is starting college, not the ninth grade. Besides, she'll need all of her money just to cover those expensive ass textbooks that she's going to need.

"Has she met with her advisor yet?"

"She's supposed to have orientation in December."

I can't wait.

Angel joins us in the living room and the conversation continues.

"So, Angel, what do you plan on majoring in?" I changed my major three times in college.

"I think I want to study Journalism." She looks excited when she mentions it.

Before I can ask her anything else about the subject, her father shuts it down.

"She's going to study nursing. We want her to be a registered nurse. Maybe a nurse practitioner."

How thoughtful of him.

I didn't have this problem when I went to college. My mother supported all of my decisions. She was mostly just proud that I decided to go. My older sisters initially went to trade schools after they graduated. My oldest sister is a Medical Assistant, and my *older* sister is a Licensed Practical Nurse. The latter is going for her RN now and wants to continue on until she receives her BSN. I hear my sisters talk about their jobs all the time, and I know that if you go into nursing without wanting to really be in the field, then the patients suffer.

"Daddy, I told you that I don't wanna do that." She sounds so frustrated.

I should leave them alone, but this is my house.

"And I told you, that's not a guaranteed income. People are always going to get sick. That's a fact. You need to let go of that journalism mess. When you're paying for school, then you can decide."

I hate to agree, but he has a point.

"I got scholarships and loans. Am I supposed to let the loan people decide what I should do?" Complete with neck action.

I'm a grown woman and I don't talk to my mother like that. Someone is obviously unfamiliar with the disciplinary functions of a leather belt. Although she should have been more respectful, she's right. If her parents aren't paying for her education, they should let her decide her major for herself.

"Who do you think you're talking to like that? Don't think that just because you're not in my house, that makes you grown. I'm paying for books. I'm paying for food. I'm paying for clothes. You want to act like you're grown, you think you're my age? Get a job. Take care of yourself. There's a hell of a lot more to being an adult than just getting a scholarship." He seems a bit out of breath, but otherwise looks stern.

"Okay, daddy." She's not even looking at him when she says it and the sarcasm is heavy as hell.

I would have been slapped already. My mother would have taken that as straight up disrespect. My mother raised Donovan, so it confuses me that his outlook isn't the same on this. I decide to interrupt. I do not need the drama.

"So, Aunt Mae would like Angel and me to go to dinner at her house on Saturday. She wants to get to know you. She thinks it'll be good for you to meet her family, just so that you know that you have other people here that you can depend on."

She looks relieved that I changed the subject. She should be. She'd better not try the neck movements and sarcasm with me. I am not above slapping someone else's child.

"Okay. What time on Saturday are we going?"

Before I can answer, in jumps Captain Plump. "Why? You got plans or something?"

They are just snippy as hell.

"No, I just want to know what time to be ready." She sounds like she's talking to a four-year old.

"For what? It's a family dinner, not a date. You don't need to get dressed up for this," he snaps at her.

He is a pain in the ass. I still think that Angel is rude, but he's trying my patience and he isn't even talking to me. They start the verbal back and forth again, and thankfully, my cell rings. I leave the room and answer it.

"Hello?" I don't know why I have a Caller ID function. If my phone rings ninety times, I look at the Caller ID maybe seven times out of those ninety. I'm hopeless.

"Hey, baby. Did your cousin get there yet?" Jonah's voice comes over the line and calms me immediately.

I needed to call him anyway to let him know that we've been shanghaied. Looks like he beat me to it. "Yeah, she got here nearly an hour ago. My uncle has informed me that he's spending the night, they've argued about her major, and now the latest is a bickering session over dinner at my aunt's. He's nitpicking."

"You poor thing. He'll be gone tomorrow. Just keep repeating that like a mantra. You'll be fine."

Isn't he the concerned one?

"My aunt wants me to bring you to dinner on Saturday." Let's see him come up with a calming mantra for that shit.

"Why would she want to do that?" He sounds scared.

Punk.

"I have no idea. Apparently, my mother told her that you're a good guy. She wants to see for herself. Now would be the perfect time for you to go away on business."

"Do I embarrass you? Should I be offended?" His voice is filled with mock outrage.

It's not him that I'm worried about. I love my family, but they can be overwhelming.

"Of course, you do. That should have been a given."

"I am totally going to dinner. I might even wear my shirt with the bowling balls on it."

"Can I give you a mohawk?" That would be priceless.

"Yeah, I'll even die my hair blue."

"Really?" That would be hilarious.

"No. Are you insane? I want these people to half like me."

Such a wimp.

"Why?" I don't care if my family likes me. It makes things easier if they do, but it isn't the end of the world if they don't. We are not really in any position to throw many stones.

"Because, I intend to be with you for a long time."

That's news to me.

"Seriously?"

"Dead seriously. Didn't we talk about this over the weekend?"

I don't remember a longevity conversation. "No. We talked about our mutual aversion to marriage."

I was tipsy, not drunk. We couldn't have had an entire conversation that I forgot.

"Exactly."

Men speak a completely different language.

"How does two people talking about never getting married equate to a long-term relationship?" Have I become slow?

"That is a major life issue that we both agree on. And I didn't say that I never want to get married, I said I didn't know if I would ever be ready to get married."

I don't see a difference.

"Well, I'm never getting married." I obviously need to clarify that.

"We'll see."

He is a very confused individual.

"What, are you going to consult a magic eight ball in five years to see if you've changed your mind about marriage?"

This dude is unreal.

"I prefer the psychic network. Or at least a vintage looking ouija board."

I'm trying not to laugh. This is such an insane discussion. "Dinner's at seven. Be here by six."

"No problem. Should I bring anything? Wine, flowers, tranquilizers?"

"Only if you have a dosage large enough to take out an elephant."

"Sorry, I never filled that prescription. How about enough to stun a large gopher?"

"Nah. No point in only doing a partial job."

"Okay. I'll bring wine."

"Just bring some flowers for my aunt."

"And would you care for some overpriced smelly weeds?"

He is such a romantic.

"I have allergies." No point in wasting the man's money on something that's just going to make me feel like I've gotten hit in the face with a hammer.

"So, lilies then?"

I could love him. "Not this time."

"Fine, just turn me down on all fronts tonight. Will you be turning me down on Saturday as well?"

Ah, back to basics.

"You don't need to buy me flowers to get laid. Shoes will do just fine."

"What size do you wear?"

He's such an eager little beaver.

"Like I would trust you to pick out a pair of shoes for me." I laugh just imagining what he would choose. He must be deranged.

"What's so hard? Just pick out something that's strappy, with a heel that looks impossible to maintain balance in, and there I go."

Feminine foot fashion summed up in typical male speak. Idiots.

"You are an idiot."

"Only on Tuesdays, on Wednesdays I'm a moron. I'll thank you to remember the distinction in the days."

This is why I'm keeping him.

"How thoughtless of me."

"Listen, I gotta go now. Working. I'll see you Saturday."

"See you then. Bye." I hang up the phone with a smile on my face. As I re-enter the room to my uncle and cousin's continued arguing, my smile falls with the return of my headache. He needs to leave.

Chapter Eighteen:

My uncle and his daughter argued until midnight. I finally put the kibosh on the bullshit by handing my uncle a blanket and telling him to get some sleep so that he could get an early start. When I left for work the next morning, he was still there. When I came home, the blanket that he used was on my living room floor, there were damp and dirty towels on the floor of my hall bathroom, and there was a sink full of dishes. I had a very detailed discussion with my squatter regarding the rules about cleaning up in my house. I don't like to clean. Luckily, I work long hours, and I can't cook. These facts eliminate most garbage and dishes. Because of my childhood, I know what it's like to live with roaches. Never again.

The spare bedroom in my house has a large closet with shelves, but there isn't a dresser. There is a television stand with a 42" television on it, thanks to a sale at Target. This girl is glaringly unfamiliar with hangers and shelves. I know this, because her clothing is all over the floor in my guest room. January can't come fast enough.

I am currently waiting for Jonah to get to my house so that we can go to my aunt's. I breathe a sigh of relief when there's a knock on the door. When I open it, Jonah is standing there looking only slightly nervous. He's wearing a pair of fitted blue jeans and a maroon button-down shirt with long sleeves that are rolled up to just below his elbows. He has opted for dress shoes over sneakers. Smart man.

"Hey, am I too early?" He's looking at me with a confused expression on his face. Is he trying to make a comment on what I'm wearing?

"No. We were just waiting for you, why?" I'm wearing black skinny jeans with my black Harley Davidson boots and a purple hi-low blouse. I think I look good.

He motions behind me, and when I turn, I'm shocked. This girl is wearing a dress that she could have fit in the fifth grade. I am not walking into my aunt's house with her looking like that.

"Angel, are you ready to go?" I keep my voice controlled.

"Yeah, I'm ready." She nods and smiles flirtatiously at Jonah.

She really isn't.

"Angel, please change your clothes. Your uncle is a preacher. You're going to a family dinner, not the club. You cannot wear that."

She gives me a disgusted look, and stomps back up the stairs to change. When she turns around, I can see her underwear.

"I take it you're not enjoying your adventure in babysitting?" Jonah wraps his arm around my waist while he's talking, and I lean into him.

"That girl is the reason that I'm never having children." Little bastards.

"You don't like kids now?" He's rubbing my stomach.

Why is he doing that?

"I like kids. The ones that go home are especially appealing. It's the ones that you have to keep all the time that don't sit well with me." I have nieces that I love. My oldest sister has three daughters. They are all smart, beautiful, well-behaved children, and I love them to death. More so because I can send them home. That makes a huge difference.

"So, no marriage, and no kids?"

This is not a difficult concept to grasp.

"That's right. I'm like a modified *Scarface*."

"You think if you change your mind about marriage that you'll change your mind about kids?"

Where is this coming from?

"I'm not going to change my mind about marriage. My mind is made up on that front."

He is being particularly dense in regard to this topic.

"But, if you do, will you change your mind about kids?"

I turn to face him. "Why are we having this conversation if neither of us wants to get married?" This is becoming annoying.

"Because, if we're still together five years from now, and I consult a Ouija board, and it tells me that I should get married, and I manage to convince you to change your mind and marry me, then I'd like to know that we'll have children."

I need a drink. A strong drink. I try to take a step back, but he keeps his arms locked around my waist. "You'd seriously ask someone to marry you based on the advice of a Ouija board?"

"It could be a very bad idea to ignore advice that comes to you from the hereafter. Wouldn't want to tempt fate." He leans down and nips my neck. He is definitely one of a kind.

"I tell you what, if we're still together in five years, and the Ouija board is consulted, we'll cross that bridge then."

Angel walks into the hall more appropriately dressed in a jean skirt that hits her mid-thigh and a polo shirt and we head out.

Is it me, or has Jonah become the woman in this relationship over night? I'm pretty sure that I'm just his white whale. I suppose that, for a man that doesn't want to settle himself with one woman, finding a woman that isn't remotely interested in marriage can be a pleasant shock. My view on marriage has been shaped by the relationships that I've witnessed. My grandparents have an amazing relationship. They each have faults, they argue, they are interested in completely different things, but when they're together, you can see why they're together. My grandfather looks at his wife as if she's still the most beautiful woman that he's ever seen. My grandmother talks about her husband and makes him seem ten feet tall. They are also from a different time. When sacred things, stayed sacred. In this day and age, it seems that nothing is sacred.

My best friend is a man that was and is having an affair with another man, who is married to a woman that he has children with. Neither of them seems to give a shit about the vows that were taken. The word sacred died with the word chivalry. There are men that will hold your door and pick up the check. They'll see you home safe and may not even push the 'no kissing on the first date' rule that some women have. But I think for me to change my mind about marriage, I'd need the guy that's going to lay his new coat over a puddle, just so I don't get my feet wet. I don't think they make that guy anymore.

My parents have a very screwed up relationship. I have at least three friends that grew up in the same circumstances as I did. One is married, one is a baby mama, and one has a live-in girlfriend. My oldest sister is married, but her husband sleeps in a separate bedroom. They don't want to get divorced because they want to maintain a level of stability for their kids. There are so many things wrong with that theory. My other sister has been in an on again/ off again relationship with her boyfriend since she was thirteen years old. She is twenty-eight. This is the relationship that confuses me. She has a stable job, she is training in a profession to increase her income, she has her own home, with a mortgage, and she's in an uncommitted relationship with a thirty-year-old man that lives with his mother and can't keep a job. Every time I talk to her, which hasn't been very often as of late, they have either just gotten back together, or she just caught him with another chick.

My last relationship ended that way. I came home, he was in our apartment balls deep in another chick, and I went a little nuts.

Not right away. At first, I was in shock. I had dated this man throughout my last year of college and graduate school, and I came home to him with the chick from the laundromat. The one that sells the soap behind the counter. I went to my friend's house, and stayed with her until after graduation in December, then I moved back to Long Island and started looking for a job in line with my degree.

It is because dysfunction has become the norm that makes me steer clear of the whole matrimony trap. This is something that I decided when I was in junior high school. The ending of my previous relationship did not contribute to this decision. It did reinforce the decision. I was more angry than I was hurt though, which is why I poured bleach on everything that I had purchased for him. The things that he purchased for me got the bleach treatment. I pawned the jewelry. I did this while he was at work, of course. He is a big dude. He probably would have called me and cursed me out, but he left his iPhone at home and I dropped it into the toilet tank. You may think that being a college educated and self-aware woman makes me above these petty actions. I assure you that I am not at all above petty shit. I didn't want to marry the man, but I deserved better than to be cheated on in my own home.

Jonah and I are going to have to have a serious talk about this relationship. I like him, but he needs to tone it down. He went from zero to eighty overnight. I want to be his girlfriend. I love spending time with him. He is an amazing person, and a talented lover, but I don't want to be Mrs. McInerney. This is completely childish. He only wants to contemplate marriage to me in the future because it isn't even a consideration. We've been dating for a sketchy month. Time to pump the brakes.

We're approaching my aunt's house now. We drove the whole way in verbal silence. The radio is playing, but I don't think that anyone is listening to it. Thanks to the wonders of modern technology I didn't need to give Jonah directions. Angel, whose name I'm realizing is an insult to all ethereal beings, is sulking in the backseat because I wouldn't let her wear the slut suit. Jonah looks like his nervousness is increasing. I'm sure that this will be a pleasant and comfortable dinner for everyone.

I'm lying. I may not need to have a conversation with Jonah regarding clinginess. Depending on this evening, I may never see him again. As he's parking the truck in the driveway, my aunt opens the door. She must have been watching for us in the window. I reach for my door handle and Jonah gives me a look that could freeze an active volcano. Evidently, he's on his best behavior tonight. Don't get me wrong, he does open doors for me, just not all the time. He climbs out of the truck and opens my door and even lends his hand in helping me out. He then opens Angel's door. I'm slightly shocked when she thanks him.

When we reach the door, I greet my aunt with a hug. "Hi, Aunt Mae. This is Donovan's daughter, Angel." I pause for her to give her niece a hug. She may want to slip some holy water into her juice at dinner. Angel has her innocent face firmly in place. "And this is Jonah."

She smiles and shakes his hand. He actually brought her flowers. I didn't notice until now. He gives her a dozen begonias. Nicely handled. My uncle Earnest is standing in the foyer behind my aunt and immediately sweeps me into a hug.

"Where have you been, baby girl?" He finally lets me go but keeps me in front of him. "We haven't seen you in church in a month of Sundays. You wanna tell Saint Peter that sleepin' in was more important than your everlasting soul? You never know when you're gonna get called home. You want the northern address to be on that invitation when it comes, you understand? Hell is not a vacation spot, or an unpleasant layover. Youth doesn't mean immortality."

My aunt breaks into his sermon that he has decided to give in the front hall. "Now, Earnest, these children came for dinner. Let's save preaching for the pulpit. Autumn brought company. Her boyfriend, Jonah, and our great niece, Angel."

He hugs Angel and then grasps Jonah's hand. "Biblical name; are you a saved man, Jonah?"

I wonder if there will be alcohol. After all, Jesus did turn water into wine. I'll take moonshine at this point. You should know that my overly Christian preacher of an uncle refers to my friend Mark as the fairy. But he likes Mark, because Mark will talk to him about football and Jesus. How ridiculous is that?

"I'm Catholic, sir." Jonah looks stable.

"So, not saved then." My uncle seems to be sizing him up. You'd think that we were about to do a gift registry at Nordstrom's or something.

"Generally, when I'm feeling lost, I speak to my father or my mother," Jonah jokes.

Two points for the white boy.

"How well do you know your bible?" My uncle gives him an appraising look.

Is he entering a seminary?

"Very well, sir. Catechism classes, first communion, bible school, the whole shebang."

If he asks him to do a Hail Mary, I'm going home.

"Baptized?"

What the hell?

"And Christened."

Is this a weird southern ritual that I was never informed about?

"Welcome to the family." My uncle smiles broadly at him.

Whoa!

"Dinner. You only need to welcome him to dinner," I hastily clarify. Now they're all looking at me as though I'm the nut in this fruit cake. What the hell?!

"You all came just in time. Dinner is about to be served, and Daniel is already here with Delanya," Aunt Mae breaks in with a smile. She is so sweet.

Delanya is the stripper girlfriend's real name. Not much better than Delightful if you ask me. My uncle takes her hand as my aunt leads us into the den.

"Autumn, why don't you help me in the kitchen?"

Jonah is unable to contain his laughter. Prick.

"I'm sorry. Are you sure you want her to help you?"

He is such a jackass. My uncle and cousins are finding this funny. Why wouldn't they?

"It'll be fine. We're just taking things out of the oven and setting the table in the dining room."

What, like I'm going to blow up the oven or something? I can cook! Breakfast food counts. I don't care what Mark says. Eggs and bacon are really all you need to survive. Of course, you'd die of a heart attack from the cholesterol of your diet, but that isn't the point.

I follow my aunt into the kitchen, and we make short work of everything. Angel sets the table. She's being very polite to everyone. It's a ruse. Everyone sits at the table and begins to eat after a five-minute prayer from my uncle.

My aunt starts the dinner conversation, and I'm happy that it centers on Angel.

"So, Angel, I hear that you'll be attending school in the spring?" My aunt is looking at her expectantly.

"Yes, Ma'am. To study Journalism," she says brightly.

I am making the decision not to even touch this topic.

"That's very interesting. Have you been writing for a long time?" Aunt Mae is smiling with real interest. She honestly does want this girl to feel welcome.

Angel is smiling at her with all of her false innocence and genuine enthusiasm. "Only about a year. I was on my school newspaper my senior year of high school and I fell in love with it."

My cousin Daniel, whose presence I have been trying to ignore, clears his throat. "Speak8ing of love, I have an announcement." The smile freezes on my Aunt's face and my Uncle pauses mid chew. "Del and I were married at the justice of the peace yesterday."

I think I'm on an acid trip. That is the only reasonable explanation for this hallucination.

My Aunt's hand is shaking. When she speaks, her voice sounds forced. "What?"

She's about to blow.

"We were married yesterday. She's your daughter in law. We're going to need to stay here. Just for a few weeks until we find a new apartment." He says that like he's talking about the weather. And his wife is wearing the biggest smile that I've ever seen on a human. It's not smug, or gloating. It's ecstatic.

My Uncle places his fork on the table and speaks calmly and slowly. "You went and got married at a court house, to a woman that we don't approve of. To a woman whose own family will not deal with her because of all the things she's done. And now, you have the audacity to tell your mother and I that the two of you will be living with us for a few weeks?"

This is how massacres start.

Jonah is looking at me with this shocked expression and I'm positive that I'm making the same face. I look at Angel and see that she's bowing her head in an attempt to hide her laughter.

"If you're upset about the stripping, you should know that she's quitting," Daniel says defensively.

This is not a conversation to be had in front of company.

"This is not about the stripping. This is about the drugs, and the fraud, and the petty larceny." Uncle Earnest has come half out of his chair and is leaning forward and looking pissed.

News flash! I was unaware of these things. I would like to stay unaware of these things.

"Those things are in the past, Dad." Daniel sounds firm.

Delanya's smile has disappeared. I feel sorry for her. She's a pretty girl, now that I actually look at her. She's about five seven, with a honey complexion and short reddish hair. She has light brown eyes, the color of new pennies, that have long lashes. She has full lips and a small, pert nose. She looks like she wants to cry and is trying very hard not to. Daniel is holding her hand.

"How far in the past Daniel? Because a year doesn't seem that long to me." My Uncle is not looking convinced.

Delanya looks at him and speaks up for herself. "Aren't you saved? Wouldn't the Christian thing be to welcome me into your family and give me a chance to prove myself? People aren't perfect, or were you born saved, Reverend Lucas?"

Got 'im. I wonder what he'll say to that.

He looks ready to lose his religion when Mae brokers a peace treaty. "This isn't really the time for this discussion. But, Daniel, there *will* be a discussion. Delanya, welcome to the family; in the meantime. Now, let's finish dinner like civilized people."

I realize that when we leave, my aunt is going to behave the way my mother would. I almost wish I could be here to see it.

My Uncle turns to Jonah. "So, Jonah, what do you do for a living?"

Here we go. I guess that since his wife called off the air strike against his new daughter in law, he's moving the ground troops in on my boyfriend.

"I'm a web developer and a graphic artist." Jonah reaches over and squeezes my hand.

This is about to get uncomfortable, I can feel it.

"And, do you make a good income doing that?" My uncle asks the question like he already knows, and is displeased, by the answer.

That isn't rude at all.

"I do." Jonah's tone is conversational.

To give Jonah credit, he doesn't seem to be getting offended. I am. He's calmly eating his pot roast and answering directly. I feel like we're at a job interview.

"So, you'd be able to support a family without needing to move in with your parents for a few weeks?" My uncle cuts his eyes at Daniel.

Amazing how he manages to conduct this interrogation and make a dig at his son at the same time. Let's hear it for Christian multitasking.

"Yes sir, I would." Jonah actually seems amused. He was also amused when Mark accused him of being a serial killer. His sense of humor can be inappropriate at times.

"Do you own a home?"

Sweet Lord! This needs to stop.

"Uncle Earnest, I think that we should just eat dinner." I'm trying to remain respectful, but this man is not my father. And, he doesn't get a say in who I sleep with.

"It's okay. We're just having a polite conversation, I don't mind." Jonah gives my hand another squeeze.

I think that Jonah may be a masochist. It would explain why he asked Kaylin to marry him.

"Thank you, Jonah. Now, do you own a home?" Earnest continues like he never stopped.

"No."

I would love for this conversation to end.

"How old are you? If you don't mind me asking."

I'm going to be sick.

"I'm thirty."

What is the point of this? Why do men feel the need to ask and answer these types of questions? Do they think that women are too stupid to weed out the losers from the winners? This is not some, D rate celebrity looking for love on a mediocre channel, show. This is my life, and I don't appreciate the questioning. The problem is that my aunt has done a lot for me, and I really don't want to be disrespectful. She needs to rein her husband in. I send her a look, and she gives me a helpless one in return. Like I don't know that she runs this house? Angel is very interested in this topic from what I can tell. This sucks!

"Did you know that Autumn is only twenty-five?"

So now he's acting like I'm a child? Jonah wasn't exactly trolling school yards for prepubescent girls when we met.

"Yes, I know that." Now Jonah looks a little confused. Welcome to my world buddy.

"That's a rather large difference. Once you pass thirty, age doesn't really matter, but in your twenties it's a big deal."

He is smoking something powerful, and I wish I could have a hit of it. Once again, I interrupt. "Uncle Earnest are you aware that I'm an adult?" I just need to make sure that he hasn't totally lost his mind.

"Now, baby girl, this is your first time on your own, and I want to make sure you're making appropriate decisions," he says patiently.

My first...what?

"I lived in Philadelphia for seven years without any of my family members in attendance, and I managed." I keep my voice light.

"From what your aunt tells me, you were dating a young man there that you caught cheating on you. I just want to be sure that you aren't repeating old mistakes. I also want to be sure that this young man isn't just fulfilling some fantasy of sleeping with a black girl."

And I'm done. Placing my napkin on the table, I turn to my aunt. "Thank you for having us, but I think we'll be going now. I believe that everyone at this table has had enough drama to last at least a week." Turning to my uncle, I continue with barely managed politeness. "I appreciate your concern, but I would suggest you direct it toward your congregation tomorrow, and more immediately to your son and his new wife tonight. I would also ask you to be conscious of the type of man you have raised and released on society before you attempt to choose a suitable man for me."

Turning from the table, I head for the front door. I don't stop until I get outside and realize that we brought Jonah's truck. Thankfully, he and Angel come out of the house a few moments later with my aunt behind them. Tomorrow, I'll feel bad about the way I spoke to my uncle. Today, I'm still pissed off. Jonah opens my door, and helps me in. My aunt stands on her porch as we drive away.

Chapter Nineteen:

I'm sitting in Tomo with Mark recounting the dinner of disaster. It's amazing how little has changed. You would think that after everything that happened with him, Mark would be a new man. Maybe he needs to have a little more therapy first. He's sitting here listening to me, and I can't help but feel selfish. He has more important things going on in his life. My problems are miniscule.

"Do you want to talk about something else?"

He looks at me in surprise. "Why would I want to talk about something else? For once, your life is full of drama, and not just my drama, because drama by association is in no way sexy or meaningful. I am thoroughly enjoying this. Daniel actually married the booty bouncer? Why didn't you invite me to dinner?"

Leave it to Mark.

"Because, I thought that you wanted to spend some alone time with Henry this weekend. And that's not even the worst part. My uncle by marriage had the gall to grill Jonah over dinner."

"Needed to make the distinction in the relation huh? Define grill." He takes a bite of his sashimi and leans forward in anticipation.

I start to get pissed off at the situation all over again. "He interrogated him."

Mark is looking at me as if I'm overexaggerating. I assure you I am not.

"Autumn, interrogated? Really?"

I very rarely exaggerate. Not out loud anyway. What I do in my private thoughts is another story, and wholly my own business, slash issue.

"Yes, interrogated, quizzed, questioned, cross-examined, brow beat." How much clarification can one person give?

"What's the matter? Did you run out of synonyms?" he deadpans. He is such a smart ass!

"We only have a half an hour left for our lunch. Be serious. It was so ridiculous."

"I don't know, I've seen Jonah." He shakes his head and frowns. "The man is gorgeous, and he looks too innocent. Add to that the fact that you can see his dick through his jeans, and there is cause to find out his intentions."

Got to love this man's way with words.

"You cannot! And, have you met me? I'm not exactly clamoring to be a baby popping Susie homemaker. They should be more concerned about my intentions." *They are, for your information, completely dishonorable.*

"Baby, I am more than aware of your intentions. And considering the fact that you went without long enough for your coochie to gather cobwebs, I would like to salute you. Is the boy scout aware of your unholy designs? You know the fact that you aren't willing to make an honest man out of him? Oh, and you can absolutely see that anaconda from across a room." He's smirking at me. This newest bit of information will make his gossip happy heart burst with excitement.

I roll my eyes at him. "Considering the fact that he's already done the engaged and nearly married thing, I'm pretty sure that he has no problem with being a little corrupted."

He looks like he's about to scream. "He was what?!" It comes out in an over the top stage whisper.

I never knew that a person that looked so masculine could behave so femininely.

"Yeah, the once again soon to be married hose beast crashed our weekend together." I didn't tell him about Kaylin last week. He was still in the hospital when the weekend was interrupted, and then the day after he got home, my unwanted house guest, who is becoming a bigger pig by the day, showed up. I had a busy week.

"This past weekend?" He's building up for the guilt trip.

"No, last weekend. Which is also when I found out about the previous engagement. It seems that Jonah didn't feel that it was necessary information."

"Why are you just telling me this?"

He's killing me.

"What was I supposed to do, call you at two in the morning at the hospital to bitch about my boyfriend's ex?" I look at him like he's crazy. Mark lives on another planet sometimes. It's occasionally necessary to bring him back to earth.

"Yes, you were supposed to call me in the hospital. Because you can be certain that if anything even remotely upsetting happened to me, and you were undergoing lifesaving surgery, I would come to the recovery room and bitch to you."

He wouldn't, but I get the point.

"I'm sorry for not telling you sooner."

"That's alright. Now, what did she look like?"

To be cruel or kind? That is the question.

"She looked like the love child of the guy from Twisted Sister and the Taco Bell Chihuahua." That's as kind as I'm prepared to be.

"The main guy or one of the back-ground guys?"

I love that he's trying to picture her. "The main guy."

"Ick. He dated something like that? I mean Chihuahuas are cute, but I wouldn't stick my dick in one."

"I think it's illegal to screw a small furry animal."

"They don't have that much fur," He says offhandedly. He goes from super queer to frat boy so fast that I get verbal whiplash sometimes.

"They have enough."

He smiles at me. "So, our boy Jonah took quite a few steps upward." Mark is signaling for the check.

"Put it this way, if she's the starting point, then I'm the summit of Mount Everest." Yes, that was mean and conceited. You are not hallucinating. I don't like that bitch.

"And the claws come out. I didn't know you had it in you. Amazing what good sex will do for a person's attitude. I like it." He winks at me. We split the check for lunch and head back to the daily grind.

I am one of only twelve women in this office. Of the twelve women in the office, five of us are black. When I talk about the office, I'm only speaking about the areas where the teams work. Not the mail area, or the accounting division, or the executive offices, just the teams. There are two females in executive offices, and one on the vice-presidential level. None of them are black. There are several female secretaries and personal assistants, I'm sure that there are a few in the mail room as well. The thing about females is we can be very catty. We love to pontificate about girl power and female empowerment, but that's often more of an i2deal than a reality. Women are sometimes emotional, and jealous, and more than a tad spiteful. This is a hard truth, but it is a truth. Women are more territorial than men and will protect what they feel is theirs more ferociously than any male would dare.

Women of color, I say of color because I'm including all women that are not white in this, have to work four times as hard for what other women work twice as hard to get. Respect in the work force. You would think that being aware of this condition we would try to help each other. Sadly, that isn't always the case. I'm not sure if the reason for this is because we know that in a given situation, there is only room for one or two of us, and we want to secure a spot by dragging someone else away from it, or if the reason is simply part of the jealous nature that is within most people. Perhaps we're projecting our own insecurities onto the women that resemble us as well as the women that don't, and that's the reason for our behavior.

Keyana and Chelsea are the only two black female team leaders in this office. There are two black female team players besides myself in this office, and I have somehow found myself in an unadmirable position. I have previously stated that Chelsea hates me. That hasn't changed one bit, even given her almost polite conversation with me a few weeks ago. Keyana, though not a huge fan of mine, never fully hated me. Until recently, that is. Keyana has all but lost her mind in my opinion. This chick has told her new stat person that I can't be trusted. She has actually warned this man to stay away from me, because I may try to get him to do my work for me. She also tried reporting me to our human resources department for creating a hostile work environment. She told them that I've been making comments to her. Thankfully, she has no proof or witnesses, so after speaking to me for my side of things, they're leaving the matter alone. If I get fired because of this bitch I will choke the life out of her young acting ass. She made her accusations on Friday; I was called into an office on Monday to deal with the issues. It's Wednesday. I feel like just running her over in the parking lot and calling it a day. I can't do that, because there are cameras down there, and I was not built for jail time.

"Did Chelsea eat a small child for breakfast this morning or something? She is scary happy." I look up at Mark leaning over my cubicle wall when I hear his voice.

"I don't know; she's been like that since last week." I told you it was strange.

"Maybe she got a new vibrator, I'm sure that there isn't a man alive that would venture knowingly into her lady garden," he says out of the corner of his mouth.

This is why I missed him so much.

"One man did. She was married before," I remind him. That is still shocking.

"Maybe the years of being a final frontiersman are what gave him the stroke."

Stranger things have happened.

"Be nice." I feel that I should try to be the voice of propriety.

"Seeing her naked would give me a stroke, and impotence." He's holding in laughter and I have to stop looking at him to keep my own humor in check.

"I highly doubt it. I've seen pictures of some of the mutated turtles that you've called lovers in the past. It would take a dosage of anthrax and a nuclear explosion on top of your penis to cause impotence for you."

"I can't help it if I'm virile."

"Viral."

"Bitch."

"Keep it up and I'll cancel your subscription to Seventeen," I warn him. He gets it delivered to my house. I have no idea why.

"You wouldn't."

"I absolutely would."

"Fine, truce. Are Henry and I still invited to be poisoned on Saturday?" Mark wants Henry to spend time with Jonah and me. He thinks that it's what couples do.

"We're eating at The Cheesecake Bistro." Because...cheesecake.

"Awesome. I should pretend to work. I'll call you from my desk." He walks away as I'm shaking my head at him. He is such a priceless person.

At 4:30 this afternoon, the answer to Chelsea's happiness is made known to all of her coworkers. She is leaving the company. She has gotten a new position, in what I will assume is a greener pasture, on a near executive level. What the hell is a near executive level? In my opinion, you are either in an executive position, or you aren't. By the same degrees, you either want to be at the top of your game, or you don't. I am good at what I do. Correction, I am great at what I do. I fully intend to be in an executive office before I'm thirty. I went from being a team member, to a stat position in three months. The amount of time that you are supposed to wait before changing your job title or description in this office is a year, and the goal for me is to end up an executive in this or another company.

In college I majored in accounting and marketing. Neither was offered as a minor, so I double majored. I minored in advertising. In graduate school I received a master's degree in marketing research. In a way, I can absolutely understand the cheating boyfriend from college's point of view. I was focused on school, internships, and my family. I really only noted his presence when I was horny. He used to tell me that I should have been born a man. I could not tell you when our anniversary was. I have no real memory of our first date or first kiss. Valentine's Day isn't even a blip on my radar. I wasn't interested in knowing his likes or ambitions. I never saw the relationship as something that would last beyond our school days. He wanted marriage and kids eventually. I was very honest in telling him that his future dreams were not something that I shared. I stated that from the beginning of our relationship. I don't blame him for wanting something else; I blame him for cheating and lying to me. I shouldn't have needed to catch him in the act for the relationship to end. He should've grown a sack and told me that he was moving on. I could've bought a vibrator and gotten over it.

The cheating just brought up all of these physical and emotional insecurities. I knew the real reason, but the weaker part of me needed to put the blame on superficial things. My breasts were too small, my thighs were too big, I wasn't freaky enough, I can't cook—you know, all of those things that are likely true, but totally inconsequential in the grand scheme of things.

I am in a position now to be a better girlfriend. I'm not living in a library or cramming for exams. I'm not trying to maintain a certain GPA to keep scholarships or reading up on and applying for all applicable grants while working a full-time job. I work sixty hours a week as opposed to twenty-four hours a day. This isn't likely to change, but it's better than it was. I'm not sure if it's enough to sustain a meaningful relationship. I'm not even sure if I want to sustain any type of relationship of a romantic nature with anyone.

What I want is to make enough money to take care of my mother. I want to be able to build a house that she can live in during her old age. I want to be able to afford a nurse to live in her home. I want to buy her all of the things that she deserves to have. This is the woman that would go hungry to ensure that me and my sisters could eat. I never went without anything because my mother wouldn't allow us to go without. I decided a very long time ago that I would take care of her as soon as I was able. I am very aware that time is forward moving, and so I need to be in a position to secure my mother's comfort as soon as possible.

My mother is forty-nine. She is by no means elderly, but she has lived a hard life, and I'm afraid that her life will be over before I can give her any rest. When I was in college, I would call her in the middle of the night to hear her voice. She thought that I was home sick; in truth I was terrified that I would call one night and there wouldn't be an answer. I was afraid that I would get a phone call from one of my sisters telling me that she was gone. I'm sure that my need to take care of my mother and my desire to remain unattached can be explained after a few thousand dollars worth of therapy. I have no desire to lie on a couch and open old wounds. I'll remain uncured, thank you.

Chapter Twenty:

When I walk into my home, my stereo is blasting current pole music. I walk into my living room and see my cousin practicing her stripper audition. She has moved the furniture and is bouncing in a split. I have had too long of a day to even broach the subject in front of me. I am absolutely fine with turning up in the club or at a party, and I am not opposed to doing a strip tease for your significant other. But after I've had a long day to come home to this in my living room, really?

The girl cooks but doesn't put the dirty dishes in the dishwasher. She washes two shirts at a time in my washing machine and then forgets to put them in the dryer. She forgets to turn off lights, or the television, when she leaves a room. There is hair all over the counter and floor in my guest bathroom. Dirty underwear in the middle of her floor. Ugh! This chick is a nasty beast. Walking over to the stereo I turn it off. Not down, off. I have been at work all day. I still have work to do. I refuse to crunch numbers for an account while some teletubby with a twang, who couldn't ride a beat if it came with training wheels, talks about how much money he has. The little interloper gets herself up off of the floor and has the nerve to put her hands on her minimal hips before speaking.

"Is there a problem?"

"Why can I hear this stereo from the parking lot? Are you hearing impaired?" There are not enough hours in the day. If I have to deal with this shit, the earth is going to need to slow its rotation and give me some more time.

"It wasn't that loud. Anyway, ain't it a little early for you to be here?"

Did I not just walk into my house? I could swear that I pay the bills in here. Why is a visitor questioning the time that I get home?

"It was that loud. I assure you. And, this is my house. I am allowed to come and go as I please."

"I can see that."

"Excuse me? Little girl you are testing the hell out of my patience."

"I'm sorry. I'm not trying to be rude or disrespectful. I'm in this house all day, I get a little bored. The music thing won't happen again."

I'm not even about to buy into that bullshit apology. I invented the innocent act, and I was much better at it when I was her age. I am not her father. She doesn't need to placate me, but she will not disrespect me. She's letting the designer clothes and briefcases fool her. I will jump on this child.

"Look, whatever. I have work to do."

She doesn't recognize the dismissal. "Why do you work at home if you spend like twenty hours a day at work?"

I'm not in the mood for this.

"Because, I have a lot that needs to get done. If I want to reach my goals, I need to be willing to work for them. Sometimes you have to put in extra to get out extra." If I could have avoided bringing this home with me, I would have.

She's looking at me like she has no clue as to what I'm talking about. "But you don't get paid for working at home."

"Actually, I do. I put in the extra work. My team's presentation is superior. We get the account, we get the bonus. You have to work hard to play hard." Does she think that millionaires earned their money by only working forty hours a week? She'd better wake up.

"You don't play hard. From what I can tell, you hardly play at all. No offense."

I'm a shopaholic. The mall is my Vegas. And, I put a large amount of my money into an account for my mother. That is the other reason that my savings account occasionally flatlines. She doesn't need to know all of that though.

"Different strokes. Now if you'll excuse yourself so that I can work?" There is such a thing as necessary rudeness.

"No problem." She starts to leave the room but stops at the door. "I'm not gonna be here this weekend, I'm visiting a friend."

Uh huh?

"What friend?" She's eighteen, but still...

"My friend Aubrey. We went to high school together. She goes to West Georgia."

Nine times out of ten, Aubrey is a dude, and they're going to spend the weekend funking up his dorm room. I'm her cousin, not her parole officer.

"Have fun," I say while moving my couch back into place.

She looks surprised. Do I look like a Gestapo agent? She's an adult. I'll treat her like one. She just won't be having random dudes spending the night here. My home is not the best little whore house in Georgia.

"That's it? No lecture?"

I don't have any children.

"What do you want me to say?"

She's just standing there. Staring at me with skepticism. Like I care?

"I don't know. I mean, I thought that my dad asked you to keep an eye on me. I figured that you'd have some questions about Aubrey."

Is she for real?

"Okay, fine. Is Aubrey really a girl?"

Now she looks uncomfortable. What an idiot.

"Not really, no."

She actually admitted it. Wow.

"Do you plan on having sex with Aubrey?" I don't really want to know.

"I don't know. I'm not really sure if I should."

I need a drink.

"You are going to spend the weekend with a dude, and you have no money or independent transportation, and you don't know if you want to sleep with him?" No one is this stupid.

"I mean, I like him. He's cute and he's nice to me. I've known him for a really long time. He's in college, so it's not like he's a bum or anything. I just don't know if I should have sex with him. I don't want him to get the wrong idea about me."

When did I become the cricket on her shoulder?

"Have you had sex before? With anyone?" No one should lose their V Card to a questionable encounter.

"Yeah. But I'm not a thot or anything. I only had sex with ten people. Not at the same time or anything. I was in relationships with them. At different times."

"Is Aubrey your boyfriend?" What the hell is the matter with teenage girls? I lost my virginity when I was sixteen because I thought I was in love. I was a pot head. Biggest mistake ever. Don't get me wrong, I love sex, but I should've waited until I was older to have it. When you have it too soon in life, you become jaded. There are emotions that come along with that action that not all teenagers are mature enough to cope with.

"No, he's a friend. He was my best-friend Tasha's boyfriend, but they broke up like a month ago."

You do not fuck your best-friend's ex. Angel is a hoe.

"You don't think that it would be wrong to have sex with him since he dated your friend?" There could be a very good reason for her behavior.

"Why? If she can't keep him, that's her problem. I'm supposed to let a good black man slip through the cracks 'cause he used to be with my friend?"

I am dumbstruck. I have never even considered dating anyone that ever dated a friend of mine.

"Why did they break up?" I don't know what makes me ask this question.

"She says that he cheated on her with some Spanish girl at his school."

I could lecture her on the fact that having an education, or receiving an education, does not make a man a good catch. Faithfulness should be in the equation.

"Alright, well, enjoy your weekend. You may want to stop for some condoms just in case, or you can take the unopened box that's in my bedside drawer. If you used any dishes today, put them in the dishwasher before you leave." I'm turning on my laptop and preparing for a night of work and pizza.

I'm pulling up the numbers for a current client's account when I hear a knock at the front door. I stay where I am because I already know it isn't for me. That is probably king ding a ling to pick up Angel.

"Autumn, this is my friend Aubrey. I know that you're working, but I thought you two should meet."

I look up and see Angel standing there with a young man. She is wearing a lime green sweater some purple skinny jeans with bright green legwarmers and some old school FILAs. Who brought back eighties fashion? Some things should stay in the past. Slavery, segregation, inequality, leg warmers, just to name a few.

"Hello, ma'am."

He's a very good-looking boy.

He stands around 6'1" and has very dark skin. I'm talking midnight blue skin tone here. That always makes for a beautiful smile. Got to admit, I love a dark-skinned man. He has very low-cut hair, beautiful teeth behind full lips, a strong nose, and chocolate eyes that slant towards the end. He has angry eyebrows. The kind that make him look like he's frowning all the time. When he smiles at me—and it is a gorgeous smile—I see one dimple in his left cheek. He's channeling his inner rock star in a pair of skinny jeans with a v neck t shirt, also on the tight side, and a pocket chain. There is a pair of sunglasses hanging from the neck of his shirt. How very *Miami Vice* of him.

I stand and walk over to them. "Hello, Aubrey, it's nice to meet you."

He takes my hand and actually looks me up and down before releasing me. Is this little boy serious? This is the problem with good looking men that know they're good looking. The same goes for women.

"The pleasure is all mine." He gives me this half-lidded smile and licks his lips. Yuck!

My idiot cousin is just standing there. She is either blind, or she's pretending not to notice him licking his lips. That is not always a turn on. Every man is not LL Cool J. I decide to ignore him.

"So, Angel tells me that you attend West Georgia? What year are you in?"

Angel smiles at me. I guess she's happy that I'm being nice.

"I'm a sophomore. Are you married?" He tilts his head to the side and gives me a half smile.

The hell?

"And what's your major? Angel tells me that she's interested in journalism." The aforementioned is currently giving her possible sex partner a very annoyed look.

"I'm majoring in International Economic Affairs."

Nice.

"That must keep you very busy. What language are you concentrating on?"

"Japanese. It's a beautiful culture. Do you mind me asking what you do for a living?" He looks around the room.

This conversation is taking too much time.

"I work for an advertising firm. Angel, do you have everything ready for your weekend?"

She stops shooting holes into the side of her maybe man's head to look at me. "Yeah, I just need to grab my bag."

She looks hesitant to leave us alone. She has to be kidding.

"Okay well, you two have a nice time. Be careful." I say the last with a look directed at Angel.

She nods in my direction, though she isn't looking at me. I head back to the couch to finish my work. A few minutes later, I hear the front door close. I am slightly concerned for her safety. The boy openly ogled me in front of the little moron, and she still went with him. She has to know that she's a booty call for this dude. The fact that she's willing to set aside a friendship on the slight chance that he may make her his bottom bitch (crude but accurate) says a lot about what little character and class she has. He's an attractive young man. Possibly with a bright future. But, loyalty is important and neither of them seem to possess that quality.

I can remember being that young, but I cannot recall being that stupid. Maybe it's because I was never looking for a man to improve my life. Or, it could be that I've never seen any relationship that I've had as being permanent. Even the so-called love of my life that I slept with at the ripe old age of sixteen. I never pictured marrying him or having his children. I never doodled his name with mine in a notebook. I knew him since I was seven, and I knew that his life wasn't going anywhere since I was thirteen. The funny thing is, he knew it too. He frequently asked me what I was doing with him. He would say that I could do better if I wanted to, and somewhere inside of me, I knew it was true. We frequently discussed our break-up. We knew that it would happen when I went away to college if not sooner. He knew that I wanted to be more than my surroundings, and that he didn't. He was perfectly content with hustling between prison stints to make ends meet, and he knew that he would need a woman that would fit his lifestyle when the time was right. It went without saying that I was not that woman.

We broke up my junior year of high school. He is currently a father of three and serving a bid in Syracuse. A part of me will always love him for being the first person outside of my mother to ever tell me that I deserved more. We remained friends for a very long time after our break-up. His last girlfriend married him in a prison ceremony. She is the mother of his three children, and they live with her mother.

Chapter Twenty-One:

I've gotten so caught up in my work that the time has seemed to pass without me realizing it. When the telephone rings, and I reach for it, I glance at the clock and receive a surprise. It's three in the morning. It isn't very often that this happens, but it does happen. I'm going to be exhausted tomorrow. My uncle's wife's name is showing on my Caller ID. She has never called me, and I don't know if I should be worried or annoyed considering the hour.

"Hello?"

"Hey, Autumn. It's Angel...I'm sorry if I woke you up."

I suddenly feel like I'm in a television crime drama.

"I wasn't asleep. What's wrong?" I sound disgusted, but I can't help it. I knew when she left with that clown that something was going to go wrong. You may be wondering why I didn't stop her. Any answer that I give would be a lie, so I'll leave the question in the air.

"Can you pick me up? Please?"

"Where are you?" Hopefully he didn't drop her off at some gas station.

"I'm at the college still. At one of the dorms."

"Which dorm, Angel?" It is three in the fucking morning. No one wants me to sleep.

She asks me to hold on for a second and then comes back with the name of the building that she's in. "It's near the east entrance to the campus. Like an hour from your house."

I should leave her dumb ass there.

"I'll google map it. Be outside in an hour. I'm on my way." I hang up the phone and look up the address to the campus.

I need to invest in some thigh high boots and a cape. I'm still wearing the clothes that I wore to work. Not the jacket, but the skirt and blouse. I grab some sneakers out of the front hall closet and make my way to rescue the jump-off in distress. This is why, when you go anywhere with another person, you should have your own money and mode of transportation. If the other person drives, then you should have enough cash to take a cab home from wherever you are going. My mother taught me that lesson when I was in junior high. Apparently, my uncle didn't see fit to pass that knowledge to his daughter.

It takes me an hour and a half to get to Angel. She walks out of the building when I pull up. She doesn't look hurt or frightened. Just pissed off. She had better have some well concealed bruises somewhere if I had to pick her up before the sun hit the snooze button.

She climbs into the passenger seat with her bag on her lap and takes a deep breath. "Thank you for picking me up." She says it softly and without looking at me.

"Why am I picking you up?" I start driving, waiting for her to answer. It is close to five in the morning.

"That sorry ass fuck boy lost his mind."

What happened to 'good black man'? Regardless, that wasn't an answer to my question.

"How so?" I have a feeling that I don't really want to know.

"Promise not to tell my father?"

I definitely don't want to know what happened.

"I don't make promises without being fully informed of circumstances. What happened?"

She seems to be thinking over what to tell me, and then she starts talking and I'm nauseous.

"So, on the way over here, he pulls out his dick in the car, and makes this motion with his head. At first, I was like 'no', but he caught an attitude, so I did it. Then we get to his school, and we get something to eat. Everything is cool until his roommate gets there. They start making jokes about girls just wantin' to have fun, and I ignored it. Then his roommate leaves, and we start gettin' into it, and everything gets all x rated. So after, he goes to take a shower, and his roommate comes in talkin' about how Aubrey told him that he could have a turn. So, I told him to get the fuck away from me with that bullshit. He starts callin' me a tease, and I'm like, 'how I'm a tease, when I never said I was tryin' to let you beat?'. So, he leaves the room, and Aubrey comes back in tryin' to yell at somebody. This dude talkin' about I'm makin him look bad, and if I'm not gonna let his man get some ass then I need to be up out. So, I was like, 'are you serious?', and he was, so I told him he was a fake ass Tyrese, and I got my shit, and left his room. I don't have no money, and I don't really know anybody around here, or else I wouldn't have even called you. So, thanks again for pickin' me up, but please don't tell my father."

What do you say to that? She is eighteen. She gave her friend's ex-boyfriend that she hasn't seen in three months head while he was driving. Can you say STI?

"Did you use a condom?" I ask her.

Please say you used a condom.

"For what?"

I look at her with a raised eyebrow. Clearly, she sees it, because she rushes to answer.

"He said that he's allergic."

"To latex or lamb skin?"

She looks confused. You should not be allowed to be stupid and sexually active.

"They make condoms out of lamb skin? Isn't that animal cruelty?"

Is she fucking kidding me? It would be inhumane for her to procreate.

"I take that to mean that you didn't use a condom."

"He pulled out."

Well, then that's okay. Fucking moron!

"You know that there's still sperm in pre-cum, right? And are you not aware that pulling out doesn't prevent STI's?"

"Okay, fine. I'm not having kids right now, so that's why they invented abortion. And he said that he was clean."

I feel like kicking her out of my car.

"Abortion. Really? Can you afford an abortion? Because from where I'm sitting, you can't even afford a fucking cab ride. And, it's nice to know that the trustworthy guy that you sucked off in a car, who after fucking you, tried to pass you off to a stranger, says that he's clean." If I ever have a daughter, and she turns out this stupid, I'll drown her in a shallow puddle.

"Well, adoption then. And I'm sure that he wasn't lying."

She cannot stay in my house. She can't. This chick has got to go. It's after six when we get to my house. The end of the drive was silent, thank God. I go straight to my room and get ready for bed. I'm calling my mother when I wake up and telling her that her brother needs to come and get his daughter. I'm thankful that she's safe. There are a hundred different ways that this night could have gone. But I have no intention of being stressed out over her actions every time she leaves this house. I'm asleep before my head hits the pillow.

When I wake up, it's after noon. I would have slept longer, but the sound of Drake being in his feelings forces my eyes to open. My wall is actually trembling. This bitch has got to go! I reach for my cell phone on my bedside table and search for my uncle's phone number. I was going to pass on the job of calling him to my mother, but screw that. Reaching his name, I hit the send button.

The phone rings four times before he answers. I can barely hear him over the background music coming from my spare room.

"Hello?" he's shouting into the phone.

"Hello, uncle Don. Hold on a second please." Walking to the spare room, I open the door and walk over to the stereo that Angel brought with her and turn it off. She looks up from her laptop when the noise stops, and I put my phone back to my ear. "Come and get your child."

That is as nicely as I'm prepared to make this statement. She has a look of shock on her face. She has been here for a week and a half, and I have had enough.

"I'm sorry, what? What happened?"

Before I can reply, his unwelcome child is running over to me.

"What did I do?"

Is she serious? What did she do? She is filthy, rude, lazy, and I woke up to my house as the staging ground for Coachella. She honestly looks confused.

"She only been there a week. What could possibly have happened to make you wanna turn your back on family?"

I love how some members of my family are only family when they need something.

"More than a week. And I'm through. She doesn't know how to clean up after herself. She's inconsiderate, and highly irresponsible." I won't get into her sexual behavior, because he, no doubt, already knows.

"I know she can be a little messy, but that's her mother's fault. Kids do what they see, and you know Robin doesn't clean up that often. I'm sure you're talking about the music with the irresponsible thing, and I'll talk to her about that. I really would appreciate you letting her stay until school starts for her. She really does need to be around a positive woman."

Was I signed up for a mentoring program without my knowledge?

"Autumn, come on, you can't make me leave. I'm sorry about the music."

Do these people really think that I'm only pissed about the music? I worked nearly seventy hours this week. I am exhausted. My intention last night was to work on a few budgets before heading to bed. I have a date tonight where Jonah will meet Mark's boyfriend, Henry. I still have work to do, and I now have a headache. The work from last night having been interrupted when I had to take on the role of Captain Save-a-Hoe, and the headache being caused by what she had blasting from the speakers. The music was so loud that the words were unintelligible. I have neighbors. Did this little jackass even think of that? I live in a townhouse. There are units on either side of mine. If I receive a noise complaint because of this tramp, I'll shove a box of lamb-skinned condoms down her throat.

"The music? You think this is only about the music, which is so loud that it can probably be heard in North Carolina? You don't think that this is about your dirty underwear in my bathroom? Or your filthy dishes on my counter? Or me needing to pick you up after four in the morning because you left with a lothario that I warned you about?" I have completely forgotten my uncle on the phone. My voice is getting louder and louder, and I am having a hard time not slapping this girl. How can anyone be this stupid?

"What's a lothario?"

That's all she got from my rant? I won't even pretend to be surprised.

"You have got to go." Remembering my uncle on the phone, I address the statement to him. "She has got to go. Be here by tomorrow to pick up your child, or I'm putting her on a bus." Hanging up the phone, I look at Angel. She still looks confused. I am not pleasant when I wake up.

Perhaps, if I had awakened to a quiet and clean home, I would have reconsidered my position of last night. That was not the case. This room is so dirty that there's a smell emanating from it. I grew up in a home infested with roaches. I will not ever live with those disgusting insects again. Being in this room is making my skin crawl. She needs to pack her shit, 'cause she is leaving my house.

"So, that's it? You're not even gonna give me a chance to change? If I knew that the cleaning bothered you, I would have taken care of it." She has the nerve to be offended.

"It's the lack of cleaning that bothers me. You are a guest in this house. You do not leave filth in your wake in someone else's home. I don't need to give you a chance to change. Before my home was offered as your personal frat house, I hadn't spoken to you or your father in seven years. You people want to throw the word family at me like it's this fundamental game changer, when none of you even remember the people in your bloodline until you need something. Give me a fucking break. People in this family would bend over backward for you, if they knew you. You can't call when you need something and ignore people when you don't. I am your cousin, very much removed. I am not your maid, chauffer, or financier. Pack your shit."

I walk into my bedroom and find some jeans and a t-shirt to wear. Grabbing some underwear, I head for the shower. You may think that I'm wrong to kick her out after only a week and a half. You may be right, but I never wanted her in my house to begin with. It would be different if she were at least clean. But she isn't. I grew up with roaches, and my house was never dirty. My mother mopped the kitchen floor every day. We didn't own a vacuum and had carpet throughout the house, and my mother would sweep the entire house twice a day. We were given buckets of soapy water and sponges on Saturdays so that we could wash the walls. We didn't have a dishwasher, we had hands and rags. This little girl is a slovenly mess. Hell yeah, I'm kicking her ass out.

Chapter Twenty-Two:

I became more and more eager to get to the Cheesecake Bistro after I decided that I deserved a slice of caramel pecan cheesecake considering the day that I've had. Jonah and I are waiting at a table of the Bistro in Atlantic Station for Mark and Henry. I told him about the earlier incident with Angel. She stayed in her room for the rest of the day. Hopefully she's packing. Jonah thinks that I should let her stay. His argument is that she's young, and everyone makes mistakes when they're young.

"Baby, you can't expect her to know what she's doing wrong if you don't tell her." He wrinkles his forehead at me.

Yes, I can.

"People should not need to be told to clean up after themselves. And, she slept with her best-friend's ex a month after they broke up! That is just trifling." My tone makes it clear that I don't want her in my house.

"Some people do need to be told. Your uncle is right, children do what they see. Maybe being around you will change her a little. And the sleeping with the friend's ex is wrong, but you don't know her friend. Stop looking for reasons to kick her out," he chides. He's being reasonable.

I hate him, and I need a drink. Looking up, I see Mark and Henry. Thank God. I stand to give Mark a kiss on the cheek and introduce Jonah to Henry. I don't like Henry. But I love Mark, and so I am civil to Henry. So, I'm a bit of a snob when it comes to other people's sexual behavior. Mark is well aware of my disdain for Henry. He thinks it's hilarious that I can't stand Henry because of his cheating on his wife, while I still consider Mark to be a good person, and my best friend. I am aware that I can be a bit hypocritical. I'm only human.

"So, what's with all the tension?" Mark gestures between me and Jonah as he takes a seat.

"Autumn wants to kick her cousin out," Jonah answers him with an affectionate eye roll in my direction.

Private conversation. Not that I wouldn't have told Mark anyway, but damn.

"Autumn doesn't want to do anything. I already did it." This is not a topic that needs to be put to a vote.

"Automatic...on what grounds are you evicting the little cherub?" Mark asks curiously.

Cherub? There is nothing angelic about that hell spawn.

"On the grounds of filthiness and whoredom." I'm mentally banging my gavel.

"How old is your cousin, if I may ask?" This is from Henry. It's rare that he and I converse.

"She's eighteen. Old enough to know better." I'm staying firm on this.

"Not if she hasn't ever seen better." This is from Mark. That benedict Arnold.

The waiter arrives before I can issue a rejoinder. He's a young black man. He is bald (shaved not natural) and has skin the color of brown sugar. A little short for my taste, but still a good-looking man. I notice Mark appreciating the view and I hide a smile. Henry places his hand on top of Mark's on the table and gives it a light squeeze. Affection or warning? I'll lean toward affection. Mark can so take Henry.

"Good evening. My name is Canaan, and I'll be your server this evening. Would you like to begin with beverages?" He has a very smooth voice.

He should be a DJ for a jazz station. I love a man with a deep voice. My ex, the adultering bastard, had a voice so deep that you practically had to strain to hear it. It would rumble through his chest when he was excited. Very sexy. Bastard.

I decide to start. Ladies being first, and Mark not counting as a lady. "I'll take an appletini please, frozen." I plan on having at least four of those.

"I'll have a Sam Adams." Jonah is a total beer man. I'm not sure, but I don't think that he even has a preference.

"I will join the lady and have an appletini, also frozen." Mark shoots me a smile after giving his order.

"Blackstone merlot, please." Henry. He just had to be the old head.

It's probably strange for him to be here with the rest of us. I mean, he's technically me and Mark's boss, and he's old enough to be every other person at this table's father. The waiter walks away after assuring us that he'll return shortly with our drinks.

"Now, getting back to the subject at hand, being a slut is only grounds for immediate ejection if she's balling strangers in your house or trying to fuck your man. Is she?"

It would have been too much to hope that Mark would have let this subject drop.

"Not yet. That could change. I'd rather she leave before it does." I should reconsider my taste in friends.

"Autumn, baby, she's just a kid. Don't you think that it would be better to let her stay with you, after laying down some rules, than it would be to dump her back into the environment that created her?" Jonah is still trying to be reasonable.

They are ganging up on me.

"I am not comfortable with her in my house. I work all day. God only knows what she could be doing while I'm not home. Most nights I get in after nine."

"Then make her get a job. That way, she's not just sitting around your house all day dreaming of dick." Now there's the Mark I know and love. Crude and to the point.

"She has no transportation. How would she get to work?" I'm just asking; I still don't intend to let her stay.

Mark, of course, has an answer for that too. "There's a Kroger around the corner from your house. She can walk. What, are you afraid that you'll walk in on her christening Mr. Jonah?"

Yeah right. "Not at all."

"Confident?" Mark raises a brow at me.

"Extremely," I say with a smile.

The waiter walks up with our drinks. After depositing them, he takes our dinner orders. I just know that as soon as he walks away Mark is going to start again. The waiter leaves the table, once again with the assurance that our meals shouldn't take long. As soon as he turns his back to the table, Mark starts talking. See? I know my friend.

"So, Mr. Jonah, should our little Autumn be confident?"

Jonah looks at me before he answers Mark with a smile. "I believe that she should be."

We're having sex tonight. He'll have to stay at my house; I have church in the morning. What? God knows that I'm a sinner. That's why I go to church; I'm working on my spiritual well-being.

"I really don't think that this is appropriate dinner conversation." Henry the stick in the mud is uncomfortable.

He doesn't ever come out with us. He'd be positively mortified to know that I have been informed about every intimate detail of his and Mark's relationship. According to Mark, he makes a sound like a chipmunk when he comes, and if they gave accolades for giving head, he'd be summa cum laude.

"On the subject of your cousin, I think that you should give her another chance, at least set some rules, and if it still doesn't work, then kick her out. Everyone deserves a second chance."

Why is he giving me advice?

"Subject change." This from Mark, he knows that I won't take any advice from his lover kindly. I believe that if your life is in shambles, it should be illegal for you to give advice. He and Mark are living together, he's still married, and he and his wife are going to marriage counseling. Yeah. So dysfunctional.

"Fine, go." I'd love to hear this new subject.

"Halloween party at my friend Joshua's house. Gays and straights invited, you must come in costume. I was thinking that you could be red riding hood, and I could be the big bad wolf."

Awesome.

"I'm there." I notice Jonah staring at me oddly. "What?"

"What about me? Can I come too?"

Oh yeah. Boyfriend, right. "Mark can Jonah come too?"

"Of course. Wait, aw fuck, what was a good three some?"

Jonah chokes on his beer.

"Mark, you of all people should be able to answer that one," I say teasingly.

I see the devil in his eye before he opens his mouth.

"Now Autumn, you're the one that had the threesomes."

Does, in confidence, mean nothing? He's like a fucking school girl sometimes. I take a large gulp of my appletini and pretend not to see Jonah staring at me.

"You had a threesome?" His voice is a scandalized whisper.

Isn't that what Mark just told the whole table?

"In college. Too much tequila." White girls aren't the only ones that experiment. All that I learned from the experience is that I'm one hundred and fifty percent straight.

"And in graduate school," Mark helpfully mentions.

I'm going to punch Mark in the head.

"Didn't count." Why is my sex life being used in conversation?

"How does a threesome not count?" Jonah asks the question. Henry looks like his head is about to explode, and Mark is smiling at me.

"It was after the break-up, and sexual contact with the female was limited to her giving me oral without reciprocation and I only came once." If you're having sex with two other people and you only experience one orgasm, then you've been ripped off and can omit the experience from your sexual tally. I see our waiter and signal that I need another drink.

"Would you do it again?"

Not even in his most erotic fantasies.

"No. I try to stay away from tequila." I lean over and give him a kiss when he pouts. He's more than welcome to have a threesome with his next girlfriend.

"So, Autobot, you gonna let the designated homeless stay with you or what?" Mark sips his appletini and waits.

I'm going to regret this.

"Yeah, but she fucks up, and she can walk to her parents' house." I take out my phone and send a text to my uncle letting him know that his beast can stay. His reply is an immediate 'thank you'. Yeah, whatever.

Chapter Twenty-Three:

It's Halloween, and I'm at Joshua's apartment for the party to end all parties. There are strobe lights going, a smoke machine, and very loud house music blasting from the speakers. I'm going to trip the next person that runs past me waving a glow stick. Since Mark couldn't think of a threesome that he deemed sexy enough, because I refuse to dress up like a little boy in a brotherly rock band and sport a purity ring, we are wearing separate costumes. I am a naughty schoolgirl, complete with white thigh highs and Mary Jane's. Ever notice how Halloween is just an excuse for women who are not yet haggin' baggin' to dress like whores without being judged negatively? Mark is a doctor, a proctologist to be exact; he keeps pulling out this silver sex toy and calling it his rectal probe. Jonah decided to be a werewolf. Henry hasn't called yet to demand Mark's immediate attention. We've been here for two hours. I expect the call to come very soon.

I've been dancing nonstop, and my feet are killing me. I'd sit, but the couches are occupied by heavily groping couples, and I wouldn't want to be accidentally molested. Imagine a man's surprise; there he is, reaching for the southern regions of someone else's anatomy, fully expecting to find a raging hard on, and encountering a not so welcoming vagina instead. It would be too traumatic.

"Some guy just grabbed my crotch." Jonah looks very put upon.

I've been getting hit on by some very butch women since the second we stepped through the door. None of the pretty ones are coming on to me. You don't see me getting all pissy.

"Keep your crotch away from him then." Simple as that. I can't tell through all the wolfishness that he has going on, but I'm pretty sure that he's wearing his annoyed face.

"Am I supposed to unscrew my dick from my body or something? You would think someone would wanna see a person's face in decent lighting before they just decided to cop a feel. What if I looked the same without all this shit on my face?"

"Who said you don't?" I'm not a hundred percent happy with Jonah. He canceled on me on Friday, because Kaylin was having personal issues. If I hear the phrase "personal issues" one more time, I'm going to go all Amityville horror on somebody.

"Like you would have slept with me once if I looked like a distant cousin of Chewbacca."

So, I'm shallow. Name at least three people that aren't.

"What are you complaining about? You spend your entire day at home with your computer. Pretend that it was a chick and shake it off."

"Why are you still mad at me?"

I refuse to believe that another life form could be this dense. He might as well be a fucking amoeba.

"Autumn is always mad. That's why I never bought her a mood ring. It would be a sheer waste of money."

Mark, that prick, has walked up to me with a nurse on his arm. Upon further inspection I realize that the sexy nurse costume has been donned by a man. This is a huge relief, considering the fact that he makes the ugliest woman that I've ever seen.

"I am not always mad." My voice is going to be useless tomorrow. I'm practically screaming to be heard above the music. Gay men tend to have amazing taste in clothing, but their taste in music is always hit or miss.

"You were, then you started getting laid, then you weren't, then he popped up with the interloping ex, now you are again," Mark shrugs.

How very well stated.

"I need a drink." I walk over to the bar setup and prepare to order a screw driver.

Joshua does throw a good party. There's a DJ spinning classically loved gay tunes, and a bar with a bartender steadily pouring the booze. I order my drink, and as I'm waiting for it, I feel a tap on my shoulder. Turning around, I see the butchest broad on the planet. She's dressed as a New York Knick. She's about 6 feet tall, with corn braids to her shoulders, and painted tattoos covering her upper arms. When I look at her, she leans down to whisper in my ear.

"Hey, beautiful. I followed those hips all the way across the room. You here with anybody? Or is this my lucky night?"

Wow! Corny pick-up lines really aren't just reserved for straight men.

"Sorry, not interested." I turn back around to retrieve my drink and feel a way too female hand on my ass.

She leans down again for her next attempt. "You don't need to be shy. I think we should get to know each other better."

I turn around a push her out of my personal space. I have had just enough alcohol to think that I can beat this big bitch's ass, and I am about to test the theory.

"You put your hand on another part of my body, and you're going to wish that the Knicks were here to pull me off of your big butch ass. I am not interested. Back the fuck off!"

Before she responds to my threat, Mark is there. "Autumn are you having a problem?"

Jonah is standing behind him waiting.

I look at the she beast as she walks away. "No, I'm fine."

Mark just smiles at me and orders a drink. There are a few people still looking at me, so I grab Jonah and we go off to dance.

The next hour passes without incident, and then, the call that I knew would be coming, does. I can see Mark making his way onto the balcony with his phone on one ear and his hand on the other. This means that we'll be leaving soon. Henry is quite possibly the most insecure man on the planet. Though, he is up in age, and not very good looking, so perhaps he's just realistic. Mark is over twenty years younger than him, and hot. He's also known for his love of drama. I can see him flailing his arms about throughout his conversation.

"Okay, I think that I've been really good considering, but I really can't take any more of this. We need to leave." Jonah is having some sort of break down.

What the hell?

"What are you talking about?" I'm standing in the dining area when he approaches me. I didn't realize that I walked away from him when I saw Mark heading outside.

"No less than ten men have come on to me. I'm starting to think that they're playing some weird game called: let's scare the straight guy. Can we please leave?"

He is such a baby.

I get how having someone of the same sex come on to you can be a little disconcerting, but it isn't that bad. All he has to do is say that he's not interested. I'm practically being mauled. Lesbians are apparently much bolder than some straight men I know. Especially these manly ass chicks that Mark and his friends hang out with.

"At least they were all good looking." See? A bright side is found.

"Are we having sex tonight?"

Okay, total topic switch. "Why?"

"Because, if we are, I'm more inclined to let you give me shit about my sudden homophobia. If we aren't, it would be appreciated if you just got your coat so that we can leave. Don't make me go back there and get that Patrick Ewing looking chick that was trying to feel you up at the bar to give you a ride home."

I'm sure that it says something about my psychological makeup that I get turned on when he's a dick. I told you, I have issues.

"Rude! And, we're about to leave anyway. Mark is arguing with Henry." I turn back toward the balcony in time to see Mark throw his phone into the night.

Mark chucked the Samsung? Has the world completely skewed? I decide to go and talk to him. As soon as I move, Jonah grabs my arm.

"I need to talk to Mark."

"You are NOT leaving me here alone!"

One or two gay men and he's fine, a room full of them, and he becomes Brent Rinehart.

"Then come with me, but you can't come onto the balcony." You would think that he was a twinkie at a weight-watchers meeting or something.

"I had better be getting laid later." He looks so annoyed.

"Isn't that what those kind gentlemen were offering?" I ask sweetly.

Now he looks angry. It's coming through the wolf get up loud and clear.

"Autumn...you are really pushin' it." His tone holds a warning, and I'm tempted to keep teasing him just to see what'll happen, but I back off instead.

"Fine, sex later. Talk to Mark now. It's on my mental 'to do' list." I walk to the balcony doors with Jonah following me. When I step out, Mark has his back to me.

"Hey, McDreamy. Why'd you go all Naomi Campbell on the listening device?"

He turns to look at me when I start to speak.

"Henry can be a very controlling person. It gets to be a bit much. Do I really love him, Autumn? Or am I just in love with the idea of a committed accepting relationship?" He looks sad. I'm not comfortable with Mark experiencing sadness ten stories up. You know, in light of recent events.

"You're asking me about relationships? Okay. Here's what I think, and keep in mind that I'm stunted in this area. I think that you love Henry. I think that that love has been bolstered by the excitement that came with him being married and your boss. I think that you're gonna have to work harder at the relationship now that it's just the two of you. And, I think that Henry is very insecure because he knows that you have a lot of romantic options, and even though you wouldn't explore them while you're still with him, they're still there." I really don't like Mark's boyfriend, but then again, I don't have to.

"It just pisses me off that he can't give me one night. We've been together damn near every day since he moved in with me, I asked him to come tonight and he didn't want to. I like to go out. I like to have a good time. That doesn't mean that I'm gonna let some random guy blow me at a party." He's getting angry.

What is with the men in my life tonight?

"I know that, sweetie. But maybe Henry doesn't."

He gives me this really strange look. "Explain that."

"Maybe it's hard for a man that has committed infidelity with a person that was a knowing participant to believe that entering into an exclusive relationship with that person guarantees monogamy."

"So, you think I'd cheat on him, too?"

Did I say that? "No. But I'm not Henry."

"So, what? It's my fault that he doesn't trust me?" Mark is outraged.

Hello, my name is Autumn, and I'm a verbal punching bag.

Hello, Autumn.

"Partially, yes. You were a willing participant, Mark. So, now there are trust issues."

"Since when are you a goddamned expert on gay relationships? Hell, on relationships period?"

Is that not how I started my response? Still, that was uncalled for.

"You know what? I'm calling a fucking mulligan. Are you okay?"

He takes a deep breath. "I'm sorry. I'll be okay, I just need to go home, and have a talk with Henry."

"Please do. Now, give me a hug. I've got to get out of here before Jonah tries to sew his asshole shut."

He laughs and gives me a hug.

Mark comes back inside with me so that we can all leave together. Jonah drove. Inside of the apartment, I find Jonah standing just inside of the dining room with his back against a wall. Poor little breeder. I walk up to him and take his hand leading him to the room where the coats are. He is walking insanely close to me, and I have to struggle to keep from falling forward. When we enter the room, our eyes are assaulted by the all-female threesome that is happening on top of the bed where the coats are lying. I spot our coats, thankfully on the floor, and go to pick them up. When I turn back toward Jonah, I notice that his homophobia has been seemingly cured. He has removed his mask; his jaw has gone slack and he is staring entranced at the bed. I throw his coat at his head, and grab his hand dragging him from the room. I literally have to put all of my body weight into moving the pig. I bet if there had been three men in that bed, he would have run screaming. Mark sees me dragging Jonah and follows us out the front door.

Once the door closes behind us, I turn and smack Jonah in the head. "Pig!"

"Ow! Fuck, Autumn. I was... shocked into immobility."

This is the best he can come up with? He should have just blamed his reaction on male hormones.

"How are you my boyfriend?" I seriously need to re-evaluate my choices.

"I threw my phone." This comes from Mark. He sounds confused.

"Yeah, like the opening pitch at a Braves game," Jonah snickers.

Mark looks at Jonah like he wants to throw him too. I can't say that I'd stop him if he tried.

"Autumn, how could you let me throw my phone?! Do you have any idea the amount of shit I have stored in that phone?! What were you thinking?!" He's yelling at me and looking as if he's expecting an answer.

Is it a full moon or what?

"I was like twenty feet away from you when you threw your phone! I don't know what the hell kind of crazy juice you drank tonight, but you need to calm down. You're fine. All of your information is okay, because you backed it up on your computer. Or, at the very least, it's in the cloud." I'm nodding while I'm talking and he's looking at me like I'm a mental patient.

"Backed it up?"

Sweet Jesus. "Yes. You did back it up, right?"

He's shaking his head at me. "No. Why would I do that?"

Let's see... before I can be sarcastic, Jonah answers Mark's idiotic question. "You know, in case it's lost, or it gets wet, or it gets broken."

"Or you throw it off of a tenth story balcony!" I snap. I swear I couldn't help it.

Mark looks at me and just shakes his head. "How the hell was I supposed to know that?"

"Did you read the manual?" They both give me a look. The 'what the hell kind of question is that' look. I guess some things, like not reading instructions or asking for directions, apply to all men. Meanwhile, Jonah was just giving me shit about throwing out the manual to my voicemail.

"Okay, so bottom line, you're screwed. We'll go to the store tomorrow and get you a new phone. Hey, maybe you can get an iPhone and we can finally facetime each other." See, I am just Mrs. Brightside tonight.

Things are quiet until after we drop Mark off at home.

"You staying with me tonight?"

I should. I really don't feel like going all the way home. But I can't. "Nope. Got to go home."

He looks at me and then back at the road. "You're still pissed about the Kaylin thing?"

That's a given.

"Um...yeah! But I need to go home because I don't trust the demon alone in my house overnight." She's been acting better since I almost kicked her out, but I still don't trust her.

"Autumn, come on. It's late. Just stay with me tonight and I'll drive you home in the morning."

Tempting...but not a chance. "I want to, but I can't."

"Please."

"Jonah..."

"Come on, baby. You know you don't wanna take that ride all the way to Peachtree City tonight. I haven't seen you in two weeks."

"Whose fault is that? You cancelled on me." I point to myself and lean back against my door. Personal issues my ass. It wouldn't have been so bad, but he was out of town on business most of the week after that. It's one thing to have phone sex when he's in another state, it's another thing to have phone sex when he's only an hour away!

"I'm sorry! She showed up at my house crying, what was I supposed to do?"

He doesn't want me to answer that question. I will anyway. "Point her sobbing ass in the direction of her fiancé maybe? Tell her that you have plans with your girlfriend? Don't answer the door? Drop her off with a female friend? Give her the number to a decent shrink? Shall I go on?"

He lets out a loud sigh. "Would you cancel on me if Mark was having a problem?"

We've been over this. "Mark wouldn't ask me to. As a matter of fact, the first time we went out Mark was having a problem. And, his problems are usually more serious than his boyfriend not allowing him to go with the photographer that he wanted for his wedding."

She showed up at his house crying because of that bullshit. Personal issues. Right.

"They had a very bad fight. She was a little emotional, and she didn't want to be alone."

"So, I get to be alone, because your ex-girlfriend doesn't want to be alone?" I don't do second place.

"She's a friend, Autumn."

He sounds angry.

Good, we match.

"You cancel on me one more time for her, and we'll just be friends too," I say seriously. This shit needs to stop.

"Are you asking me to choose?"

I'm really not a fan of ultimatums, but sometimes they're necessary. I'll be overlooked for his career, because he gets overlooked for mine and that's just fair. But I will not be put to the side for another female. Friend or no friend, especially when I know that she still wants to sleep with him.

"I think you're going to have to."

He might not choose me. In that case, I'm probably better off without him anyway.

"You need that decision right now?"

"I need you to take me home." I'm not doing this anymore.

"Autumn..." He sounds frustrated.

"Take me home."

"She's been my friend for damn near a decade! What do you want from me?!" He slaps the steering wheel.

"I want you to take me home. That's all. Just take me home." I'm calm on the outside, but inside, not so much.

"You know what? Fuck it, fine!" He makes the turn onto 285.

We don't speak for the rest of the drive.

Chapter Twenty-Four:

I'm sitting at my desk trying to finish up the numbers for this report before I leave for the day. It's six thirty on Friday. Mark is already gone for the day. He and Henry had a very in-depth relationship talk after we dropped him off. Things have been going a little better since then. For them anyway. I haven't spoken to Jonah in a week. He sent flowers, and I threw them out. He sent candy and I gave it to Mark. He has called and texted me four times, and I have either hit ignore, answered with a rude gif, or hung up the phone. I realize that I'm being a bitch. The truth is that I care a lot about Jonah. Possibly more than I'm comfortable with seeing as how we haven't been together very long. I don't want to devote any more of my time, or emotions on a person that places his engaged ex above me on the totem pole. I can do better than that.

Shutting off my computer after finally finishing for the day, I gather my things and make my way home. On the drive I decide to order Chinese for dinner. The spawn shouldn't be home. The little idiot has a date with Aubrey. You remember him, don't you? He's the one that slept with her and then tried to pass her on to his friend. Apparently, he called and apologized, so all is forgiven. I gave her some money for a cab, a box of condoms, some pepper spray, and told her to be careful. You can't cure stupid. She's supposed to be going home to her parents the week after next for Thanksgiving. I cannot wait. I need a little peace and quiet. She's better at cleaning up after herself, but the music thing is a constant struggle and I've already received a noise complaint.

Pulling up to my apartment, I receive a surprise. Jonah is sitting in front of my door. I can honestly say that I didn't see that coming. I contemplate just staying in the car, but I'm hungry, my phone is dead, and I need to order my food, so I make my way to the door. He stands up when I approach.

"Hey." His expression is hesitant.

"Hello. Excuse me; I need to unlock the door." I move past him, but he places his hand on my arm.

"You gonna talk to me?" His tone of voice has this cajoling quality to it, and I can feel my resolve to never speak to him again crumble.

"Sure. Come in." I open the door and lead the way inside. Picking up the phone, I hit the speed dial button for the Chinese restaurant.

Jonah stands in the entrance to the living room while I give my order to the woman on the phone. I decide to order enough food for two people, just in case. Hanging up the phone, I take off my jacket and un-tuck my blouse. That is as comfortable as I'm prepared to get in his presence at the moment. I sit down on the couch and motion for him to have a seat. He sits at the opposite end of the couch and turns toward me.

"So, where's your cousin?" he rubs his hands along his legs and looks around the room.

"She had a date."

"This early? It's like seven thirty."

"Yeah well, she's going to be spending the weekend out," I shrug.

"Oh. You look good." He scratches his eyebrow and looks me over. He's nervous.

This is the worst conversation ever.

"Thank you. You look tired."

He does. He looks like he hasn't been sleeping well. I hope he hasn't been sick. I find myself worried about him before I can help it.

"Yeah. How have you been?"

Miserable, bitter, dejected, lonely, the list goes on.

"Great, how about you?" So, I'm a liar, so what!

"I miss you."

He looks sad.

When did this relationship become miss-able?

"Jonah..." I don't really know what to say. It's not that I didn't miss him. I did. Just ask Mark. He kept telling me that I should just call him and talk about things. How pathetic is it when Mark is giving sane relationship advice? But I don't want to be a casualty of whatever the fuck is going on between him and the Viking witch.

"Look, I know that we barely saw each other, and I didn't make you feel like you were important to me, but you were. You are. I miss talking to you every day. I miss listening to you fall asleep on the phone. I miss you stealing my dessert when we go out and you arguing with me over something completely senseless. Tell me you don't miss me," he dares me.

"I don't miss you." I'm going to hell.

"You're lying!"

He seems amused. He's smirking at me.

"No, I'm not!" I'm getting angry, or happy, it's very confusing. I'll repent for lying later.

"Yes, you are. You miss me; you just wish that you didn't. Believe me, I wish that I didn't miss you. You are the most infuriating person on the planet." He's shaking his head as if he really doesn't understand his own reasoning.

I hate the fact that he's right. Fuck! He is an unplanned event in my life. I don't like unplanned events.

"Thank you. You piss me off too."

He moves closer to me while I'm talking. I'd retreat, but my back is already against the arm of the couch. His tongue traces along his bottom lip and he reaches forward so that his hand is in my hair. "I'm gonna tell you something, and I don't want you to freak out on me, okay?"

I nod jerkily. I'm a little apprehensive. He is very close to me now.

"I love you."

Not possible. 2

"No, you don't." Cleared that up.

"Autumn, baby, don't tell me how I feel. I love you." The way he says it is so...steady. Like he's just stating a fact.

There hasn't been enough time for him to love me. I dated someone for over three years, and I could never honestly say that I loved him. We've been together for two months tops.

"You can't love someone after two months." It's a fact.

"Baby, I loved you after two minutes. And, it's okay if you don't feel the same way. You don't have to. Not right now. I know you, even if you do feel the same way, you won't admit it. Just...I just need you to know how I feel. I also need you to know that I spoke to Kaylin, and I let her know that I can't be her designated shoulder all the time. I can't stop completely being there for her, but I will never put her before you again. So, the question is, do you still want me?" He brings his other hand up to my cheek and brushes his thumb across my bottom lip. And there go those tingly butterfly feelings. Before I can answer, the doorbell rings.

"Do you want to stay for dinner?" My voice sounds breathy.

He smiles at me, and I get up to answer the door. Am I in love with Jonah? No. I definitely care a lot about him. I like him more than I've liked any other man that I've dated. I am sickeningly attracted to him. And I miss him whenever I'm away from him. Love is more complicated than that. Right?

I pay the man at the door and take the food to the living room. I haven't used the dining table at all since moving in. Jonah starts unloading the food while I pick a movie from the shelf. I decide on a Jet Li classic. *Thai Chi Master*. One of the best martial arts movies ever. I have a shelf full of martial arts movies, everything from *Enter the Dragon* to *Seven Deadly Venoms*. I blame my mother. When I was a little kid she was obsessed with Bruce Lee. Thus, opening the door to the world of martial arts cinema.

After setting up the movie, I sit down and take off my shoes. Jonah is staring at my legs.

No way buddy.

"Keep your hands to yourself, I'm hungry." I reach for the orange flavored beef.

"Me too." He bites his bottom lip. He's such a pervert.

I laugh before I can stop myself. "I mean it. Have you ever seen this movie?"

He looks at the screen for all of three seconds before he's looking at me again. "No. So, can I ask what you did with the flowers?" he asks as he's opening up the chicken and broccoli.

"I'm allergic to flowers," I remind him.

"That's why I sent lilies. They're hypoallergenic. What did you do with them?"

"I threw them away."

He chokes on his broccoli and I start pounding on his back. "Do you need a drink?"

"You threw them away? Why would you do that?" he asks incredulously. He's a bit out of breath but seems otherwise fine.

It's not like they were going to live forever anyway.

"Because you sent them, and I wasn't exactly feeling all warm and fuzzy where you were concerned at the time."

"Fair enough. Did you throw away the chocolates too?"

They were Godiva chocolates. I wouldn't throw those out. "Mark ate them."

He just shakes his head at me. "It's a good thing I didn't send jewelry."

"That, I would have kept," I laugh. Like I'd give away jewelry? Yeah right.

"Forgive me yet?" He leans closer and puts his hand on my thigh.

The material of my skirt feels non-existent and I'm having trouble breathing. "I'm getting there."

He leans his forehead against mine. "Wanna stay my girlfriend?"

I don't think I ever really stopped wanting that. "I'm considering it."

He kisses me, and I slide my fingers into his hair, holding him to me.

"You know," he whispers against my lips, "with making up, comes make up sex. And as engaging as a night of Jet Li and orange flavored beef can be, I'm positive that I can do a better job at entertaining you."

How can I argue with that logic? "We should start making up then. Where do you want to start?"

"I was thinking that we could make up a little here, then we could make up some more in the shower, and then we could finish making up in your bed. I'll even make you pancakes for breakfast."

"Deal." We've got to argue more often.

Now that I think about it, I'm not really that hungry. Grabbing him by the front of his shirt, I pull him to me, and he smiles against my mouth.

I've never been big on kissing. Not even when I was in junior high and spin the bottle was one of my favorite games. Don't get me wrong, I do like it and I've been told by a lot of people that I'm very good at it, but it's always been something of a chore. An obligatory thing that you do when you're in a relationship with a person that makes the difference between being just a friend and being a girlfriend. With Jonah though, I enjoy the kissing just as much as I enjoy the sex. I could kiss him for hours. Crazy, right?

Jonah makes kissing an erotic experience. His tongue strokes along mine and I feel it everywhere. He sucks my bottom lip and runs his tongue along it, and my panties are soaked. He likes for me to bite his tongue. Not hard, just a light nip of pressure. When I do it, he groans into my mouth and moves even closer. I feel his hand between my legs just before his wicked fingers push my panties aside and tease me. He's not pushing them inside of me. Not fully, anyway. He's using just the tips of his fingers to spread my wetness up to my clit.

"Fuck, baby, you're drenched. I gotta taste you." That's all the warning I get before he slides down to the floor, pushes my skirt up, and presses his face between my legs.

"Ahh!" I am officially non-verbal.

Jonah's tongue should be dubbed a wonder of the world. He licks up and down my opening before pulling my clit into his mouth and sucking. My hands find their way into his hair and I force myself to loosen my grip before I rip it out of his head when he thrusts his tongue into me and does this twisting thing with it. Holy fuck! And then I feel his fingers joining his tongue and I'm moving my hips to match his rhythm. I lose all control of my body when I come. I hear myself screaming and I think my arms and legs might be spasming, but who could give a fuck about any of that when I can see suns being born on my ceiling?

Jonah sits up and helps me out of my clothes. I expect him to get naked, but after he takes off his shirt, he picks me up so that my legs wrap around his waist and takes us up to my bedroom.

Once we get there, he lays me on the bed and then maneuvers me so that I'm on my knees. He starts kissing me along my back, and I feel his tongue on my spine and hear him opening his pants and taking them off. He bites me on my ass just before he brings his hand down in a hard swat. I moan before I can stifle it. He laughs, and I can hear him opening and sliding on a condom. He grabs my hips and drives straight into me and I cry out loudly.

Jonah usually starts slowly. He knows that he's big. He knows that it can take me a few seconds to adjust to him being inside of me. Tonight, he has no fucks to give as he wraps an arm around my waist and fucks me like he's trying to make sure that I feel him in the morning. The orgasm that shoots through me makes the one that I experienced on the couch in my living room seem meek in comparison.

I hardly catch my breath before he's pulling out of me and flipping me over onto my back. I gasp as I feel him enter me again; his right hand grips the back of my thigh and pulls my leg higher on his hip. I'm holding onto him for dear life as he places his left hand on my face and his gaze locks onto mine. Looking into his eyes I find myself wondering how I thought I could live without this. Thankfully, before those thoughts can take root in my mind, I can feel that exquisite pressure building within me again. He kisses me, and I scream into his mouth as my body spasms around his with an orgasm that nearly rips me in half.

God, I love make-up sex.

Chapter Twenty-Five:

It's Monday. In an unusual turn of events, I am in an amazing mood and Mark is acting like the grinch. We're on our lunch break, and in exchange for treating him to dinner tonight, Mark is looking at an apartment with me and skipping the food. I need to move. My lease was only for six months and is up at the beginning of January. I have to give them thirty days' notice if I decide not to renew, and it's the middle of November now. I love my townhouse. It's large, and inexpensive, and in a quiet and safe town. It is also over an hour away from my job in rush hour traffic. After working an eleven-hour day, the last thing that I want to do is take that drive home. Granted, rush hour is generally over by the time I leave work, but the drive is still a solid hour.

On top of that, my bestie, and my on-again boyfriend live near my job. Which is why Mark and I are currently touring the available units at the 17th Street Lofts. They are more expensive than my current apartment, but I'll save on gas and oil changes. There is still a good amount of space. The apartment that we're in reminds me a lot of Jonah's place, except that it isn't on the ground floor and there isn't carpeting. All hardwood. The dining room isn't enclosed either. Not that I really plan on using it all that much anyway.

"Autobot, you sure you wanna move here?" Mark is coming in from the balcony when he asks the question.

"You don't like it?" I find that hard to believe. This place is amazing, if a little expensive.

"I do! Very much actually. But what is this gonna do to your mommy fund?"

Mark knows that I put a lot of my money into an account that is set aside for my mother's future care. I send her money every month, and between what I send her, and what my sisters give her, we manage to pay her utilities and a portion of her rent. I tried to get her to come down here with me when I moved, but she didn't want to leave Long Island. More than likely, she didn't want to leave my father. They have the most bizarre relationship.

"Well, I figured that I could keep sending her money every month, cut back a little on the savings, and a little on the 401K, and I'll definitely have to ease up on the shopping for a little while. But, it's doable." I know what he's going to say before he says it.

"You could just let go of the mommy fund all together."

We've had this conversation.

"You know that that isn't an option. I can more than afford this place." I can. If I cut back on other things, it just gives me a little more breathing room.

"I know that. I'm not arguing that point with you, but since when does it fall on the youngest child to take care of the parents?"

This is an upbringing thing. Some people have absolutely no problem with putting elderly family members in a nursing home. Other people view such places as a last resort. Somewhere that you only send a family member that has absolutely no recourse.

"My sisters are helping my mother too. Mark, this isn't something that I have to do, it's something that I want to do," I explain for the umpteenth time. My mother appreciates what we do, but she has told all of us on more than one occasion that we should stop giving her our money.

"So, you're taking it?"

"Yeah, I'm taking it." Looking around this apartment I know that I want it.

I have been putting money into an account for my mother since I was fifteen years old. Twenty dollars here, fifty dollars there, and as I made more, I saved more. When I was in college living off of Ramen noodles I never once touched that account. My personal savings account gets pillaged on a regular basis, but after ten years of saving, there is roughly thirty thousand dollars in my mommy fund. She doesn't know that though. She'd try to talk me into using it to bail out every family member that we have that has financial issues. I figure that by the time that she's sixty-seven, I'll have saved just under a hundred thousand. With the damage that she's done to her body, she'll need quite a bit of care by then.

"You could always ask Jonah if he'd like to live with you. Split expenses."

Has he been drinking?

"Why would I do that?" I don't want to live with another person. And, I've only been dating Jonah for two months.

"Well, he did tell you that he loves you."

I'm really going to stop telling him shit.

"Did I say that the feeling was mutual?" I ask. A noise near the door draws my attention, and I realize that we've completely forgotten the person that is showing us the apartment.

"You don't have to say it for it to be true." Mark sings. He loves love. Love, drama, shopping, and sex. Not necessarily in that order.

I roll my eyes at him and address the woman at the door. "I love this apartment. Will it still be available the first week of January?"

Mark follows me as we head toward the door.

Love was invented by Hallmark and Harlequin. In actuality, it's really just another four-letter vulgarity. I firmly believe in the love that is shared between parents and children. I believe in the love that is shared between friends. I do not believe in the romantic love that Mark is talking about. I think that kind of love existed sixty years ago. My grandparents have it. But in today's world, where committing infidelity is as simple as logging into an app? Love is dead.

I told you, I'm waiting for the guy that'll lay his coat over a puddle just to keep my feet dry. I love romance in movies and books. It's believable there, because you know it isn't real. The past inventor would never fall through a time portal into the future and meet his true love. The successful millionaire would never turn the Hollywood hooker into his high society housewife. That's all for entertainment. I care about Jonah. He is probably everything that I'd want if my priorities were different. I don't have time for love.

We're heading back to the office when Mark decides to throw more salt into the mix. You'd think that he didn't constantly complain about how far away I live.

"So, you're gonna cut back on shopping to afford the apartment, the mommy account, and the monthly support payment?"

He acts like I'm taking care of a child that isn't mine or something. This is my mother that we're talking about. And, I only send her about two hundred and fifty dollars a month. My sisters give her around the same amount, so it isn't like I'm doing everything alone.

"I told you that it's doable."

"You realize that you're moving to the middle of Atlantic Station, don't you?"

His point being?

"So?"

"So, that's like an obese person going on a diet and moving to the snack aisle of the Walmart."

I have self-control. Except when it comes to shoes. Mostly, I shop online for clothes. I have been known to go online for my more expensive shoe purchases as well.

"It's all about restraint and will power."

He snorts at me in a very un-diva like fashion. "You don't have any restraint."

I beg to differ.

"I haven't slapped you yet." Emphasis on the 'yet'.

"I am so abused." He's leaning his head back like he's awaiting salvation.

"Now Mark, you know you like it rough."

"Do you kiss your mother with that mouth?"

"You'd be surprised what I do with this mouth," I say with a grin.

"That's only because you never wore braces."

I can't hold in my laughter. What would I do without Mark?

When I get home it's after ten at night. Mark and I went straight for dinner after work and the time just slipped away. We had an amazingly clueless waitress that kept flirting with him. She even wrote her phone number on our check. The man ordered a cosmopolitan for God's sake. You'd think she would have caught on, but no. Not even his talk about Jason Mamoa playing a super hero in a movie and the sexiness of that sheer fact clued her in. She actually joined in on the conversation and winked at him when she left the table. The really ridiculous thing about her actions was the fact that they pissed me off. I mean, yeah, Mark is a bigger queen than Freddie Mercury, but she obviously didn't realize that, so her overtures to Mark were very disrespectful to me. He is a man, I am a woman, and we were having dinner together. Her hitting on him was just disrespectful as hell.

The waitress hitting on Mark would have been more insane if it didn't happen all the time. Women hit on him constantly, so do men for that matter. He's usually very polite in turning women down. He never tells them that he dates men; he just says that he's in a relationship. He thinks that they'll be embarrassed if they find out that he's attracted to the same thing that they are. I think that if a person is adult enough to approach another person, then they should be adult enough to hear the reason that they're being shot down. Though, I have occasionally lied and told particularly annoying men that I'm a lesbian. Mark swears that I'm going to say that one time too many and be overheard by a feminine admirer.

The apartment is quiet when I get in, and I almost let myself believe that Angel isn't here. But then I hear a sniffling sound coming from the living room. Why me, Lord?

I know that she wants me to go in there and ask her what's wrong. If she didn't, she'd be in her room—correction, my spare room, crying. I wish that she would have just done that because I'm certain that I don't want to know what's going on with her right now.

Against my better judgment I find myself walking into the living room. The room is completely dark, so I turn on the light. Angel is sitting on the couch with her head buried in her hands sobbing like a new born baby. She looks up at me and tries to wipe her face. I hand her the box of tissues from the end table and wait for her to gain a little composure. When she looks like she's as in control as she'll become, I ask the question that I shouldn't.

"What happened?"

"I...I can't tell you. You'll probably just tell my father on me." She blows her nose loudly and looks away from me.

Raising my head, I stare at the ceiling for a moment. Why is she crying in my living room if she doesn't want me to know what's going on? Screw it.

"Do you know when you'll be moving into the dorms, because I'm moving out of this apartment the last week of December." Not that I owe her any explanation for wanting her out of my house.

"Can you lend me five hundred dollars?" She asks the question like she didn't just hear what I said.

I'm experiencing an acid trip. I thought you had to drop acid to do that, but apparently that isn't a prerequisite. That question really just popped on in out of nowhere. "Repeat that?"

She takes a deep breath and looks away before facing me again. "Can I borrow five hundred dollars? Please?"

I did not see that coming.

"You know that when you borrow money, you have to pay it back, right?" I can never be too sure where her level of understanding is concerned.

"I'll pay it back. I'm gonna get a job after I get back from Thanksgiving in Jersey. And the financial aid that I'm getting is more than my tuition, so if you want, I can use some of that to pay you back."

I don't want to know why she's asking to borrow money from me, but I hear myself ask anyway. "Why do you need it?" I'm not really comfortable with contributing to the delinquency of an idiot.

"I really need you not to tell my father."

I'm trusting this situation less and less. "Why do you need the money?"

"I need to get an abortion when I go home for the holiday. I can get one in Trenton where nobody knows me."

I knew it. "How are you going to get to Trenton?" Not the most important of the questions that are slamming through my head right now, but whatever.

"My best-friend Jayda said she'd take me. She went with her cousin before." She shrugs one of her shoulders and waves a hand dismissively. She's making it sound so simple.

"Is your friend Aubrey the father?" Somehow, I doubt it, but I had to ask.

"No. I don't think so. It doesn't matter; I'm not ready to be a mother. I can't take care of a baby."

That's the first intelligent thing I've heard her say.

"So, you want me to lend you abortion money?" Huh. I'm really not sure how I feel about that.

"I want you to help me out. Please? I know that you think I'm irresponsible, and this whole thing probably isn't helping, but I can't have a baby." She's crying again and I'm trying to feel sorry for her. It isn't working.

"Do you know who the father is?" I swear that she'd better not say she doesn't.

"Yeah. He's a lot older than me. We were getting up before I came down here. He wasn't really my boyfriend, but he kinda was. I think it's his."

"If the only thing that y'all were doing was having sex, then he wasn't your boyfriend." I try not to say it too condescendingly. This girl really needs to learn that there's more to being an adult woman than just spreading her legs. And, she *thinks* it's his? Seriously?

"We did other stuff. We talked a lot. He thought that studying journalism would be a good idea for me, and he thought that it would have been a good idea for me to go to St. Johns or NYU, but I wanted to get away from my parents."

I'm pretty sure that Angel wouldn't have gotten in to either of those schools, but then again, my mother always says that people with a lot of book sense lack common sense. Angel has absolutely no common sense, so academically, she must be a genius.

"Angel, I really don't know if I can do that. Maybe you should ask the baby's father to help you." I'm trying to move into a more expensive place and I just resigned myself to spending less money.

She bites her lip before looking at me again. "He can't give me the money. Not that much money at one time."

She was sleeping with an older man that couldn't take care of his responsibilities? What was the point?

"Why can't he help you?"

"He has a wife and kids. His wife would notice that much money missing."

Seriously?! How did I not see that coming?

"Ask him anyway. Actions have repercussions, the same way you have to deal with the results of your actions he should deal with the results of his." I'm not going to ask who the married man is because he's clearly a lot older than her and even more responsible for this trifling mess.

"You're not gonna lend it to me, are you?" When I don't answer her, she sucks her teeth at me.

"Keep it up little girl. Your face is not pregnant, and I will slap you. If you would make people wear condoms you might not be in this predicament."

"If you're not gonna help me then you can save the lecture. I'll figure out a way to get the money. Thanks for nothing."

I need to leave this room. Walking over to her where she's sitting on the couch, I barely keep my hand from closing into a fist before it connects with her cheek. I understand that she's scared right now. I get that this is a lot for any woman to handle, especially at the age of eighteen, but when children act like adults, this is what happens.

"I have been helping you since you walked through my door you ungrateful little hussy. You created this situation. There is a man in New Jersey that I'm sure holds large shares of the blame for what you're going through, but you do not get to disrespect me because you're being forced to be a woman. If you're having an abortion, then that's your decision, and I'm not about to judge you for it, but I'm not going to pay for it." I leave the room before I hit her eye rolling ass again.

Chapter Twenty-Six:

It's the Saturday before Thanksgiving and I'm sitting in Mark's living room waiting for him to finish getting dressed so that we can go shopping. I need some new sweaters. I look up when someone enters the room. Unfortunately, it's Henry. He barely acknowledges me sitting on the couch on his way to the kitchen. Whatever, it isn't like I'm his biggest fan or anything. Henry really only speaks to me if Mark is in the same room. That could be due to the fact that he knows that I don't like him. It's hard not to notice. He's bent over with the top half of his body buried in the refrigerator. It's like that scene from *Mary Poppins* when the top half of her body disappears into her purse. Amazing. He's rummaging around in there, and the back end of his body is moving jerkily around. I'm utterly transfixed.

"Uh hum!" Mark's exaggerated cough next to me makes me jump. I didn't hear him come into the room.

"Is he stuck?" I say it in a stage whisper and Mark gives me what should be a stern look, but it's ruined by the upturn of his mouth.

He nudges me in the arm and then directs his attention to his lover in the kitchen. "We're leaving now. I'll be back around six."

I get up from the couch and follow Mark out of the apartment. Every time I see the two of them together, I'm amazed by just how much opposites really do attract. I'm pretty sure that strangers think the same thing when they see me out with Jonah. We decide to take Mark's car since he's the one with the curfew. We both know that if he isn't home at least five minutes before he said he'll be back, Henry will be sending out a search party. This is one of the reasons that I'm firmly against living with your partner, unless of course you're married. My ex was like that. He'd always question where I'd been if I stayed out too late, as if I had the time to cheat on him. He would actually get annoyed that I never felt the need to question his whereabouts. It isn't like I was his mother.

Mark looks over at me from his position behind the wheel; I guess I've been inside my own head for too long. "What's going on with you? The demon baby pissing you off, or are you having problems with Mr. Jonah?"

I haven't told Mark the latest about Angel. He would flip out. The man is firmly against abortion. I decide to keep that information to myself. As much as I detest Angel's irresponsibility, I don't want Mark to hate her. And the abortion issue will make him hate her. I think his issues with abortion stem from his experience with the married woman. Mark should probably delve into that with his therapist. After I calmed down, I told her that if she spoke to the baby's possible father, and he refused to give her the money that she needed, then I would lend it to her. I also stressed to her that this was the only time that I would help her with a situation like this.

"Autumn? What the hell, since when are you so quiet?" Mark glances quickly at me and then back at the road.

"I'm sorry. I guess I'm having Jonah issues. This relationship shit is for the birds." This really is only a small untruth. I am having Jonah issues.

Mark huffs a little. "Is this still about the Thanksgiving thing?"

Jonah wants me to meet his family on Thanksgiving. I am very against that idea. It just seems like such an official couple thing to do. Besides, his first meeting with members of my family didn't turn out so well. I'm not eager for an encounter like that with his family.

"I don't think I'm up for that. Besides, I thought that you wanted to come with me to my aunt's house on Thursday."

Apparently, Henry is spending the holiday with his children and he doesn't want to upset them by bringing Mark.

I see the smile on Mark's face before he starts speaking. "It seems that my brother's wife is practicing acceptance and wants me to join them for Thanksgiving dinner."

How do you tell a person that something they obviously want may be a bad idea?

"Are your parents going to be there?"

Mark shakes his head. I can tell that he's making an effort to keep his voice neutral. "They aren't speaking to Patrick because he still wants to be a part of my life. My father actually told him that if he could accept having a fag for a brother, then maybe it was because he was a fudge packer too. Eloquent, isn't he?"

I really want to crack that man's skull. And he's a preacher? If that man is a Christian, then I'm a nun. Turning to Mark, I try to keep the sympathy out of my voice. He doesn't like when I feel sorry for him.

"The man sure knows how to colorfully express himself. So, I guess it'll just be you and your brother's family?"

I'm glad to hear that his voice is clearer when he responds. "It looks that way. His wife's parents are going to visit her sister in Missouri."

"Shit, so this means that I'm going to have to deal with my crazy ass family all alone. Thanks for nothing." I love my family, even my uncle, but it's always nice to bring a guest as a buffer.

Mark reaches for the radio and searches for a suitable station. "You could always ask Jonah to go with you. You could spend part of the day with your aunt's family and part of it with his family. That is what we grown-ups call a compromise. Come on, say it with me, com-pro-mise."

"If you weren't driving, I'd punch you in the head." I turn up the volume to drown out his laughter.

I really should reconsider the idea of living in Atlantic Station. This mall trip is proving detrimental to my Visa. How am I going to control myself when some of the stores that I love are right outside my front door? We're on our third store and I am currently holding four shopping bags, and before you ask, no I haven't bought any sweaters. But I did find the cutest boots in Aldo. Mark really isn't any better. If he picks up one more ribbed shirt, I may have to head an intervention. He's trying on his umpteenth pair of jeans and I'm considering telling him that they all make him look fat so that we can take a break. I'm hungry. I ran out of those frozen breakfast pastries and I haven't eaten today. I wonder if Mark would notice if I disappeared.

Mark comes out of the fitting room and turns around once. "How about these? I don't know if I like the wash."

I swear that he can be worse than a seventeen-year-old girl sometimes. "Mark, honey, you already have those jeans."

He actually looks offended. "I do not. I think I'd know."

"Yes, you do. You bought those exact same jeans two months ago. You weren't sure if you liked the wash then either," I tell him. He seriously needs to take stock of his closet.

"Are you high? I do not have these jeans. Maybe you're becoming delirious." He seems to be really considering the possibility.

I take a deep breath to keep from screaming. My belly button is touching my spine right now, and he wants to argue with me about a pair of jeans that he already owns? I should just let him waste his money. "Mark, you bought those pants two months ago when we went shopping at the outlets. You weren't sure if you liked them, but they were sixty percent off, so you bought them. Now if you don't take those jeans off and come with me to the food court so that I can get something to eat, I swear to God, I will key your car!"

I notice that there are several people staring at me, but the sound of my stomach growling drowns out all logic as I push him back towards the fitting room.

I have decided that Farmer's Basket has wonderful food. They also had the shortest line when we got to the food court, so I was able to get something to eat quickly. I'm half buried in my plate and barely listening to anything that Mark is saying when a shadow falls over our table. People are so rude.

"Autumn?"

I look up at the sound of that voice and wish I hadn't.

Mark gives me a curious look and I reach for a napkin to wipe my mouth before I turn to the walking sore that has interrupted my meal.

"Kelvin. What are you doing here?" By here, I mean this state. I left this jackass in Philly, that's where he should be right now. *Dear Lord, did I think this son of a bitch up?*

He smiles at me. This clown actually has the nerve to smile at me. "My wife's family lives in the area. We're spending Thanksgiving with them."

Mark nudges me with his foot and I remember my manners. "Oh, Mark this is Kelvin Williams. Kelvin, this is my friend, Mark. Go away."

Kelvin laughs and rubs his head in what used to be an endearing gesture. "Still blunt I see. But then, that was always part of your charm."

I'm really not in the mood for this.

"Shouldn't you be getting back to your wife?" I look around for the other woman. Hopefully I'll recognize her outside of the laundromat. The only other time I've seen her was when she was face down, ass up on my couch.

This, if you hadn't already guessed, is the boyfriend that I caught cheating on me. Kelvin is 6'4", the darkest of dark chocolate complexions, and very broad in the shoulders. When we first met, I thought he was a football player. The man was two hundred and fifty pounds of muscle. I hate that he still looks the same and that I still find him attractive. It's been a year since I last saw him, but it feels much longer. In a moment of childishness, I consider throwing my food at him. Bastard.

Kelvin waves someone over and I experience a moment of disbelief. Is he actually pretending that we're friends? I choke on the soda that I'm swallowing when his very pregnant wife waddles over to my table. It's the soap slut. When she realizes that it's me that he's talking to, she puts her arm through his and leans up for a kiss. Yeah, he's still attractive, but I'd rather fuck a rabid squirrel than make a pass at this man.

He actually introduces her. "Ta'Kendra, you remember Autumn. And this is her friend, Mark."

This situation is just too ridiculous. I see Mark shaking his head in confusion. I've told him about this man. I'm glad to see that I'm not the only one finding this entire meeting bizarre. I really cannot pretend to be friendly with these people. I wasn't in a true love relationship with him or anything, but we were dating, and sleeping together for three years. I haven't seen him since I caught him cheating on me, and I'm supposed to be warm and friendly now?

"Okay, correct me if I'm wrong, but didn't I walk into the apartment that we were sharing as a couple and find you fucking soap girl on my couch?" I look from him to her with a raised brow. What is wrong with these people?

Kelvin places a calming hand on his wife's back. "Autumn, we're all adults. We should be beyond that now".

Again, it's been a year. Am I over him? Yes. Am I over it? No. I felt like such an idiot after things ended. How didn't I know that he was cheating on me? How long had it been going on?

"Keep telling yourself that. And really, congrats on the new addition. I'm really happy that you two were able to find deep and meaningful love while you were screwing around behind my back, but right now, you're ruining my meal."

Mark stands from the table and faces them. "Maybe you two should leave. All this tension can't be good for the baby."

Kelvin ignores Mark and looks at me. "Autumn, I really was hoping that we could be friends eventually. Three years is a long time. I'm not proud of the way things ended, but that shouldn't cancel everything else out."

His wife is squeezing his hand in what could either be warning or support. I really don't care which. I have no interest in being mean to a pregnant person, and I have no interest in being civil to a cheater.

I manage to keep from raising my voice when I speak again. "Kelvin, that is a very nice thought, but I don't like you. What you did was dirty, and low, and disrespectful to me and any friendship that we had. Have a nice holiday, I hope that you have a healthy baby, but I really don't see us being friends. Now if you don't mind, we were eating."

He looks like he wants to say something else, but his wife starts to pull him away. He keeps looking back and I turn my attention back to my food. It doesn't taste as good anymore.

Mark settles back into his seat across from me. "Hey, you okay, Autobot?"

I give him a smile and say around a mouth full of chicken, "I should have gotten extra gravy."

He reaches over and squeezes my hand before continuing his own meal and the one-sided conversation that we'd been having before the interruption. It only takes him about three minutes to stop pretending that everything's alright. "You don't have to act like that didn't bother you." His face seems more understanding than sympathetic.

I run a hand across my forehead before looking up at him. "I just wasn't expecting that."

"Did you know that he married her?"

Unfortunately, I did.

"Yeah. I heard about it from a friend that still lives in Philly. I was okay with it." As long as I didn't have to see it.

"I can't believe he cheated on you with that sea donkey." His tone is so baffled that I can't help but laugh. I dab at my eyes with a napkin. Mark is priceless.

"Everyone is beautiful to someone." At least that's what my mother says.

Mark just frowns and turns up his nose. "I hope that baby doesn't come out looking like her."

He is so mean. Hilarious, but mean.

"Stop it. Maybe she makes up for her looks with her personality." Yeah, sure.

Mark raises an eyebrow at me before speaking. "Right. Because fucking another woman's man says so much about her personality."

"Mark, you were fucking a married man. Actually, you're still fucking a married man." It seems necessary for me to point that out.

He waves that off as if its insignificant. "He's separated, and he's gay. It isn't my fault that he was trying to convince himself that he was straight and married a woman. It also isn't my fault that his wife didn't know that he was gay. Hell, I knew he was gay the first time I saw him."

You would think that it would be easy to point out Mark's hypocrisy. The problem is that he knows that he's a hypocrite, but he feels that it's justifiable. He should have been a politician.

"You did not know that he was gay." I decide to focus on one part of his statement as opposed to the whole thing.

"I suspected. He kept making cow eyes at me. I thought that only fifteen-year-old girls did that."

Well, Henry does kind of look like a cow.

Mark narrows his eyes at me as if he can read my mind and I make my expression as innocent as I can.

"Anyway, are you gonna tell Jonah about your ex showing up?"

"Why would I do that?" Yeah, seeing Kelvin upset me a little, but it isn't exactly about to affect my life or anything.

"Oh, I don't know. He may be interested to find out that the man that you spent three years of your life with would like to be your friend."

I hate it when he gets all know-it-all on me.

"I really don't think that that will be necessary since I have no intention of being Kelvin's friend. They're going home after Thanksgiving, and God willing, I'll never have to see either of them again." Don't we have enough problems with Jonah's pain in the ass ex?

Mark shrugs a shoulder. "You didn't think that you'd see them now. And, how do you know that they aren't moving here? They're starting a family. She could want to be closer to her parents."

This conversation is pissing me off. "This isn't really a small state. Even if they move here, there's nothing saying that I'd ever bump into them again. And if I do, I'll just ignore them."

He'd better hope that I don't start ignoring his earth disturbing ass.

"So, if you see them out in a few months with their baby, say at a restaurant, and you're having dinner with Mr. Jonah, you'll be able to just ignore them and enjoy yourself?"

"Unless the calf that the sea donkey is carrying starts shrieking at the top of its lungs. It's really hard to enjoy a meal over the sound of a screaming zoo creature." I'm sick of talking about this.

Mark breaks off a piece of his biscuit and throws it at me.

"You throw like a girl."

"Bitch."

I laugh at him and finish my food. We have more shopping to do, and I have a few things to think about.

Mark and I hit five more stores before leaving the mall and I think that I'll have to burn my credit card when I get home. There really is no way to justify spending a hundred dollars on a shirt, but its silk and it's from Michael Kors. That store is my kryptonite. I can't walk past it. I get weak as soon as the entrance draws near and the next thing I know, I'm in the fitting room with the maximum number of allowed items. My credit card is getting dangerously close to its limit. Especially considering the thigh high stretch boots that I just paid two hundred and seventy dollars for last week. In my defense, they're Stuart Weitzman and they're insane.

"Have you thought at all about pulling back on your Mommy fund?" We're almost back at Mark's apartment when he changes the subject from our recent purchases to my finances.

"I thought about it. I decided that I'm going to put a little less away in that account per month for a little while." It was really a no brainer. Pulling back on that account is the only smart way to increase my cash flow.

Mark glances at me and sighs. "I know that you don't wanna do it..."

"It makes sense. I'm still going to be putting away money for her, just not as much. Besides, I should be able to get the job that I really want in about four more years and then I'll be able to make up for slacking on it." I really hate to have to do things this way, but I can't really avoid it.

"Why don't you talk to your sisters about putting some money away with you? She's their mother too." Mark doesn't understand why I want to do this alone.

I wish that I could explain to him my reasons for not involving my sisters in my savings plan, but it would just make them look petty. It would turn into a, "who put away more money?", or a, "we should all have access to the money!", situation. I don't want that. Besides, knowing them, they'd tell my mother about the account, and that is unacceptable. It would be empty in no time from her loaning it to friends, or worse, giving it to our father.

"It's important to me to do this myself." I'm sure that he knows that there's more to it, but since he knows me, he won't ask. Not right now. He'll just bring it up again and again until I cave and tell him everything.

Mark's cell phone rings just as the clock on the radio reads ten to six. Henry really needs to be less of a clingy pain in the ass. I'm actually surprised when Mark doesn't answer it. That is a definite first. Maybe he just doesn't want to risk getting pissed and tossing the new iPhone out of the driver's side window.

"You know, your idea about splitting Thanksgiving might just work." I'm pretty sure that he doesn't want to talk about the middle-aged insecure man that's blowing up his phone, so this is a safe topic.

"Might, nothing. You can either sit through another uncomfortable dinner with your Aunt's family, or you can duck out early to meet Jonah's. Think of it this way, if his family is half as insane as yours, you can stop feeling mortified by your uncle's behavior." Mark says the last with a smirk.

"I wasn't mortified, I was pissed off. I mean, his son marries a shady stripper at the justice of the peace, and he grills my boyfriend. 'Cause Jonah was clearly the suspect person at the table." I know it happened over a month ago, but I still get pissed off when I think about that dinner.

"I really wish I could have been there. Why can't you take a video with your phone at those dinners or something?" He's serious. There isn't the tiniest hint of a smile on his face.

"Yeah, that would be normal. I'll just tell everyone to ignore me panning my phone around the table. I'm sure that they'll understand your reluctance to miss out on the drama." I roll my eyes at him. He can be so unreal sometimes.

His phone rings again and he makes an annoyed sound. "Henry can be such a suffocating bitch."

I'm sure that I'm not supposed to say anything, but I can't help it. "Only always."

I can tell that he wants to refute my statement, but he doesn't. Instead he just turns on the radio and focuses completely on the road. I feel like I was just given a time out.

Okay, so maybe I'm not exactly overly supportive of his relationship with Henry, but can you really blame me? The man is living with him while going to marriage counseling with his estranged wife. How encouraging am I supposed to be?

When we get back to Mark's apartment, I'm still trying to decide if I should leave or come in. That is until I see Henry standing in the parking lot. Remember when you were a kid, and you stayed out past curfew and your mother or father was waiting just inside the front door when you came home, ready to hand out a serious ass punishment? That's what this reminds me of. Henry has on his stern 'father' face, and it's ridiculously creepy. Who wears that expression with their lover? Well, unless you're doing some role playing. You know, teacher with naughty student, or judge with unruly defendant?

Hey, these are just examples.

"You want me to go or hang out?" It's no secret that Mark can probably take Henry's head off, so I'm not concerned about Henry pulling any kind of physical violence, but I figure he'll tone down the bitching if there's an audience.

Mark ignores Henry and looks over at me. "Don't you have a date tonight?"

Shit! That's right, I do. With the whole, popping up of the ex, thing I had totally forgotten that I have a date with Jonah. But I can always get ready here and call Jonah to tell him not to pick me up. "Yeah, but I can get ready here. I'll just wear some of the new clothes, and I have a pair of shoes in my car that I ordered from this website. They came when I was about to leave my apartment, so I put them in there."

"If you stay, you have to behave. No baiting Henry," he says sternly and wags a finger at me.

Where's the fun in that?

"Not even a little?"

"Autumn..."

"You can't just make me quit cold turkey, and it isn't even like I'm ever blatantly rude." Really, I'm usually on my high school behavior with Henry. The time that we went out to eat was the most civil that I've ever been to him.

Mark just rolls his eyes at me and gets out of the car. I take the hint to follow him when he grabs a few of my bags from the back seat and starts walking toward Henry. As soon as I'm out of the car, I can hear Henry's annoyed voice.

"...called you three times. You know, I really don't appreciate you spending an entire Saturday out. These are the only free days that we have together."

I bite my tongue and stay out of it. We were gone for a while, but it isn't like we do this all the time. This is the first time we've done this at all since he and Henry moved in together, and we used to spend nearly every weekend together. I suppose that maybe I resent Henry because of that. Mark is my only close friend here, and I hate sharing his time. It was different when Henry was still living with his wife; he and Mark barely saw each other. But now, it's like he needs Mark to sleep in his back pocket to be happy.

Henry gripes all the way into the apartment. I'm waiting for him to tell Mark that he's grounded or that his video game privileges are revoked. I just keep looking at my friend and shaking my head. Who puts up with this shit? Cohabitation is the devil. You would think that it was six in the morning and not six in the afternoon. I don't even know what the over the hill dick chaser is complaining about. Mark told him that he'd be back at six, and he was. What is there to take issue with? If he didn't want him to leave in the first place, why not say something before we walked out the door?

I take my bags from Mark and pull out the heather grey silk sweater and the destroyed skinny jeans that I just bought. I just need to touch up my make-up and I'll be ready. With the exception of my sneakers, but the shoes are in the car.

Henry stops mid-rant when I take out my phone and call Jonah. I pretend not to notice him looking at me and focus on my phone call. I can't really help the smile that comes to my face when Jonah answers the phone, and you have no idea how much that annoys me.

"Hey, baby. You're not calling to cancel on me, are you?"

"No, I'm just calling to tell you that I'm at Mark's still and I'll meet you at your place in about an hour. I didn't want you to drive all the way out to my apartment for no reason." That would have been nearly an hour of wasted time. I can't wait until I live closer.

"Okay, so I'll see you in an hour. You're spending the night, right?"

Wrong. "Actually, we need to sleep at my house tonight."

"What? Why?"

What, do I live in a hovel or something? "Because I need to go to church tomorrow. If I miss one more service, my Aunt's going to come by my house while I'm sleeping and try to perform an exorcism on me."

"Alright, fine. At least tell me that you have food."

I wonder if frozen pizza counts. I'm sure that in his mind it doesn't.

"We can stop at the supermarket before we get to my place."

"The things I do for you."

I roll my eyes at his beleaguered tone. "Yeah, you're a real martyr."

"See you soon."

"Bye." I hang up my phone and continue to pretend to ignore Henry's glare. He should really try to calm down before he has a heart attack or something. The man is a blob, it's amazing that he hasn't had one already. That's another thing that confuses me about Mark's relationship with him. I mean, yeah, beauty isn't everything, but come on. Mark is a gorgeous specimen of maleness, and Henry's just a specimen. He literally looks as if he were grown in a petri dish as some weird experiment, but he managed to land an attractive wife (I've seen pictures) as well as a really hot younger boyfriend.

Henry turns his glare to Mark. "I really would like to talk to you in private."

Mark rolls his eyes at him. "Okay, well then we'll talk when Automobile leaves."

I smile brightly and nod when Henry looks at me. "Yeah, it'll take me less than an hour to get ready."

Henry looks as if he wants to say something, but instead he stomps his foot before leaving the room in a huff. Okay, who over the age of five does something like that? This is a grown ass man who is slowly inching his way toward a senior discount, and he just had a small tantrum. I would laugh if I weren't so disturbed by his actions.

"So, have you talked to Mr. Jonah about your move to the new place?" Mark sits down on the couch with a flop. He looks a little stressed. I blame Henry. Mark was fine before we got back to this apartment.

I decide that it would be best not to voice my thought and instead answer Mark's question. "No. I'll tell him tonight. We're going to the movies at Atlantic Station, so I can bring it up without it seeming random."

"Why haven't you told him already?" Mark is frowning at me and I just know that he's reading way too much into this.

Why does there have to be some drama filled ulterior motive to everything?

"I don't know. It just hasn't come up."

Mark shoots up from the couch with a look of surprise on his face. "Are you thinking of breaking up with Jonah? Like, for good this time? Autumn..."

"What?! I didn't say that. I haven't told him about moving because I haven't told him. I promise that if I consider ending my relationship with Jonah, I'll tell you."

"Be sure that you do. It'll give me some time to talk some sense into you. I think that Jonah is perfect for you; you're just scared because he told you that he loves you and you aren't ready to admit that you love him back."

"You don't get paid for thinking. I have to get dressed." I toss a throw pillow at him when he sticks his tongue out at me and leave the room.

The truth is that I've been thinking a lot about my relationship with Jonah since we got back together. Everything is moving along fine, if you discount he fact that he keeps telling me that he loves me.

Now he wants me to spend a holiday with his family. Everything is becoming so real between us, and I don't have time for it. Yeah, he met my family first, but that was a very random dinner on a regular day that banks and malls do not close for. He wants me to come to a dinner that his parents, siblings, and a few other relatives could be at. If it were a regular Sunday dinner, I'd be fine with it, but this just seems so...couple-ish. And yes, before you point out the obvious, I know that we're a couple. Just...I have to get dressed.

Chapter Twenty-Seven:

J onah and I have just come to the street level of Atlantic Station after leaving his car in the underground parking lot. I almost invited Mark to come along with us. As soon as I left his apartment, I could hear Henry telling him how inconsiderate he is. If that isn't the pot calling the kettle pitch black. That man is a hot mess of ridiculousness.

As soon as we round the corner I tug on Jonah's hand and point up. "That's where I'm moving to in January."

He looks puzzled. "What?"

How much more straight-forward could I possibly be? "I'm moving into that building in January when my lease is up."

"When did you decide this?" He pulls me over to a bench and sits down. I continue to stand.

Is it wrong that I decided this over a week ago? I don't think it is.

"The Monday after you came over to my house. Mark went with me on our lunch break to check the apartment out, and it was awesome. I already called a moving company to do the heavy lifting, 'cause I do not have the back for that," I joke.

He doesn't even crack a smile. "Why're you moving?"

"Because my place is in Guam. I'm completely separated from everything that I need to be close to, and I can afford the apartment here," I explain. What, like he doesn't know that I live too far away from my job and my friends.

He nods and seems to accept my reasons. "Okay. It'll be nice to have you closer. You know this means that you'll have to wake up earlier on Sundays for church, right?"

I really hadn't thought of that. But waking up a little earlier once a week is better than waking up at the butt crack of dawn every morning. "I can deal with that."

"And this also means that I'll be seeing you a lot more. Yay for me and my sex life." He tugs on my hand until I sit next to him on the bench.

"Don't get too excited, I'm still gonna be working a million hours a week. Your sex life probably won't change that much. Even with you being closer, I doubt I'll be in the mood to come home, shower, change, and drive to your apartment after I've had a full day of Chelsea the wonder bitch." I'm just trying to be honest. Usually, when I leave work, I just want to relax at home in my bed. It rarely happens that way, but I can hope.

"You could move in with me," he suggests.

Everything around me is frozen for a second as soon as that sentence leaves his mouth. I wonder if this is what it feels like when you have a near death experience. People are always saying that time slows down just before you die.

I realize that he's staring at me as if he just made the most natural suggestion in the world. Is he on crack? "Huh?"

Huh? Eloquent, Autumn. You really expressed yourself well there. What I meant to say was, are you out of your rabbit ass mind. What came out was, huh. And he's smirking at me, the bastard.

"I'm buying a condo in that market village that has that restaurant that you like near Mark's apartment. My apartment is a good size, but I wanna own something. What do you think?"

He's stroking his fingers over the back of my hand, and the fact that I can feel it is the only thing keeping me from thinking that I've slipped into some warped day dream.

I really don't want to have an argument with him right now. If we were in the movie theater, we could just sit quietly and watch some really bad romantic comedy play out in front of us and make occasional comments to each other about the predictability of the plot, but we're still sitting on this uncomfortable ass bench in the middle of Atlantic Station with people walking by us, completely oblivious to what we're talking about, and he's looking at me waiting for me to say something, and I wish I could be just another one of those oblivious people walking by.

"I think that owning a condo would be a good step for you. You don't really have the time to devote to a house, with you traveling for work sometimes. You're at an age when most people begin to purchase property. So, yeah, I think that moving to a condo would be a good thing for you and the area that you're thinking about is great." I'm channeling my inner politician.

Jonah sighs a little and rubs his head. "But not for you."

What the fuck, man? I can't even commit to meeting his family on Thanksgiving and he wants me to move in with him? Are we even in the same relationship? "Jonah..."

"Listen, I'm not talking about right now. My lease on my apartment isn't up until March anyway. I've looked at the unit that I'm interested in once, and I wanna see it again before I make an offer."

"Why are we talking about this at all?" I flap my hands in the air. Dinner and a movie, that's what I agreed to. Talking about cohabitation, not so much.

"Because I want to live with you. I want to wake up with you and go to bed with you without needing to pack an overnight bag."

That simple? Nothing's that simple. I need a drink. We should just skip the movie and go to the sport's bar.

"Jonah, I thought that you understood how I feel about marriage."

"Who the hell said anything about marriage? There are more stages to a relationship than just dating and marriage," he says, motioning side to side.

Good point. How to put this nicely? "Jonah, I've lived with someone that I was dating before, and it didn't work."

Jonah nods slowly. "Yeah, because he was cheating on you and you didn't see the relationship as long term."

Who said that I see this relationship as long term?

"You do realize that we've been dating for less than two months, right?"

Now he looks frustrated. Well good, because I feel frustrated.

"Where did you learn to tell time? And why does that even matter?"

I am ready to be done with this entire conversation. "We're going to miss our movie."

"Fuck the movie, Autumn! This is more important than a goddamned movie! I love you. I wanna live with you." He looks angry. Like, really angry.

"Do you not realize that you're springing this on me in the middle of the street? What do you want me to say here? My lease is up in January. The apartment that I'd like to take may not be available if I wait too long on it. What am I supposed to do until March? Am I supposed to move into a new apartment and then break my lease to move again in March?"

"There will always be apartments available. You could just move in with me now, and we could move into the condo in March. We can get a storage unit and put some of your furniture in there and I'll put some of my stuff in there too and make room for the things that you bring so that you don't feel like a guest. If you don't wanna do that, you could just do a month to month thing at the townhouse."

He's really serious! I have never wanted the ground to open up and swallow me more than I do now. I'm trying not to just scream in frustration. Mainly because we are in public and there are cops walking around patrolling the area.

"I really don't think that this is the place for this talk."

"Baby..."

"I'll think about it. Just give me a few days and I'll let you know on Thanksgiving. Okay?" I hope he agrees, because this is the best I can do.

Jonah nods reluctantly. "Fine. Thanksgiving."

He takes my hand again and we walk over to get our tickets. I'm on total autopilot. Mark would laugh if he heard me say that. I have no idea what movie we saw or who was in it. One minute the previews were playing in front of me, and the next thing I knew, the credits were rolling. I really like the apartment that I saw with Mark. I already pictured myself in it and everything. I imagined working in the living room and then soaking in the tub before going to bed. I pictured myself shopping in Atlantic Station, eating at the Cheesecake Bistro and then walking home.

"I wanna see the condo." We're sitting at California Pizza and there's a waiter standing next to our table, and before I know it the words are coming out of my mouth.

"Okay. When?" He doesn't seem at all surprised by my request.

When? Good question. I hadn't thought about that. "How about next week? Sometime after the holiday."

"I thought you were gonna give me a real answer on Thursday." He's starting to piss me off.

"I'd like to see the condo before I decide whether or not I'm willing to adjust my life and live there."

"And if you don't like it? What then?"

Why do people always want quick answers to important questions? You would think that they'd appreciate a person putting careful thought into their decisions. "Jonah, I'm not going to live in a place that I hate."

"Fine, I wanna know what we're gonna do if you hate the condo."

He can't be serious. This has got to be some really bad practical joke. How did I get into this situation? We just got back together for Christ's sake.

"I don't know. I don't know if I want us to live together, though I'm pretty sure that I don't, and you can't really peer pressure me into changing my mind on this."

The waiter has apparently realized that neither of us is ready to order, and so has decided to allow us a few more moments to read the menu. Or argue.

"If you've already made up your mind—"

"I haven't already made up my mind, I just—"

"You just said—"

"I said that I'm pretty sure I don't—"

"Which is a, no!"

"It's not a, no! It's an, I'm not sure but I'm leaning toward no based on where I am in my life and my past experiences with living with people!"

People are staring at us. Our voices have gotten a little loud. Jonah looks around and seems to notice that we've acquired an audience. He smiles apologetically at a few people and when he starts talking again his voice is a lot lower. "You're thinking about you and I'm thinking about us. Maybe that's the problem."

"The *problem?* The problem is that you just spring something like this on me and then get all pissed when I don't start jumping for joy. Have you only just met me? I'm trying here. That's why I'm waiting to see the place before I make a decision."

He shakes his head at me. "The place shouldn't matter. I'm asking you to live with me. Whether it's this place, or the apartment that you saw with Mark, or someplace else, the setting shouldn't matter."

How very romance novel of him. I don't subscribe to the notion of love conquering all, or the whole, *we can live in a cardboard box as long as we're together*, crap.

"It does matter. So, can we at least wait until I've seen the condo to have this argument?"

"Alright. You coming to Thanksgiving dinner with my family?"

WHAT THE FUCK! I feel like banging my head against the table. Do people not believe in casual relationships anymore? How did I get sucked into this?

"Jonah—"

"What is the big deal? I've already met your family. I even endured an interrogation! This won't be like that. I promise." He softens his voice and looks at me like he's trying to read my mind, "this is important to me."

God dammit! Just shit! All I can hear is my grandmother's voice in my head telling me that I need to learn to pick my battles. And he's right, he did meet my family and I did make him talk to my mother on the phone, and there were interrogations, and he endured it all with a polite smile and without running for the hills. Fuck!

"Fine, but we have to stop at my aunt's house before we go to your parents'. She invited me to dinner, and I can't not show up."

He manages to keep his relief from showing too much. "Okay."

Chapter Twenty-Eight:

After talking to Mark, I decided that meeting Jonah's family wouldn't be the end of the world. So here I am, trying very hard not to throw myself from the moving vehicle as we approach his parents' house. The thing is that I genuinely care a lot about Jonah, way more than I'm comfortable with. I think I mentioned that before. I've never felt this way about another person, and I'm not sure how to handle it, but I am aware of this constant paranoia that something will go horribly wrong between us. Not the best feeling, let me tell you.

We pull up to a two story, brick front house that looks nearly identical to at least half of the houses on the street. Got to love sub-divisions. Jonah gets out and opens my door, and for the life of me, I cannot make myself get out of the truck. My hands are literally gripping the seat as if I'll float into the stratosphere if I let go. I also feel like I'm going to throw up. We were already at my aunt's house, and thankfully nothing crazy happened. Well, not really. My uncle did give a prayer that sounded a lot like a sermon that focused on virtue. Unfortunately, that has only fueled my belief that the sky is going to fall.

"Baby, get out of the truck." He's looking at me like I'm being ridiculous.

Like I don't know that I look crazy? Closing my eyes, I take a few deep breaths and manage to convince my hands to unclench. A few more breaths and I step down out of the truck. Jonah takes my arm and pulls me forward while closing and locking the doors.

"It's gonna be fine. I promise." He's trying to be soothing.

I look at him and I'm sure that the doubt is written all over my face. "Uh huh."

He shakes his head and gives me a half smile before leading me up the path and through the front door. Why was I expecting him to knock or ring a doorbell? This is his parents' house for Christ's sakes.

When we step inside, I start to take in my surroundings. There are family pictures everywhere. Hanging on the walls and sitting on side tables; mostly all of them are of Jonah and his siblings at various stages. Everything from baby pictures to graduation photos. The house feels warm. Not in temperature, more like in essence. I can hear multiple conversations going on, and I can smell food cooking, it smells like coconut in here. I love that smell. I also smell bananas. This could be okay.

Walking further into the house, I take in more of my surroundings. There's a family room with two comfortable looking couches and a sliding glass door across from us with curtains that are open and show a deck that has an outdoor dining set and one of those green egg grills. The mantle full of pictures is above a large brick front fireplace and has a 60" TV mounted above it. The walls are painted amber, and there are floor plants in every corner of the room. The conversations that I heard happening were courtesy of the three men standing in the family room and the commentators on the television. One of the men in the family room, I recognize. Jim. Why the fuck is Jim here? I give Jonah a questioning look and he quickly shakes his head at me. He doesn't know what's going on either.

An older man looks over when he notices us enter. His face stretches into a welcoming smile. If it weren't for the light brown hair and eyes, I'd say I was looking at an older version of Jonah. He comes over to us and pulls Jonah into a hug, and then pulls back and gives him two hard slaps to the back of his shoulder. "You finally got here!"

Jonah laughs. "Yeah, I told mom that we needed to stop at Autumn's aunt's house first."

"You better have left some room. Your mother will kill you if you don't eat anything," he says jokingly.

Jonah rolls his eyes and pulls me forward. "Dad, this is Autumn."

I give him what I hope is a warm smile and extend my hand. He uses it to pull me into a hug. Well, okay.

"We're huggers in this family," he says when he lets me go.

"I see that," I laugh. "It's very nice to meet you, Mr. McInerney."

"None of that. I'm Patty. The lummox over there is Jonah's brother, Ethan. And that's Jim."

Ethan gives me a smile and a wave. He looks like he could be in the WWE main line-up. "Very nice to meet you."

I return his smile, but my wave to him is a bit distracted as I turn my attention to Jim. I was under the impression that both he and Kaylin have large families that live in Georgia, so what the fuck are they doing here? I'm about to ask, but Jonah beats me to it.

"Hey Jim, fancy seeing you here." He says it pleasantly.

I probably wouldn't have. And, come on. We all know that I can be a bitch, but I don't want that side of me coming out during Thanksgiving with my boyfriend's family.

Jim looks uncomfortable. "Yeah, sorry we didn't give you a heads up. Kay's not really talking to her mom right now, and her whole family is at her parents' place, and she didn't wanna drive down to Valdosta to do the holiday with my parents, so she called your mom and here we are."

Patty clears his throat and breaks into the awkwardness. "Well, the more the merrier. Especially with Kayden having to miss the holiday."

Kayden is Jonah's youngest brother and he's in the Navy. From what I've been told, he went to college, partied extremely hard and got kicked out. Moved back home but continued to drink and stay out late until Jonah's parents told him to shape up or get the fuck out. He decided to get the fuck out and couch hopped from friend to friend for a while. After he had alienated almost everyone he knew and got a one-night stand pregnant, he joined the Navy. Turns out, the Navy was his true calling. He's stationed somewhere near Japan and it seems he couldn't get leave.

"Where's Arihi?" Jonah asks.

Arihi is the baby of the family and the only girl. She's home for the holiday but attends college in California where she's studying marine biology.

"She's in the kitchen with your mother and Kaylin. She was wholly uninterested in our talk about Heisman contenders," Patty says with a smirk.

Jonah sighs before taking my hand and leading me to the kitchen. He looks like he wants to say something, but he's not sure how to word it. That makes two of us. I knew that shit was going to go left.

When we enter the kitchen, Kaylin and who I assume is Arihi, are sitting at the island together while an older woman that I'm guessing is Jonah's mother is pulling something out of the oven.

Kaylin notices us first and goes on defense before anyone can say anything. "Jonah, hey! You finally got here. I was wondering when you would. Wasn't it so nice of your mom to let me and Jim spend Thanksgiving with y'all? Me and my mom are at war again," she shakes her head and gives an exaggerated eye roll. "But then, you know that from our talk yesterday."

And then, as if she's only now seeing me, she pastes a fake as fuck smile on her face and addresses me. "Hey, Autumn. It's so good to see you again. Love those shoes."

Jonah slides his arm around my waist and rests his hand on my hip. He gives me a subtle squeeze, and I force myself to be nice. "Thanks, Kaylin. It's so good to see you again as well. How are the wedding plans going?"

She heaves a put-upon sigh. "They're going. I swear, it'll be great when all the planning is done, and the wedding is over."

I doubt that she really feels that way. This bitch loves being the center of attention while playing the harassed victim. She'll be one of those women that does some over the top gender reveal party when she gets pregnant, followed by an over the top baby shower. The wedding planning probably would have been done already if she didn't have a tantrum over every little thing. I swear, when I get married, I'm going to do it on a beach in Turks and Caicos. It'll just be me, Mark, my friend, Aiyana, from New York, Jonah, and whoever he decides to bring.

Wait, what? What the fuck just blasted through my mind? Marriage and Jonah. Hell fucking no! Please God, let there be wine tonight.

"So, this is Autumn," the older woman says. She comes around the kitchen island and pulls me into a hug. When she pulls back, she holds on to my arms. "It's wonderful to finally meet you."

"It's wonderful to meet you as well, ma'am. I've heard a lot about you," I smile at her. She is beautiful.

Jonah's mother is taller than me and very curvy. My heels put us eye level with each other. She has dark brown eyes, long dark wavy hair that's pulled away from her face in a hair clip, a small round nose, a cupid's bow mouth, and bronze skin. When she smiles, small wrinkles appear at the corners of her eyes and around her mouth.

"None of that, Ma'am, stuff. I'm Lulu." She smiles at me before squeezing my arms and letting me go. "The one over there eating more than helping is Arihi." She motions to her daughter who's still sitting at the kitchen island.

I smile and nod in her direction. "Hi."

She smiles around a mouthful of what looks like rice but smells like coconut. Putting her hand in front of her mouth, she laughs. "Sorry. I'm starving. I live with three other girls and no one cooks."

"No one does laundry either," Lulu says while cutting her a look.

Arihi just shrugs and then turns to Jonah and raises her eyebrows. "So, big brother, how ya been?"

"I've been great. How much do you need?" Jonah gives her an affectionate smile while stepping more fully behind me and wrapping his other arm around my waist.

I lean back against him. Jonah is very touchy-feely. He's always kissing me on my forehead or pulling me into his lap. I never thought I'd like that. Whenever I saw couple's that always had to be touching, I would think, *God that seems suffocating*. Now, it feels natural to slide my hand into his or lean back against him and let him take my weight against his body. I feel...safe with him. It's nice. It seems to be annoying Kaylin, though. I notice her pinched expression as well as his sister's smirk.

Arihi's smirk turns into a full-blown smile. "I only need fifteen hundred dollars."

I try not to show any reaction to that, but did she just hit him up for fifteen hundred dollars? And did she say, only? Hell, my whoring cousin asked me for five hundred and I gagged! Jonah and I don't ever really talk about money, so I have no idea how much he makes or what he has saved, but I know that he works hard and has been self-employed for nearly eight years.

"What for?" Jonah sounds exasperated.

"Okay, well there's this oceanography institute in Mexico—"

He cuts her off. "Why are you hitting me up for this?"

She rolls her eyes. "Daddy already said no, and mommy won't help me try to convince him. Ethan doesn't have that kind of money, and Kayd has child support. I already have half of it, I just need the other fifteen hundred."

He drops his head down to my shoulder and groans. "Fine, but this is the last time. I swear, you better discover something amazing and name it after me."

Arihi squeals and jumps up from the table. Rushing over, she pulls Jonah into a hug that squishes me between them. She's nearly the same height as Jonah, so my face is pressed into her breasts for a second before she hops back.

"Best big brother ever!" then she fingers my sweater. "Wow, this is really soft. Nice!"

I promise that I'm trying not to look at her like she's crazy. "Thank you."

Lulu comes over to us and pries Jonah off of me. "Joe, go play with the boys in the other room. And tell your father to get the pig."

Jonah looks from me to Kaylin and hesitates. "Uh..."

I look at him and silently promise not to shove his ex hag into the oven. "Go do the guy thing. I'm good."

He gives me one more doubtful look, but then kisses me on the side of the neck and leaves the room.

I turn back to the women in the room and see his mother and sister eagerly studying me. Kaylin still has her phony smile in place. I really am fine with this. I can talk to anybody. My mother used to be afraid that someone was going to steal me when I was a kid because I treated every stranger like I'd known them forever. Any discomfort I'm feeling has more to do with Kaylin being here than anything else. I am seriously tired of this chick.

"Now, Autumn, tell us a little about yourself. Jonah said that you're from New York?" Lulu sits at the kitchen island and offers me a seat, and a margarita. I already love her.

I thank her for my drink and take a sip. It's a little strong, but still tasty. "Yeah, I'm from New York. Long Island, actually. My family is still there, but I got a job offer here and so I relocated."

Arihi leans forward and rests her chin on her hand. "What part of Long Island? Like, the Hamptons?"

Yeah right.

"No, Amityville."

"Horror house, Amityville?" Arihi asks. "Did you grow up near that house?"

I hate this question. I get it every time I mention my home town. I really wish they'd stop making movies and documentaries about that shit.

"No. I grew up on the other side of Amityville." I take another sip of my margarita.

Arihi is still curious. "But have you, like, ever gone in the house? Do people live there?"

"Ari, Jesus! I do not want to talk about a family massacre over Thanksgiving dinner," Lulu chastises her. "Anyway, Autumn. What is the job that brought you to Georgia?"

"Oh, Autumn's in advertising," Kaylin chirps.

I really don't think I'm imagining the snottiness. And it seems that I'm not the only one that notices it. Lulu shoots her a look before taking a sip of her own margarita. The look that she gives her is the look that your mother gave you when you were a child and started acting up when company came over. That look that let you know that if you didn't start acting right, you were going to get embarrassed in front of the people that you were showing out for.

Clearing my throat, I address Lulu. "I work for an advertising firm in Atlanta. My aunt retired from there, but she still has a few friends in the firm and when an opening became available, she let me know. I had just finished my masters a few months before, so I was excited for the opportunity."

"What college did you go to?" Kaylin asks. "Jonah and I talk all the time, but he never really mentions you."

Yeah, she wants me to curse her out. But I was raised not to disrespect other people's homes, so I'll do the politely impolite thing. I smile at her. "Yeah, I know you guys are really close, but it makes sense that he wouldn't talk about me too much with you, considering everything. I mean, he knows how stressed all this wedding planning has you, especially with all of the problems and fights that you and Jim have been having. No real friend would just flaunt how happy they are in their relationship when they know how unhappy their friend is in their respective situation. By the way, are you keeping any ideas that you had for the wedding that you were planning before Jonah ended things, or are you starting all over? Even if you are going in a totally different direction theme wise, at least you still have the information that you must have gathered for the vendors from the last time, right? And to answer your question, I attended Temple University for my Bachelor and Masters' degrees."

My comments about her wedding plans and Jonah dropping her ass have disconcerted her. I managed to come off as both curious and sympathetic. It's a gift.

Arihi gives Kaylin a curious frown. "Did you and Joe even get to the planning stage? You guys were only engaged for five minutes."

"Four months, Arihi," Kaylin huffs.

"Well, it hardly matters now," Lulu says diplomatically as she refills both of our drinks. "That was how many years ago? And you're happily engaged to be married to a very nice man, and Jonah has moved on as well. That's what makes it so easy for the two of you to be such good friends."

"No, yeah, of course," Kaylin stammers and brushes some hair behind her ear.

"Autumn, would you mind telling the boys that dinner is ready? The table is already set, so everyone just needs to wash their hands," Lulu says, standing up and going to the oven when the timer goes off.

I stand up, making sure to bring my margarita with me. "No problem."

The conversation in the family room seems to have moved on to college football championships and the surprises that happened this year, as a game plays out on the huge television over the mantle. Mark has tried to pull me into these types of conversations in the past. I've reminded him repeatedly that he has his brother for sports talk and me for fashion, and never the twain shall meet. Don't get me wrong, I enjoy sports. I was a cheerleader from junior high through high school, but that doesn't mean I'm trying to join a fantasy league. Football in Georgia is like a way of life. These people are obsessed.

"Gentlemen, I have been asked to inform you that dinner is ready and if you don't wash your hands, the women are eating without you." That gets everyone's attention and I laugh when Ethan and James practically race to the hall bathroom to wash their hands.

Patty chuckles and shakes his head, then he slaps Jonah on the back. "I really like her."

Jonah grins. "Yeah, me too."

I roll my eyes at him and turn to head back to the kitchen. I feel his arms wrap around me from behind before I take a step. How unfair is it that I'm wearing five-inch heels and he's still about half a foot taller than me?

Lowering his head, he kisses me on my neck. "Are you behaving?"

I lean back against him. "What do you think?"

"Well, I didn't hear any screams, and there doesn't appear to be blood under your finger nails, so I'm hoping things are going well."

I turn to face him, forcing him to loosen his hold a little. Bummer. "If I make it through this night without slapping that decaying blonde breadstick that you inexplicably asked to marry you at one point, then I feel that I should be nominated for sainthood."

He laughs a little before leaning down to speak into my ear. "Instead of a nomination for sainthood, what if we play sexually frustrated executive and underachieving employee later. You can make me stay after work to give you an oral presentation."

And now I'm wet. Just great. "Jonah..."

He keeps going. "In fact, we don't even have to wait. I'm positive that I can get you off in less than five minutes if you'll just come with me into the bathroom."

As tempting as that sounds, I'm not about to let this man go down on me during Thanksgiving dinner at his parents' house! Do you have any idea how hard I would judge a chick for some shit like that? If we were at Mark's house, then I'd be down for that, but here? I'm meeting his family for the first time, and I'm a screamer. I didn't used to be. Alright, so every once in a while, I would have an orgasm that made me moan a little loudly. Every orgasm that I have with Jonah has me screaming like my body is on fire. There is no way that any near naked freaky shit is happening in this house. And, I'm wearing jeans.

He nips my lip. "You know you want to. Your ass in those jeans has me hard as fuck."

Before I can give in to my inner slutbag, Lulu interrupts us. She clears her throat behind me and when I turn around, she has this look on her face that says she knows exactly what her son was trying to get me to do. I breathe a sigh of relief when she smiles at me after shooting a censuring look at Jonah. He laughs before kissing me on the side of my head and leading me into the dining room.

The dining room is nearly all table and there are more family pictures on the walls. The food has been placed in the middle of the table so that we can serve ourselves. There's a roasted pig in the center, that coconut rice that Arihi had in the kitchen, fried plantain, some fish dish, green beans, what looks like sticky buns, and roasted yams. Everything tastes delicious, and the conversation mostly centers around what everyone has been up to lately. It seems that Ethan recently broke up with his girlfriend, but no one is surprised because he's a man whore. Like, getting tested for STIs all the time, man whore.

Arihi appears to be the family princess. I actually mean that in a nice way. It's obvious that she's used to everyone catering to her, but she seems genuinely nice. She's turning twenty in January, her birthday is close to mine, and she's on a full ride scholarship at Berkley, which is great since their mother retired a few years ago and her parents are paying for her apartment and car. It also explains why her father would veto giving her fifteen hundred dollars for something that she waited to spring on them until coming home for the holiday.

I'm biting into a fork full of my coconutty rice when Kaylin decides to take another run at being phony.

"So, Autumn, how are you liking the food? I mean, I'm sure it's a lot different than what you're used to having." She gives me her faux innocent eye flutter.

How could she know what I'm used to having? I'm from Long Island. I grew up eating everything from pierogi to jerk chicken. "I'm not sure what you mean. But everything tastes great."

The only one that seems to be paying any attention to what's happening between the two of us is Arihi. Jonah, Ethan, and Jim have gotten into another football debate and Patty is fully engrossed in his meal while Lulu is trying to talk to him about a cruise.

Kaylin nods, still smiling. "Yeah, but it must be a significant change from fried chicken and watermelon, right."

It's like a record scratched and all conversation around us grinds to a halt. Did this broad really just say that shit to me? It is very hard for me not to jump across this table on her and snap her little phony ass neck. I don't even like watermelon! And who the fuck eats that shit in November anyway?

"Wow, way to generalize and marginalize an entire group of people with one sentence. My mother typically makes Cornish hens and ham for Thanksgiving since no one in my family really likes turkey. There's also stuffing, green beans, candied yams, and baked macaroni and cheese. As far as watermelon goes...I'm not sure if anyone eats that at Thanksgiving, but I've never been a fan." I take a bite of my pork and wait to see what tiki torch barbie will say next.

She manages to look offended. "Are you implying that I'm racist? I'll have you know that my best friend in college was black. From Africa. And fried chicken and watermelon is a southern thing."

"I see. So, you having one black friend means that you're in no way racist. Got it. But how does the southern excuse apply here?" I should get an Emmy for this. My voice is not betraying any of the hostility that is coursing through me and I keep my expression impassive.

"Well...it was just that...what do you mean?" she flounders.

"I'm from New York. It's not really located in the southern region of the United States," I explain slowly.

She looks over at Jim and he throws on his cape and swoops in to pull her out of the hole.

"She didn't mean nothing by it. It was just an innocent question." He laughs awkwardly and puts up his hands in mock surrender. "No need to pull the race card."

My mouth literally drops open in shock. That's his defense? Accusing me of pulling some mythical card that only exists in the world of the small minded?

Jonah has come out of his chair and is half across the table before I've even managed to close my mouth. He looks pissed.

"What the fuck did you just say to her?"

Oh shit. I don't really know what to do. Jonah looks like he's about to pile drive Jim through the table even though Jim has about twenty pounds on him. Ethan stood up when Jonah did, but he's not trying to hold Jonah back. It's like he's waiting for Jonah to take a swing so that he can join in and get some hits in on Jim too. This may be a good time to mention that Jonah has been boxing since he was nine. His mother insisted on it after they moved to Georgia and he got cornered by some aggressive and racist kids on a school bus.

Kaylin stands from the table and pulls Jim up with her. "Maybe Jimmy and I should just leave."

"Bye," Arihi snickers.

Kaylin looks at Jonah like she's waiting for him to apologize and ask them to stay.

"I think that's a great idea," Jonah says while glaring at Jim.

She gasps. Actually places her hand to her heart and fucking gasps! This is so Scarlett O'Hara. Who the fuck acts like this? She looks at me like she wants to say something but changes her mind and stomps away from the table.

Patty stands from his seat and jerks a thumb in the direction of the front door. "I'm just going to go and lock the front door behind them."

And now everyone is staring at me. I'm not sure what they're expecting me to say. Am I supposed to assure them that I'm okay? Give some rendition of a Martin Luther King Jr. speech about us all being judged on the content of our character? Recite the lyrics to *I'm Black and I'm Proud*?

I don't have anything like any of that running through my mind right now. To be honest, and I cannot explain this to you, my feelings are hurt. Not because of what Kaylin said, but because of what Jim said. I actually liked him. I thought he was a nice person. I felt bad for him because his fiancé keeps running to her ex every time they have a problem, and I'm sure that it makes him feel inferior. So, his whole, "race card", comment caught me off guard. I am not surprised at all by Kaylin's thinly veiled racist comment. Nothing else that she had said or done tonight seemed to faze me, so she tried to go all the way low without appearing to. I've learned that immature people tend to do that. If their more subtle insults don't leave a mark, then they fall back on racism or homophobia or something else just as vile. When I was much younger, I responded with violence. It didn't take long to realize that they were getting their desired reaction out of me, so I adjusted.

Patty comes back into the dining room with a fresh beer for himself and the margarita pitcher. After refilling my glass, he walks back to the head of the table and takes his seat. He turns and looks at Lulu and his expression is all about the 'I told you so'.

She throws up her hands. "What was I supposed to do? She called me crying and saying that she needed somewhere to spend the holiday!"

Patty takes a swig of his beer. "Why did we have to be that somewhere? Restaurants are opened on Thanksgiving, you know."

"Seriously, mommy," this from Arihi, "I thought we were done putting up with her when Jonah wised up and dropped her skinny ass."

Patty points his beer bottle at her. "Watch your mouth in front of your mother, young lady."

Arihi puts her hands up in apology. "I'm very sorry. But that woman is exhausting, and I don't care about her problems or her wedding."

"Why are you even still friends with her anyway?" Ethan gives Jonah a dubious look.

I would also love to know the answer to this question. From what I've seen, little miss Kaylin has not one redeeming quality. I turn to him, patiently awaiting his answer as I take large swallows of my margarita.

Oh, we have gone way passed the fucking lady like sips portion of the evening.

Jonah looks around the table at all of us and visibly tries to come up with an answer. He has been on the receiving end of racist comments. His mother is Samoan, and he grew up in a predominantly white area with kids that couldn't tell the difference between a Polynesian and a Mexican. He was called all kinds of half breeds and spics by kids when he was younger, so I know he gets it. Therefore, I am not expecting what comes out of his mouth.

"She's really not that bad."

If my eyebrows could hit my hairline, they would. I pick up my glass and drain it before standing from the table and looking at his parents and siblings. "Thank you very much for having me and allowing me to be a part of your holiday. The food was wonderful, and I really enjoyed meeting all of you."

I walk out of the room without looking back, though I hear Jonah getting up from the table and Ethan calling him a fucking idiot.

Where the shit did I put my purse? I don't even remember putting it down. I spot it on an end table and grab it. My phone is in my purse, and I need it to order an Uber.

"Autumn, will you wait a minute?" Jonah calls from somewhere behind me.

I'm not doing this. There is no way that I'm about to go in on him at his parents' house on a holiday. Did I expect him to say that he had just realized what a vapid succubus his ex was and declare that their friendship was over effective immediately? No. But I expected something. Something like, 'I'm sorry that my continued association with her has placed you all in this situation' or 'I'll talk to her about leaning on my family and making racist comments to my girlfriend'. Fuck this whole entire situation sideways. I keep walking and head out the front door while opening my Uber app. I'll wait for my ride outside.

He grabs the door when I try to pull it closed behind me. "Autumn, baby, will you stop?" He sounds a little panicked.

I don't have any fucks to give about anything that he has to say. He wants me to move in with him, but he's okay with his ex being a complete bitch to me whenever we're around each other. Granted, he was ready to bust Jimbo's mouth wide open, but that big dumb ass was just co-signing the ice vagina's comment.

He steps in front of me and I almost fall when I pull up short. I'm wearing five-inch heels and I probably shouldn't have deep throated that last margarita. He reaches out and helps to steady me. As soon as I feel like my balance is good, I slap at his hands to make him let me go. He does, but he snatches my phone out of my hand so that I can't order a ride.

"Give me my fucking phone," I growl at him.

"Baby, please just—"

"No! I don't want to hear anything that you have to say right now. I'm not even sure that I want to hear anything that you have to say ever again." I try to snatch my phone back.

He falters. It looks like the wind has been knocked out of him. "You wanna be done with me?"

"I'm not sure. I need to think about things." I hold out my hand. "Give. Me. My. Phone."

"If you wanna go home, then I'll take you."

I'm shaking my head before he's even done talking, and it's really fucking up my tenuous balance. "I don't want to be around you."

"Baby, she's—"

"Not that bad. I know. I heard you. I get it. She's just a misunderstood, put upon, paragon of pure white virtue, and she didn't mean anything by the fried chicken and watermelon comment. I'm just being overly sensitive. Kaylin Antebellum with all of her southern charm and manners would never think a racist thought, let alone verbalize one. I read way too much into it and pulled out my magic race card and slapped that shit down like the big joker in a spades game!"

Asshole!

"When did I say that? I would never say somethin' like that!" Now he looks like he's getting angry at me.

The utter fucking gall!

"So, you won't say it, but you'll say that her saying it isn't that bad?"

"I didn't say that neither! I said that *she* ain't that bad. The shit that was said tonight is not somethin' that I'm tryin' to excuse. I'm pissed that she even thought that shit, let alone said it." He takes a deep breath and I can see him trying to calm down. "How could you think that I'd be okay with that?"

"Because the people that you surround yourself with say a lot about the kind of person that you are. You know that she's a manipulative twat, but you're still friends with her!" I wish I had something to throw at him. Well, there's my purse, but it's not very heavy. "Why are you friends with her? What do you have in common other than the fact that you used to fuck each other?"

"Will you please just let me drive you home and we can talk about this?" He's begging.

I usually find begging to be pathetic. Why don't I find it pathetic or at least annoying when he does it? This has to be because of the alcohol in my system. I'm a very horny drunk. It would explain why instead of holding on to my anger, I'm feeling all tingly at the sound of his voice and that fucking begging. I look down in an attempt to clear my thoughts. I can't locate my very justifiable anger if I keep focusing on his eyes and his lips and his hands. Fuck, fuck, fuck!

"No," I shake my head and mentally congratulate myself on not stumbling.

"Baby, please, just let me take you home."

I feel his hand on my cheek. This is what I get for looking away. I should have kept my eyes on him and then he couldn't have snuck closer. I take a deep breath and his scent fills me. Damn it! Jonah isn't a big cologne guy, but he does use aftershave. It smells a little like cinnamon. I love that smell. Just damn it!

"Okay, you can give me a ride home. But while you're driving, you're going to need to be telling me something other than 'she's not that bad' if we're going to be okay." I snatch my phone out of his hand and walk over to his truck.

He must have already told his parents that he was leaving, or he's afraid that if he goes back in the house for any reason, I might pull a Flo Jo and set a record getting the fuck away from this house. He helps me into the truck and walks around to climb in on the other side. My vertically challenged, tipsy ass was not going to be able to climb up in this thing without some help. Jonah drives a Silverado with tires that are in no way factory standard. Just one more thing that proves he's an asshole. Who the hell needs a vehicle that sits up this high?

He starts talking as soon as he pulls away from the house. "I'm her only actual close friend at the moment."

I sit up. "What?"

Jonah groans and scrubs a hand roughly down his face. "Kaylin. You once asked me if I was her only friend and I said that I wasn't. She doesn't have any other close friends anymore. There was a falling out earlier this year and she lost a lot of friends. She's got sisters and cousins, but I'm her go-to friend right now."

That is not a surprise. "Why do you think that is?"

"Because she's fucking impossible. I know that. She needs to be the center of attention for every person in her life and she has tantrums when she doesn't get her way." He shakes his head at his own words.

I'm waiting for him to continue with a positive attribute, but he doesn't say anything else. "How the hell did you date her for four years?"

He rubs a hand across his forehead before gesturing. "It was off and on. My friend's girlfriend hooked us up. I knew the relationship was doomed pretty early on and I ended things, but then we got back together after we hooked up at a party where I'd had a few too many. Every few months we'd break-up and then we'd get back together after she'd start calling me or her friends would start calling me, or there'd be a drunken hook-up...I always knew we weren't suited though."

"Then why did you ask her to marry you?" Their relationship sounds like a version of hell.

It takes him a full two minutes to answer me. "Because she was pregnant."

"Oh." *Yeah, that's what I said. He tells me that they were going to have a baby, and my response is, 'oh'.* That admission actually manages to stir some jealousy in me. Which is just bizarre. Trying to shake it off, I wrap my arms around myself and take a deep breath. "She lost it?"

"No. After we got officially engaged... you know, I bought her a ring and we told our families and friends, she had an abortion. She didn't wanna get married after the baby was born because she didn't want all of her neighbors and church missionary board members and the fucking clerk at Kroger to judge her for having a baby before she was married, and she didn't wanna just go down to the courthouse because she had this whole perfect picture of a June wedding in her head," he laughs sardonically.

"You broke things off because she had an abortion?" We've never really talked about our views on this subject.

"Yes and no. I wasn't ready to be a father, and I damn sure didn't want to marry her, but it seemed like the right thing to do when she came to me crying about being pregnant and alone. We weren't together when it happened. Not really. We were still sleeping together sometimes, but she wasn't my girlfriend." He glances at me like he's trying to gauge my reaction. I raise my eyebrows and wait for him to continue.

"If she'd have told me that she wanted to have an abortion...I can't honestly say if it would have upset me. She was twenty-four, with no job, and pregnant by a guy that wasn't even her boyfriend." He rubs a hand over the top of his head. "She had the abortion a few weeks after she told me she was pregnant, but she didn't tell me that she had it until damn near four months later. She knew I was only marrying her because of the baby, and she only told me because I told her that I wanted to tell my parents about the kid before she started to show. She was sitting in my living room showing me samples of wedding invitations when she admitted it."

"How in the hell can you still be friends with her after that?" I wouldn't let her anywhere near me.

"I said some really cruel shit when I ended things, and she thought that I was angry because she ended the pregnancy. I wasn't angry about it. I understood. Like I said, I wasn't ready to be a father and our relationship had way too many problems for it to work for very long. There was no way that I was gonna marry her if there wasn't a kid involved in the situation. I threw her out of my apartment and then I got a call from her mom that night saying that she had taken a bunch of pills and was in the hospital."

"She seriously tried to kill herself?" Given the situation with Mark a few months ago, I begin to feel some sympathy for Kaylin.

"After she got out of the hospital, she started seeing a therapist. I went to a couple of sessions with her, and she finally got that I didn't hold anything against her. After a lot of very long talks, she started saying that she only had the abortion because she knew that it was what I wanted, and while I told her that I didn't wanna be with her ever again, I agreed that we could stay friends. Shit had been going okay." He shrugs a shoulder and rubs his thumb along his eyebrow.

"Define, okay." I'm still not believing that they were able to have a functional friendship.

"We hung out sometimes. We'd grab lunch together every once in a while. Her family likes me, so I would go to barbecues and birthday parties for them, I even went with her to a few of the games for the team that Jim coaches, she helped me pick out my dining room set. Typical friend shit."

"So, then what changed?" What, one day they were all kumbya-ing it over dining room sets and varsity games, and the next day she's being clingy and racist?

He thinks about it for a minute before looking over at me. "I met you."

Um... "I'm not the first female that you've been with over the past three years."

"No, you're not, but I haven't talked to her about anyone but you. I talked to her after I met you for the first time and I was going on and on about how pissed off I was at myself for freezing up the way I did. That had never happened to me before. When I saw you at the club, I was there with a few of my friends and decided to take a shot at talking to you and hoped that I wouldn't freeze again. I was fucking ecstatic after you gave me your number. I wanted to call you that night. I told her about it the next afternoon when I saw her."

"And then she called you with an emergency at the butt crack of dawn and you rushed right off," I snark.

He heaves a sigh. "Yeah, something like that."

Not something like that, exactly that. This girl is acting like they're still a couple and I'm trying to steal her boyfriend. "I think that the issue is that she still sees you as her boyfriend."

"That's insane. I haven't been with her in over three years and she's engaged."

I turn in my seat to face him more fully. "Okay, I'm a little nice right now, so I'm going to do my best to explain this to you clearly. You dated this broad—"

"Broad?" He laughs.

"Yes, broad. It's slang for prostitute." Fun fact.

He looks at me wide eyed. "Seriously?"

"Okay, so in the 20's, cards were called broad backs or broads for short. They started referring to prostitutes and showgirls as broads because they were often on their backs. Get it?"

"Huh. You learn something new every day." He nods.

"Getting back to my point. You dated the broad for four years, off and on. You kept fucking her even after you ended things with her. You asked her to marry you and reluctantly resigned yourself to having a family with her. Then you ended things after she decided to terminate the pregnancy without telling you, but she guilt tripped you, and you agreed to be her friend. You kept attending her family functions, going out to eat together, and didn't appear to be dating anyone else, but you weren't sleeping with her anymore. I'm assuming here?" I wait for him to confirm my assumption.

"No, I wasn't sleeping with her anymore." He sounds annoyed that I sought confirmation on my assumption.

'Cause it was totally unreasonable. Right. "So, you're not doing the grown-up anymore, but she's the main female in your life outside of your family members. She's even helping you pick out furniture. She meets Big Jim and starts asking you to accompany her to games that he coaches and gets you to do various other third-wheel shit. She gets engaged, you get a girlfriend, and she becomes needy as hell."

"Nice synopsis. Do you have a point?" He glances at me and then back at the road.

Do I have a...? "Yeah, dick, I do! She has been waiting around this whole time for you to realize that you still love her and want to marry her. She started dating the coach to make you jealous. That's why she invited you to his games and on their dates. He asked her to marry him and she said yes, probably thinking that it would snap you out of your reluctance to do the couple thing again and make you realize that if you didn't do something then she would be out of reach forever. Instead, you start dating some woman that couldn't be more polar opposite of her if we were created by DC to be archenemies," I ignore his laughter and continue, "so, she reacts by creating personal drama and pulling you into it in an effort to sabotage both of your relationships."

He reaches out the window to put in his gate code, and that's when I realize that this sneaky bastard did not take me home. Not to my home, anyway. I should have been paying attention to my surroundings instead of trying to untangle the jumbled-up Christmas lights of a friendship that he has with female Doofenshmirtz. While we had initially planned to spend this four-day weekend together, I feel that in light of recent events, that plan needs to be reconfigured. This conversation that we've been having has not changed the fact that I'm angry and hurt and want to go home.

Jonah pulls up in front of his apartment and gets out of the truck. I watch him reach into the backseat and grab my bag with my clothes before coming around to my side. I cross my arms and stare straight ahead. I'm not getting out of this truck. I hear him huff as he closes my door. Then I watch him open his front door and go inside. With. My. Bag. What in the hell? I know he doesn't think that I'm gonna get out of this truck and follow him inside just because he's kidnapping my clothes!

He comes back out and opens my door. I keep staring straight ahead. He reaches across me, unbuckles my seatbelt, forces me to uncross my arms, pulls me out of the truck, throws me over his shoulder, grabs my purse from the truck, pushes the door closed, and carries me into the apartment.

What in the caveman hell?

Tossing my purse on an end table, he continues on to the loft.

"Jonan—"

He slaps my ass when I try to straighten up. "Shut up and be still before you make me drop you."

Has he lost his mind? "Put me down!"

He begins climbing the stairs. "I plan on it."

"This is really uncomfortable." Bouncing on someone's shoulder with a stomach full of margaritas is not something that I would voluntarily do or ever recommend. Just a piece of friendly advice.

"Then I guess next time you'll get out of the damn truck!" He drops me onto the bed and reaches down to remove my shoes.

I want to kick him, but I don't actually want to hurt him. My feet release their own sigh of relief when my stilettos drop to the floor. Next, he's unbuttoning my pants and pulling them and my panties down my legs. He tosses them over his shoulder, and then he's pressing his face between my legs and thrusting his tongue into me.

Fuuuuuck! I can feel my anger, which had already gone from a boil to a simmer, evaporating. I slap at him in an attempt to hold onto it, but he reaches up, pulls down the cup of my bra, and pinches my nipple with one hand while he sucks my clit into his mouth and pushes two fingers from his other hand into me. My anger flashes me the peace sign and jumps on the train to orgasm junction as every muscle that I have clenches and releases. I'm probably screaming, but there's no sound on the planet right now, so I really can't be sure.

My body goes limp and I close my eyes. He's not done. He removes the rest of my clothes and I hear the foil package opening. I moan as he kisses his way up my body. Reaching my mouth, he nibbles my bottom lip before licking it.

"Open your eyes and look at me." He breathes the words against my mouth and my eyes open as if his wish is my command. He strokes his thumb along my cheek and stares into my eyes. "I'm sorry and I love you so fucking much that it feels like I can't breathe without you."

He's inside of me before I can even begin to digest his words. He tells me how much he loves me again and again while he moves slowly inside of me. Fuck, he's so big. Isn't my body supposed to adjust to this feeling at some point? I'm not so sure. All I know is that he's so deep in me that it almost hurts. He's all I can feel and all I can see and all I can hear, and he's driving me higher and higher until I scream my orgasm into his mouth.

Jonah keeps moving. He starts thrusting harder, moving faster, holding me tighter. The headboard is beating out a steady rhythm against the wall and I bite down on his shoulder as another orgasm rolls through me. Jesus Christ!

Jonah groans against my neck. "Fuck, I love makin' you come. You feel so good on my cock, baby."

"Jonah...Oh God!" Those are the only words that I'm capable of speaking.

He shifts his hands to my lower back, sits up on his knees, and pulls me up and into his lap. Wrapping his arms around my waist, he holds me tightly to him while thrusting up into me. Sliding my hands into his hair, I move up and down on him. I feel myself pulse around him when he slaps my ass.

"I'm gonna come so fuckin' hard in you." He licks his way into my mouth, and I feel his finger rubbing against my clit. His cock jerks inside of me and I feel myself falling over the edge again. My body is still trembling when everything goes dark.

Chapter Twenty-Nine:

Today, we're meeting with the realtor to see the condo that Jonah wants to buy. Thanksgiving was a week ago. To my knowledge, Jonah hasn't spoken to Kaylin even though she's been calling him and posting shit to Facebook. Before you ask, he tells me all the time that he loves me, and I haven't said it back. Fucked up, right?

I care a lot about Jonah, but love is a big word. I never thought I loved the ex, and after everything went down in flames and enough time passed for me to look at things objectively, I realized that while I cared about him, I was more used to him than anything. And I spent three years with that man. I didn't cry when we broke up. I was angry. I broke some stuff and bleached some stuff and donated his PS4 to Goodwill (I bought that damn thing as a birthday gift for him a month before I caught him cheating on me). But there was no heartbreak over the ending of the relationship. Even when I saw him with the suds slut recently, I wasn't hurt. I was outraged that he thought that we could be friends. He's been private messaging me on Facebook since the run-in and I haven't responded. I'm hoping that if I just ignore him long enough, he'll get the hint and go away.

Jonah pulls into a visitor's space in front of the building and gets out of the truck. It's not far from my job and there are restaurants and clothing stores in walking distance. Not like the stores near Atlantic Station, more like small boutiques and bistros. I like it.

Coming around the truck, he helps me down and leads me over to the sidewalk where a woman in a grey skirt suit is waiting for us. She has her hair pulled back in what can only be referred to as a severe bun. It's so tight that I'm not sure how she's managing to open her eyes. It's not the best look for her. She has pale skin, almost paper white, and jet-black hair. She smiles at us as we approach, and it does a lot to improve her appearance.

"Mr. McInerney, I'm glad that you decided to have another look at the property. And, this must be Ms. Blaire. I'm Shelby Richards." She offers me her hand.

Shaking her hand, I return her smile. "Hello, it's nice to meet you. And thanks for coming out at the end of the day. I know it was probably a pain."

She waves that off. "It's really no problem. I'm a realtor. There are no set hours, and the seller was happy to accommodate."

We follow her into the building and wait for her to use a keycard to open the interior door. There's a comfortable looking sitting area, with a few couches in burnt orange and butternut yellow leather and coffee tables. She waves at a man sitting behind what looks like a concierge desk and leads us over to another set of doors. Out comes the keycard again and we're walking through the doors and waiting for an elevator. She hits the button for the twentieth floor and starts rattling off facts about the building's construction and the neighborhood. All the different shops, the schools, the fitness room, security measures, and pools. When we get to the door of the condo, I'm sure that I could pass a test about the area and the building.

Stepping into this condo, I have every intention of saying that it won't work for me and sticking with the apartment that I've already chosen for myself. That conviction flies south for the winter when I step into the large open space. The entire front wall is a window. The view is amazing. I can honestly see for miles from up here, and I am not a girl that is normally fond of heights.

"Wow."

Jonah wraps an arm around my waist. "Beautiful, right?"

"It's nice," I say. He responds by laughing under his breath at my obvious understatement.

The floor is a light hardwood. I'm going to guess its oak. It's aesthetically pleasing, but I have concerns.

"You know that I tend to go barefoot when I'm at home, right? Does this hardwood go throughout the entire condo? That's going to be cold."

Ms. Richards addresses that concern before Jonah can even open his mouth. "There's radiant floor heating throughout the unit."

She just shut that concern all the way down. I ignore Jonah's smirk and take in the rest of the space.

At the far end of the room is a fireplace set into the wall and surrounded by white and gray granite. There's a dining area that's separated from the kitchen by an island of the same color granite, and the kitchen has gray, glass front cabinets, black stainless-steel appliances and a wine fridge. There's a laundry room just past the kitchen. This place has three bedrooms, but I know that Jonah wants to use one as an office. There are two guest bathrooms, both with a bathtub and shower, a granite vanity, and subway tile. There is also a half bath or powder room near the laundry room. The master bedroom has a fireplace and that same floor to ceiling wall length window. The master bath is a thing of beauty. Heated floors, claw foot tub, huge shower with a bench seat, a walk-in closet with built in cedar drawers and shelves. There's also a large closet in the actual bedroom.

When I look at Jonah, the expression on his face says that he knows that he has me.

"Damn it!" My Atlantic Station apartment waves goodbye and fades into the distance.

He fist pumps. "I knew you'd love it!"

In an attempt to appear in control of this situation, I place my hand on my hip and stand firm. "This is my closet, and I'm not cleaning those windows."

Jonah grabs me and kisses me. "Deal."

Ms. Richards clears her throat. "Does that mean that you'd like to make an offer? The owner of this unit is looking for a closing date around the second week of January. She doesn't want to give possession before that. She'll be moving out of the country for work and has a considerable amount to do before then."

Holding my hand, Jonah smiles at her. "Yeah, I'd like to make an offer."

Her face lights up, but she quickly puts her professional face back on. "That's wonderful! Now I do think that she'll be willing to cover the closing costs on this, but I think that you should offer her asking price. This place is listed at ten thousand under what other units in this building have gone for."

He squeezes my hand and pulls me in front of him. "Yeah, that sounds good. If she's willing to pay the closing costs that's great, but if not, it's not a deal breaker."

We look around one more time before the realtor escorts us out. I can't help but bounce a little in my excitement. Crazy, right?

Two hours later, we're sitting in Jonah's living room, me with a glass of wine and him with a beer, talking about the condo. I have kicked off my shoes and taken the pins from my hair, letting my coils fall free. There's a lot that needs to be worked out. My lease ends in January, but his doesn't end until March. The buyer is looking to relinquish ownership in January, which is good for me but not practical for him. Also, I hadn't intended to buy property anytime soon, but I can't live with him and not take on some of that responsibility.

"Baby, it's not like I'm expectin' you to sign mortgage paperwork." Jonah takes a sip of his beer and leans back into the couch.

I sit my glass down and fold my legs under me. "Okay, but then what are we doing?"

"What do you mean? We're movin' in together. You already agreed. No backin' out on me."

I swat at him when he squeezes my thigh. I am not trying to let him distract me right now. Thankfully, I'm still on my first glass of wine and can fight the temptation to throw my panties at him. Jonah is all about the celebrating right now. I guess he didn't think he'd be able to get me to say yes to living together, even with a potential move-in date that's a month away.

"I mean that we've been together for two months, so moving in together is crazy as hell, but I'm still willing to do it, as long as we can work some things out." My words end on a laugh as he wrestles one of my legs from under me and nearly falls off the couch. He did manage to keep his beer from spilling.

He takes another sip and then sits his beer next to my wine. He studies me for a second and then tugs my ankle until I slide closer. "First of all, we been together for longer than some two months. Second, you don't need to sign any mortgage papers, but we can split utilities and food costs. Once we move in, if you wanna pay a portion of the mortgage, then great. If not..." he bites his lip and smiles at me, "well I'm gonna need you to learn to cook somethin' that ain't breakfast food."

Did I ever tell you that Jonah gets the cutest country accent whenever he drinks? It really is adorable. His accent is usually really light but get a few beers in him and he goes full CMT.

"I'd honestly rather pay a portion of the mortgage than try to learn to cook." I am totally serious. "And, it has only been two months."

"Autumn, baby, it's been damn near four months. We spent the night together at the beginnin' of August, and even though there was no sex, there were definitely orgasms." He leans forward and nips at the side of my neck. "Several orgasms."

I squirm and try to keep to the topic at hand. "Yeah, but then you dropped off the planet on me, and then there was that week that we weren't speaking..."

"That week that you wasn't speakin'," he corrects me. "I was callin' and textin' you the whole time. I even sent flowers and chocolates. Not that any of that matters 'cause we been together for just under four months, and by the time we move in together, we'll be at five months. Why does that matter anyway?"

It matters. It does. I know that it does. It's just that he's gone back to kissing my neck, and I can feel his erection, and so I'm having a very hard time formulating a thought. I didn't even know that he was unbuttoning my blouse until his mouth closes on my nipple. Sliding my hands into his hair, I resolve to continue this conversation later. I'm sliding a hand toward his belt when someone rings his doorbell. At first, we ignore it, but whoever's on the other side starts pounding on the door and ringing the doorbell incessantly. I have a feeling that I know who it is.

Jonah pushes himself off of me with a curse and goes to answer the door while I button my blouse. I hear him saying that this isn't a good time. I hear him saying that she should call him next week. I hear him let her in. I cannot locate the manners that I was raised with. Both my mother and my grandmother would be so ashamed. In an attempt to squelch the flame steadily growing in my stomach, I pick up my glass of wine and down it as they come into view.

Jonah's expression is once again full of apology and it gives me pause. Is this what I'll have to deal with if I move in with him? Her just popping up all the time and interrupting whatever life we're trying to have together? Do I want to deal with that? Would it be right for me to ask him to cut her completely out of his life? I mean, his family doesn't really like her, and his other friends give her a wide berth from what I understand, but none of them live with him. She isn't as big a pain in their asses as she's certain to be in mine if I have to deal with this kind of thing all the time.

Kaylin looks at me and flutters her eyelashes while placing a hand to her chest. "Oh, Autumn, I'm so sorry to interrupt. I had no idea that you'd be here."

And it's in that moment that I realize the gift that I'd be giving her if I decided not to move forward with Jonah. All the things that I would be giving up if I walked away from this gorgeous, funny, and successful guy just because I hate his ex. That can go right to hell.

Standing up, I give her a huge smile. "How could you have known? I mean, it isn't like we've moved in together yet. That's still about a month off."

I watch as she all but chokes on her tongue. Jonah gives her a strange look and pats her on the back. "You alright?"

She looks like she's going to be sick. "You're moving in together?"

Walking over to them, I wrap my arms around Jonah's waist, and I couldn't stop smiling if you paid me. "Yup! Isn't it great? We went and looked at the condo today. It's gorgeous!"

Jonah gives me a kiss. "You're gorgeous."

My heart flutters. It actually flutters. The last time my heart fluttered was in the seventh grade when Devon Jenkins kissed me on the cheek and said that I was the most beautiful girl in our school.

She takes a few steps forward, looking lost. "You looked at a condo? Together? You're buying a place together?" Kaylin's purse drops to the floor with a clunk. "Is there wine?"

I nod happily, pretending not to notice her discomfort, and pull Jonah back over by the couch. "Of course, we were just celebrating. I'll bring you a glass."

When I get to the kitchen, I hear Jonah excuse himself before following me. I turn around humming *Scars to Your Beautiful* and holding the wine glass that I grabbed for the unwanted one. Grabbing the stoppered wine bottle from the fridge, I raise my eyebrows at him in question and wait to hear what he has to say.

"Enlighten me." He looks at me curiously and leans back against the counter with his arms folded.

Putting my collected items next to him on the counter I lean into him and wrap my arms around his neck, linking my fingers together. "I came to a realization."

"About...?" He wraps his arms around my waist and spreads his legs a little so that I can get closer to him.

"I hate the fact that your ex-girlfriend seems to pop up whenever something significant is happening between us. It's like she has hidden cameras planted in your apartment." I'm only half joking about that. "And, I started thinking, do I want to live like this? Do I want her just popping up to our home that we share the way she does here, especially given the Thanksgiving debacle?"

He looks wary now. "And?"

I shrug. "And, she's not the biggest part of your life. You're smart and funny and caring..."

"And capable of givin' you screamin' orgasms," he says with a grin.

"There is that," I laugh before becoming serious again. "The fact is that as much as I can't stand her, I'm not willing to sacrifice our relationship just to be rid of her. That being said, when we do move in together, if she pops up in the middle of the night because of personal issues, she is not coming in."

He leans down and kisses me. "I can agree to that," he whispers against my mouth.

Going up on my tip toes, I kiss him back. I love the way Jonah kisses. His lips are full and firm, and his tongue moves into my mouth like he's taking ownership of it. Every time he kisses me it's like a silent conversation is happening between us.

Him: *Are you really choosing this, choosing me?*

Me: *Absolutely and without a doubt.*

Him: *This is only the first step toward everything that I want with you.*

Me: *I know, but you have to be patient with me. Give me time.*

Him: *I want so much more with you. I want everything.*

Me: *What if I can't give you everything?*

> **Him:** *You can. You want to. You're just afraid, but you don't need to be afraid with me. You're already mine, you just need to admit it.*

A throat clearing behind me breaks us apart. I stare into his eyes, breasts heaving as I try to catch my breath. He strokes his thumb across my cheek before kissing me on my forehead and looking at the woman that interrupted us. Again.

Kaylin's voice is filled with censure. "I hate to interrupt, but I was starting to feel abandoned."

Turning to the counter, I unstop the bottle and pour a liberal amount of the merlot into the glass that I grabbed for her. Suddenly, I'm happy that we didn't get champagne. I would hate to waste the Moet on her.

"Sorry about that. We got distracted." Handing her the glass, I leave them in the kitchen and take the bottle with me to refill my own glass. I'm going to need it. I'm a mellow drinker. The more I imbibe, the more I love everyone.

When I sit down on the couch, Jonah's phone starts ringing, and I see the realtor's name on the screen. Before I can yell for him, he comes running into the living room and answers the phone. I take a sip of my wine while I listen to his end of the call.

"She accepted? ...yeah...yeah, I'm fine with that. I have a person that can do the inspection. Wonderful, yes...thank you again!" He hangs up the phone and beams at me. "We got it!"

I take a large gulp of my wine, sit the glass down, and launch myself at him. He hoists me up and I wrap my legs around his waist. I can't believe that I'm so happy about something that I didn't even think I'd want when I woke up this morning. I was all set to take the apartment in Atlantic Station and keep grabbing scraps of Jonah's time and throwing him scraps of mine.

If I'm honest, I h8adn't seriously given any thought to us living together even though I told him that I'd consider it. Shitty, right? But then I saw the condo and actually pictured myself living there with Jonah. Not having to fall asleep talking to him on the phone, unless he was away on business. Not having to pack a bag just to spend time with him. Not getting home from work and wanting to see him but being too tired to take that drive. Laughing when he gets annoyed with me because he's trying to cook, and I keep snacking on his ingredients. I am so ready for us to live together.

Jonah is laughing against my mouth. "Tell me that this ain't just 'cause of the closet."

Smiling, I waggle my eyebrows at him. "Oh, this is totally because of the closet."

"I love you, too."

"So! I take it that congratulations are in order?" Kaylin is standing just inside of the living room and takes a drink of her wine as if she's trying to rid her mouth of a really bad taste. "You'll have to tell me where you're registering for your housewarming."

I refuse to let her ruin my good mood. I'm sure that my mother, grandmother, sisters, and my aunt will have a lot to say about my decision to live with a man that I've been with for all of three and a half months, according to Jonah's timeline, but I'm an adult and I've made my decision.

"Do you want to have a housewarming?" I direct the question to Jonah and wrinkle my nose.

He shakes his head. "I really don't think that's our style."

I agree. We're really not housewarming people. "Your dad's going to do the inspection?"

Kaylin decides to give her unsolicited opinion. "If you're buying a place, then you obviously have to have a housewarming."

Jonah turns to face her with me still wrapped around him. "A housewarmin' is not required for purchasin' property. 'Sides, I'm sure that my parents'll come over for dinner once we're all moved in, and we can have Autumn's mom come for a visit after we're settled. Done."

Despite Jonah having answered her, she continues to address me. "Autumn, I know that you don't really have any family here, but Jonah has family and friends that are going to want to see this *condo* that you're getting him to buy. I mean, you've known each other for about three minutes and suddenly you're buying property together? I'm sure it'll go a long way to easing everyone's minds and clear up any questions about motivations."

Jonah tenses and I wiggle until he puts me down. Little Miss Moment Ruiner is killing my buzz, so I'm going to go and take a shower and lie down before she completely kills my happy.

But first. "Look, I get that you're probably having some totally overblown and self-created drama unfolding as the rest of us are enjoying life, but I am really not in the mood to even feign sympathy for you. You are a self-centered pain in the ass, and I'm pretty sure that you have the potential to be a bunny boiler. That being said, I'm going to remove myself from this room before I waste my wine by throwing it in your face."

Picking up my glass, I top it off and take it upstairs with me. I don't even feel a little bad about the things that I just said to her. I don't feel bad about the fact that Jonah will probably have to defend or sidestep any of my words. Fuck it. This bitch couldn't even pull any southern hospitality out of her ass long enough to fake real happiness for her *friend*. I say it that way because it is still crystal clear to me that she sees Jonah as way more than a friend. And saying that I'm *getting* him to buy a condo? What the hell is that about? Does she think that just because she's a manipulative skank, all women are manipulative skanks?

By the time I reach the loft, the sound has returned to the living room. Jonah starts it and I'd feel bad for listening, but they know that this apartment has an open loft as the master suite and they're not exactly speaking in low tones, so...

"What do you mean, that she's 'gettin' me to buy? And what questions regardin' motivations? I'm a grown ass fuckin' man in case you missed it, and I'm capable of lookin' out for myself." He sounds angry.

"Really? That's what you wanna talk about? What about all that stuff that she just said to me?"

"You don't think that how Autumn feels about you is even a little bit justified?"

"No, I do not! I have been nothin' but nice to her!"

"What about that shit on Thanksgivin'?! You call that nice?" His voice is filled with disbelief.

"Oh my gawd! I told you that I didn't mean anything by the whole different food thing! Those margaritas your mom made were really strong and I wasn't thinking, and Jimmy feels terrible about the race card comment! It just came out! Some of the kids that he coaches are black. He doesn't treat them any differently that he treats the other players."

"Oh my...fuck! You really just don't get it!" He yells.

"Get what?!" She screeches.

"I'm really not 'bout to break down all the ways that the shit you just said was fucked up, 'cause you still ain't gonna get it. I'd have an easier time puttin' my head through a brick fuckin' wall!"

"So that's why you haven't been answering my texts and calls? She's playing the victim over some misplaced words and you decide to just be over our friendship?"

"Kaylin—"

"You're my best friend! And you just let her talk to me like—"

"Like, what? Like she's fed up with your shit? Newsflash, she's fed up with your shit! You came to my house with a suitcase on a weekend that you knew she'd be here, brought up our bullshit engagement, and then crashed our date! And that was the first time you met her!"

"So now our engagement was bullshit?"

"When was our engagement not bullshit?"

"Why did you even ask me to marry you if you felt like our relationship was bullshit?"

"Because you showed up to my apartment cryin' and tellin' me that you were knocked up from a night that I still can't even remember since I was smashed outta my damn mind on Jager!"

"Are you saying that you don't believe that I was pregnant? I had an abortion because it was what you wanted!"

"I never asked you to do that! And if it was somethin' that you did for me, then why the fuck didn't I find out about for four damn months?"

"Because...I...." Kaylin stutters.

"The more I think 'bout...I can't remember you even havin' any doctor's appointments for the baby."

"So, you think that I lied about being pregnant. That's basically what you're saying here, right?"

"Did you?"

"Do you really think that I'd do that, or is that just what *Autumn* thinks?"

"Autumn thinks that you still see me as your boyfriend."

"Well...maybe a part of me does, but can you really blame me?"

"Can I blame you?!" He sounds incredulous.

And with that, I walk into the bathroom, pull my hair into a ponytail holder on top of my head, and start the shower. This shit is like a Lifetime Movie, and I don't have the energy for it tonight. I've had a long week at work, I actually did end up wiring money to my cousin after my mother contacted me on her behalf. Mark signed us up to find a DJ for the office Christmas party after an email was sent out requesting additional volunteers because nothing was being done for the event. I don't even want to go, but now I've got to help plan the damn thing. Chelsea's replacement started this week. He's an idiot that is obviously either related to someone higher up or sleeping with someone higher up. I'm starting to appreciate the saying about the devil you know being better than the devil you don't.

Then I went to look at that condo with Jonah. That beautiful condo that's close to my job and Mark, and that would allow me to spend every day with an amazing man that loves me. Despite me still feeling like we need to come to an agreement on the financial aspect of us living together, I'm happy about taking this step with him. When I moved in with Kelvin it was more about finding an affordable housing solution after I wasn't chosen in the housing lottery in my senior year. He had already graduated and had started working a full-time job. We'd known each other for about a year and had been dating for half of that, so it made sense that we would take the next step and move in together. I should have gone ahead and moved into that crappy little two-bedroom apartment that my friend Brenna had found that was just off campus. Hindsight is a bitch. When I told her that I was going to move in with Kelvin, she was disappointed, but she figured that he and I were in love and wanted to be together. The truth was that his place was bigger, in a better location, and the building was filled with mostly young business people so that I wouldn't have to worry about parties happening while I was trying to study.

Turning off the water, I step out of the shower and notice the silence. I'm wrapping a towel around my body when Jonah walks into the bathroom. Raising my eyebrows at him, I wait.

He pushes his hands into his pockets. "She's gone. They'd like us to meet them at First Watch for breakfast, if you're okay with that."

I should have brought the bottle of wine with me. I pick up my glass from the bathroom counter and take a sip. "Why would I want to do that?"

"She says that they want to apologize."

I roll my eyes at him and start to dry myself off. "I'm really not interested in hearing some fake ass apology from either of those people. At this point, I'm done with subjecting myself to the Kaylin show, but feel free to attend without me."

"Come on, baby. You love First Watch," he cajoles.

"Yeah, which is why I don't want to ruin it by going there with someone that's constantly trying to ruin all of my happy moments." Seriously, how many times am I supposed to subject myself to the bullshit and sneak attacks?

"Please do this with me. This one last time and if she says anything even remotely rude, I'll never ask you to tolerate her presence again."

Grabbing my lotion, I leave the bathroom and sit on the side of the bed. "She told you that she still thinks of you as her boyfriend?"

"Yeah, but—"

I feel my eyes nearly bug out of my head. "But? How is there a 'but' in this situation?"

"***But*** I don't have any romantic feelings toward her." He sits next to me and drops his head into his hands. "Look, I need to do this, and I need you with me."

Wait, is this a closure thing? 'Cause that's what it sounds like. Maybe he's finally fed up with her shit the same way I am.

"Okay. I'll go to this breakfast, but whether she's nice or not, I don't want to be around her after this."

He nods. "I get it. Thank you."

"You're welcome," I grumble.

The next morning, I drag my feet getting ready to go out for breakfast. Putting my hair in a top knot, I pull on a pair of jeans and a t-shirt that says, *I can explain it to you, but I can't understand it for you.* Jonah raises an eyebrow at the shirt but doesn't say anything. In my defense, I packed this shirt for this weekend before this happy little breakfast was planned.

Kaylin and Jim are already sitting at a table when we get to the restaurant. They're wearing matching Christmas themed sweaters. It is literally the second day of December and they're both wearing sweaters with snowmen in Santa hats on them. Hers is pink and his is blue. It's damn near seventy degrees outside. It isn't even sweater weather! I hate these people. It's also 8:30 in the morning and I am not an early riser on the weekends. I have to force myself to move toward them and take the seat across from Jim when Jonah pulls out my chair. He sits next to me and gives my hand a gentle squeeze like he appreciates the effort that it's taking for me to be near either of these people.

Jonah hands me a menu and begins the greetings. "Good morning, Jim. How ya been?"

He looks at Kaylin before saying anything. "It's good, I mean, I've been doing good, and you?"

This is awkward. Thankfully we're saved by our waiter coming by to take our orders. I decide on a ham and gruyere omelet. If I have to sit through this joke of an apology, then I'm going to find some enjoyment somewhere.

The waiter leaves after filling our cups with coffee and letting us know that our food will be right out.

"Autumn, I want to apologize to you for last night. You know, if you were offended by anything I said?" Kaylin fidgets and bites her bottom lip before continuing. "I really don't know what came over me."

Jim pats her hand like he's trying to give her strength through this difficult encounter.

'Cause she didn't create this situation or anything.

Placing my elbows on the table, I prop my chin in my hands and give her a curious look. "What specifically are you apologizing for? Quite a lot was said last night."

She looks from Jim to Jonah as if she's waiting for one of them to save her. Jim dives in with a life preserver as Jonah leans back and takes a sip of his coffee.

"The important thing here is that you both can put aside your differences and agree to be civil to one another going forward. It doesn't matter what specifically was said as long as—"

"Oh really, Mr. Race Card? Is that how you see things? So, you don't think that her actual words should be apologized for, I should just be thankful that she's willing to apologize? And what the hell have I said to her that I need to apologize for?" I'm happy to report that I kept my voice down and while my tone was drenched in disdain, there were no traces of aggression. Positive steps.

He looks at Jonah like he's waiting for him to rein me in. Jonah just shrugs at him and continues to drink his coffee. And now I get it. This isn't about closure for Jonah, it's about closure for me. This is about me saying what I feel like I need to say, or not say, so that I can move on from both of these people without always thinking back and wishing I had said something or that he had said something. Well played, Jonah. Well played.

The waiter comes back with one of their specialty morning drinks for Kaylin and tells us again that our food will be right out. Before he has even stepped away from the table, Kaylin takes a stab at defending her own behavior.

"I was caught off guard last night. I wasn't expecting you to be there, and I just wanted to talk to my best friend after him shutting me out for a whole week, but then I get there and you're there, and I wasn't ready to even be around you after you called me a racist. That was very hurtful to me." She uses her napkin to dab at her eyes while placing her right hand over her heart. "And then I find out that you've convinced him to buy a condo and move in with you after the two of you have been together for all of two months, and my protective instincts kicked in. I was a little upset."

I have had just about enough of her trying to accuse me of manipulating Jonah. It's on the tip of my tongue to remind her that she's the one that trapped him into an engagement with a baby. The only reason that I keep the words on my tongue from hitting the air is because it's not my place to speak them. But, I'm over her acting like Jonah doesn't have a mind of his own.

Apparently, so is he. "I already told you that I had been thinking about buying a place. That being said, Autumn didn't convince me to do a damn thing. In fact, I had to convince her to even consider moving in with me, so I don't need your protection. And when you say racist shit, people are gonna form the opinion that you're a racist."

The table goes quiet after that little gem is thrown out there. Jim and Kaylin exchange looks as if they're each trying to prompt the other to say something. Kaylin loses the silent argument. I'm sitting back and enjoying my coffee when she addresses me again. I really don't understand why she keeps doing that, responding to me instead of responding to Jonah whenever he says something that she doesn't like.

"I've already apologized for my comments on Thanksgiving. Are you planning on holding them against me for the rest of my life?"

I finish my coffee before saying anything. "I personally don't feel that you can blame people for being who they are. That being said, I don't plan on even being around you beyond this morning."

Her eyes widen, and she looks to Jonah. "How exactly is that going to work?"

The waiter arrives with our food, but Jim and Kaylin don't seem to care whether or not everyone in this restaurant knows the details of our conversation, because Jim slams his hand down on the table and addresses Jonah in a voice that carries.

"You're a shitty friend! You just gonna stop speakin' to her over some chick that you been bangin' for a few months? She's been your best friend for three years!"

In case you missed it, it would appear that I'm some chick that Jonah has been banging for a few months. Classy.

Jonah's jaw is clenched, and his voice comes out in a threatening growl. "You got 'bout one more time to disrespect her 'fore I put you on your fuckin' back."

Jim leans forward and looks him up and down. "I ain't scared of you, boy."

"You ain't gotta be scared to get yo ass whooped," Jonah says as he leans in.

Okay, wow. That was really hot. I'm not one for grown people fighting. I feel that once you pass the age of twenty-one, you should be mature enough to settle things with words, but I also know that that isn't always realistic or possible. And given the fact that my hand has on occasion flown without forethought, I can't judge anyone for taking things beyond words. I place a calming hand on Jonah's forearm and ask the waiter to please bring us boxes for our food. The waiter does me one better and takes the food away to be boxed up and says that he'll bring it to the register for us.

Jonah stands from his chair and takes my arm, pulling me up. He gives Kaylin a look like he'd hit her if she was a guy. "I'm gonna leave 'fore I say somethin' too fucked up, but bottom line, this situation is on you. You wanna know how this is gonna work? Simple. Autumn doesn't wanna be around you, and since it makes perfect damn sense, she ain't gonna be around you, so you can't just pop-up at my place anymore, and once we move into the condo, you will never be invited over."

Taking my hand, he leads me to the register where the waiter has our food all boxed and bagged. I take the bag while Jonah pays for the food and we head out to his truck in the parking lot.

Is it weird that I feel bad? I don't like Kaylin, and Jim needs to stop defending bullshit, but Jonah is probably going to lose his friend. I take friendship very seriously. I don't want him to lose someone that's important to him, I just want him to stop allowing her to be antagonistic and intrusive.

"Are you sure about this?" I ask him after he opens my door for me.

"Sure about what?"

"Jonah, I'm positive that your friendship isn't going to survive."

He looks up at the sky and takes a deep breath before releasing it and looking at me. "Yeah, you're probably right. Look, after she and I talked last night, I realized that our friendship isn't healthy. I probably never should have even agreed to remain friends after things ended between us, but I felt so guilty about everything... taking a few steps back from that is a good idea."

I let him help me up into the truck and wait for him to get in on the other side. Before we pull out of the parking lot, I see Kaylin and Jim come out of the restaurant and head over to an F-150 with those seasonal reindeer antlers above the doors. It looks like they're arguing, but I can't be sure. Maybe they're just mutually bashing us. Whatever.

I sit back and feel the tension drain out of me. "So, what do you want to do after we eat?"

Jonah grins at me while he starts the truck. "I was thinking we should finish what we started before we were interrupted last night."

"So, breakfast and then sex. I am for this plan. Honestly, I'd be for doing that all weekend. Having sex and then stopping every once in a while for food breaks."

"That's my girl," Jonah laughs.

Chapter Thirty:

Mark and I are Christmas shopping at Perimeter Mall. His phone keeps going off, and he is one text alert away from throwing it over the second- floor railing. He and Henry had a fight. Their relationship has issues on top of issues.

Okay, so Henry and his wife had planned a family vacation to everyone's favorite Florida mousey theme-park for Christmas. This was planned, of course, before Henry's wife walked in on him letting Mark check his tonsils with his dick. The therapist that Henry is seeing with his wife feels that it would be a good idea for the trip to go on as planned. I think the therapist is a loon. Mark understands that Henry wants to spend Christmas with his kids, and he's all for it. He doesn't, however, agree that a family vacation with the wife is a good idea. Mark is feeling insecure. He thinks that if Henry goes on a vacation with his wife, then that may lead to him reconciling with his wife.

The phone chimes again and Mark pulls it out of his pocket. I snatch it out of his hand and turn it off, then put it in my purse.

"Autumn..."

I hold up a hand before he can go off on me. "I will give it back when we grab ice cream."

He takes a deep breath. "Fine. Tell me more about the condo."

We've already talked about this over lunch during the week at work. Granted, I focused heavily on the condo and its accoutrements, and I was very light on my reasons for deciding to move in with Jonah.

I sip my sweet tea. "What do you want to know?"

"I get that the place is nirvana, but I thought you were dead set against moving in with the sex god?" He tugs my sleeve and directs me to J. Crew.

I ignore the nickname that he's given Jonah.

"I was."

He raises his eyebrow at me and waits.

"If I tell you, you can't give me any shit about it."

He stops just inside the store. "Okay, we're gonna need to do ice cream now. It'll make the confession you're about to make so much sweeter."

"Whatever." I roll my eyes at him but follow him to Haagen-Dazs anyway.

After getting my mint chocolate chip ice cream with a gummy bear topping (don't judge me, it tastes great), I join Mark on a bench and people-watch as I eat. He allows it for about thirty seconds.

"Automation, spill!" He points his spoon at me.

"I just realized that I don't want to miss out on anything with Jonah," I say, trying to keep my voice as nonchalant as possible. By the look on his face I'm failing. And who am I kidding? This situation is not nonchalant. This is very fucking chalant!

He grins at me and eats a big spoonful of his ice cream. I hope he gets a brain freeze.

"Shut up!" I shove his shoulder. God, I think I'm even blushing.

"Just promise me that I can be the man of honor at the wedding."

I snort. "You can quit that right now. We're moving in together, not getting married."

"Autumn doesn't believe in marriage," a voice behind me says.

I say a quick prayer that the person behind me isn't who I know it is. Standing from the bench, I turn around and there he is. Again.

Kelvin Williams. Son of a bitch! He comes around to stand in front of me and nods a 'hello' to Mark.

"I thought you were only here for Thanksgiving." I say it in a way that lets him know that nothing would please me more than him leaving the state. He rubs the back of his head and I have to mentally command myself not to punch him in the crotch.

"Nah, we moved down here. We were going to wait until the baby was born, but Kendra was really unhappy being so far from her family so—"

"I don't care!" I see people turn to look at us and realize that I yelled that at him. I lower my voice before I end up on YouTube. "Why can't you just be normal and avoid me?"

Mark stands up and inserts himself between us. "I don't think that this is the place for this."

Kelvin leans around Mark to look at me and points a finger at him. "Is this your man?"

"How is that your business?" I frown at him.

"Come on, Sweet, I just want to talk," he says, still leaning around Mark.

"Don't call me that!" I give him a look of disgust. That's what he called me when we dated. What is wrong with him? "I don't want to talk to you. I'm good, you're good, move the fuck on!"

"You can't just give me a few minutes?"

Mark moves into his line of sight and flattens a hand against Kelvin's chest. "I really think it would be best if you left her alone."

Kelvin knocks his hand aside. "I think it would be best if you kept your hands to yourself, playboy."

I insert myself between them and try to get them both to back up a little. I'm having little to no effect. I told you that I'm a whole 5'3", and I'm not wearing heels. Kelvin is 6'4" and Mark is 6'1".

"I think it would be best if you went and checked on your pregnant wife and left my friend the hell alone!" Mark raises his voice and steps forward.

"You want me to leave your 'friend' alone, huh?" Kelvin pushes Mark and shoves me in the process.

Mark pushes him back. "Yeah, I do! What the fuck do you need to say anyway? What? You're sorry that you fucked a chick on her couch and now that she's pregnant and you married her, you're thinking that maybe that shit was a bigger mistake than you realized at the time?"

I'm still between them when the fight starts. Kelvin swings first. He's bigger than Mark, so I guess he thinks that the hit will level him.

It. Does. Not.

Someone's elbow catches me in the head and down I go. I try to catch myself, but I'm pretty sure that I just succeed in hurting my wrist. Just great! The fight pauses briefly when the two dumbasses realize that I've become collateral damage.

You would think that one of them would come over and try to help me out. No. It would appear that Tweedle Dumb and Tweedle Dumbass are blaming each other for knocking me down and are seeking to settle the matter by tearing up the whole damn sitting area. Kelvin throws a haymaker at Mark, but Mark dodges by ducking and plowing his shoulder into Kelvin's abdomen. They both go down. Kelvin has Mark in a headlock, but Mark is punching Kelvin in the ribs.

Aaaaannnnndddd, here comes security. If we get banned from this mall, I am gonna be pissed. You will not be surprised to learn that everyone has their cellphones out and pointed at the two idiot grown men that just got into a fight in a mall. I didn't even get to finish my ice cream. Someone finally helps me up. I am also LIMPING! *These motherfuckers have maimed me!*

The police are called, as is an ambulance. Mark made it out of the scuffle with a few cuts and bruises, but I've got a sprained ankle and a possibly fractured wrist, so I have to go to the hospital to have x-rays. Yay, me! I manage to give Mark his cellphone before being taken to the ambulance. He's being put in hand-cuffs and I promise that I'll come and get him, but he tells me not to worry about him. An officer comes with me and asks me questions the whole time I'm being loaded up. What happened? How did it start? Who was the aggressor?

I'm trying to answer the questions in a way that makes both men look good. There's no love lost between me and Kelvin, but I'm annoyed by the way that the cops are trying to act like he's some overly aggressive thug that was looking for trouble. Yeah, he was acting like a dick but I don't want him to go to jail when he's about to have a baby. He's not a bad guy. He's a cheating bastard and I really wish he would stop trying to be my friend, but he has good qualities. He also probably has a few broken ribs. I'll treat Mark to dinner as a thank you.

They take me to Northside Hospital and after three hours, I find out that my right wrist is indeed fractured. My ankle is okay though. It hurts a little but isn't sprained or twisted. They gave me pain meds, so I'm still in pain, but I'm high so I don't mind it as much as I probably should.

I've been calling police departments since I got to the hospital in an effort to find Mark, but every station that I call tells me that they don't have a record of him, and he isn't answering his phone so I'm freaking out. I call Jonah to come and pick me up since Mark drove us to the mall and my car is in the parking lot of his apartment building.

I'm sitting in my little curtained ER cubby when Jonah walks in looking frantic. That's my fault. I didn't give him any real information. I just told him that I needed him to pick me up from the ER at Northside Hospital.

Okay, so I didn't call him. I texted him. I didn't want to answer the questions that I knew he would have over the phone.

He rushes up to me and takes in the cast on my wrist and the bruise near my eye. "Baby, what happened?"

He helps me up and frowns when he notices me favoring my left leg. I grab my release forms and lean on him. He takes the forms from me and tries to get me to sit back down.

"Jonah, stop. What are you doing?"

"I'm gonna grab you a wheelchair. You're limping." He motions to my leg. "What the hell happened?"

"Let's just go to the car and talk about it on the way home." I start limping toward the exit.

I hear Jonah sigh before he scoops me up. I would insist that I can walk, but my ankle hurts, I'm feeling kind of loopy, and I don't want to. Ignoring the looks of the other people in the area, I lean my head against his shoulder and relax.

Once we're in the car and on the road, he looks at me and waits. And waits. "You're seriously gonna go silent on me?"

I release a breath. "My ex and his pregnant wife have moved to Atlanta."

He nods slowly. "Okay...and?"

"And he keeps trying to get me to be his friend." I look over at him for his reaction.

"Uh huh." He rubs his mouth but doesn't show any other reaction.

Now I feel like I have to elaborate, which I don't want to do since I never told him about running into the ex before Thanksgiving. It didn't seem like a big deal at the time. On top of that, I'm legit high as hell right now.

"Me and Mark saw him before Thanksgiving when we went shopping. We were in the food court and he came over to us and started talking about how his wife has family here and—"

"You said, keeps," he interrupts me.

"What?"

He looks at me before looking back at the road and I can see his irritation growing. "You said, 'he keeps trying'. Define, keeps."

"He came up to me at the food court talking about how we had too much history to just stop speaking to each other. His wife was with him." I feel the need to include that fact. "And he keeps private messaging me on Facebook and DM-ing me. I haven't responded so I guess when he saw us at the mall today, he decided to try to talk to me again."

"And then?" He makes a rolling motion with his hand.

"And then I told him to leave me the hell alone. Again. And he and Mark got into it because Mark suggested that he was regretting his marriage, blah, blah, blah. They started pushing each other and I got between them and ended up getting knocked down. They took me to the hospital, and I think they arrested Mark, but I can't find him and every police station that I call says that he isn't there, and I don't know what to do because people were taking videos with their phones and he was just trying to defend me." Oh, dear lord, I'm crying! It has to be the damn pain meds.

"Fuck, baby, don't cry." Jonah looks at me like he's at a total loss. "What kinda pain meds did they give you?"

"I don't know. They gave me a shot of something," I say with a sniffle. Fuck, I need a tissue. I suddenly wish I was one of those perky, over-prepared women that always has a pack of travel sized tissues and a first aid kit in her purse.

Jonah leans over and opens the glove compartment and hands me a bunch of napkins. The tears are refusing to stop. I probably look like a hot raggedy mess. I blow my nose loudly and grab for my phone when it starts ringing in my purse.

"Hello?" I hiccup.

"Hey, Autonomic, are you okay?" Mark's concerned voice comes to me over the phone and the tears stop like magic.

"Mark! What happened? Where are you?" I slap at Jonah in excitement.

"Okay, so the mall declined to press charges, so I'm free and clear in that regard, but they banned me for two years. If I go back before the two years are up, they'll press charges on me for trespassing." He's wincing, I know it.

"Two years! Are you fucking kidding me?" I slap my leg and Jonah looks over at me in concern. He's right to be concerned. I used my injured hand. Fuck, this hurts!

"I know!" Mark sounds as indignant as I feel.

"I'm so sorry!" Aaaaand I'm crying again.

Jonah takes my phone from me. "Yeah, Mark hey, are you okay? ...She's got a broken wrist...yeah....no, I think they must have given her some really strong ass pain meds...okay, I will...yup, bye."

We drive the rest of the way in silence. Well, near silence. I can't stop crying, so I keep sniffling. I don't even know why I'm crying. My wrist hurts, but it isn't that bad. This must be what it's like to do drugs and have a bad trip.

I must have fallen asleep, because I wake up in Jonah's bed and my phone is ringing. He managed to get my clothes off of me and put me into one of his t-shirts. My wrist is throbbing and so is my head. Something tells me not to answer my phone.

"Hello?" my mouth tastes like cotton and my voice is scratchy.

"You're on the internet." It's Angel. She got back to Georgia a few days ago. I don't know why she came back. She's going back to Jersey for Christmas in a few weeks and then moving into the dorms after the new year.

It takes me a second to realize what she said, but when I do, I sit up. "The hell!"

"Yup, there's video all over Twitter and YouTube. The comments are crazy." She sounds like she's eating popcorn.

"Ugh!" I flop back on the bed. Please don't let me get fired because of this.

"According to the security guard and eyewitness accounts, two men were fighting over you." She starts chewing again. "The black guy is cute. That your new man?"

"Goodbye, Angel." I hang up the phone and then turn it off before I'm tempted to check social media. I should just delete all of my accounts, then annoying ass people that I don't want to be bothered with wouldn't be able to contact me.

Getting up, I go to use the bathroom, brush my teeth ('cause damn), and try to find some Tylenol. It's after eleven o'clock. We left the hospital over five hours ago. My ankle feels much better, but this wrist and head situation is a problem. Jonah has no OTC pain meds in his bathroom, so I make my way downstairs. Slowly. I peak in Jonah's office on my way to the kitchen and see him sitting in front of three computer monitors, but he doesn't seem to be focusing on any of them.

I cautiously make my way into the room. I never really come in here. There are the three monitors that take up the surface of a dark chestnut desk as well as a laptop on a table that sits at the same height as the desk and has file cabinets. A fax machine, two printers, and a landline sit on built-in shelves. There are movie posters in this room too. *The Incredibles* on one wall and *The Lord of the Rings* on another. There are also *Legend of Zelda* and *Guardians of the Galaxy* figures still in the boxes on the shelves. A mini-fridge is on the floor near his desk, and I know that he stockpiles red bulls and cokes in there.

He doesn't notice me until I'm standing next to him. I see him glance at the time on the monitor in front of him before he rubs his hands down his face and shakes his head.

I run my fingers through his hair and give a little tug. It's longer than it was when we met and starting to curl. "Hey."

He gives me a half-smile and pulls me down into his lap. Leaning his face into my neck he breathes me in. "Hey. How you feelin'?"

"Like fried garbage. My wrist hurts, and you don't have any Tylenol."

He fingers my cast. "I've got aspirin." Reaching into a drawer, he pulls out a bottle of aspirin and sits it on the desk and then spins the chair a little so that he can reach into the mini-fridge and pull out a coke. Taking out two pills, he hands them to me and then pops the tab on the soda so that I can wash them down.

"The doctor at the hospital gave you a prescription for Oxy, but since whatever the hell they gave you at the hospital turned you into a weeping basket case, I decided not to fill it. I shredded it," he says unapologetically.

I doubt I would have taken it anyway, but still. "You didn't want to ask me first?"

"Nope." He kisses my shoulder. "You hungry?"

Before I can say something bitchy about him shredding a prescription for medication that I don't even want, my stomach growls and he laughs. Reaching around me, he saves files in the different programs that he has running before standing up with me and shifting me around so that my legs are wrapped around his waist.

I rest my head on his shoulder. "I can walk."

He snorts. "You can limp. Shut up and let me take care of you."

"So chivalrous," I say sarcastically.

"So argumentative," he shoots back. There's no playfulness detectable in his voice. He sits me down on the couch and hands me the remote for the tv and the can of coke that I didn't even realize he was still holding before leaving me alone and heading into the kitchen.

Once I'm alone I turn on the television and stall out. I mentally go over my relationship with Jonah. Am I purposefully difficult with him?

There was the week that I refused to speak to him even though he kept calling me and sending me flowers and candy. Honestly, I wasn't even that angry anymore by the time he sent the flowers, but I threw them out anyway and didn't call him, even though I missed him and really wanted to. We've had other arguments since then. Just stupid stuff, mostly, but I've often held onto things longer than necessary just for the sake of it. I told him that I'd think about living with him, but I didn't, not until we saw the place together and then all I could think about was how great it would be for us to live together. But over the last week, I've been second guessing the decision. It would be great to live with Jonah, but what if we break up a few months or weeks into it and I'm stuck looking for a new place? And if we do last, what happens to the plans that I have to take care of my mother? What happens if another family member gets dropped on me the way Angel was? Is he going to want to deal with that?

Jonah comes back into the living room and sits a bowl of soup on the table in front of me before sitting down next to me on the couch. "What are you watching?" he asks, sounding baffled.

Focusing on the television, I see an elderly woman selling sex toys. "I have no idea."

He laughs. "Aw, baby don't be shy. I'm all for us getting some toys."

I try not to laugh but fail when he starts waggling his eyebrows. "You're such a geek."

"Yeah," he smiles. "But, I'm your geek."

I bite my lip. "Do you really think I'm overly argumentative?"

"Yeah." He's still smiling at me. "You'd argue the date of Jesus's conception with the Virgin Mary."

"I would not!" I frown. "Though if you think about it, it's not like she'd know the actual date of conception. I mean, the bible says that an angel appeared to her and told her she was going to have a baby, he didn't tell her exactly when God started the oven timer."

He looks at me like I'm crazy for a second before bursting into laughter. He's clutching his stomach and everything. I hit him with one of the throw pillows on the couch. He's such an ass.

"You are crazy as hell!" He's gasping for air. "You can't even blame the pain medication for this!"

"Can I eat now?" I hit him with the pillow one more time. So, he proved his point. So, what?

He calms down enough to pick up my soup and hold out a spoonful, but his shoulders are shaking and he's still grinning.

"I can feed myself." I probably can't. My right wrist is broken, and it still hurts too much for me to really support anything with my right hand, so I can't hold the bowl, and the coffee table is too far away for me to lean over it and eat unless I sit on the floor.

He raises an eyebrow at me and hands me the bowl. I ignore his smug look and try, unsuccessfully to feed myself. Finally, I manage to get the bowl back on the coffee table and slide onto the floor to eat my soup. Jonah laughs again and slides down on the floor to sit next to me.

"This is really good. What is it?" I ask.

"Potato bacon soup. I heated up some rolls too. Want some?" He stands up and heads back to the kitchen before I answer and comes back with four rolls on a saucer.

"I can't eat all four of those and this soup," I say as I grab a roll off of the saucer.

"We both know that you can, but two of them are for me." He takes a roll. "Now, getting back to your completely ridiculous question that you already know the answer to. Yes, you are at times unreasonably argumentative and you're also really stubborn, but I love you anyway."

"Gee, thanks," I grumble.

He shakes his head at me and grabs the remote. "You wanna watch *The Princess Bride*?"

"Since when do you have that movie?"

He shrugs and leans back against the couch. "Since you said it's your favorite movie."

Warmth literally spreads from my chest throughout my entire body. Yeah, he loves me.

Chapter Thirty-One:

I t's Thursday and the bruising on my face finally faded. I was able to cover it with make-up for the most part, and thankfully no one that I work with seems to have seen the video of that stupid fight. My wrist is still sore, but I'm able to use my hand, so all is not lost. My family members did see the video, though. It would seem that Daniel, that childish little asshole, showed it to my aunt, who told my mother about it, who then showed it to my sisters. They've all been calling and texting me trying to find out what really happened. I haven't answered my phone for anyone in my family in the past week.

Someone's Escalade is parked in my space when I get home, and I'm really not in the mood for it. The heel on my ankle boot broke when I was walking through the parking garage after work, and I spilled my latte on my silk blouse while I was driving. Burned the hell out of myself, and probably ruined my shirt, and now it's doing this slushy rain thing outside. I get out of my car and hobble quickly to my door. Dropping my things once I get inside, I pull off my shoes and start unbuttoning my blouse as I make my way to my living room. I need to call Jonah. He's out of the country on business. He left yesterday and won't be back until Monday or Tuesday. I miss him. Is it weird that I stole four of his shirts and have been sleeping in them? They smell like him.

I step into my living room and freeze. Kelvin is in my house. *How the fuck did Kelvin get in my house?* "What the hell?"

"Your cousin let me in before she left," he says while holding up his hands.

Before she left? That little demon seed let some man that she doesn't even know into my house and left? Is she really that fucking stupid? And why does he even know where I live?

"Who gave you my address?"

"I called your mother. She gave me the address and then she texted me the gate code." He looks sheepish.

Of course, she did! This is why I can't stand people. "Why won't you leave me the hell alone?"

He takes a step forward. "'Cause, I miss you."

I throw up my hands in frustration. "Well bully for you! I don't miss you! I'm good! Go away!"

He takes a deep breath and pinches the bridge of his nose.

Like I'm the problem here?

"I know that I hurt you, and I'm sorry. If I could do it over—"

"You can't! There are no do overs in real life." I notice that he's staring at my chest and I look down. Fuck, my blouse is open. I forgot that I'd been unbuttoning it when I walked in. Shaking my head at his tool bagginess, I button my stained blouse. "You need to leave."

"You really just want to throw away three years? I fucked up! It's not like I'm the first person in the history of the world to make a mistake! Sweet, come on..." he comes forward more. I hold up a hand to keep him back, and he sees the cast and winces. "Damn, baby, I'm sorry. It's broken?"

Does he think that the cast is a fashion choice? I look at him like he's stupid. "Yeah, it's broken. Goodbye."

"Dude that was with you is your man?" He seems offended by the prospect. "So, you'll give a white guy the ass, but I can't even talk to you?"

"What does one have to do with the other?" I seriously don't get the connection. "And I already told you that I wish you well, but I don't want to be friends. Good luck with your marriage and your baby—"

"I'm not even with her like that anymore!" He cuts me off.

"She's pregnant!" I say, outraged. Is he out of his mind?

"I only got with her because shit between you and me was all fucked up!" He throws his hands up and takes a few steps back before coming forward again.

"Wait, you're blaming me for the fact that you cheated on me? Shit between us wasn't going well, so instead of just telling me that you didn't want to be with me anymore, you bring a chick into my house?" I can feel the look of disbelief that is on my face. Kelvin graduated magna cum laude, he is not this stupid.

"I still wanted to be with you! I still want to be with you right now! I was just frustrated with where we were at and the fact that you didn't seem to understand how much I loved you. Come on, Autumn! I was try'na marry you. Every time I brought it up, you changed the subject or started talking about divorce rates and shit. We hadn't had sex in almost two months when I started fuckin' with her. When I tried to talk to you after you walked in on us, you fuckin' pepper sprayed me and then you destroyed half of my shit and moved out while I was at work and changed your number!"

Gotta admit, these zingers are finding targets. But they don't change the fact that he is a cheating ass dirtbag that I don't trust and that isn't the man for me.

"You know what? I will own all of that. But that doesn't change the fact that you're a liar and a cheater that I don't want to be with."

He shakes his head. "I don't believe that. We were together for a long time. Your mother and your sisters love me, and my parents still ask about you. Maybe if I hadn't seen you again, I'd believe that we aren't supposed to be together. But the fact that I keep running into you has to mean something."

"No, it doesn't mean a damn thing. I have a man that makes me very happy and I have moved on. You have a pregnant wife. Either make that shit work or find a new situation that will work for you. Either way, this is not happening." I motion to the entryway. "Please leave."

"So, that's it? I make one mistake and it's enough for you to just throw me away?" He asks incredulously. He's acting like he really can't believe my position.

That painful look of confusion has taken up residence on my face again. I can feel it. "One mistake? You cheated on me with her for who knows how long—"

"It only happened twice!" He yells over me.

"—but you were comfortable enough with the bitch to bring her into my house!" Squeezing my eyes shut I rub my temples and try to calm down. In the grand scheme of things, this probably doesn't matter, and I should be over it. I'm over the relationship and him for sure, but the disrespect of the whole him cheating on me *in my house,* **on a couch that I helped pay for, while wearing the cologne that I bought him, and DRINKING MY WINE** is a bit harder for me to brush off.

"How many times do you want me to apologize for that? You think I don't know that I never should have even entertained her? I love you! I have only ever loved you! I put a ring on her finger 'cause I thought that if I just moved forward with her that I'd get over you. It didn't work." Coming forward, he tries to take my hand.

"Try harder." I yank my hand away from him and take a step back. What the hell does he want from me? How much clearer can I be about the fact that I don't want him?

He actually laughs a little at that. "I miss that smart mouth. And you can't tell me that that white boy in the mall is hittin' it better than I was."

I could crush his ego right now, but what would be the point? "I am very satisfied, Kelvin."

He grabs my hand again and this time he doesn't let go when I try to pull away. Instead, he grabs the back of my head and pulls me into a kiss. I'd knee him in the crotch, but I'm wearing a pencil skirt and that makes things difficult. I struggle against him, but he tightens his hold and pushes his tongue into my mouth, so I bite down. Hard.

"Ahh, fuck!" Kelvin lets me go and covers his mouth.

I refuse to let him intimidate me. "Are you leaving or am I calling the police?"

He shakes his head at me. "Come on now."

Grabbing the phone off of the end table I start dialing 9-1 and give him a pointed look with my finger hovering above the last 1.

He shakes his head at me again and stomps toward the front door like an angry toddler. When he gets there, he opens it and turns to look at me. "It says a lot about you that you turn down an offer to be my queen, but you'll let some white man make you his whore."

Snatching my keys from the hall table, I push him out the door and use the pepper spray that I keep on my keychain to make my final point. I slam my door and lock it to the sound of him screaming and slapping at his face.

Okay, so what planet does he live on? I'm supposed to jump for joy because his cheating ass wants me to take him back while he has a whole pregnant wife, and I should be ashamed of the fact that the person that I'm dating isn't black? So, because I'm black, I'm supposed to feel like he's the better choice even though he cheated on me and has a pregnant wife? Even if I wasn't with Jonah, I wouldn't take him back. Trifling ass.

Grabbing my phone, I call my mother.

She doesn't answer until the fifth ring. "Hey, Reigney."

I can't do respectful right now. "Why did you give Kelvin my address and the gate code to my complex?"

"He misses you! And I don't know who the hell you think you're talking to like that!" she snaps.

"It's wrong for me to be pissed off that you gave a person that I have no interest in ever seeing again my damn address? I have a boyfriend that I'm very happy with and that I'm about to move in with!" I had planned on telling her about that after Christmas, but oh well.

"You're moving in with a man that you barely know?" She makes it sound like I'm deranged.

"No, I'm moving in with Jonah, someone that I know very well." I say it slowly while praying for patience.

"I cannot believe that you are just going to allow yourself to be fetishized by some white man, while there is a good black man that loves you—"

"Good...what?" I choke.

"Kelvin called me and begged me for your address."

"He's married to the chick he cheated on me with, and she's pregnant! Did he tell you that while he was calling and begging for my address?" I ask her as I head for my bedroom to change my shirt.

"Who told you he was married?"

Yanking off the shirt, I throw it on the floor and pull on Jonah's *Thundercats* t-shirt. "He did, when he and his pregnant wife approached me and Mark in the food court last month."

"What the hell is he doing fighting for you in a mall if he has a pregnant wife? Are you sure?" She sounds genuinely surprised.

"I'm very sure. They moved down here because she wants to be closer to her family and he's having second thoughts about his marriage since he ran into me. And I was in the mall with Mark, so he wasn't 'fighting for me.'" Going back downstairs, I look out of the front window and see a police car pulling up. Kelvin is still out there making all kinds of noise.

"I did not know that. You know I do not condone that kind of mess." One of my sisters must be there, because I hear her relaying information to someone in the background.

"Oh, and Angel let him in my house and left. I came home from work and he was standing in my living room." This is said with a lot of accusation. She is the person that forced Rosemary's baby on me. Also, I'm feeling a certain kind of way about her assumptions about Jonah.

There's a knock on my door and I go to answer it. "Hold on one second, Ma."

When I open the door, there is a policeman standing there. There's another one over by Kelvin. I give him a questioning look and wait.

"Ma'am, the gentleman over there says that you assaulted him." He's only a little taller than me with graying buzz cut hair and a wiry frame.

"I wouldn't say that." I say it calmly.

He raises an eyebrow at me. "What would you say?"

"I would say that I came home to him in my house, repeatedly asked him to leave, and when I finally got him to the door, he started calling me names and insulting me instead of leaving, so I pepper sprayed him and shoved him outside before closing and locking my door," I tell him.

The officer takes out a notepad. "You say he was already in your home when you got here?"

"Yes."

"Do you know how he got in?"

"He said that he called my mother and got my address and the gate code, and he said that my cousin let him in before she went out." I can hear my mother talking on the phone that's still in my hand.

"So, then you do know him?" he asks.

"We used to date, we broke up over a year ago. I have repeatedly asked him to leave me alone, and he got into a fight with a friend of mine last weekend at the mall." I cut a look at Kelvin. There's an ambulance pulling into the parking lot. He's acting like he's dying. *I should walk over there and pepper spray his crybaby ass again.*

The officer takes in the cast on my wrist. "That how you hurt your arm?"

"Yeah, I was knocked down trying to de-escalate the situation." I hadn't told my mother that I broke my wrist and I can hear her asking about it. She is so flipping loud.

The cop closes his notepad and looks over at Kelvin being loaded into the back of the ambulance. I fight the urge to roll my eyes. Looking at the car that's in my spot, I realize that it's his and debate having it towed.

"Ma'am, I recommend that you file for a temporary protection order. You can come down to the station and get a copy of the report that we'll write up for this incident. I would also advise you to speak to your family members about handing out your address and leaving people in your home without your permission," he tells me before closing his notepad and walking over to his partner.

Going back inside, I head up to my bedroom to change into a pair of jeans and a sweater. I hang up with my mother after I explain to her about my wrist and she assures me that she will never hand out my address again. I text Angel and tell her to pack her shit when she gets back to my house, because I'm sending her back to her parents.

Her reply? *BuT hE wAs dRiViNg An EsCaLaDe.*
Seriously?

I don't get back from the police station until nearly eleven o'clock. It's nearly five in the morning in Munich, but I pick up my house phone and call Jonah's hotel room anyway.

"Hello?" his groggy voice comes over the line on the third ring.

"Hey. Sorry for waking you up." I'm trying to find something edible in my refrigerator. Looks like a peanut butter and jelly night.

I hear him shift around in the bed. "That's okay. I was gonna get up in... two hours anyway."

"Want me to let you go?" Even I can hear the disappointment in my voice.

He laughs around a yawn. "No, I miss you. Tell me about your day."

I tell him about work and Mark's attempt to convince me that we need to hire a Lady Gaga impersonator for the Christmas party, I tell him about my shoe breaking and my latte spilling, and then I tell him about Kelvin.

"She really left a man that she's never met alone in your apartment and didn't even tell you?" He sounds wide awake and angry now.

"Yes, she did, because apparently murderers don't drive Escalades." I shake my head and take a bite of my peanut butter and jelly sandwich that I wish was potato bacon soup.

"What did he say?" His voice is tight. Yeah, he's definitely mad.

I give him a condensed version of our conversation and interaction, making sure to omit the whole part about Kelvin shoving his tongue in my mouth.

"I just got back from the police station when I called you. I had to get copies of the police report and that took forever. They didn't arrest him, but they told him that if he came back to my house that I could have him arrested for trespassing. I have to file the protection order in the county where he lives through the clerk's office, so I can't do that until tomorrow. The cop that I talked to said that I should file a stalking protective order."

"How long will that take?" he sounds like his jaw is clenched.

"They said that the temporary order will be given as soon as I file, and then there'll be a hearing within thirty days to decide whether or not to extend it. I'm not even sure that it's necessary." Just as those words leave my mouth, I get a Facebook notification.

"What? It's absolutely fuckin' necessary!" Jonah continues letting me know exactly what he thinks about me not getting an order against Kelvin as I unlock my cellphone and open up the private message that was just sent.

> **I'm sorry about today. I shouldn't have said that to you. I just hate the thought of you with someone else. I love you and I know that I hurt you, but I know you still love me too. We belong together, Sweet. I can still taste you.**

Yeah, this has to stop. His car was gone when I got home, so at least I don't have to worry about him coming back for that reason. I double check to make sure that all of the doors and windows on the first floor are locked.

"Autumn? Baby, can you hear me?" Jonah's concerned voice breaks through my unease.

"Yeah, yeah, I hear you." I start putting the food away in the kitchen. "I'm sorry."

"What happened?"

"He private messaged me."

Do I really need to get a protection order against this man for him to understand that I want him to leave me alone? That seems dramatic, even for me.

"What does it say?" he growls.

I read the message to him. "I'm feeling a little...uncomfortable right now."

"Uncomfortable, huh?" Jonah asks skeptically.

He knows that this is scaring me, and I want to act like it isn't, but that's not happening.

"Why won't he just let this go? It's been a fucking year!" Maybe Kelvin was having some kind of early mid-life crisis, or maybe he's just regretting everything like Mark said. Neither of those possibilities makes me feel better.

"Okay, go to the privacy shortcuts in your Facebook and change the messaging option to 'strict filtering'. If you aren't friends with him on Facebook, that should keep him from being able to message you. You already blocked him on Twitter and Instagram, right?" It sounds like he's moving around.

"Yeah, I did that after he kept DM-ing me." Who acts like this over a person that they cheated on?

"I think that you should move in with me when I get back." He sounds agitated.

"That would mean that I'd have to move twice in just under a month. We're moving into the condo in January." I rub my forehead. Jonah was able to get released from his lease early, but he has to pay a penalty. "That's going to be a huge pain in the ass."

"You said that most of the furniture at your place is your aunt's anyway. We can ask her if she wants it back, or if she wants us to put it in storage, or you can just bring your clothes to my place now and we'll worry about the rest of it later."

He's dead serious.

"Can we talk about this when you get back? In the meantime, I'm packing up Angel's shit and putting her on a bus this weekend." I start making my way up to my bedroom and regret not buying a dog.

"I feel like a dick for talking you into letting her stay." He lets out a breath. "I wanna read the other messages that he sent you."

Climbing in the bed, I shut the light off and settle down for sleep. "Okay."

"I fuckin hate that I'm not there right now. The thing on Sunday and Monday is more like a conference. I can miss it and come home tomorrow night."

I can tell that he wants me to take him up on it, but there is no way that I'm asking him to cut his trip short. "No, I'm fine. I promise. I'm going to go down to the clerk's office tomorrow before I go to work and file the protection order. It'll be fine."

"Maybe you should just go and stay at my place for the next few days. You know the gate code, and you have a key. And this asshole that can't take no for an answer doesn't know where I live."

"I'll think about it," I say to appease him.

"I doubt that. This is why I should be there. I could just throw you in my truck and take you to my place." I hear him flop back on the bed.

"I'm used to taking care of myself." I can't apologize for that. My environment wasn't always stable when I was growing up, so I've been taking care of myself for a very long time.

"I get that. And, I love the fact that you're so independent, but that doesn't mean that I'm not gonna wanna take care of you, too. You're scared. I know that you're scared and I fuckin' hate that I'm across the goddamn world right now instead of being there with you and makin' you feel safe." He groans in frustration.

"I'm okay. I'm annoyed that he won't leave me alone since I really don't understand why he suddenly thinks that we're some written in the stars, love match. His favorite movie is *Gangs of New York*! I should have emptied the can of pepper spray in his face." What the hell?

Jonah laughs. "That's my girl."

My laughter ends on a yawn. "He also fell asleep on *Casino*."

"You sound tired." His voice is soft.

I yawn again. "I am. Will I talk to you later?"

"Yeah. I'm gonna be leaving here tomorrow, and then I'll be in Geneva for a day and a half before I head home Monday night. The flight is over twelve hours with a layover, so with the time difference, that'll put me back in Atlanta at around four in the morning on Tuesday."

"Hmm. That's a lot of information." I'm having a hard time keeping my eyes open.2

He chuckles. "Yeah. Go to sleep, baby. I'll talk to you later. Love you."

"Okay. Love you, too. Bye." I hang up the phone before my eyes pop open. *What the fuck did I just say?*

Chapter Thirty-Two:

I am so frustrated. In case you were wondering, I was not able to get a Temporary Protection Order. Why? Because while I think Kelvin lives in Fulton county, he may not. Perimeter mall is on the Fulton/Dekalb county line. Also, while I know the idiot's full name and social security number, I don't know his current address, it isn't listed on the police report, and he has no listed address that I can find in Georgia. So even though Commander Crazy knows where to find me, I have no idea where to find him, so there's no way for them to serve him with the order. Jonah is going to go fucking ballistic. Mark has already gone on several rants about the situation and keeps trying to convince me to stay with him and Henry for the next few days. He keeps muttering about how he should have killed him at the mall. Whatever.

Mark and I are going to a Mediterranean place for lunch. Their lamb shawarma is really good, and I'm starving. The owner there gives you free samples while you're waiting in line, and that is sounding amazing to me right now.

We're sitting near the window and people-watching while we enjoy our food when I tell Mark about my conversation with Jonah the night before.

"I told him that I love him."

Mark starts choking on his falafel. I pound on his back and hope that I won't have to perform the Heimlich. He finally gets control of himself, but his eyes are watery and he's rubbing his chest.

"Are you trying to kill me?" He coughs a few more times. "You can't say things like that when I'm swallowing!"

"I thought you didn't swallow." I smirk at him.

He bumps my shoulder. "Cute. Now tell me about the grand confession."

"We were talking on the phone and were about to hang up, and he said, 'I love you', and I said, 'I love you, too.'" I take a bite of my shawarma and wait for him to say something. When I dare to look over at him, he is wearing the biggest smile I've ever seen on him. Damn it.

"I would like to reiterate that I have called the man of honor position, and I'm not trying to hear you do some bullshit like having a man of honor and a maid of honor. The hell with that. Those bitches are bride's maids." He's waving around his falafel as he's talking. "You should register at Macy's. They have really nice flatware sets and I think they give you a gift card worth like ten percent of all the stuff that people buy you off your registry."

"Can you be serious? This is freaking me out!" I snap at him.

"Why?" He scrunches his face up. "I knew you loved him when you had that hissy fit after Halloween and threw away those flowers."

"Maaaaark!" I whine. "Be serious, please!"

"I am being serious. Had you honestly convinced yourself that you weren't in love with this guy? For a smart girl, you're really dumb." He pats my hand and makes a tsking sound. "It's okay. Some relationships do work out."

My appetite is gone. It's like there's a lead ball sitting in my stomach all of a sudden. The way that I'm feeling must be showing on my face, because Mark puts his arm around me and gives me a squeeze.

"Look, I know that your parents' marriage is the stuff of nightmares. Trust me when I say that I get it. My parents have been together for over thirty years and I can't even remember them ever sharing a bedroom. Who they are isn't who we are," he says as he rubs my arm. "Jonah is a good guy that really loves you. I mean, the guy is a total breeder and he came with you to a gay Halloween party where he spent the night damn near getting molested, and then you flipped out on him over his clingy ex-girlfriend and made him take you home without you giving him so much as a hand job. He could have been pissed at you over that and just said fuck it to the whole relationship, especially since you were ignoring his attempts at contacting you, but he came to your house and waited for you to get home so that you two could work out the totally overblown situation."

"I wasn't wrong about his ex." I feel the need to point that out.

He tilts his head from side to side. "No, you weren't wrong, but you could have made your point without making him jump through hoops like a trained dolphin."

I can't argue with him since I recently had the same thought. "You know me being in love doesn't mean that I'm getting married."

Mark pulls a piece of lamb meat out of my wrap. "We should contact the botanical gardens and see if they have any openings for next June, or were you wanting to get married in a hall with your allergic to everything ass?"

By the end of the day, Mark has named all of my future children. He even threw in a Mark Jr. and a Markesha. He's an idiot, but he manages to take my mind off of the crap with Kelvin. Not that it lasts. When I get home, Angel is there and so is a bouquet of flowers.

Angel stands from the couch when I walk into the living room. "Hey, cousin."

I'm planning on dropping her off at Greyhound in the morning. I already bought her ticket. "Are you all packed?"

She picks up the flowers that are on the coffee table. "These came for you a half hour ago. The card says they're from that Kelvin dude."

I don't even want to touch those flowers. "You can throw them out if you want. Did you pack?"

"No," she huffs. "I feel like it's wrong for you to just decide that I'm goin' back to Jersey. I mean, I'm a grown woman. I can do what I want."

Oh, really?

"Fine, you don't have to go back to Jersey. But you can't stay here."

She stomps her foot and leans forward. "I don't even wanna stay here. You act like you're somebody's mother and all pure or something, but you runnin' around here fuckin two men! Ain't nobody gonna be fightin' over you in a mall and sendin' you flowers if they not blowin' your back out." She crosses her arms and gives me a smug look. "I mean, you were being all uppity about me havin' an abortion, but you around here bein' a hoe on the sneak."

I don't even correct her slutty assumption. I don't care. "Glad to hear that you don't want to stay here. You need to be out tomorrow."

"Tomorrow? Where am I supposed to go by tomorrow?" She throws the flowers at the wall and glares at me.

I shrug and give her words back to her, "You're a grown woman and can do what you want. Besides, since you don't want to stay here, I figured that you must have somewhere else to go."

She shoves by me and runs up the stairs. "You're such a stuck-up bitch!"

"Yeah, but I'm a stuck-up bitch with somewhere to live!" I yell.

Let her cut off her nose to spite her face if that's what she wants to do. I wasn't trying to put her out on the street, that's why I bought her the bus ticket. If she goes back to Jersey, which she was planning to do in about two weeks for Christmas anyway, then she can stay with her parents until it's time for her to come back down and move into the dorms. 'Cause she flat out cannot stay with me anymore. And as far as me being uppity about her decision to have an abortion? Um, hello, I'm the one that paid for it!

I can hear her upstairs slamming things around and having a tantrum. Then the stereo in her room comes on and my walls are vibrating to the sounds of The Migos. This is another reason why she needs to get the hell out. This shit is so inconsiderate. I've already gotten a second noise complaint. I love hip hop. But I barely slept last night, got up at the butt crack of dawn this morning to go and be told that I can't get a protection order against a person that has tripped off the planet, worked with a team leader that can't tell his dick from his thumb, and came to the realization that I'm in real love for the first time in my life. I want to eat something, stream my Jill Scott playlist, and take a bath before I pass out. But no. I have to deal with this child.

The music is abruptly shut off and I hear her come stomping down the stairs. Pouring myself a glass of Riesling, I pull a frozen dinner out of the freezer and toss it in the microwave. I really do need to learn how to cook something besides eggs, bacon, pancakes, and French toast.

"Can... I... talk-to-you... please?" Angel is breathing heavily, and her words are choppy.

I turn around and see that she's crying. Is it messed up that the tears aren't moving me in the least? I tip my glass in her direction. "Sure."

"I'm sorry. I should have told you that I had left someone in the house before I left, and I shouldn't have said that stuff to you in the living room." She wipes at her face and shifts on her feet.

"Apology accepted." I take a long drink of my wine.

She stands there like she's waiting for me to say more. When I remain silent, the tears pick up speed. "You—you're...still gonna...kick...me...out...?"

I nod. "Yeah. You were planning on going home in two weeks anyway."

She sits down on one of the chairs at my small kitchen table. "I just got back! If I leave now, I'm gonna be in Jersey for two weeks before Aubrey gets home for the break. He's gonna start messing with somebody else!"

I try not to look at her like she's stupid, but... "You can't trust your boyfriend to keep his dick in his pants for two weeks?"

She grabs a napkin off of the table and blows her nose, then looks at me as if I'm being naive. "Pffftt, a man can't be trusted to be faithful for two minutes."

Damn. And I thought that I was cynical. "If you don't trust him, why are you with him?"

"Because his family lives in New Vernon, his father is a surgeon, and he drives a Benz. It's a 2011, but it's still a Benz." She shrugs.

Why did I expect something deeper? This is a girl that posts weekly thirst traps on Instagram. "How does he treat you?"

She leans her elbows on the table and sighs. "Not every man is gonna send you flowers and open your door for you. It's stupid to expect that. Bitches miss their man when they try to set ridiculous, romance novel expectations."

I wrestle my facial muscles into submission to keep from looking at her like she's an idiot. "Okay, so he's not a guy that opens doors or sends flowers, but how does he *treat* you? Is he respectful? Does he care about your feelings? When you're with him, do you talk about the things that interest you?"

She looks uncomfortable. "I guess, yeah."

That's a, no. It wouldn't surprise me if he was still trying to convince her to let his friends screw her when they're together. Not that she's some innocent little flower or anything, but standards are good to have. So is clarification.

"Has he called you his girlfriend?" I know that I sound doubtful. I can't help it.

She looks away for a second before looking at me again. "No, but we haven't been together that long. Anyway, that's not the point. I just can't go back right now. If I go back in two weeks, I'll be able to spend time with him over the break. If I leave now, he's gonna end up screwing one of those thirsty ass hoes that go to his school."

He probably already is.

"You should not be stressing about a dude that's going to sleep with somebody else if you leave town for two weeks. He's not worth your time or your vagina," I tell her.

She stands up and slams her hands down on the table. "This is what I'm saying about that uppity mess! Your man is out of the country right now and probably laid up with a bitch ten shades lighter than your ass, and he was only gone for two seconds before you started fuckin some Idris Elba lookin motherfucker, but you wanna preach to somebody!"

I tell myself that it would be wrong to slap her again. It's beneath me. Still, I can't stop my hand from balling up into a fist or the image that pops into my mind of me beating her over the head with my cast.

"Jonah is out of the country conducting business. If he is sleeping with someone else, and I find out about it or have reason to believe that it's happening, I will be done with him, because I have **standards.** The person that you let into my home and left unattended while you went to spread your legs for a guy that won't even claim you, is my ex. I left him after I caught him cheating on me, and I'm not inclined to change my mind on that. Again, **STANDARDS.**"

"Whatever." She rolls her eyes and gets up to leave. "Your standards are cute, but unrealistic. All men cheat. It's what they do. If you're gonna leave a man every time he cheats on you, then you're gonna be alone forever, 'cause you work like eighteen hours a day. Men want to be catered to."

My home phone rings before I can respond, and she leaves the kitchen with a smirk on her face.

"You still need to be out by tomorrow!" I yell after her as I hit answer on the phone.

"Damn, you haven't changed." Kelvin's deep laughter comes over the line.

"How did you get my phone number?" I am not in the mood for this. I only answered because I thought it was Jonah. This is my fault for not checking the Caller ID.

"Your mother gave your number to me when she gave me your address. How did you like the flowers?"

I grit my teeth to keep from flipping out on him. "I'm allergic to flowers, and I have asked you several times to leave me alone."

"You're just being stubborn. I know you miss me." His tone is full of self- confidence.

"I really don't. Shouldn't you be decorating a nursery or buying diapers or something?" I ask snidely. He should be doing anything other than calling me and wasting his money on flowers that I don't want.

"We don't need to talk about that. You don't even need to worry about it. Her parents are taking care of all of that. We're staying with them right now, but I already told you that I'm not really with her anymore. I'm just staying here 'til I can find a place." He sounds like he's trying not to be overheard.

I can't help but laugh. "You are such a clown. No part of me wants you. Hell, I tried to get an order of protection against your ass."

"You really need to stop with all of this hard to get shit. I know you miss me. That white boy don't know what to do with that."

The thought that Mark is my man is really killing this guy. It probably burns more that when he swung on Mark he got bulldozed. I'm tempted to rub it in by telling him that Mark is gay, but I'm not interested in any further conversation.

"You think so? 'Cause I've never had to fake an orgasm *with him*." I hang up after that and check the caller ID. The number came up as Vernell Lewis. I google the name and get her address. First thing Monday morning, I'm getting a protection order.

Chapter Thirty-Three:

Kelvin's wife is as insane as he is. I was able to file a temporary protection order against him the Monday after he sent the flowers since I could provide an address for him. Unfortunately, they couldn't serve him with the order because when they went to the house, his wife claimed that he didn't live there and that she thought he had gone back to Philly. So, while I filed an order, it's unenforceable because he hasn't been served.

His wife began Tweeting and Instagramming all levels of craziness throughout the week. I blocked her and continued on with my life. She started @-ing my family members on Twitter in posts calling me a whore and saying that I was trying to sleep with her husband. After one of my sisters went all the way off and responded by telling her that her husband was the one calling my mother and begging for my information and telling her that her pussy probably smelled like disintegrating dryer lint, she decided to leave my family alone.

But she wasn't done.

She contacted the leasing office for my townhouse and told them that I was cooking meth on the premises. Fucking METH! Then, she came to my house with three other women the other night, banging on my door, calling me a home-wrecker, and pretty much threatening to beat me up. She's pregnant. I'm not getting into any manner of fight with a pregnant woman. I called the cops and let them deal with it. Unfortunately, once the police arrived and I came outside, I found out that one of the ignorant bitches that she brought with her slashed two of my tires and smashed in my rear window. When I got it picked up and taken to a repair shop, I found out that they also poured water in my gas tank. My fuel injectors had to be replaced. All told, the repairs were just under five thousand dollars with labor and that put my savings account in pain.

Needless to say, the idiot that caused all the damage was arrested. Mainly because she admitted to being the one that did the damage in front of the cops. Moron. She doesn't even know me, but she's the wife's cousin, so I guess that's enough.

After that, I started receiving phone calls from blocked and unknown numbers in the middle of the night. Who in the hell acts like this? I do not want her husband. I took out an order in an attempt to keep him the hell away from me, but she lied to the police so that he couldn't be served! How am I the bad guy here? This whole situation is unreal. I took out an order on her nutty ass too. This time they were able to serve it.

In case you're wondering, and this is totally off subject, Angel disappeared. Poofed out like she had an invisibility cloak. I woke up the morning after Kelvin called me, fully prepared to drop her off at the bus station, but when I went to wake her up, she and most of her clothes were gone. I went downstairs thinking that she was already up and waiting for me, but she wasn't in the house and her key was on the coffee table. I have no idea where she is. I tried calling her, but she didn't answer. I contacted my aunt to see if she went to stay there, but Mae hadn't heard from her. We don't have any other family in Georgia, and she has no money that I know of.

I called my uncle to let him know that his daughter was no longer under my roof. That was fun. He pretty much called me everything but a child of God for allowing his precious and innocent baby to just go off on her own. Um...hello? The girl left while I was asleep! I ended up just hanging up on him.

The fallout from the Angel situation is that my mother and my uncle aren't speaking to each other. It would seem that he called my mother after I hung up on him and tried to curse her out. If you knew my mother, you would know how ill advised that was. She went nuclear on him and talked about everything from how long it took him to learn to talk, to how much weight his wife has gained over the years. She also went off about Angel leaving Kelvin in my house and told my uncle about me having to pay for his daughter's abortion after his wife called her begging her to get me to help. My mother has no chill. My uncle then went back to calling me every few hours asking if I'd heard from Angel yet and responding poorly each time that I told him that I hadn't. So, now we are in the familial version of The Cold War.

I'm already dealing with enough shit. Now that Kelvin has my home number, he's seriously calling me every few hours. I blocked him, but he's calling from random numbers, so it didn't even matter. I called the cops, but they said that since he isn't threatening me, there's nothing that they can do. I had to turn my ringer off on my home and cell phones and ended up missing a bunch of calls from Jonah.

I tried to have his nuttier than a payday ass served with another protection order, but they said that no one answered the door when they attempted to serve him the second time. Apparently, that's all it takes for a person to avoid being served with a protection order. Reassuring, isn't it?

I really don't know what's going on with the universe. My life is normally very boring.

Right now, I'm getting ready for my office Christmas party and praying that aliens don't land in the parking garage or something. I need a break from the drama. I decided to get dressed at Jonah's apartment since I'm spending the weekend with him. We're supposed to be going to a Christmas party that a friend of his is throwing tomorrow.

Tonight, I'm wearing a red, drape-necked, spaghetti strapped sheath dress with a back cutout. The dress stops just above the knee, and I've paired it with my leopard print platform heels. I used a ceramic brush to straighten my hair and pulled it into a loose, side swept bun. Now I just have to keep from drinking too much or embarrassing myself in front of people that I'll be working with every day. Mark should be picking me up any minute now.

When I walk into the living room, Jonah is sitting on the couch and typing something on his laptop. He looks up when he hears me...and just keeps looking.

"What?" I smooth my hands down my dress and wonder if there's something wrong.

"You're dressed like that for a work party?"

"What's wrong with the way I'm dressed?" What is the problem?

He closes his laptop and I can tell that he's trying to frame his words in a way that won't piss me off. "I though corporate parties were held at the office and everybody wore the same shit that they would wear to work?"

"Some companies do that, but some don't. The invitation said cocktail attire. There's going to be a catered dinner and drinks and some recognitions, and then music and dancing," I say. In my defense, I did invite him.

He nods. "Okay...how would you feel about changing into something less...appealing?"

There's a knock on the door and Jonah hurries to answer it. I look down at myself. Less appealing? What does that even mean? Does he expect me to wear a burlap sack? He comes back into the living room with Mark, who's dressed in a charcoal suit with a red shirt and a red and grey striped tie.

"Looking fabulous, Autonomous." Mark gives me his flirty smile.

"Thank you," I say. "But it would seem that Jonah doesn't agree."

Mark turns and gives Jonah a disbelieving look. "You don't? God, straight men are so lost."

Jonah ignores him and focuses on me. "I think you look amazing. I always think you look amazing. Just...I think that you maybe look a little too amazing for an office party."

I'm not looking at Mark, but I'm certain that his expression mirrors mine, which is all about the: *what the fuck?* "So, I'm supposed to go to a work event looking like a spinster?"

"You are aware that I can see your nipples, right?" He gestures at my breasts.

Shit, I forgot to put my pasties on. "Dammit. I'll be right back."

I hurry back up to the loft and put on the pasties that I somehow forgot on the bathroom counter. Looking at myself in the mirror, I am pleased to see that my high beams have been turned down. I'd love to be all 'free the nipple', but I work in corporate America, and I'm trying to make the right kind of impression.

Going back downstairs, I grab my coat and give Jonah a quick kiss before heading out with Mark. He still doesn't look excited to see me leaving, but he doesn't say anything. Whatever. I'm a grown ass woman and I was wearing something much shorter and tighter than this when he approached me at the club.

"Mr. Jonah seems to be letting his possessive side out to breathe." Mark's voice is full of humor.

I roll my eyes at him. "I invited him to come and he said he had work to do."

"I bet he's regretting that right about now," Mark snickers.

"Probably. Can I ask if Henry is going to be at the party?" I ask the question tentatively. Mark's been on edge about his relationship lately. More so than usual.

His jaw tenses before he relaxes it. "He already left with his family for their happy little fairytale vacation. He told me that he thinks we should take a break while he's away."

"A break?"

Mark gives a humorless laugh. "Yeah. I guess he couldn't figure out how to say that he planned to fuck his wife in Florida without compromising the wonderful trust that we have in each other. So, we're on a break."

I don't know what to say that won't sound bitchy, so I don't say anything. Instead, I turn the radio on to a station that plays mostly top 40 hits and rub his leg. *Closer* by the Chainsmokers comes on and we sing along together. Halfway through the song, Mark takes my hand and I give him a light squeeze. I honestly hope that he breaks up with Henry and finds someone that deserves him, 'cause I'm coming close to slapping that emotionally deceptive son of a bitch.

The party is definitely not what Jonah would have expected. Things start out respectable. A dinner of some dry chicken and vegetables accompanied by a presentation about goals and earnings and the vision for the next year. And then, the liquor starts flowing and the music starts playing. I am pleased with the job that Mark and I did of selecting the DJ. He keeps the music to mostly '70s and '80s funk and disco and throws in a few hairbands, 90s hip hop, and some new jack swing. By the end of the night, quite a few people are drunk off their asses, someone has disappeared with someone else's girlfriend, two verbal fights have broken out, I've developed ninja dodging skills because of some guy in our IT department that won't leave me alone, and Mark made-out with someone from accounting and got a blow-job in the bathroom.

I end up driving us to his apartment, because he was barely able to zip his own fly. After getting him into bed, I call Jonah to pick me up. I was a little worried about leaving Mark alone, but he promised that he was okay, and that he'd call me in the morning.

Jonah is knocking on the door twenty minutes after I call him. He must have sped over here. I grab my purse and step outside, locking the door behind me. Neither of us speaks until we get in the car.

"How was your party?" He asks as he takes us out of the parking lot and heads for 285.

"Eventful." I kick off my shoes. I've been wearing them for over four hours and that's more than enough torture for me.

He cuts me a look. "Eventful good, or eventful bad?"

"There will be a few embarrassed people at the office on Tuesday. If they can even remember what they did," I sigh and sit back. I went to college parties that had less drama.

"Did you get a lot of compliments on the dress?" He goes for casual, but his hands flex on the steering wheel.

I turn to face him. Since when does he act like this? "What the hell is your problem?"

He looks at me and raises his eyebrows. "Are you serious?"

"What the hell is wrong with the way I look?"

"Autumn, you went out in a dress that looks like a fuckin nightgown that I could see your nipples through, and that rubs your ass like its makin' love to it!" He turns the heat up when he sees me shiver and pull my coat tighter. "And don't even get me started on your legs and those fuckin shoes."

Now, I'm offended. "You don't like my shoes?!"

"What are you, high? I love your shoes. I wanna bend you over the end of my bed while you wear nothin but those shoes and fuck you till you can't see straight." He reaches down and adjusts himself in his jeans.

Now I'm really lost, because he sounds angry. Since when does sex make him angry? "I swear I'm not drunk, and you aren't making any sense. Are you really about to be one of those men that thinks that just because you're in a relationship with a woman that she's supposed to start wearing turtlenecks and calf length skirts? 'Cause I'm not doing that. Full disclosure, I'm probably never doing that."

"Did I ask you to do that?"

"Okay, then what's your problem?" I flap my hand in frustration.

"My problem is that you went out lookin' like sex and I wasn't with you, and then damn near every single guy that you work with probably imagined bendin' you over a fuckin' copy machine or a desk while Mark was getting' blitzed off his ass. If you're gonna go out lookin' like that, then I'm gonna need you to carry some mace and a stun gun, or get a concealed carry permit for a .22, or start takin fuckin' Krav Maga, or kick boxin', or somethin'." He rubs a hand across his mouth in irritation.

Jonah's accent also gets deeper when he's angry. I should not find that as attractive as I do. Unbuckling my seatbelt, I lean over and nip at his neck.

"Baby..." His voice holds a warning.

Reaching over the console, I unzip his pants and slip my hand inside. He's already hard. Probably from all that talk about bending me over in nothing but my shoes. I tighten my grip and stroke my hand up and down his cock while he groans and fights to keep his eyes open. He reaches down and forces my hand to stop moving. I pout, but then he gives me a quick kiss and focuses his attention on getting us to the apartment.

Once we get there, we race inside, and I push him against the door as soon as it closes while he pulls me into a kiss and pushes my coat off my shoulders so that it drops to the floor. Working his pants open, I wrap my hand around him again and smile as he groans into my mouth. Breaking the kiss, I slide down to my knees and tease the tip of his cock with my tongue before pulling him into my mouth. Flattening my tongue, I take him to the back of my throat and suck hard. I feel his hands at the back of my head and begin moving up and down. I wrap my hand around the base of his cock and stroke him so that every inch of him is covered. He's huge, and I'm not a porn star, so there's no way that I can fit all of him into my mouth. I'm not sure if he's aware of all of the curses and pleas that are coming out of his mouth, but I love every filthy syllable. I take him deep again and let my teeth lightly graze the head of his cock as I pull back.

Jonah pulls me off of him and picks me up. I wrap my legs around his waist, and he kisses me and turns us so that my back is against the door. His tongue teases the seam of my lips and I open my mouth on a sigh. I feel his hands squeeze my ass as he grinds his lower body against mine. The kiss becomes more consuming and his movements become more urgent when my nails bite into his shoulders in an attempt to pull him even closer to me.

"Fuck, I gotta get inside you," he growls, "hold on."

Pushing my dress up, he braces my legs on his forearms, moves my panties to the side, and slams into me so hard that I lose my breath. Gripping his hair in my hands, I plant my elbows on his shoulders for purchase and meet him thrust for thrust. He uses his mouth to move my dress straps out of the way and licks the top of my breast. I moan and tilt my hips, forcing him deeper into me.

Fuck. I can feel him taking over every part of me. Consuming me, loving me, owning me. He's so deep that I almost can't take it. I let my head fall back against the door and try to keep up with him. It isn't long before I start to fall behind as the pleasure becomes too much and the ceiling begins to blur, so I close my eyes and just feel. I'm trying to hold on, but soon my body is splintering into a million pieces and the earth is shifting on its axis and I'm screaming his name like it's the answer to every question that has ever been asked. He buries his face in my neck and groans against my skin as he comes inside of me.

Jonah takes a few deep breaths and shifts me so that my legs are around his waist again instead of on his arms. Leaning back, he smiles at me. "Hey."

I kiss him. "Hey."

He looks at my dress where it's bunched up between us. "This dress looks amazin' on you."

I laugh, and he groans when my muscles clench on him where he's still inside of me. Turning, he starts toward the loft. I rest my head on his shoulder and yawn.

"None of that. We ain't done yet." He nuzzles his nose against my hair. "Fuck, you feel good on me."

I can feel him hardening inside of me. I suddenly realize that he isn't wearing a condom. I have never had condom free sex in my entire life. I've been on the pill since I was sixteen, and I'm very good about taking it at the same time every day, but condoms have always been an essential part of my sex life. A birth control double tap if you will. I should be flipping out. I should demand that he pull out of me and immediately apply the damn latex. Instead, I hold him tighter.

Chapter Thirty-Four:

Jonah's friend Zach is a laid-back IT specialist that lives in Duluth with his girlfriend, Molly who works in hotel management. Zach is a first generation Cambodian American and total hip hop head. When we arrived at their house for the party, Zach was in the middle of the living room with a microphone and a karaoke machine singing, 'I Left My Wallet in El Segundo'. He did not look at the machine for the words even once. Molly is originally from Kenya but moved to America when she was ten with her parents. She works for a mortgage company and seems to be one of those women that's so effortlessly stylish that you want to hate her, but she's so nice and warm that you end up liking her. They live in a four-bedroom house in a subdivision surrounded by houses that are identical to theirs. Still, it's very nice and I could probably fit the house that I grew up in inside of it. This party is considerably more casual than the one I attended last night, so I'm wearing my black Bear Paw boots with a pair of red jeggings and a black off the shoulder sweater. Jonah is in his typical jeans with a t-shirt that says, In Dog Beers I've Only Had One.

I was originally supposed to meet Zach, Molly, and a few of Jonah's other friends at a birthday party before Halloween, but plans changed when Kaylin had an "emergency" about a photographer. Jonah introduces me to everyone, and I quickly learn that he has an eclectic group of friends. There are about twelve of us here, and mostly everyone is part of a couple. They're all around Jonah's age, and for the most part they all met in college.

We've been here for about two hours and I'm talking to Paul, a friend of Jonah's who's originally from Philadelphia, about one of the bars on South Street in Philly when he freezes and stares at something over my shoulder.

Turning to see what he's looking at, I spot Kaylin and Jim and another woman that I don't know coming into the house. Just fucking spectacular. I was actually enjoying myself.

"Fuuuuuck," Paul groans. "I was hoping that she wasn't invited to this."

I feel the same way but stop myself from saying so. Instead, I take a sip of my wine and look around for Jonah. He's talking to Zach and another guy, a caramel colored man with hazel eyes and dreadlocks named Keon, about some new software company or something. He's been really good about staying by my side most of the night, but since I got involved in a conversation about Philly with Paul and he got pulled into a separate conversation, and the night was going really well...not that it matters now.

Turning back to Paul, I try to ignore the new arrivals by keeping the conversation going. "Are you going back for Christmas?"

He looks back at me and takes a drink of his beer. "Nah, I thought about it, but the weather up there is really shitty right now and I don't want to risk getting stuck. I gotta be at work on Tuesday. What about you?"

"Same." I say. "It kinda sucks though since I've never been this far away from my family during the holidays and I didn't go back up for Thanksgiving."

"Autumn, hi!" Kaylin's fake chipper voice sounds out from over my shoulder and I shoot Paul a look for not warning me. He gives me a look of apology in return.

Facing her, I give her a polite smile (I'm in someone else's house, after all) and return her greeting. "Hi, Kaylin. How are you?"

Her smile is practically pasted onto her face and it's reminding me of the tattoo that the Joker had on the back of his hand in *Suicide Squad*. Creepy.

"I'm doing just great, thanks." She bats her eyelashes at me. "I mean, I've barely spoken to my best friend in weeks, but other than that, I'm peachy." She grabs the hand of the woman that came in with her and pulls her forward. Jim is nowhere to be seen. "This is my sister, Paige."

Paige is about the same height as Kaylin, making her taller than me. Her hair is dyed red, but the eyes are the same as her sister's and she has slightly fuller lips. While Kaylin is wearing jeans and a cable knit sweater with a pair of black kitten heels, Paige is wearing a blue sweater dress with cut outs along the arms and the cleavage area that stops just under her ass with a pair of knee-high combat boots.

I shake the hand that is held out to me. "Lovely to meet you."

She looks me up and down after releasing my hand. "Wish I could say the same."

"Excuse me?" I'm actually surprised. Did this bitch really just say that?

She puts her hand on her hip like she's about to deliver a reality tv level read. "After the shit that I've heard about you—"

I hold my hand up to her face silencing her. "I'm really not about to give any life to anything that you have to say."

I turn back to Paul and excuse myself. Walking away from whatever dramatic moment the two of them have planned, I go over to Jonah and catch his eye. When he looks at me, I motion to the area near the dining room where I was just talking to Paul and he sees Kaylin and her sister. Jim is standing with them now, and Paul has walked away to talk to Molly.

Jonah snags me around my waist and pulls me to him. "I didn't know that she'd be here."

Zach overhears him and looks over to where Kaylin and her small entourage are standing and staring daggers at me. "Shit, man, I'm sorry. Molly must've invited her. I didn't even know they were speaking again after that shit that happened last time. It seemed like everyone was pretty done after that."

I don't know what he's talking about, but looking over at Molly, it doesn't look like she's so happy to see Kaylin either. So, the question is, what the fuck is she doing here? Did this chick really crash someone's Christmas party?

"Sorry, sorry, this is my fault," Keon's girlfriend, a really sweet brunette named Carly, says as she approaches us. She seems to have had a bit too much to drink and leans heavily against her boyfriend. "She texted me asking about what our plans were for tonight and if we wanted to go out with them for a bite and I told her that you and Molly were having a Christmas party so that we could all get together before the actual day and that she should stop by."

Keon looks annoyed with her. "You invited her to their house after what happened with her and Molly without clearing it with them first? Are you crazy?"

"I thought they made up!" she says defensively.

I'm the only person out of the loop. I want to ask what happened, but Jonah gives me a squeeze and shakes his head no when I look up at him. Hopefully, he fills me in later.

Zach excuses himself and goes over to talk to Molly while someone cues up the karaoke machine again. Jonah sits down on the couch and pulls me onto his lap while two women start singing Bad Romance.

"We can leave if you want," Jonah says in my ear.

I shake my head without even considering it. "No. It's fine. I like your friends."

He slides his hand under the hem of my sweater and strokes my stomach. "They like you, too."

Before I can respond, Carly is pulling me up and over to the karaoke machine where another woman whose name I can't remember is waiting.

"We need a third person. You're it." She laughs and hands me the microphone. *What a Man* starts playing and I do my best Salt impersonation. Molly jumps in and is apparently embodying all of the members of En Vogue as she does the chorus. We continue our group performance with *Let's Talk About Sex*, *Red Light Special*, and *When Doves Cry*. The last one isn't exactly a group performance song, but we killed that shit.

Molly asks me to help her with something in the kitchen, and since Jonah is talking to Kaylin and I have no intention of losing my temper, I agree. I'm really not interested in being around that woman.

Once we're in the kitchen, Molly turns to me and puts her hands on her hips. "Why are you still allowing him to be friends with that bitch?"

Whoa! I was not ready. "I'm sorry?"

"Kaylin. She is toxic. I'm sorry that I ever introduced them. Worst mistake! But, why are you still allowing her to be a part of his life?"

I point to myself. "Because I don't have the right to tell him who he can and can't speak to."

"Well, you're better than me. I don't understand how it is that Jim can't see that she's just using him to try and make Jonah jealous." She has this look of confused disgust on her face.

I'm just glad that I'm not the only one that realizes it. "Look, Jonah knows how I feel about her, and we've already talked about how she won't be invited to the condo when we move in—"

"What condo?" Her eyes go wide.

I assumed that he'd told his friends. I guess not. You know what they say about making assumptions. "Jonah's buying a condo and asked me to move in with him."

"Congratulations! That is great news!" She gives me a genuinely happy smile. "We should all go out and celebrate after the closing."

"That sounds good to me, I'll run it by Jonah."

"And since you don't like that hyena in a skirt, she won't be there to ruin your celebration the way she ruined mine," Molly huffs as she grabs a bottle of pinot noir out of their wine fridge and opens it.

"She ruined your closing party?"

"No." Molly pours each of us a glass. "She ruined my engagement party. She stood her drunk ass up and gave a speech about how it was about time that Zach stopped getting free milk and that everyone should expect a pregnancy announcement from me soon since that's the only way he'd propose."

My mouth drops open. Just unhinges and hangs there. I force it closed and take a sip of my wine before I attempt to say anything. "This was at, like, an official engagement party?"

Molly nods looking pissed off. "Yes. We had it at this great wine tasting place in Atlanta. Everyone was having a good time, and then her drunken jealous ass had to ruin it."

I shake my head. "I'm sorry, but how long have the two of you been friends?"

"I met her in college during my freshman year. She seemed like such a sweet person."

So, Molly is the black friend that disqualifies Kaylin from being racist. I almost mention that, but Jonah walks into the kitchen looking irritated.

"What happened?" Molly asks him as she sits her glass down on the counter like she's expecting to charge out of the kitchen.

He gives her a tense smile. "Nothing. Everything's fine. Can I talk to Autumn for a minute?"

She looks from him to me and back again before picking up her glass. "If you're leaving my party because of that fake bitch out there, I'm going to be very offended. No one wants her here. I can just tell her to leave." She shoots a smile at me. "Besides, Autumn promised to perform another song with us." With that said, she leaves the kitchen with her glass and the newly opened bottle of wine. I really like her.

I wait for Jonah to tell me what has him looking so pissed off, but he doesn't say anything.

"What's going on?"

He scrubs his hands down his face and paces before looking at me. "Why didn't you tell me about the shit with your ex's wife?"

What the shit? I didn't tell him about the stuff with Kelvin's wife because it's childish and stupid. "Because it isn't important."

"It isn't important that she's going batshit on Twitter because her husband left her for you?" He looks at me like I'm crazy.

"He what?!" I ask, shocked. *What the shit?*

"It would seem that his wife is operating under the belief that her husband is moving in with you." He leans on the kitchen island and looks at me like he's waiting for me to dispute the ravings of a lunatic on Twitter.

And I would, but I don't feel like I should have to. I don't even know how he's come across this craziness. "Why are you acting like there's any validity to that?"

"Autumn, there are fuckin' screenshots of this man callin' you the love of his life and describin' the way your mouth feels on his dick and how good your pussy tastes!" He growls. I can't tell if it's because he's angry or because he doesn't want to be overheard.

"Again, why are you acting like this holds weight?" I snap. I have blocked Kelvin and his crazy ass wife on social media. I'm barely on social media anyway. I'm blocking numbers on my phone left and right like I'm Neo blocking bullets in *The Matrix*. I have tried to get protection orders against both of them. What the hell else does he think I can do?

He straightens up. "You don't see why this would make me wanna find 'im and stomp a mudhole in his ass?"

"Yes, I do, but I can't control what people post online. I don't want to be with that man and since I've blocked both of them, I don't know what he or his psycho wife are posting online!" I flap my hand in frustration.

"This is disrespectful as fuck! It's disrespectful to you, it's disrespectful to me, and I'm ready to find 'im and shove his phone down his fuckin' throat!" He slams his fist down on the island.

"I agree that it's disrespectful, but what do you want me to do? How did you even see that mess?"

"Kaylin was out there showin' me screenshots of posts that were made right after I got back from Geneva—"

"And you're not questioning why messy Bessie is following my ex and his wife on Twitter?" I cut him off. Of course, Kaylin. Why is this bitch in my business?

"The question is, why is she the one showin' it to me? You told me that you were able to file the order against him after he called your house, but you ain't said shit else about it."

Am I supposed to cry to him every day about the fact that Kelvin is annoying? How would that help anything?

"I haven't said anything else because there's nothing else to say. He called me, I told him to leave me alone, I got the address from the number on my Caller ID, I filed the order, they tried to serve him, but his wife claimed that he didn't live with her, so the order isn't valid. I tried to have him served again, but no one answered the door. So, he keeps calling me from unknown numbers and I don't answer. Then his wife and some of her hood rat ass family members showed up at my apartment, after my sister went ham on them on Twitter, and they vandalized my car. I pressed charges, filed an order against the wife, and got my car repaired. I told you about my car—"

"You told me that your car was in the fuckin' shop!"

"It was," I say lamely. Okay, so I didn't tell him exactly what was going on. This shit has been draining and I really just don't want to deal with it. Jonah is my escape. Lately, since he took a step back from the clinger, we've been able to just enjoy each other and I'm not trying to bring any bullshit into that.

He gives me a 'cut the shit' look. "Why didn't you tell me that they couldn't serve the order?"

"Because I knew you'd be pissed about it."

He clenches his jaw and looks up at the ceiling before looking back at me. "You know we're talkin' about this when we get home, right?"

"Jonah—"

"No, fuck that! We. Are. Talking. About. This. When. We. Get. Home."

"Look, I know that I should have kept you informed about everything that's been happening with Kelvin's wife, but it just seems like junior high bullshit that I don't want to give any of my energy to. And as far as Kelvin goes...I honestly had no idea that he was posting shit about me on Twitter. I blocked him, and I'm not on there that often anyway," I explain. I don't want to argue with him about this crap. It's not important.

"You can't just keep shit from me because it'll make me mad. I woulda been pissed about some chick comin' to your house with a group of women and vandalizin' your car, yeah, but you still shoulda told me about it. And you abso-fuckin-lutely shoulda told me about them not bein' able to serve your ex with that protection order." He looks less angry now, but I can tell that he still has a lot that he wants to say about this subject.

"You're right. I'm sorry." I really am. If the shoe were on the other foot...let's just say he's being much calmer than I would be, and we both know it.

"I love you, and I get that this whole, allowin' somebody into your life, thing is new for you, but this is what it means to be in a relationship. We share the good and the bad, baby. You get that, right?"

"I do." I feel like I need to buy a *Relationships for Dummies* guide.

"Good. Then, no more omissions. We keep it a hundred with each other, or this don't work." He waits for me to nod before taking my hand and pulling me out of the kitchen and back into the party.

Kaylin is standing by the kitchen with her sister when we walk out, and Jonah maneuvers us so that I'm in front of him and a little to the right. I think he's trying to make sure that I don't throw my drink on her nosy ass. I wouldn't do that. First off, it would be a waste of good wine, and second, I already told you that I was not raised to act a fool in other people's homes. I do cut her a look though and can't help but snicker when her sister takes a step forward like she's going to try something. I roll my eyes at both of them and sip my pinot.

Jonah gives me a squeeze and speaks into my ear while moving us further away from his ex. "Behave."

I give him a look of wide-eyed innocence. "You mean, you don't want me to find accusations about Kaylin on social media or tell her fiancé that she stood in your living room a few weeks ago and said that she still sees you as her boyfriend?"

He releases a sigh and tips his head. "Touché."

I notice that Kaylin and her sister are making their way over to us and feel my body tense. Jonah wraps an arm around my waist as if he's expecting me to go all Love and Hip Hop at any second. James is sitting on the couch with a plate full of finger foods and talking to Keon. He should probably come and get his future wife before she starts a problem.

I'm waiting for whatever passive aggressive trollness that she's about to let fly out of her mouth when her sister stops directly in front of us and addresses Jonah.

"Wow, talk about a downgrade," she says loudly.

Jonah tightens his arm around me as all other conversation dies down. We have become the center of attention. Yippee. I feel Jonah pull me back and realize that I've taken a step forward. While I was raised to be respectful of people's homes, I was also raised to beat bitches up. Unlike Kelvin's wife, this chick is not pregnant, so I am well within my rights to ragdoll her ass.

"Shouldn't you be hooker bopping on a street corner somewhere?" I look her up and down with a raised eyebrow. "You look like a bag of STDs."

Someone laughs and Kaylin's sister lunges at me. I'm holding my wine glass in my left hand, and I'm not about to waste my wine, but in my effort to preserve the pinot, I forget that I'm wearing a cast and ball up my right hand and let it fly. Down goes Stripperella. Pain explodes down my arm, but before I can fully process it, Kaylin is grabbing my hair!

Fuck that!

Dropping my glass, I reciprocate and tangle my left hand into her hair and start punching her with my right hand. I can hear Jonah and a few other people yelling and I feel them trying to untangle us, but I am not letting go. I yank as hard as I can, and she screams and lets go of me just as I feel her hair come loose in my hand. I'm left standing there, chest heaving, hair a mess, arm throbbing, and holding a handful of her weave. Jonah is in front of me, Zach is on my left, and a guy named Juan is on my right. There's a wall behind me. I am literally boxed in. They're all taller than me, so I can't see anything, but I can hear everything.

"Get off of me!" Kaylin shrieks.

"Why did you come into my house, uninvited, and start trouble?! This is the reason that I stopped speaking to you!" Molly yells at her. "You need to be the center of everything, and you don't know the difference between good attention and bad attention."

Then I hear Jim.

"You can't blame her for protectin' her sister!"

Jonah takes an aggressive step forward. "Her sister wouldn'ta needed to be defended if she wasn't runnin' up on people lookin' for a fight!"

"Nobody was lookin' for no fight!" Jim scoffs. "Paige made a little comment to your *girl* and she got violent for no reason."

Is he serious? I got violent? What the hell kind of blinders is he wearing?

"Autumn defended herself," Jonah says slowly.

"Autumn needs to be on a leash!" Jim yells.

And we have the second fight of the night when Jonah swings. I hear the hit. I also hear the next few hits since Jonah keeps swinging. The men that had been keeping me boxed in rush forward to try and break up the fight while Kaylin stands there screaming like an idiot and someone has to haul Paige away when she tries to jump in. When they're finally separated Jonah has a cut on his lip and his shirt is torn at the collar, and James is bleeding all over the place. He's got a cut on his eyebrow, and his nose and mouth are bleeding.

Jonah tries to push himself free of the hands that are holding him back. "I told you about disrespectin' her, you fuckin' redneck piece of shit!"

Kaylin and Paige try to help James up. He's looking a little dazed. Kaylin is a crying disheveled mess as she glares at Jonah. "God, what is wrong with you?"

"Are you fuckin' serious?!" he yells, and she flinches.

Going over to him, I put a hand on his arm and try to move him toward the kitchen. The guys holding him realize what I'm trying to do and help me. We have to practically shove him in there. I grab a bag of frozen ravioli out of Zach and Molly's freezer and hold it against his mouth.

He pushes the bag away and grabs my right arm in concern. "How's your arm?"

I give him a half smile. "Hurts like a bitch."

Paul slaps him on the shoulder. "Welp, at least we know that if your current career choices don't pan out, you guys could totally go into wrestling and have a successful career as a tag team."

Jonah laughs a little and looks at me. "A bag of STDs?"

They all start laughing and Keon throws an arm around my shoulder. "That was funny as hell. And that right cross?"

Juan gives me a bright smile. "That was a thing of beauty. Elbow in and straight from the shoulder. You take boxing?"

I shake my head. "No, but my father taught me how to throw a punch when I was four."

Juan claps his hands together and points at me excitedly. "That's what I'm talking about. My wife and I got a daughter that's four and Maria keeps talking about girls not fighting and wearing pretty dresses and shit, and that's all well and good, but I feel like she needs to know how to defend herself."

Jonah kisses me on the top of my head. "I guess I don't have to worry about you goin' out in nightgowns."

Molly comes into the kitchen looking very apologetic. I have no idea why. We fought in her house. My mother would have thrown us all out by now.

"I am so sorry about all of that. I should have asked them to leave when they walked through the door, but I was trying to avoid drama." She bites her lip at the irony. "Anyway, they're gone now so please feel free to come out of the kitchen and try to enjoy the rest of the night."

"Are you sure you don't want us to leave?" I ask her.

She looks surprised. "Of course not! We're going to perform Bodak Yellow in a minute. And come with me and I'll give you a comb and some bobby pins."

I smile gratefully and follow her from the kitchen. "I really am sorry. I was not raised to fight in someone's home."

She waves my comment off and leads the way down the hall to the master bathroom. "Please. I understand that. I was raised the same way, but you can only take so much. You think I didn't have to be held back at my engagement party? And what were you supposed to do when Paige came at you with her claws out, stand there and be attacked?"

She has a point, but still. "Well, I'm still sorry. Especially about dropping my glass. That's going to leave a stain. I will absolutely pay for any cleaning or repair that needs to happen because of it."

Molly laughs and shakes her head. "Are you kidding? Zach is over the moon about that stain on the carpet. He's been trying to convince me that we need wood floors and I've been resisting because wood gets cold in the winter. He's hoping that the stain ends up being so bad that it'll give him a reason to argue for new flooring."

"I had that same concern about the floors in the condo, but turns out that they're heated, so you guys could do that. I looked into it and they're not very expensive and they save you money on your heating costs," I tell her.

She leads the way into the master bathroom and lays out a comb, a brush, and some bobby pins. Molly is awesome.

I look at myself in the bathroom mirror and grimace. There's a scratch on my neck that I didn't feel, and my hair is looking very Sideshow Bob. I take a few minutes to gather it into a knot on the top of my head and pin it in place. After taking a deep breath, I head back to the living room for some wine and Cardi B.

Chapter Thirty-Five:

Jonah and I are moving into the condo this coming weekend. I already moved out of my townhouse and have been staying at his apartment. I asked my aunt if she wanted her furniture back or if she just wanted me to put it in storage. She said that they already own a storage unit and that I could put anything that I didn't want to keep in there, but to feel free to keep anything that I wanted for the new condo. Daniel and his wife are still living with them and she joked that if he and his wife ever got around to getting an apartment that she'd give them whatever I didn't want for myself.

We spent Christmas eve at my uncle's church and Christmas day lying in bed and watching *A Christmas Story* over and over again. I love that movie. Jonah's parents were visiting Arihi in California since she took a job at the Albany Aquarium and wasn't able to get off work for more than the actual holiday, so he skyped them all Christmas morning, and I called my mom, and his brother came over and had dinner with us.

I found out from my mother that Angel popped up at my uncle's house on Christmas looking a mess and with nothing but the clothes on her back. I have no idea how she got there or where she was after she left my house, and I don't care. I'm happy that she's safe, but other than that, I'm done with that girl. My mother actually asked me if I'd be willing to help pay for her books! But that's my mother. She can hate someone and still give them the shirt off her back if they're cold. I did not inherit that personality trait.

We had a very informal gift exchange since Jonah doesn't have a tree. I told him that we are absolutely having a tree next Christmas.

He got me a charm bracelet and a stun gun that looks like a tube of lipstick. The man is priceless. Right after I opened it, he showed me how to use it and made me charge it. The bracelet is really nice. It's white gold with a locket and a watch pendant. He wants to add a new charm every year. My inner cynic rolled her eyes, but I have to admit that it made my heart flutter.

Since I found out that he's obsessed with Monopoly, I got him the Nintendo edition Monopoly board game and a few t-shirts. His favorite one says, 'If At First You Don't Succeed, Call It The BETA Version'. We made dinner together (meaning that he cooked, and I drank wine and handed him stuff when he asked for it) and when Kayden came over, we ate in the living room while we watched *Die Hard*.

I could do that every Christmas. Definitely.

Today, I'm in court to see if a judge will extend my order of protection against Kelvin's wife. Jonah wanted me to hire a lawyer, and I agreed to do it even though I feel like it's unnecessary. The lawyer had me give him screenshots that I printed out of the Tweets that Kelvin's wife has been writing about me. I have a copy of the police report from the day that she and her family members came to my house and the bill from the mechanic with the list of repairs done on my car.

Jonah is here with me and I can feel the tension radiating off of him. I'm more nervous about Kelvin showing up with his wife and Jonah trying to attack Kelvin than anything.

See, Kelvin has started reliving our past sexual exploits on Twitter and Facebook. He posted about the time we had sex in a restaurant bathroom. He posted about the threesome that we had. He posted about the time we had sex in the campus library. He's like a fucking walking PSA for abstinence. In between reminiscing about the mediocre sex that we had (because while I was giving him something he could feel, he was not doing the same for me), he's openly fantasizing about fucking me up the ass while he chokes me unconscious. Isn't that sweet? I mean, if that's what you're into, then rock on. Me? I'm not particularly turned on by the thought of Kelvin's dick in my ass while his hands are wrapped around my throat and my life is flashing before my eyes. I would be happy to never think about his dick near me ever again.

My lawyer is a middle-aged man with thinning hair and sharp blue eyes. I met with him after Christmas and discussed the situation and after seeing the Tweets, he feels that it shouldn't be a problem to get the order extended to twelve months. I hope he's right. I realize that she's the lesser problem, but one thing at a time.

Following him into the courtroom, I sit beside him at a table on the left side of the courtroom and Jonah takes a seat on the bench behind me. Kelvin's wife comes in with an older woman and sits alone at a table on the right side. She's wearing a baby blue maternity dress and ballet flats and looks for all the world like an innocent vessel of life.

We rise when the judge comes in and then it's down to business. The judge is a petite woman, around fifty years old, her hair is cut into a bob, and she's wearing horn-rimmed glasses.

"We're here to decide on the matter of Blaire vs. Williams. Ms. Blaire is seeking to extend a temporary stalking protection order that was filed against Mrs. Williams." She looks down once more at the papers in front of her before looking from me to Kelvin's wife and back again. "Ms. Blaire, I see that you are represented by counsel today. Mrs. Williams, do you have representation or are you seeking to represent yourself at this time."

Kelvin's wife clears her throat. "I will be representing myself, your honor."

The judge nods. "Alright. Mr. Abrams, will you inform the court as to why Ms. Blaire feels the need to ask that this order be extended?"

My attorney stands up. "Yes, thank you, your honor. Since Mrs. Williams has been served with the temporary order, she has continued to attempt to contact Ms. Blaire via social media. She has continued to call her home and has begun posting sexually explicit rumors about Ms. Blaire on social media. My client had to get a temporary order against Mrs. Williams after Mrs. Williams' husband falsely told her that he was having a sexual relationship with Ms. Blaire, at which point Mrs. Williams along with a group of her family members went to Ms. Blaire's home and threatened her and vandalized her car."

The judge looks at Kelvin's wife before addressing my lawyer again. "Do you have proof of these claims, Mr. Abrams?"

He holds up the folder with the printed tweets, police report, mechanic's bill, and phone records. The bailiff comes over and takes the folder and hands it to the judge. She takes a moment to look through the papers.

"Mrs. Williams, do you have a response?"

She stands from her seat and folds her hands in front of her. "Your honor, I admit that my behavior has been unacceptable to an extent, but Ms. Blaire is not innocent. She sent police to my home in an attempt to harass my husband and force him to admit to an affair, even though she knows that I'm pregnant.

"I went to her home in an attempt to confront her about her affair with my husband, and my family members accompanied me to make sure that things didn't get out of hand. When we got to her house, she refused to come out and speak to me and a few of my family members became upset and acted out.

"Since that incident, she has continued her relationship with my husband who has since moved out of our home. I'm pregnant with my first child and I've had some medical issues, and so I kept calling Ms. Blaire because I know that he's staying with her and that's the only way that I can get in contact with him, but I haven't gone to her home since the order was filed."

I know that there's a look of shock on my face. My mouth dropped open halfway through her little speech. Does she honestly think that her husband is living with me? She was standing in the food court when I told that man to stay away from me!

The judge looks down at the folder again and I see her pause. "Mrs. Williams, while I understand that the situation that you're in is not ideal, that does not excuse the amount of damage that you've done to Ms. Blaire's property or your harassment of her and her family."

She should see some of the tweets that Kelvin has posted. There's a recent one where he talks about branding his name into my thigh. That one scared me.

Kelvin's wife looks over at me and waves a hand in my direction. "She's sleeping with my husband!"

The judge looks at me. "Do you currently have a relationship with her husband, Ms. Blaire?"

I don't know if I'm supposed to stand up, but I do. "No, I don't, your honor."

"Do you know why she would believe that you do?"

"No. She was with him when he approached me at Perimeter Mall, and I wished them both well and told him that I didn't want to see him again. He started trying to contact me online and I ignored him, then he and a friend of mine got into a fight at the same mall when he tried to approach me again and I ended up with a broken wrist." I raise my right arm out of habit. The cast came off last week. "I filed an order of protection against him after he showed up at my home and started calling me. I've blocked him on social media and haven't had any contact with him in weeks even though he keeps posting things about me."

"Do you follow Mr. Williams on social media?" she asks me.

"No, ma'am."

"Then how did you come across these tweets that you say he's posting?" she's looking down at the folder and not at me. It makes me uncomfortable.

"I was at a party with my boyfriend and one of his friends showed them to him, and he told me about what was being posted. More recently, my sister saw some and called me."

The judge nods, still not looking up. I can't tell what she's thinking or which way she's leaning. She closes the folder, folds her hands, and looks at Kelvin's wife. "Mrs. Williams, while I do sympathize with your situation, I feel that you have misdirected your anger toward Ms. Blaire. You've continued to attempt to contact her and have posted potentially damaging messages about her on social media even after you were served with a protection order, showing a disregard for the law. That being said, I am ruling to extend the stalking protective order against you for a period of twelve months. I am also ordering you not to contact or reference Ms. Blaire on social media or call her home or place of business. You are also ordered to reimburse Ms. Blaire for the cost of repairing the damage to her vehicle," she looks down at the folder, "which comes to five thousand three hundred and eighty-three dollars and forty-two cents."

Kelvin's wife looks outraged. "This is bullshit! That bitch is sleeping with my husband! He has abandoned me and our child for her!"

"If you violate this order, Mrs. Williams, you will be subject to incarceration. You should take this matter very seriously," the judge warns her.

Kelvin's wife shoots me a look of contempt before facing the judge. "Of course, your honor."

She looks completely composed after that. She doesn't look in my direction as she leaves the courtroom, and the woman that came in with her follows her out. The lawyer tells me that I'll need to update my address with the clerk's office once I move so that she can be informed. She has to know where I am so that she'll know where she isn't allowed to go. I feel like you're safer when crazy people don't know where to find you.

I took the day off, so after we leave the court we go back to the apartment. Jonah keeps asking me if I'm hungry, but I have absolutely no desire to eat anything. I should feel good to know that the order has been extended, but I feel unsettled. Going up to the loft, I kick off my shoes and lie down on my side while he goes to his office and checks his messages.

"She's sleeping with my husband!"

That sentence keeps playing in my head. I don't get it. She is utterly convinced that her husband and I are living together and having a relationship, which makes me wonder exactly what he's been telling her. The fact that she thinks that he's with me means that she doesn't know where he is either, and for some reason that scares the hell out of me. I honestly thought that Kelvin would get tired of this unrequited love thing and go away after a while.

If you could see some of the things that he's posted...yeah, we were together for a long time, but we weren't ever supposed to be forever. I told him all the time that I didn't want to get married and that my ultimate goal was to take care of my mom. He met my family and I met his. We were together for three years! It was unavoidable! We weren't looking at daycares and picking out China patterns.

Kelvin's mother was a stay at home mom, and that's what he always said he wanted in a wife. He constantly complained about me not knowing how to let a man be a man. He wanted to be the breadwinner and sole provider, and he wanted to marry a woman that cooked and cleaned and gave him at least four children. Were we in separate relationships? How the hell did he ever think that we would be able to have a marriage? It seems like he's got what he claimed to want in his wife, so why is he fixating on me? He also complained about my Mommy Fund, because I refused to dip into it for anything.

Jonah comes up the stairs and lies down behind me, wrapping his arm around my waist. "You okay?"

I nod. I'm really not, but I don't want him to worry.

He pulls me closer. "Liar."

I don't say anything. What is there for me to say? As soon as his aggravating ass ex stops being a problem, my ex's cheese slips off his cracker and he goes full on football helmet and cowboy boots on my ass, and so does his wife. I'm definitely not okay. I've got all kinds of images of that nut breaking into my house or hiding in my parking garage playing in my head.

Threesome and occasional public sexcapade notwithstanding, I've led a pretty conservative sex life. In terms of partners, if you don't count the women in the threesomes, I've only slept with five people. In this day and age that practically makes me a nun. It's just my luck that out of the five men that I've slept with, one of them would turn out to be nuttier than a jar of Planters.

"You gotta eat something." His voice is full of concern. I didn't eat dinner or breakfast because I was too nervous. This is the longest that he's ever seen me go without food. I did have coffee, but I doubt that he feels like that counts.

I rub his arm. "I will. I want to take a nap and I'll eat something after."

He kisses my shoulder. "Promise?"

I nod. I doubt that I'll have much of an appetite when I wake up, but I'll force myself to eat some crackers or something so that he doesn't freak out on me. I've learned that Jonah can be a mother hen when he gets worried about someone.

"How do you feel about the fact that I save money so that my mother can live with me when she gets older?"

"Are you kidding me? I love that about you," he says against my shoulder.

"Really? You don't think it'll bother you if things get hard and I refuse to use any of the money to help us out?" I turn to face him so that I can study his reaction.

He pulls back a little and frowns in confusion. "Why would I expect you to? You told me that you've been saving that money for almost ten years and it has a very specific purpose. It wouldn't be right for me to try to get you to use it for anything else. Besides, I've got a good amount in my savings and some investments in case shit gets tight."

"Okay, but what if..."

Jonah maneuvers me so that I'm on my back and he's leaning over me and brushes my hair away from my face. "Hey. Where's this coming from?"

"I just need to know that you understand what my goal is," I say with a shrug. We're moving into the condo in three days and I want him to know that at some point, we're probably going to go our separate ways.

He looks at me intensely for a minute before saying anything. "You know that my family's close, right?"

"Yeah, I know."

"My parents are basically planning to travel once my dad retires. They've saved a good chunk, and they plan on hiring a nurse to live with them when they get too old to take care of themselves because they don't wanna feel like a burden to anyone. Maybe getting a smaller house or a condo." He rubs his hand along my arm. "From what I understand about your mom, she hasn't been able to save any money or plan anything like that for herself."

I swallow, feeling self-conscious. Our upbringings were very different, and while I've never been ashamed of where I come from, I'm suddenly feeling inadequate. I shake my head when he continues to look at me as if he's waiting for me to say something.

"So, that means that what you're doing, saving money and planning to take care of her, is right. I mean, she basically raised you and your sisters by herself and it's not like she asks you for anything or even expects anything. I get that it's important to you to take care of her when she needs it. Families are supposed to do that for each other, baby. And, come on, she's your mother." He gives me a sort of, *why wouldn't you wanna take care of your mother?*, look.

"The plan is for me to save up enough money to buy a house and move her in with me and pay for her medical care when she gets older. She's had a lot of problems, so that could only be ten years off," I explain. I don't want him thinking that this is something that's going happen at some far-off time.

"That *was* the plan, but plans change. When she needs to live with us, then she will. It'll either be in the condo or some ranch style house with exposed beams in the ceiling and a huge master closet for your shoes." He says the last part with a grin.

"Jonah..." I'm going to cry, and I am not a crier.

"Taking care of your mother is important to you, so that means that it's important to me." He makes it seem like it's the most natural thing in the world.

I grab him and hold on tight. I can't even tell you how much what he just said means to me.

Jonah hugs me back and drops a kiss on the top of my head. "I love you, too."

Chapter Thirty-Six:

Two days later, I'm sitting at my desk and trying to focus enough to rework the numbers for a new campaign when the phone on my desk rings. I wish you could ignore work phones the way you can ignore cell phones, but it could be my team leader or someone from another department, so I have to answer.

"Good afternoon, this is Autumn Blaire." I sound as tired as I feel.

"Sweet." Kelvin's voice is a purr in my ear.

I jerk away from the phone like it just turned into a serpent and hang it up. *What the fuck? How did he get this number?*

It rings again not even a full minute later. And keeps ringing. Finally, my new team leader comes over and raises an eyebrow at me and motions to my phone like it's an air raid siren and furiously whispers for me to answer it.

I cringe as I lift the receiver from the cradle. "Good afternoon, this is Autumn Blaire."

"Don't hang up!" Kelvin barks at me. It sounds like more of a warning than a demand.

I rub my forehead. "How did you get this number?"

"You're on LinkedIn. I came by your place the other day, but there's some guy staying there, and he said he doesn't know you. Where you been?"

"Kelvin..." I feel like throwing up. I cannot even begin to understand why he thinks that this is okay.

"Look, sweet, it's time for you to stop being stubborn. I already left my wife for you."

"Did I ask you to do that?" I realize that I've raised my voice when I notice a few people looking at me. Leaning closer to my desk, I lower my voice. "I had to get a protection order against your crazy ass wife! Why won't you leave me alone?"

"Look, I'm sorry about that shit. I told her about us—"

"There is no us!" I say through clenched teeth. "You have a wife and a baby on the way! I have a boyfriend that I'm very much in love with and who wants to run you over with his truck because of the shit you've been posting online!"

"You're really still with that dude?" He blows out a breath. "This is because of her and the baby, isn't it?"

"You know what? If that's what you need to hear in order for you to leave me alone, then yes. That's what this is about," I tell him.

It's not. It has nothing to do with his wife and kid. Yeah, the cheating means that I would probably never trust him again, but I've moved on with my life and I'm in love for the first time, so anything to do with Kelvin and his relationship isn't even a blip on my radar.

"Listen, I know that you always said that you didn't want kids, and I know that this situation would be hard to manage, but you would be an amazing mother to my son. You're hardworking and caring. You always used to put my needs first... I'm going to file for sole custody and you won't even need to be around Kendra."

I frown into the phone in confusion. "Why do you think I would want to be involved in your child's life?"

"You don't think you could love my son like he was yours?" His voice is trembling.

I think he's crying, and sadly, I don't care about his feelings. At all. I just want him to stop bothering me. Maybe if he hadn't attacked my friend in a mall or popped up at my house calling me a whore or posted all that shit on every social media site there is, then I'd care that he's upset. It would bother me that he was hurting because even though he cheated on me, I did spend three years with him, and I would still want good things for him. But now? Not even a sliver of sympathy.

"Kelvin, I don't love you! How am I going to love your son?" I'm trying to keep my voice down, but it's hard.

"Why the hell are you doing this to us? Do you have any idea how much I love you? You know what I would do for you? And you over there saying that you can't accept my son?"

"Kelvin, you cheated on me and we broke up over a year ago! I. Have. Moved. On. You need to do the same. And, even if I were to want to take you back, the fact that you are having a baby would be a deal breaker for me. I'm not ready to be anyone's mother, and I certainly don't want to have to worry about your child's insane mother every day for the rest of my life. I want no parts of you or your situation." My head is starting to throb thanks to this conversation.

"You know what? Fuck you, you fuckin selfish bitch! You don't care about anyone but your damn self! Talking about how you moved on. Bitch, please with that bullshit! You need to be thanking me for even wanting to fuck with you. You think I don't know that you fucked Nate and Celia like a week after we broke up?"

"Do you think I care what you know? You think I'm ashamed of that or something? I'm not."

This is the threesome that I feel doesn't count since my contact with the female was limited. Besides, I only did it to piss Kelvin off.

"OF COURSE, YOU'RE NOT ASHAMED, YOU'D HAVE TO STOP BEING A TRIFLIN' BITCH FIRST! I GOT FIRED OVER THAT SHIT!" He's literally screaming in my ear.

I take a deep breath to keep from screaming back at him and getting myself fired. "So, you got fired from your job and that's on me? Okay? You think I'm a selfish bitch? I'm glad that you feel that way. Now, maybe you can move on. Don't call my work, stop posting shit, and tell your wife's family members to leave me alone!" I hang up the phone. There is the slightest sense of relief when it doesn't ring again.

I work for about two more hours before stopping and calling a friend of mine in Philly that I haven't talked to in a few months. She's dating a friend of Kelvin's and when he and I were together they were our companion couple. You know, the people that you do relationship things with. After we broke up, she and I didn't talk for a while since she and her man were on Kelvin's side about everything, but she hit me up after I moved back to Long Island, and now we text each other every once in a while.

I ask her about Kelvin's claim that he got fired over me sleeping with Nate. Turns out that he got fired this past September after he went to work and punched Nate in the face during a morning meeting. She doesn't know the specifics, but Kelvin and his wife ended up moving here to live with Kendra's mother because they couldn't afford their apartment anymore and he couldn't get hired at another company in Philly after what happened. Kelvin had been a financial adviser.

How the hell is he laying his getting fired over assaulting someone at my feet? Maybe if he had gotten into a fight with Nate a week or two after we broke up, it would lend credence to his claim. But a full year later? Nuh uh. That doesn't make sense to me. Especially given the fact that by then Kelvin was married with a pregnant wife and I was long gone. The nosy Rosie in me would love to know what their fight was really about, but I don't care enough to try to find out.

BY THE TIME I GET HOME I'm exhausted. Moving in with Jonah was definitely a good call. He lives much closer to my job, so it only takes me twenty minutes to get home. That means that instead of walking in the door at nine, I get in at a quarter after eight. And believe me, after the day I've had, I'm ready to just lay down in the entryway and go to sleep. Dropping my purse and coat on a chair in the living room, I look toward the hallway and the stairs that lead to the loft. I cannot manage that distance right now. I make it to the couch before I pass out. I didn't even manage to unbuckle the straps on my shoes.

I wake up in bed. Jonah must have brought me up here. He even managed to get me out of my shoes and the dress I wore to work, but he left me in my bra and panties.

The clock on the nightstand says that it's after one in the morning. I probably would have slept through the entire night if I wasn't hungry. I've been exhausted since going to court on Wednesday. Jonah is asleep next to me, so I make sure to be quiet as I leave the bed, take off my bra, throw on one of his shirts, and make my way to the kitchen. Hopefully there's something in there to eat. We cleared most of the food out after I took a nap on Wednesday. It made perfect sense and seemed like a good idea at the time, but now that I'm starving, I feel like we should have left everything edible alone until we were ready to walk out the front door. There are some things still in there. Mostly sandwich stuff, coffee, soda, and wine. I'm thinking a turkey sandwich and a bottle of Moscato.

A few of Jonah's friends, along with Mark, will be coming over to help us move at around ten. I really don't think that we need that much help, but Jonah can't move all of the heavy things by himself. Don't get me wrong, I am fully intending to help with the heavy lifting, or at least I had been, but when Jonah and I talked about it over the weekend, he acted like I was out of my mind. We don't even have that much to move. There's his bedroom set, my bedroom set, the set in his spare room, his office stuff, the televisions, washing machine and dryer, clothes, dishes, Jonah's workout shit, and the small appliances. Most of my furniture belonged to my aunt, so it's already in her storage unit and we decided to donate the living room, spare bedroom, and dining room sets that belong to Jonah.

I know what you're thinking, and the decision to get rid of the living and dining room sets wasn't mine. I was all for keeping them in the interest of saving money. I mean, yeah, I'll splurge on shoes and my car was a huge splurge that I was able to get because it was used, and I put a good chunk of money down on it since I'd been staying with my sister for the six months following my graduation and all she was making me pay was three-hundred dollars a month. Jonah wants us to get new furniture so that the condo will feel like us, not just like him or me. I think he's been reading relationship articles or something. So, because he's being all cohabitation guru, we're going furniture shopping on Sunday. He's thinking Haverty's, but I'm thinking Ikea. One is way less expensive than the other.

"What're you doin' up?" Jonah's sleep heavy voice comes from behind me.

I raise the loaf of bread in answer and turn back to the counter where I've laid out the sandwich fixings.

He yawns and comes over to me. Leaning against the counter, he quietly watches me for a bit. I'm doing my best to ignore the probing look that he's giving me. He's going to want to talk about the Kelvin situation. After the phone call at work earlier, I don't even have the energy. Putting everything away, I grab my sandwich and the bottle of wine that I took out and turn to head for the living room.

9I take two steps before Jonah redirects me to the kitchen table, pulls out a chair for me, and takes my bottle of wine. I glare at him, but he just shrugs and puts the bottle away before handing me a can of soda.

Sitting across from me, he places his hands on the table and waits. When I don't say anything, he scrubs a hand down his face and groans. "Will you fuckin' talk to me?"

I take a bite of my sandwich. "About?"

"Well, you've barely eaten in three days, and now you're up at two in the morning making a sandwich and trying to drink an entire bottle of wine. You gotta tell me something here, baby."

"It's just been a long week." And, it has. I've had a lot to do at work and we've been packing up for the move.

"And...?"

"And, I'm under a lot of stress. I've got a new team leader at work and he's a moron, we've been packing most of the week, Kelvin's crazy ass wife finally stopped tagging me, but her family picked up where she left off, so I just deleted my Twitter altogether, and now Kelvin's psychotic ass is calling me at work." Looking at my half-eaten sandwich, I grimace and push it away from me.

"He's been callin' you at work?" Jonah sits up straighter.

I shouldn't have said anything. I don't want him getting pissed off about this crap all over again. "No, only today. Well, yesterday now, I guess."

"What did he say?"

"Same thing he's been saying." I rub my temples.

"How'd he know where you work?" He asks suspiciously.

"I'm on LinkedIn." I drop my head onto the table. *Social media is the devil.*

I hear his chair scrape against the floor and look up. He looks really tired. I have no idea what time he went to bed since I passed out on the couch three seconds after I walked through the front door. He was at the condo earlier because someone had to be there when they came and connected the internet and cable, and I'm sure that it took hours.

He holds out his hand to me. "C'mon. We're goin' back to bed."

I let him pull me up and throw out the rest of my sandwich. "He was talking about me and him raising his son together, and then he started cursing me out."

Jonah stops walking toward the bedroom and looks at me over his shoulder. "He threatened you?"

"No, he just called me a selfish whore. Or something. I don't know," I say and wave it off. The things that he said aren't important. The fact that he won't stop bothering me is, though.

"You know if I ever come across 'im, I'm gonna whoop his ass, right." He says it like it's just a fact.

I lean into him and rest my head against his chest. "I don't want to think about that. Bed now?"

He drops a kiss to the top of my head and laces his fingers through mine before leading us back up to bed. As soon as I lie down, he pulls me into his side and sighs. There's a tension surrounding us, and I hate it. I've never felt tense or removed around Jonah. Even when I've been pissed at him about something, I never felt like there was any emotional distance between us.

"You know I love you, right?" I look at the shadowed silhouette of his face as I say it.

Jonah rolls over on top of me and I open my legs as he shifts around and gets comfortable. The room is dark and I'm sure that he can't really see me that well, but I can feel his eyes tracing over my face. He lightly runs a finger along my bottom lip before kissing me softly.

"Yeah, I know." He presses the words against my mouth as he kisses me again.

His lips are firm against mine as he continues kissing me. I feel my skin flush as the tension in the room slowly shifts and becomes something else. It goes from being about everything that I'm not saying to everything that he's making me feel. There is security in the weight of his body on top of me. There is comfort in the way that he caresses my face with his fingers. There is assurance in the steady thrum of his heart beating against mine. His hardness pressing into the juncture between my thighs is a grounding force that keeps me from being swept away by the emotions that are flooding through me.

I whimper when he moves back in order to remove his shirt and the shirt that I'm wearing as a nightgown and smile against his mouth when he comes back to me. I'm impatient to feel him moving inside of me, but Jonah is not about to be rushed tonight.

Kissing his way down my neck, he teases his tongue along my flesh until he reaches my breast. I'm expecting to feel his mouth engulf me, but instead he kisses and licks around my nipple without taking it into his mouth. His hand covers my other breast and he uses his fingers to tease my flesh. Jonah has taught me that pleasure, like pain, can be excruciating. I rock against him in an effort to ease some of the pressure building inside of me. He finally takes my sensitized bud into his mouth and I moan and arch into him.

Jonah returns to my mouth and kisses me deeply, exploring me as he slides his hands down my sides and hooks his fingers into the waistband of my panties. I lift my hips to help him remove them and slide my hands down his back to push his boxer briefs down. Once our underwear are out of the way, I feel the head of his cock, all hard and smooth rubbing against me.

"Jonah, please," I beg against his mouth. Even I can hear the desperation in my voice as I plead with him to move into me.

Jonah uses his hand to guide himself inside of me, and then he's sliding deep. He's thrusting slowly, driving me crazy, his skin rubbing against mine in a constant kiss. Lacing our fingers together, he brings our hands up above our heads to rest on the pillow and keeps them linked as he moves into me harder but still just as slowly. I'm moving with him. Climbing to that peak that he's taken me to countless times over the past few months.

"Jonah, fuck!" My voice breaks and I tighten my hold on him as that pressure that had been building inside of me bursts free.

"That's right, baby. Give it to me." He breathes against my mouth.

Jonah's thrusts pick up speed and he pounds into me as he chases his own orgasm. He presses his face into my neck and growls as his cock pulses inside of me. He kisses me along the side of my neck and nips my skin lightly where my neck meets my shoulder. Taking a deep breath, he rests against me for a moment, completely surrounding me, before moving off of me and pulling me into his side again.

My heart is pounding, my skin is humming, my head is swimming, and I've never been happier.

It's terrifying.

I don't personally know any genuinely happy people. There are people that seem happy, but you scratch the surface on that happiness and there's typically a mine field full of shit that they're not dealing with. Am I doing that? Kelvin is stressing me out and today he scared the fuck out of me. Am I just using these moments of happiness and peace that I have with Jonah as a throw rug to cover the Kelvin shit?

"When he called me, he was talking about me being a mother to his son." My voice comes out in a whisper. I told you before that I don't deal well with heavy emotions and part of me is hoping that Jonah is asleep. That for once, he'll be a normal guy and pass out after he comes. No dice.

"Should I be worried that we just had sex and you're thinking about your ex?" He doesn't sound worried.

I press a kiss to his chest. "No. It was a six degrees of separation thing."

He trails his fingers along my arm and sighs. "Okay, then. So, he called you while you were at work and talked to you about his son?"

"He was saying that we could raise his son together and that I'd be a great mother. I told him that I didn't want to be with him and that I didn't want to be a mother to his kid." I shake my head a little remembering how he went from fawning over me to berating me. "He started screaming at me and calling me selfish, and then he brought up the fake ass threesome that I had after he and I broke up."

"He knows about that?" Jonah asks almost incredulously.

Disclosing shitty things about yourself is never easy. Taking a deep breath, I sit up and reach over to turn on the bedside light so that I'll be able to see him while we talk. Am I ashamed of what I did? No. Do I recognize that it was shitty? Yes. Would I do it again? In a fucking heartbeat.

"Okay, so a few days after I caught him cheating on me, I went out with some friends and ran into a guy that he worked with and his secretary at a club—"

Jonah holds up his hand. "Kelvin's secretary or the guy's secretary?"

I pinch my lips together to keep from laughing at the question. I don't know why I find it funny. "Kelvin's secretary."

He nods and motions for me to proceed.

"Anyway, I ran into them and we started hanging out and having a good time that night, and I slept with them. Well, really him, but she did go down on me. I really only did it because I knew that Kelvin would find out and I wanted him to. I knew that it would piss him off because the guy had just received a promotion that Kelvin wanted, and the secretary was terrible at her job, but she was related to someone in the company, so he couldn't get her fired." I cautiously meet his eyes and wait for his reaction.

Jonah tilts his head to the side and bites his upper lip. I am feeling judged. And now my feelings are hurt. I shift away from him, but his hand stops me from leaving the bed.

"Hey. Don't...I'm not being a judgmental dick here, okay? I've had a good amount of one-nighters, so I can't say anything about you having sex with a guy that you weren't in a relationship with. I just have a question." He pulls me closer and waits for me to give him the go ahead to ask his question. "So, this guy? He was a friend of Kelvin's, or...?"

I snort. "No. Kelvin fucking hated him. The guy, Nate, was really likeable and attractive...Kelvin felt like he was phony and that no one else could see it."

"And you expected him to tell Kelvin about it?" He looks at me like I'm crazy.

"No, I expected Celia to talk about it. I figured that she'd gossip about it with someone at work and the gossip would eventually reach him," I explain.

Jonah nods slowly and looks me over skeptically. "And you weren't trying to hurt him at all, just piss him off?"

Alright, so maybe I wanted to hurt him. Even though I wasn't in love with Kelvin, I was aware of the fact that he was in love with me at one point. I did care a lot about him, I just always thought that we were heading in different directions. But, honestly, I wasn't trying to break Kelvin's heart or fuck up his world when I had sex with Nate. Considering the fact that he was cheating on me, I didn't think that I had that power over him anymore. Bottom line? I felt betrayed and I wanted him to feel betrayed.

I shrug by way of an answer because I'm not sure what to say.

Jonah blows out a breath and pulls me into him. "Come on. We're goin' to sleep."

I lean back and look at him a little surprised. "That's it?"

"Yeah." He shrugs. "Whatever happened between you and your ex, happened between you and your ex. You and me? We're getting up in a few hours, moving everything out of this apartment, and moving forward with each other. Anything and anyone that came before, doesn't matter."

"Okay. But this particular 'anyone/anything' is a problem—"

"And we're dealing with it," he says, cutting me off. "I love you. All of you. The good and the bad—and make no mistake that you sleeping with some guy that your ex hates as a way to make him hurt, was fucked up."

"I get that, but I don't regret it." I'm trying to be completely honest with him.

"I figured." He stretches and tries to pull me down again.

I shake him off. There's a reason that I brought this all up. "I'm scared."

He sits up, and this time when he pulls me into him, I go without a fight. Jonah drags me into his lap so that my back is to his front and wraps his arms around me.

"Baby..."

"I know that he doesn't know where I live, and even with him knowing where I work, it isn't like he can just walk into my office or even get into the parking garage to do anything to me. I get that. But I don't know where he is or why he won't leave me alone and before it was just annoying, but when he called me today, he flipped out on me, and that shit was scary." I rub my fingers along Jonah's arms where they're wrapped around my middle. "He went from talking about me being a mother to his son to screaming at me and calling me a selfish bitch. It was like a switch got flipped," I say quietly.

Jonah kisses my shoulder and squeezes me a little. "I think that once we get everything into the condo and everybody leaves, we should call the cops again."

"Jonah, it's not like everybody's going to be gone in an hour. We have to move an entire apartment and drop off furniture to Goodwill, and set up the bedroom, and eat at some point."

"Okay, but police departments are open twenty-four hours a day. If we gotta call them at midnight, just so that they can have a steady record of this shit, then that's what we're gonna do." 2

"Alright," I agree. I can't see a problem with making sure the cops where we live know about everything that's been going on.

Jonah reaches over and turns off the light. I lie half on top of him and pull the covers over us. It takes me a little while, but I finally fall asleep. Unfortunately, I have nothing but nightmares about Kelvin popping out of bushes and from behind pillars in parking garages. When I wake up, it's after nine in the morning and I feel like I haven't slept at all.

Chapter Thirty-Seven:

Lying on the floor of my new living room, I look around at all of the boxes littering the space. You never realize how much shit you've actually accumulated until you have to box it up and move it someplace else. I'd only been living in my townhouse for six months, and the majority of the furniture there had belonged to my aunt, yet I still had boxes upon boxes of clothes, shoes, pictures, bedding, dishes, knick-knacks, small appliances, and movies that needed to be moved. It's going to take forever to unpack all of this crap. On the good side of things, moving everything over only took a little over three hours. Jonah and a few of his friends went back to the apartment for a twin bed along with the living, kitchen, and dining room furniture and are going to drop it all off to Goodwill. While they're doing that, Mark and I are supposed to be unpacking.

We set up the furniture in the master bedroom. We decided to use Jonah's bedroom set since his bed is a California king and mine is a queen. After we got the bed re-assembled and the dresser and night stands all arranged, we stalled out. We did get the wine fridge stocked before we collapsed on the floor, but we'd better get up and do a little bit more before everyone else gets back.

"Okay, let's start putting the dishes away and we can move Jonah's office stuff into the spare room that's closer to the living room. He wants to set that room up himself, and then we can put my bedroom set into the other room and get that set up." I say, pushing myself up from the floor.

Mark groans but gets up and starts looking for the box that has the dishes in it. "I swear that when I moved into my apartment, it took me a year to finish unpacking. The way you're working me, we'll have this place done before dinner."

"Yeah, well my mom is supposed to be coming down for a visit in a few weeks, and since Jonah travels so much, we're trying to get everything unpacked as soon as possible. That's why we're going shopping for living room and dining room stuff tomorrow," I tell him.

"You guys should go to The Dump. They have a lot of designer stuff for like seventy percent off," he says, gesturing at me with one of the wine glasses that he's putting away. "I got my bedroom set there."

"I love your bedroom set," I sigh.

"I know." He studies the glass in his hand. "What are the odds of us opening up one of those bottles of wine?"

"Focus." I roll my eyes at him. "Once the guys get back, we're going to treat everyone to food and drinks as a thank you for helping us."

"Are we talking a sit-down meal or..."

"Jonah wants to do Fogo de Chao, but that would require everyone getting changed, so I'm leaning toward Tin Lizzy's."

Mark moves his head from side to side in consideration. "I could go for some lobster tacos."

"I'm saying."

By the time Jonah gets back with Zach, Juan, Keon, and Ethan, Mark and I have unpacked the entire kitchen, put Jonah's work stuff in his office, and set up the beds, dressers, and night stands in the spare and master bedrooms. We've also moved the boxes with the clothes and shoes into the master closet. We can be very efficient with the proper motivation, and lobster tacos and margaritas are just the dangling carrot that we need.

"Damn, baby, you guys were not messin' around," Jonah says as he takes in the space.

I look up from where I'm unpacking pictures. "I told you that Mark and I could handle it."

Coming over to me, he smiles and gives me a quick kiss. "Tin Lizzy's, huh?"

"Yup," I laugh.

Thankfully Tin Lizzy's isn't too crowded when we get there and we're able to get a table that fits all of us. It's not until we get there that I realize that I'm the only female in the group, but the guys don't seem to mind. Conversation centers around the condo and the fact that Jonah was closer to SunTrust Stadium when he was in the apartment. Not that it matters. He's not a big baseball fan, but he is very into football and soccer.

"Y'all really gotta stop all of this movin' in together shit. Y'all are making me look bad as hell," Keon jokes. There are a few groans and Zach throws a nacho at him.

It seems that he and Carly have been together for over two years and she's been pushing for them to live together, but he's been holding off on her.

"Will you nut up and just move in with the woman already," Jonah tells him.

"I like havin' my own space," he defends. "It's great that y'all were ready for that step, for real, but I'm not there yet."

I'm staying all the way out of this conversation. Keon seems nice, Carly seems nice, and that's all I got. I don't know either of them well enough to chime in on their relationship. I take a long drink from the straw of my margarita glass and steal a piece of Jonah's shrimp. Jonah shoots me a look and slides his plate away from me. I pout, and he slides it back, but takes a piece of my beer battered lobster. He laughs when I slide my plate away from him because he knows that I won't be sliding it back.

Ethan orders celebratory shots for the table, and when the waitress drops them off, I notice that the napkin that she placed under Jonah's shot has a note written on it. It says, 'call me' and there's a phone number. I raise my eyebrows at Jonah, and he gives me a kiss and pushes the napkin over to the side. I find it offensive when I'm out with Mark and women approach him. Mainly because, even though he's gay, the women don't know that and it's rude for them to hit on him while I'm with him. In this case, I'm the only female at a table full of guys, and I could be dating one of them or none of them, so it was a shot in the dark. Still, I'm tempted to write, 'don't hit on your customer's boyfriend', in the tip space when she brings the check.

Zach laughs and mutters something that sounds like, "every time", under his breath. I see Juan jab him with his elbow before shooting me a smile and I turn to Jonah again, one of my eyebrows nearly to my hairline and my facial expression all about the: you'd better elaborate, now.

Jonah just shrugs. "I have no idea what he's talking about."

"So, you don't have a drawer full of napkins with waitress's phone numbers on them?" I'm only half joking.

He puts his arm around me and pulls me closer. "Nah, I threw 'em all out around the time I was buying *The Princess Bride* on Vudu."

I don't say anything, but I move my plate closer to his on the table. A part of me wants to ask some questions about how often women are approaching him and tossing him phone numbers, but that seems crazy. Jonah is attractive. Hell, I was transformed into a staring moron the first time I saw him, and he was dressed like a basement dweller. And, come on, men hit on me all the time and he deals. It's only a problem if he starts taking women up on their offers.

See? I can get a handle on the jealous and the crazy. For the most part anyway.

"You're staying with us tonight, right?" Jonah is talking to Ethan. He had three beers before the shots, and he had two of those since Zach passed on his. Ethan lives in Fayette. That's kind of a drive from Dunwoody.

"Nah, I figured that you two would wanna christen the new place tonight. I'm gonna go home with her." He points to a blonde that's sitting at a table on the other side of the room. She waves at him when he points to her and motions for him to come over.

Mark and I exchange looks and take sips of our margaritas. We're both thinking the same thing. He better double up on the condom with that one. She's practically throwing her panties at him from across the room. Hell, they may not make it to her apartment.

Ethan stands up and braces his hands on the table. "I'll be right back."

"What are the odds that he's going to call you in the middle of the night to pick him up? Isn't his car at our house?" I ask while watching him cross the room.

"Don't worry about it." Jonah takes a sip of his beer. "He'll probably stay with her the whole night and then take an Uber to our place to grab his car in the morning."

Our waitress stops by to check on us and see if we need anything. I manage to get her attention, (which is a feat since she's more interested in mentally fucking my boyfriend than doing her damn job) and order some churros.

She nods at me and then puts her hand on Jonah's shoulder and starts rubbing him. "And, can I get you anything?"

I lean around him to get her attention as he's leaning away from her. "Yeah, you can get your hand off his shoulder. Physical contact is not necessary."

She snatches her hand back like she accidentally touched a hot stove. "Sorry. Just being friendly."

I smile sweetly at her and pick up the napkin with her phone number on it. "I noticed. By the way, you dropped this."

Blushing, she looks from me to Jonah and takes the napkin from my hand. "I'll be right out with your churros."

I roll my eyes as she rushes away from the table and take a sip of my margarita. I notice that the table has gone quiet and look around. "What?"

Juan snickers and it seems like that's all the provocation that everyone else needs. They're all laughing like there's a comedian at our table giving us a private show. I really don't know what the hell is so funny. I was willing to let the napkin thing slide, but then she came back and practically humped his leg. How thirsty is this chick?

Mark nudges my shoulder. "Honey, that was a thing of bitchy beauty. The claws were definitely out."

I just shrug. Jonah felt a kind of way over a dress that I wore to a work party. This is way different than that. Who just starts stroking some stranger's shoulder? And there are six other people at this table! Her tip is just shrinking more and more.

By the time we leave, I am nicely buzzed, Ethan has left with two women, Mark has ignored five calls and two texts from Henry, and Jonah and I have been invited to a painting party at Zach and Molly's house next weekend. All in all, it was a good time. We compromised and left the waitress a fifteen percent tip.

When we get home, the situation with the waitress is heavy on my mind. I've never been jealous in a relationship before. It always seemed silly to stress myself out over things that may or may not be happening between the person that I'm dating and another woman. I always felt like there were too many men in the world for me to get into any kind of conflict over one. Besides that, I've been drinking. Typically, when I drink enough to feel buzzed, nothing fazes me. I'm able to laugh everything off or just not let things get to me. Right now? I feel like going back to the restaurant, dropping into a three-point stance, and blitzing that bitch. What the fuck is wrong with me?

Jonah tosses his keys on the counter and groans. "This day was long as hell. I'm ready to just take a shower and pass out."

"How often do women hit on you?" I blurt out.

He looks over at me near the door and raises his eyebrows. "Clearly you're not."

"Jonah." I sound serious. Apparently, I am very interested in the answer to this question. I didn't know that until just now.

He walks over to me and locks the door. "Baby, do we really have to do this?"

"Look, I probably wouldn't even care, but you spend a lot of time in other countries and states, and—"

"And I'm not the guy that cheated on you, so how about not treating me like I am!" he interrupts me.

I'm not doing that! Am I doing that?

"I know that! But thanks. I'm just asking a question. I think it's understandable for me to want to know if you've ever had sex with a random while you were away on *business*. How is that unreasonable?"

"I have not been with anyone else since we've been together." He states it calmly while holding my eyes with his.

"That didn't answer my question." I narrow my eyes at him.

He throws up his hands and walks away from me before turning back around. "Autumn...look, I don't need to know how many times a day other men hit on you, and I definitely don't need to know how many guys you had sex with before we met or what the circumstances were. That shit isn't important as far as I'm concerned. What happened before me was before me. Fuckin' end of story!"

He has made a valid point, and yet, I can't let this go. I have no idea why I'm pushing this. I'm not even sure that I really want to know the answer to what I'm asking, but I can't leave it alone.

"Have you, or have you not slept with women that you are likely to see again while you've been away on business?"

He clenches his jaw, and I don't think he's going to answer my question, which honestly would be the answer. But then, he does.

"Yeah."

I nod. I feel like crying. Seriously what the fuck is wrong with me? Did I think he was going to say no? I'd have to be stupid to think that Jonah had never slept with anyone while he was on one of those trips or at one of those conferences. And why the hell did I ask whether he was likely to see them again? I don't want to know that. Fuck! I'm going to blame this on the alcohol and pray that I don't remember any of it in the morning.

Walking around him and making sure to avoid any form of contact, I decide to take his initial suggestion and head for the shower in the master bathroom.

As I stand under the steaming water, I wonder how the night ended up here. Don't get me wrong. I realize that I started us down this path with the drunk ass jealous questions, but I really don't know why. I have personally known people that have not only slept with men that I've been in relationships with, but I had a three-some with Kelvin and was in the bed while he fucked the other chick, and at no time was I jealous or upset!

Jonah was engaged to that walking carton of rapidly souring milk, Kaylin, and I never felt jealous about that. I was annoyed that he didn't tell me before I met her, and the fact that he cancelled on me for her at one point had me livid, but not out of jealousy. Mainly it was because her so called emergencies were bullshit and I felt like she was manipulating him into spending time with her.

This feeling that I have now is completely foreign to me. I don't like it. Does being in love make you an insecure and overly emotional basket case? If it does, then I don't think I want it. I've never been an insecure person. Ever. So, what is going on with me?

I get out of the shower and go into the closet to rummage through one of the boxes of clothes for something to sleep in. Grabbing one of Jonah's t-shirts, I throw it on and head to bed. He isn't in the room and it makes me wonder if he decided to sleep somewhere else. Before I can decide if I should find him and apologize for being a psycho, he comes into the bedroom. I watch as he walks into the bathroom and closes the door, and then I hear the shower come on. Maybe I'll get lucky and we'll just pretend that none of this ever happened.

I must have dozed off, because I wake up when I feel him slide into bed with me. He fits his body to mine, his skin cool and damp where mine is dry and warm. One of his arms slides under my head while the other slides around my waist and pulls me even closer.

"I love you so fuckin' much," he says against the back of my neck.

I reach back and slide my hand into his hair. "I know."

"Then you gotta trust me, baby. I'm not gonna cheat on you. Hell, I feel like I've waited my whole life for you."

"Honestly, I don't even know where all of that came from." I really don't.

The problem is...I'm still feeling like a jealous psycho. Like, I want to ask for names and dates and pictures, even though I really, truly do not want any of that shit.

Jonah strokes his hand over my stomach. "You're stressed. There's a lot of shit going on right now."

I laugh. "Are you making excuses for my crazy?"

"I'm not excusing it, I'm understanding it. You've never done this before. Shit, neither have I. But I trust that when I'm away for work, you're not here with some random guy. I mean...fuck, I can't even think about that shit." He rubs his face against my shoulder and releases a breath.

"Jonah..."

"You have an ex that keeps reminiscing about sex with you, on social media. It's like a bad fuckin' car crash. I don't wanna see it, but I know it's there and I can't stop myself from looking. And every time I look, and he's posting' about something' y'all did together—"

"I'm sorry." Truer words were never spoken. I need a Way-back Machine so that I can go back in time and stop myself from ever dating Kelvin. If I had to read the kind of things about Jonah that Kelvin has been posting about me, I'd be homicidal by now.

"For what? For being hard to get over? That ain't your fault." He kisses my shoulder. "I'd be a basket case if you ever left me. I wouldn't be posting shit online, but I'd definitely be wrecked for a long time. Maybe forever."

"I'm not going anywhere," I promise. And I mean it. I take a deep breath and snuggle back into him. Seriously, I'm losing my shit over hypothetical situations, and he's dealing with Kelvin reliving our past in a public meltdown.

Thanks a lot, perspective. Where the fuck were you an hour ago?

Turning my head, I pull him forward and give him a kiss. I mean for it to just be something to seal my promise, but when I go to pull back, Jonah holds me to him. His hand moves under the shirt that I'm wearing and travels to my breasts, sliding between them. He holds me and cuddles me before moving his fingers to my nipple and pinching me until I gasp into his mouth. He lets go of my breast and moves his hand down to cup me between my legs. His fingers slide into me and my muscles contract.

Jonah groans into my mouth. "Fuck, baby. You get so wet for me."

He gets me right to the edge with his fingers and then leaves me hanging on the precipice while he helps me out of my shirt. I move to lay on my back, but he turns me so that I'm on my side again. He moves my leg up and out of the way, and then he's sliding into me. He keeps his arm wrapped tightly around my waist as his body moves against mine.

Pushing back against him, I feel him slide deeper. He moves harder into me and I reach back and tangle my hand in his hair. "Oh, God, Jonah!"

Jonah kisses me on the side of my neck. "Damn, I love you!"

"Jonah!" I can feel my orgasm building. Growing bigger and bigger inside of me. Expanding until it becomes too big, too wide, too much for my body to contain. The force of it bends me in half as it barrels through me. Jonah's arm is a steel band around my waist as he pistons into me until he comes with a shout.

He pulls me up so that our bodies are flush against each other again. I can feel his smile against the back of my neck as he tries to catch his breath. "Condo... Christened."

Laughing, I kiss his arm that's still resting under my head. "The bedroom is. We've still got to christen the bathrooms, living room, kitchen, and other bedroom, and your office. Ooh, and the laundry room!"

"When we go shopping tomorrow, we need to get a really sturdy table for the dining room," he sighs. "I'm gonna make chicken parmesan this week, and I wanna have you for dessert."

I fall asleep with a smile on my face. Being in love is great.

Chapter Thirty-Eight:

I have moved to a state that loses its collective mind over a snow flurry. I was at work on Wednesday, and it started to snow around one o'clock. I didn't think anything of it, but pretty soon people started freaking out and they were telling us all to go home and to keep checking our email to find out if the building would be open the next day. I kept thinking that it was a joke. It was not.

I got home relatively quickly, and Jonah acted like it was a miracle that I'd arrived safely. My confusion grew. I watched the news and they were calling it "Snow-mageddon Part Two". There were seriously three inches of snow.

Three. Inches.

People were abandoning their cars on the interstate because this state can't handle three inches of snow. There were eighteen car pile-ups. This is the craziest shit that I have ever seen. I grew up on Long Island. We got feet of snow every year. It wasn't strange to see huge piles of snow in mall parking lots that were still melting in June. Then I went to college in Philly, and there is no such thing as a snow flurry in Pennsylvania. You either got a few feet or you got nothing at all. So, to see nearly an entire state grind to a halt over a few inches of snow is just surreal.

My office closed on Thursday, and then it *gasp* snowed again in the middle of the night, so I've been working from home for the past two and a half days. Jonah and I were able to go grocery shopping and find furniture at The Dump on Sunday, and they delivered everything on Tuesday, so at least we got to be snowed in in comfort. We got a cream-colored leather living room set that could comfortably seat Paul Bunion, and a very sturdy dining room set.

The chicken parmesan was delicious, but dessert was better.

I hear Jonah rummaging around in the kitchen before he comes over to the living room where I'm working. I've got my laptop open in front of me and papers spread out everywhere while I try my damnedest to force the numbers for this latest campaign to work. It's not happening. Part of the problem could be the fact that I've been on the phone with Mark for the past hour attempting to calm him down. He and Henry have been trapped in an apartment together for the past few days, and he's reached his breaking point. It seems that he went to the gym that is located at his apartment complex, and Henry flipped out about it.

Okay, so Henry told Mark that he wanted the two of them to take a break during Christmas, because Henry was going on a vacation with his wife and kids and he was confused about what he wanted. Mark was hurt but agreed. Then Mark got drunk at the company Christmas party and made out with some guy from another department and let the guy blow him in the bathroom. When Henry came back from his family vacation, he told Mark that he had slept with his wife while he was away and that it happened three times, but Henry swore upside down and cross ways that he loved Mark and that he still wants them to be together. Mark, in an attempt to be completely honest, admitted to the Christmas party hook-up. It did not go over well.

Despite the fact that Henry had sex with his wife three times while they were on vacation, and despite the fact that he's the one that wanted them to take a break, he keeps bringing up the blowjob and calling Mark a cheater. Henry's argument is that since he slept with his wife, it's more forgivable because of the relationship that he has with her, but since Mark's hook-up was random, it was a disgusting betrayal. I cannot even process that level of bullshit.

Henry is now convinced that every time Mark is away from him, he's with the guy from the Christmas party. He doesn't even know who it was, because Mark won't tell him, so he has accused Mark of being with nearly every man in our department! He really thinks that Mark somehow managed to get around all of the stalled traffic and icy roads to get his dick sucked by the Christmas party guy, or CPG, while he was supposed to be at the gym.

Now, CPG *did* contact Mark via his company email. He basically just told him that he wanted to continue their conversation that started at the Christmas party, and asked that Mark give him a call. He included his personal number in the email and left it at that. Mark called him and told him that he was kind of in a relationship, and CPG fell back. He told Henry that, too. Despite Mark's reassurances, Henry is convinced that Mark is still in contact with CPG and fucking him on a regular basis.

When Mark called me, I could hear Henry in the background yelling, "Who are you talking to?! Is that him?!"

I thought I was being a psycho the other day when I got all upset about the fact that Jonah had ever slept with anyone else, but this shit is James McAvoy in *Split* level crazy. I would tell Mark to come over here, but there's no way that he can get here. It started snowing again and even if it hadn't, I'm sure that him leaving for any period of time would just make things worse.

"Mark...Mark!" I rub my hand across my forehead. He and Henry are arguing, and it sounds like it's becoming volatile. "Mark, remove yourself!"

"And go where? I'm stuck in this apartment with this *insufferable bitch*!" he finally addresses me, but it's clear that he's talking to Henry.

And now they're both yelling again.

"Mark...sweetie...MARK! Go into the bedroom and lock the fucking door!" I yell into the phone.

I hear a door slam, so I think that he did what I told him to do, but they're still arguing. If they keep it up, I'm sure that their neighbors are going to call the cops on them.

"Mark...?"

Jonah comes over and stands in front of me, giving me a questioning look. I just shake my head. I can hear Henry yelling, "let me in", and it sounds like someone is banging on a door. Finally, things go quiet.

"Mark?"

Mark clears his throat. "I can't do this anymore. I did not survive an attempt to fucking kill myself and get another shot at living for me to put up with this shit!"

I nod even though I know he can't see me. "Okay. What do you need me to do? Do you want me to come over there once the snow stops so that you can tell him that you want him to leave, or do you want to take some time and rethink things—"

"As soon as the roads are clear, I want you outta my apartment!" Mark yells.

And now Henry is banging on the door again and they're screaming back and forth.

"Hey," Jonah taps my forearm, "what's going on?"

I put my phone on speaker and hit mute so that Mark won't hear me. "They've been in the apartment together for three days and Mark went to the fitness center at the complex, and now Henry is accusing Mark of cheating on him."

Jonah looks at me like I'm crazy. "This is an adult?"

"You met Henry, remember? From the Cheesecake Bistro?" I prompt.

"I remember. Isn't that guy like fifty?" Jonah asks, and then his eyebrows shoot up when the argument that we're listening to over the phone ticks up again.

The word, selfish, is being thrown around and peppered with varying obscenities. I'm pretty sure that they're still yelling at each other through the door. I'm also pretty sure that the only reason that the police aren't knocking on their front door is because they can't get into the parking lot.

"Whoa!" Jonah takes a step back and his mouth drops open at a particularly harsh insult that was tossed out there by Henry. It involved the older woman that Mark slept with as a teenager and the baby that she didn't have.

Violence in relationships is never okay, but I would totally understand if Mark kicked his ass. Henry is abusive. No, he's never assaulted Mark in any way, but he knows exactly what to say to light up every one of Mark's emotional pain sensors.

I look up at Jonah. "Can your truck make it to Mark's apartment?"

He stares at me for a minute and sighs. "Yeah, let me get my keys."

"Mark?...MARK!" I yell his name into the phone.

"Yeah?" he responds in a way that lets me know that he's only half listening to me.

"We're coming to get you. Be there in ten. Stop responding to him. I'm going to use the key you gave me to get in so that you don't have to come out to answer the door. Pack up some clothes, okay? You're gonna stay with us through the weekend." My tone is very matter of fact. I am not hearing him staying in that apartment with that asshole anymore.

He's quiet for a minute, but I can still hear Henry alternately begging him to open the door and verbally abusing him in the background.

"Alright."

I'm wearing a pair of Jonah's sweatpants and a tank top, and my hair is tied up in a head scarf. I didn't think that I'd be leaving the house today. I look out the window to the city below and see that huge flakes are falling slowly, but it doesn't look like they're sticking. Still, there are no cars on the road. Mark only lives five minutes away from us, so hopefully we can get to him and get him back here quickly.

Jonah hands me a pair of socks, my Bear Paw boots, and my coat. I smile a thank you at him and hurry putting them on. It feels like it takes forever for us to get to the parking garage, and even longer for us to make our way down to the street level. My legs are bouncing in my impatience to get to Mark and get him out of his apartment before he does something that he'll regret. I'm still on the call, and I keep telling him that we're almost there. I can hear Henry yelling again, and then it sounds like something is slamming into the door.

When we reach Mark's apartment and Jonah pulls into a space, I fly out of the truck before he even turns the engine off. I can hear Henry from outside. I'm sure that everyone in the entire complex can hear Henry.

"I'm here! I'm unlocking the door right now!" But my hands are shaking, and I can't get the key in the lock.

Then Jonah is there. He takes the key from me and gets the door open, but he grabs me and pulls me back before I can run inside. Moving in front of me, he keeps me behind him and enters the apartment.

"Hello…!" Jonah calls out.

It's like someone pulled the plug on the volume in the apartment, because it goes completely silent.

Henry comes down the hall breathing heavily, face flushed, and points a finger at Jonah. "You are trespassing!"

I hear the bedroom door open down the hall and then I see Mark come out carrying a duffel bag. He looks wretched, and I lunge for Henry. Jonah catches me and holds me back.

Henry is so lucky that I forgot to grab my keys with my pepper spray.

Mark moves around Henry and grabs my hand, giving it a squeeze. "I'm okay, Autobot. I promise."

I look up at him, breathing hard and fists trembling, and try to get myself under control. I squeeze his hand in response, because I don't have any calm words right now.

Mark nods at Jonah before turning to Henry. "I'm gonna stay at Autumn's until Sunday. You need to be gone when I get back, or I'm callin' the cops and havin' them remove you."

Henry looks like he wants to say something, and I wish he would. One word out of his mouth, and I'm going to channel my inner Incredible Hulk and pile drive him all the way to the center of the fucking Earth! He shoots me a look before he looks over at Mark and just nods. I doubt that it'll really be that simple, but for now, I'll take it.

Jonah leads the way out of the apartment, keeping me in front of him. Once we're out in the corridor and Mark has locked the door behind us, Jonah relaxes his hold on me.

"One of these days, I'mma have to post bail for you, I just know it," Jonah says as he steers me toward the parking lot.

I keep looking back at Mark like I expect him to evaporate into thin air or something. He's clearly upset but musters a smile for me anyway. I take a deep breath and try to drag my mind away from all of the ways that we could kill Henry and dispose of his bloated corpse so that I can focus on my friend.

When we get to the parking lot, I realize that there's a huge slush puddle on the passenger side of the truck. How the fuck did I manage not to step in that thing when I jumped out and ran to Mark's apartment? I hear Jonah hit the key fob to unlock the doors and try to figure out how the hell I'm going to manage to extend my stubby ass legs over that thing. As I'm resigning myself to the ruination of my boots, Jonah takes off his coat and throws it over the puddle before opening my door.

I swear to God, time slows down.

I'm sitting in the passenger seat with my mouth hanging open in shock when Mark climbs into the back seat and says, "Close your mouth, honey. You're catchin' flies."

Jonah seriously threw his coat over a puddle for me. Once he closes my door, he grabs the coat, a London Fog three-in-one that he just bought two weeks ago, off of the ground and tosses it in the truck bed. He's wearing a dark gray, long sleeved Henley with a hole at the hem, some old faded blue jeans with a tear at the knee, and work boots that have paint spatters on them. He needs a haircut, he hasn't shaved today, and he is the most beautiful thing I've ever seen.

Jonah starts the car and then shifts into reverse, but he must feel me staring at him, because he looks over at me with a quizzical expression on his face. "What?"

Mark sighs wistfully from the back seat. "Just when I thought that romance was dead, Mr. Jonah comes along and throws his coat over a puddle for my little Automotive."

Chapter Thirty-Nine:

I have been replaying the coat over the puddle incident in my mind for four days. Is it weird that I can't get over it? I nearly proposed to him right then. And he acted like it was no big deal.

We got home, and he threw the coat into the washing machine and started cooking comfort food for Mark while I got him settled in the spare bedroom. I should have been comforting Mark and making sure that he was okay, but all I could talk about was that coat dropping onto that slush puddle. Mark was more than happy to focus on my relationship than his and started talking about center pieces for the wedding that he's planning for me and Jonah in his head. We're going to have floating cymbidium orchids and lilies, and our colors are blush and mint.

Mark is priceless.

He's also heartbroken. When he went home Sunday evening, Henry was gone but he had left a lot of things behind. I helped Mark box it all up and we took it to FedEx after work on Monday and shipped it to Henry's wife's house since that's where Mark figures he went. I thought that we should have burned it, but I was overruled.

Mark called his therapist and had an emergency session with her about what happened with Henry and she agreed that ending the relationship and cutting all ties was for the best, so Mark blocked Henry's phone number and email address. I really hope that he sticks with this decision because Henry is a toxic jackass. Not that Mark doesn't have his own shit to work out but having the person that you love tell you that it's a good thing that someone chose not to have your kid because you're too selfish to ever be a real parent anyway, is just beyond the pale.

Jonah was great throughout all of the drama. He made us fried chicken and baked macaroni and cheese, then after we all ate, he gave me a kiss and went back to his office to work so that Mark and I could talk. He worked most of the day Saturday too, but he hung out with us once he finished up. We watched *Harry Potter and the Deathly Hallows: Parts 1&2* and then, because we needed to laugh, we watched *Coming to America.*

I'm praying that things will calm down now.

Kelvin hasn't posted anything or tried to contact me since the last time I spoke to him and I am relieved. Maybe me telling him that I didn't want to be a mother to his child was the wake-up call he needed. One can only hope.

I'm on my way home for the day at just after six (which is very early for me) when I get a phone call from Jonah.

"Hey, babe. You'll be surprised to hear that I'm on my way home," I say as I put the phone on speaker and sit it in the mount that's attached to my vent.

"Hey, I was trying to catch you before you left work. I was hoping you could stop by the store on your way home."

"For...?" I ask, pulling out of the parking garage.

"We're out of bread."

"The multigrain bread or the cinnamon swirl bread?" I care about replacing one of those much more than I care about replacing the other. Would you like to guess which one?

"The multigrain. I know you're not a fan, but I use it for my turkey sandwiches. Stop making that face," he says with a laugh.

"How do you know that I'm making a face? You can't even see me," I point out. But he's right, I was making a face.

"Because I know you. Now, can you grab bread on your way home? Please?"

"You've been home all damn day. Why couldn't you go out and get your bread your damn self?"

"For the same reason that you sat watching that damn alligator documentary that you didn't wanna watch the other day until I came in the room and you asked me to give you the remote."

In my defense, I accidentally left the remote on the kitchen island and the kitchen and living room are really far apart in the condo. I groan. "Ugh, fine. I'll stop at a store and grab you some nasty ass multigrain bread."

"Thank you, baby. I'll see you when you get home."

I blow him a kiss and end the call. I don't understand how he eats that bread. It tastes like cardboard to me, but to each his own.

I get to Kroger and find a space that isn't too far from the entrance. I find it crazy that a few inches of snow had this state on complete lockdown just about a week ago, and now you can't even tell that there was any snow anywhere to begin with. Hell, by Sunday it was basically all gone.

After grabbing Jonah's cardboard bread, I get a bag of chips and a four pack of Chobani Flips before heading to the self-checkout and hurrying back to my car. It may not be as cold here as it was on Long Island or Philly, but my slacks are thin, and the wind is biting into my skin.

When I reach my car, what I see there makes me think that I should have never gotten out of bed today. Kelvin is standing there and he's staring straight at me. A few months ago, I wouldn't have hesitated to just ignore him and get into my car. Now, in light of his recent flip out over the phone, it seems safer to retreat.

I turn around and head back to the store, but he reaches me before I've taken more than a few steps, and his hand locks around my forearm. I can't even pepper spray him because my keychain is in the hand that's attached to the forearm that he's damn near crushing in a vice grip. He doesn't say anything, just starts trying to drag me towards his car. The heels that I'm wearing aren't helping me dig my feet in, so I start screaming and swinging the grocery bag in my other hand at him. The bag rips and the few groceries that I bought spill out onto the ground. My voice is so loud that it's echoing, and I see people stopping. I feel my purse slide down my arm and I can't catch it before it hits the ground. My stun gun is in my purse. I try to reach down to pick the purse back up before he gets me too far away from it, but he yanks me back and I start clawing at his hand that's holding my forearm.

"HELP ME!" I'm screaming like a banshee and finally the people that had stopped to watch are running toward us.

Everyone stops rushing forward when Kelvin pulls out a gun and starts waving it around.

He's going to kill me.

What seemed like an overblown fear before is a glaringly obvious reality now. Kelvin is crazy, and he's going to kill me. So many things rush through my mind.

Who's going to take care of my mother?

Will Mark be okay?

I hope he leaves my body somewhere that it can be found. It'll break my mother's heart if after he kills me, she can't bury my body.

Jonah.

I'm never going to see him again. I'm never going to have another Christmas with him, or argue with him, or miss him when he goes away for work. I'm never going to marry him or have children with him.

He gets me to the passenger side of his truck and starts trying to shove me inside, but I'm kicking and flailing and making it as difficult as I can. I have to believe that someone called the police and if I can just keep us here, they'll come before he can do anything to me. That plan is scrapped when he slams me in the side of the face with the gun. That scene from *Sin City* inexplicably pops into my head. The one where Clive Owen's character is trying to recover the cop's head from the mercenaries, but then someone tosses a grenade. All I can hear is his voice saying, *"and everything seemed to be going so well"*. Then, everything goes dark.

Chapter Forty:

I come awake slowly. It takes a few seconds for me to recall what happened, but the pain in my face hastens my memory. I can't open my left eye, and both of my ears are ringing, but there's a piercing pain in my left ear that makes the ringing seem insignificant. We're in Kelvin's truck, I have no idea what time it is, but it's still dark out and the car seems to be moving really fast.

"You up?" His bass-like voice is gruff and comes from beside me, I think. When I don't reply, he shakes my shoulder and the pain in my face gets worse. "I said, are you up?"

"Yeah," I yelp, sitting up straighter in the seat. We're on an interstate, but I don't know which one or which direction we're going in. There's an off ramp approaching, but I don't recognize the name of the town when we're close enough for me to read it.

My coat is gone. I was wearing a coat when he grabbed me, but I feel a draft against my skin, and I realize that I'm only wearing my blouse, and the buttons are opened so that my bra is exposed. I feel sick. Was he feeling me up while I was unconscious?

"What the fuck is wrong with you? Why were you screaming like that?" He takes his eyes from the road to look at me, and he seems genuinely confused.

Is he crazy? *What the hell am I thinking, of course he's crazy.* "Where are we going?"

He looks over at me again as if I'm the one that's out of my mind. "We're going home."

Okay, I can handle this. He's calm right now, so maybe he can be reasoned with. "Kelvin—"

"You know what I been through for you, sweet?" He shakes his head. "It was hard, but you know, I had to do it. I had to make sure that it would just be us."

What the fuck is he talking about?

"I don't understand."

"It's going to just be us, like you wanted. I thought about it, and I was mad at first, that you would want me to do that for you, but I love you and I knew that if I took care of them, then it would prove it." He smiles at me and it's chilling. "And now we can go home and be together."

I'm going to throw up. What did he do? What the fuck did he do, and why does he think that it's what I wanted?

Before I can ask him what he's talking about, the smile slips off of his face and he glares at me. "Why did you scream like that? Why did you fight me? You made me hit you!"

I see his hands tighten on the steering wheel, and then his right hand is tangled in my hair and he's rag dolling me so hard that I'm sure he's going to snap my neck. "Why did you make me hit you?!"

"I'm sorry! I'm sorry!" My voice is high pitched and terrified. If I didn't hate him before, I do now.

He lets me go and shoves me so hard that my head hits the window and I see fireflies for a moment.

There's nothing sharp in the front seat. Nothing that I can ram into his neck or his ear. I'm certain that he's going to kill me, and I'm just as certain that if that's the case, then he's dying too.

"It's okay," he says after a few minutes of silence. "Everything's okay now. We're going home and we're going to get married. It was hard, getting rid of my son, but it was for the best. We're going to have a son, and it'll be better, because we aren't a mistake. What I had with her, that was a mistake. Everything with her was a mistake, so I took it back."

I can't tell if he's talking to me or to himself, but I wish he'd stop talking. My hands and legs are trembling, and my teeth start to chatter. I think I'm going into shock.

Fuck! I can't go into shock! I can't kill him if I go into shock! What happens if I find a pen or something? I can't jam it into his eye if I'm in shock! *Fucking get it together, Autumn!*

"Are you cold?" He reaches over and turns up the heat.

I clear my throat. "Where's my coat?"

"I threw it out." He says it like it makes perfect sense. "I wanted to see you."

He wanted to see me? *How much of me did he see?*

"What's wrong?"

"I...I have to... use the bathroom," I say.

He looks down at the gas gauge. "I have to get gas anyway. You hungry?"

I shake my head. I couldn't eat anything right now if my life depended on it.

He laughs under his breath. "That's a first."

It gets quiet again for a moment before he says anything else. "Were you living with that guy from the mall? Is that why you moved out of your place? Were you with him?"

I try to make myself smaller somehow. Like I can somehow shrink until I fade away. He grabs my hair again and pulls so hard that I'm surprised that it's still attached to my scalp.

"No! No! I was staying with my aunt!" I cry. I know that if I tell the truth, he'll probably kill me right here.

"Why?!" He yanks my hair again.

"I—I—I got evicted! There were noise complaints because of my cousin, and then your wife called the leasing office and told them that I was making drugs in the unit, so they voided my lease!" I've never prayed so hard for someone to believe a lie.

"Were you still with him after I called you last time?" He pulls harder.

Tears are streaming down my face. "No, no I broke up with him! I broke up with him!"

"You told me you were still with him!" He shakes me.

"I lied!" I scream. "I lied because I was mad that you were with someone else!"

He lets me go and takes a deep breath. "Damn, sweet. I'm sorry about the spot. It was really nice, and I know that you always wanted something like that. Remember that townhouse that I looked at that time that I was talking about buying us a spot? We'll get something like that when we get back home."

It's like dealing with Dr. Jekyll and Mr. Hyde. He's flipping back and forth so fast that I'm sure he's faking his psychosis. This CAN NOT be real.

He looks over at me like he's waiting for me to respond, so I nod and force myself to smile as if I'm looking forward to whatever future he's envisioning. I see another off ramp with a sign for a rest stop, and I'm hoping it's a gas station with a bathroom that has a lock.

I force myself to take his hand and give it a gentle squeeze. "Baby, I really have to pee."

He strokes his thumb over the back of my hand and laughs a little. "We'll go to this rest stop coming up."

The sign says that the rest stop isn't even half a mile away.
A half a mile never

seemed so far or took so long to travel. My whole body trembles in relief when I see that it's a Quick Trip and it's completely lit up. There are two other cars in the parking lot when Kelvin pulls up to a pump.

He grabs my hand before I can get out of the truck. "Wait a minute." Reaching into the backseat, he grabs a hoodie that's lying on the seat and hands it to me. "Put this on and put the hood up. Your face is swollen and your hair's all messed up."

I pull the hoodie on over my head, and the smell of his cologne on the thing makes bile rise in my throat. But I manage a smile so that he'll believe that I appreciate his thoughtfulness. I pull the hood over my head and he hits the locks to open the doors.

He grabs my arm again, and pulling me over to him, he kisses me hard on the mouth. "Hurry up in there. Don't make me come in and get you."

"Okay," I nod quickly and jump out of the truck, hurrying across the parking lot. There's a female clerk behind the register. I look to the window that shows the parking lot and see Kelvin watching me, so I hurry to the bathroom. I go inside of the women's room, hoping that there will be someone in there with a phone. I can ask them to call the police. Or maybe I can just lock myself in and hope that someone will call the cops to get me out.

The room is empty, and I deflate. I turn to lock the door, but the latch is broken. I can't hide in here. I have to go back out. I leave the rest room and stand in the small hallway at the back of the store trying to figure something out. Maybe I can find a piece of paper and pass a note to the clerk?

Before I can head back to the front of the store, the door to the men's room opens. There's an older Hispanic man coming out, and I grab his hand before he can walk past me. "Sir, sir, please, do you have a phone?"

He looks at me like I'm crazy and tries to pull his hand out of mine, but I clutch harder and he panics. "Señora, no hablo inglés!"

"Fuck!" I look behind me and pray that Kelvin isn't coming, but I don't see him. Searching my memory, I try to recall everything that I learned in my high school Spanish class. "Por favor! Por favor, uh...um...yo necesito...ah...yo necesito...llamar a la policia! Necesito el...telefono! Tienes un telefono?"

He's looking at me wide eyed, and then I hear Kelvin's voice and I start to cry.

"Autumn!" His voice is an enraged bark that bounces off of the walls of the store. "Get over here!"

My hands start shaking and I drop my grip on the stranger that I was hoping would be my lifeline. The man looks from Kelvin to me, and then he pushes me inside of the men's room, locks the door, and hands me his phone. I can't see through the tears that are pouring down my face and my hands are shaking so badly that I can't keep my grip on the phone. He takes it back and I experience a moment of crippling panic. What if he thinks that I'm crazy and unlocks the door and lets Kelvin take me?

But then he's dialing 9-1-1 and speaking in rapid fire Spanish. I can only understand a few words: woman, hurt, angry man, scared, help.

I want to tell him that Kelvin has a gun, but my throat won't work, and I don't know how to say gun in Spanish.

Something slams against the door and I scream and run to the corner of the room that holds the sink and crouch beside it.

"OPEN THIS FUCKIN' DOOR! OPEN THIS FUCKIN' DOOR, YOU DIRTY BITCH! YOU THINK I CAN'T GET IN THERE?" Something slams against the door again.

The man that helped me has pushed the heavy trash can across the room and jammed it beneath the doorknob and is yelling into the phone and motioning to the door. I can't move. There's nowhere for me to go anyway. There's a loud bang followed by another and I realize that Kelvin is shooting at the door. I don't know if the clerk is still out there or if she managed to leave, but I'm hoping that she's okay. I'm hoping—praying that we'll all be okay.

He goes back to pounding on the door. He must be out of bullets. The doorknob is shaking. I think he's kicking it. "OPEN THE DOOR!"

I flinch so hard that my elbow slams into the wall at my back. I don't even feel it. The good Samaritan that I dragged into this ID Channel episode is shooting looks from me to the door and back again as he gives, what I assume, is a play-by-play to the 9-1-1 operator.

"Sweet, I promise that I won't hurt you if you just open the door," Kelvin cajoles. When I don't answer, the pounding starts again. "OPEN THIS GOD DAMNED DOOR!"

Just as I'm starting to think that the police are never going to get here, and that Kelvin is going to bust through the door, drag me out of here, and turn me into a lamp shade, I hear two new voices.

"Drop the weapon! I said fucking drop it!"

"Sir, drop the weapon and kick it over here!"

"On the ground, now!"

"Hands, behind your head. Lace your fingers together and don't fucking move!"

"Got him!" There's more talking, but I can't make anything out. After a moment, I hear voices fading.

There's a knock on the door. "Open up! Is everybody okay in there?"

The Samaritan edges cautiously over to the door, shoves the trashcan out of the way, and throws the latch on the deadbolt. It takes a moment for him to get the door open since Kelvin messed up the knob on the other side, but he does, and once it opens a police officer comes in followed by an EMT.

The Samaritan starts gesturing to me and to the door and speaking quickly. The cop looks over at the EMT, but the EMT returns a confused look and shrugs. Apparently, neither of them speaks Spanish. The cop gestures for the man to be quiet and approaches me where I'm still crouched next to the sink.

He holds a hand out in front of him like I'm a wounded animal and kneels down. "Ma'am, are you hurt?"

Am I hurt? I realize that the hoodie is still covering most of my face, and I reach up and pull it off. He just nods and motions to the EMT.

I find my voice as the other man makes his way over to us. "Where am I?"

They both freeze. I get that the question probably seems crazy, but I still need the answer, so I explain. "He...he took me. He took me from the parking lot of the Kroger in Dunwoody. In Georgia. He hit me and knocked me out. I don't know where I am."

The cop clears his throat and shoots a look at the EMT before answering me. "You're in Tennessee, in a town called Smyrna. I need you to come with me, okay?"

I nod, but I don't move. I can't move. My body is literally locked in place. "How far away from Georgia is that?"

"'Bout two hundred miles give or take I believe. Now, ma'am, please come on out from under there so that my friend can have a look at you. Your face looks like it's hurt pretty bad." He reaches a hand out to me again, but I can't make myself take it.

"Señora," my Samaritan moves closer to us and gives me an encouraging smile, "este es un policia. Él te va a ayudar. Estas salvo ahora."

I take a deep breath and allow the officer to help me up. Unfortunately, as soon as I'm vertical the world goes wonky on me, my eyes roll into the back of my head, and I pass out.

Chapter Forty-One:

I wake up as I'm being loaded into the back of an ambulance. There's a paramedic sitting beside me, hanging an I.V. bag on a small pole.

"You back with me?" He shines a light in my eyes. "I'm pretty sure that you have a concussion and I'd be surprised if your cheekbone isn't fractured. How many fingers am I holding up?"

I look at the fingers that he's holding up in front of me. "Three?"

"Good girl. Now I need to know if you're experiencing any pain anywhere other than your face. How does your left ear feel?"

"Hurts," I say. "Feels clogged. Ringing." I feel like I'm going to pass out again.

"Okay, stay with me, honey. Keep your eyes open." His voice is firm, and I want to do what he says, but it's like there are anchors on my eyes.

"What's your name, honey?" He pats me on the hand, and I flinch. "You're okay. You're okay now. Can you tell me your name?"

I lick my lips and try to focus. My name. Okay. "Autumn...my name is Autumn."

He writes something down. "That's my favorite season. How about a last name, Autumn?"

"Blaire," I say. I can barely hear myself.

"Okay, Autumn. We're almost at the hospital, okay? Can you give me a next of kin that they can call for you?" He asks.

"Jonah McInerney." Shit, he's probably losing his mind right now. Does he even know that Kelvin took me?

He's checking machines that I didn't even know that I was connected to. I think that he's just trying to keep me talking, but I hope that they really will call Jonah. I should call my mother, too, but I don't want to worry her when she's so far away. I can hear the EMT talking to me, but he sounds too far away for me to make out anything that he's saying. It feels like I'm under water. My teeth start to chatter and my body begins to shiver. I feel cold, but that makes sense. It's winter time.

"Autumn, Autumn, sweetheart stay with me! Shit, she's going into shock!"

The next time I open my eyes, I'm in a hospital bed. There's a person that I'm assuming is a nurse writing in a chart. She looks to be in her late thirties, with blonde and black hair that's pulled back into a ponytail. She's wearing white uniform bottoms and a pink top with multicolored hearts all over it. My face is throbbing, and my ear feels like someone shoved an ice pick in it. It takes me a few seconds to remember what happened.

Kelvin took me.

"Look who's awake." The nurse's gentle voice brings my eyes over to her. "I'm Tammy, I'm your nurse. You've been through a lot, haven't you?"

"Where am I?" My throat is dry, and my voice is scratchy.

"You're in the emergency room of Smyrna General. You were brought in by the paramedics after the incident at the gas station."

"What time is it?" I don't see a clock anywhere.

"It's about a quarter after two in the morning." She pats my hand. "I'm going to let the doctor know that you're awake and he'll come in to see you. There were also police officers here earlier. They asked me to give them a call when you woke up. They've got some questions for you."

I nod for lack of anything to say. She leaves, and I lay still trying to wrap my mind around everything that happened. This is surreal.

It feels like I'm trapped in a bad dream. I keep expecting to wake up in bed next to Jonah and hit snooze at least three times before I get up and rush off to work. How did any of this happen? Up until last week, I didn't even think that Kelvin was dangerous, and even then, I was convinced that I was being paranoid and ridiculous.

I spent three years with Kelvin, and he was never violent. He was the definition of a gentle giant. The first time that I'd ever even seen him in a fight was when he hit Mark in the mall. And where the hell did he get a gun? He hates guns.

I have so many questions. I remember him saying something about his wife and son. Taking them back or sending them away? I can't remember his exact words. I can't remember a lot of what happened in the truck. I just remember being afraid and telling him that I needed to use the bathroom. Then there was the man in the gas station that didn't speak any English, and saved my life. The ambulance. Someone was talking to me and I asked them to call Jonah.

The curtain at the end of my bed moves and a man walks in wearing green scrubs, a white lab coat, and holding a clip board. "Miss Blaire. Hello, my name is Dr. McEttrick."

"Hello." I have to clear my throat, and when I do the pain in my ear sounds off.

"Is it okay if I have a look at you?" He comes closer as he talks, and I try not to shrink away from him.

"Yeah, that's fine." I can hear the nervousness in my own voice, and it makes me sick.

He watches me for a moment before saying anything. "Would it make you more comfortable if I had one of the nurses come in while I look you over?"

"Yes." The word is out before I fully process the question, but I know that it's right.

He walks back over to the curtain and leans out. "Would you mind coming in here with me, please? Thank you."

He waits there until the nurse that was in here when I woke up walks into my little curtained off area and comes to stand next to the bed. He asks me to lean back, and he prods the side of my face. I wince and jerk away from his hands.

"Okay, that is definitely broken," he says, and it sounds more like he's talking to himself than to me.

After that, he takes a thing with a light on it and looks into my ear. "Alright, you have a ruptured eardrum. Lot of drainage happening. I'm going to give you some antibiotics to keep you from getting an infection while that heals. I'm also going to order a CT scan for your cheekbone and then we'll proceed from there. We're going to give you something for the pain, okay."

"I need to call my boyfriend. I stopped at the store on my way home. He doesn't know where I am," I say without even acknowledging his comment about pain medication.

"Okay, we'll get a phone in here for you so that you can call him," he assures me.

"Thank you." I lean back against the bed. I don't even remember sitting up.

The nurse squeezes my hand and then follows the doctor out. It takes a while for her to come back with a phone. So long that I thought she had forgotten me. It's a cordless, and she presses it into my hand and steps out while I try to figure out what to say to Jonah before I place the call.

I dial the number slowly. Jonah answers on the first ring.

"Hello?" His voice sounds frantic.

"Hi... I'm sorry about the bread." That was so lame, but it's the only thing that I can think to say.

"Oh, thank God." I can hear the relief in his voice. "Baby, where are you? Are you okay?"

"I'm in a town in Tennessee. Smyrna. I'm in the hospital."

"In the hospital," he repeats. "Fuck, baby..."

"I'm sorry." I don't know why those words come out of my mouth, but I feel like I need to apologize to him.

"What? Don't...baby...fuck! I'm on my way, okay? I'll be there as soon as I can. I love you."

"I love you, too," my voice cracks and I start to cry. I've never been a crier. I wasn't raised to cry about the things that happen. Good or bad, you deal with shit and move on, but I feel so...broken.

The nurse comes back in with a man wearing white scrubs. "Sweetheart, we've gotta take you down for your CT Scan now."

I nod and clear my throat. "Jonah, I have to go. They have to take me for a cat scan."

"Cat Scan? Shit, okay. Just...I'm leaving the house now, okay?"

"Okay," I nod.

"I love you so much." I can tell that he doesn't want to hang up.

"I know. I'll see you soon." The words are more for me than for him.

"See you soon," he says.

I hang up before either of us can say anything else and hand the phone back to the nurse. I expect her to leave me alone with the tech, but she doesn't. She helps me into a wheelchair and then accompanies me down to have the Cat Scan. This woman is a fucking angel, and possibly clairvoyant, because it's like she knows that if she leaves me alone, I'm going to lose my shit. And she's right.

Chapter Forty-Two:

My cheekbone is shattered. Not broken, not fractured, shattered. They're going to repair it by making an incision inside of my mouth and using metal plates and pins to put it back together. I can't get the surgery until the swelling in my face goes down some, so it'll happen in about a week at a facility in Georgia. I'm not looking forward to being put to sleep for surgery, but it isn't like I can be awake for it.

I expect the police to come and talk to me, but instead there are federal agents. Kelvin took me from Georgia, and once you drag someone across state lines, your crime becomes a federal offense. I told them everything that I could remember about the things that Kelvin was saying in the car, and they said that they would check on his wife. It's as they're leaving that Jonah walks into my room. I was moved from the ER to a private room after my CT Scan.

I'm sure that it's way past visiting hours, so I don't know how he managed to get in here, but I've never been happier to see anyone in my life. He ignores the agents and walks straight to me. Taking me in, he makes a noise in the back of his throat before touching the side of my face that isn't swollen and bruised and kissing me on my forehead.

The agents come back over and introduce themselves to him. They're very cliché with their dark suits and cropped haircuts. They told me their names, but I can't remember what they were, so I've dubbed them Agent Smith and Agent Smith Jr. in my head. Jonah accepts their handshakes and takes their cards.

"You called the police, Mr. McInerney?" One of them asks him.

Jonah shakes his head. "No actually. The supermarket is really close to our house, and it was takin' Autumn a really long time to get home, so I called her phone and...uh... a cop answered."

He looks down at me and touches my face again. "When he grabbed you, there were a lot of people around and they called the cops, so they were already lookin'. I'm not in your phone as your 'in case of emergency person', so they didn't call me."

Why does that make me sad? Not that they didn't call him, I know why that thought upsets me, but the fact that he doesn't have a special designation in my phone. It hurts that someone looking in my phone would never know that Jonah isn't just another contact.

"I'm sorry."

"Don't do that." His voice is stern, and I must look afraid, because his face falls and he leans down and kisses me. "Fuck, baby, I'm sorry. Just...I don't want you apologizin' to me. Not while you're in a fuckin' hospital bed 'cause I asked you to go to the store for some bread that you don't even like."

I'm in a hospital bed because Kelvin is crazy, and I wanted to believe that he wouldn't really hurt me. I ignored that voice in the back of my head that told me to be careful. I forgot to call the police after we were moved into the condo to tell them about him calling my job because I was too busy being a jealous nutjob over the unfounded thought that my boyfriend might go away on business and hand out free orgasms. None of this is on Jonah.

"Did you call the police in Georgia to tell them that she had been found?" One of the agents, Smith Jr., asks. Isn't that something that police here would have done?

Jonah looks away from me to answer his question. "No. When she called me I just...grabbed some clothes for her and headed out the door."

"You brought me clothes?" For the first time, I notice that he's carrying my overnight bag.

"Yeah, and your hair stuff." He shrugs like it was the most natural thing in the world for him to do.

"We'll contact the police in Georgia to make sure they've been updated, and we'll be in contact with you again soon. Let us know when you're being released from the hospital," the agent instructs.

I nod and watch as they leave.

There's a chair beside the bed and Jonah pulls it closer, sits down, and takes my hand. He kisses my palm and I stroke the side of his face. I finally feel like I really will be okay.

"Well, it's official. I'm never lettin' you out of my sight again," he jokes.

I laugh. I thought it would take longer for me to find anything funny. "Don't worry. I think it'll be a while before I'll go anywhere by myself anyway."

He looks down and runs a hand through his hair. "I was so fuckin' scared that I wasn't ever gonna see you again."

"Me too," I say quietly.

He looks at me and folds his hands together and presses them against his mouth. I can tell that he wants to ask me what happened, but he doesn't want to upset me. Is it weird that I'm more worried about upsetting him? I lived through it and I already had to relay everything to the agents that just left, so I don't have a problem telling Jonah. I want to tell Jonah. I feel like, the more I tell it, the freer I am from it. Like every retelling fixes something inside of me that Kelvin broke.

"He was standing by my car when I came out of the store, but I didn't see him until I was too close to get away, and my shoes weren't exactly made for running," I try to smile. "I turned around and tried to go back into the store, but he caught me and started dragging me to his truck. I screamed like I was trying to crack the sun and a bunch of people came running, but he started waving a gun and they stayed back. I was kicking and screaming, and he couldn't get me into the truck, so he hit me in the face with the gun and knocked me out. When I woke up, we were driving."

Jonah clenches his jaw and his leg starts bouncing. "He hit you in the face with a fuckin' gun?"

"Okay, so my eardrum is ruptured, my cheekbone is shattered, and I have a concussion. But I'm alive so I don't think I should be complaining. He said that he did something to his family." I'm trying not to think of what that means.

"How'd you get away?"

"I told him that I had to go to the bathroom," I say simply.

Jonah looks baffled. "And he believed you?"

"We were talking. He kept yelling at me and he grabbed me by my hair...I told him that I wasn't with you anymore. I think I promised him that I'd stay with him? I can't remember everything. I remember holding his hand. We went to one of those gas station convenience stores and I went inside. There was a man coming out of the bathroom and I asked him if I could use his phone, but he only spoke Spanish, so I asked him in Spanish to call the police." I laugh, and Jonah looks at me like he thinks I may be becoming hysterical. "I'm sorry, it's just...I haven't spoken a word of Spanish in eight years."

Jonah takes my hand again. "Maybe we oughtta send some flowers and a thank you note to your high school Spanish teacher."

I know he's trying to lighten my mood, but he could have a point. That woman was practically a drill sergeant. I remember always feeling like she took everything way too seriously. She would always say, "what's going to happen if you're stuck in a situation where you need help, and no one speaks English?"

How insane is that? I remember thinking, *where the hell am I going to be stuck in this country where no one speaks English?* It seemed absurd. Not so much anymore.

"Kelvin came in looking pissed off and started yelling, and the man could tell that I was afraid, so he pushed me into the men's room and locked the door and he called the police. Things get a little blurry after that. I know that the cops had to have come and arrested him, but I think I passed out before they did. I think I came to in the ambulance, but I'm not sure if that really happened or if I dreamt it." This is a more condensed version than I gave the agents. They kept making me repeat myself and trying to get me to remember specific details.

"They arrested him," Jonah states. He sounds disappointed, and I don't need to guess why.

"Jonah..."

He presses his face into my palm. "I'm sorry, I'm just...he needs to fuckin' die."

"Did you call Mark?" I'm trying to change the subject before Jonah finds whatever police station that they took Kelvin to and gets himself shot.

"Shit, baby I completely forgot. I'm sorry. I was just thinkin' about gettin' here and seein' you." He pulls out his phone. "I can call him now."

"No. I shake my head. We'll call him in a few hours. At like eight so that he doesn't worry when he gets to work and I'm not there." I yawn and enough pain flares in my face to make my eyes water.

Jonah notices and tenses up. "When's the last time they gave you something for the pain?"

"I don't want anything," I say quickly. "The pain meds make me loopy and things get confusing and I can't tell what's real. The whole time I was with him, I felt like I was trapped in a bad dream and everything still seems pretty surreal."

He nods. "You think you can get some sleep?"

"I'm not sure." I really don't want to go to sleep. What if this is all a dream and I'm still in a truck with Kelvin and driving down the highway to hell?

He looks at me for a second before standing up and kicking off his shoes. Putting down the arm rail on the bed, he climbs in beside me, lays on his side, and wraps his arms around me.

Safety. This is what safety feels like.

"I'm going to marry you, you know," he says after kissing me on the head.

"I know," I sigh.

"Try to sleep. I've got you," he strokes my arm. I don't think I'll be able to fall asleep.

Turns out, I'm wrong about that. Not that it matters. The concussion means that Jonah and the nurse keep waking me up every so often and asking me questions.

Chapter Forty-Three:

M ark and Jonah were both there the last time the nurse woke me up, and I only had to stay in the hospital for an additional day before they let me go home.2 Jonah told me that he called my mom while I was asleep and that she would be coming down to Georgia as soon as we were home. My sisters will be coming a few days after. That news simultaneously made me feel better and worse. I love my family, and I wanted them here with me after everything that I'd been through, but they can be overbearing.

I had to call my job and tell them that I wouldn't be in for a few days at least. They already knew. Everything that happened was on the news, and they released my name and description the night that Kelvin snatched me in hopes that someone would spot me and call the police. For some reason, I'm embarrassed by that. I hate that everyone knows what happened. I'm dreading the day when I finally leave the house, and someone recognizes me and brings it up.

Jonah wants me to go to therapy. He thinks that I need to talk to someone about what happened. Normally I would be against that, but I woke up screaming last night and it took me nearly five minutes to realize that I was home and safe before I stopped trembling. After that I turned on every light in the house and triple checked all of the locks. I know that he took me from a parking lot full of people, and so I should feel safe in my house, but I don't. I'm fucking flinching at every creak and squeak and shying away from dark corners.

My mother is getting here today. We were supposed to go to the airport to pick her up, but I freaked out when we got to the parking lot of our building and had to go back inside. I tried, unsuccessfully, to convince Jonah that I was okay after a few minutes, but since he's not an idiot, he didn't believe me.

He called my aunt, and she agreed to pick up my mom from the airport for us and bring her to our condo. They should be here any minute, and I'm not ready. My face is still bruised and swollen, and though my left eye isn't swollen shut any more it's still black and blue, and my ear hurts like a motherfucker. I haven't been able to eat anything, I keep crying, and I'm terrified that Kelvin is somehow going to be released from jail despite what he did to me and this time there won't be someone willing to help me. This time he really will kill me.

I'm sitting in the living room in a pair of yoga pants that have never seen the inside of a yoga studio and one of Jonah's old Georgia Tech sweatshirts. This is as presentable as I could force myself to become. Jonah is cooking manicotti in the hopes that I'll finally eat something. I probably won't. I have no appetite, and every time I try to force myself to eat something, it comes back up.

"Hey."

Jonah is kneeling in front of me. I didn't even hear him come over. Worse, he's directly in front of me and I didn't notice him until he spoke.

"Your aunt just texted me to say that they're here."

"Do we need to go down and let them in?" I could do that. I think.

He shakes his head. "No, baby. I just had to call down to the concierge desk to let them know that they're here for us and the man down there'll let them up."

I knew that. "Right. I'm sorry, I don't know what I was thinking."

"I really need you to stop apologizing to me."

I catch myself before I can apologize again. I don't even know why I keep doing it. I just can't seem to stop. "When are you leaving for Boston?"

He blows out a breath and seems to brace himself. "I'm not."

"Jonah—"

"It's fine. I told the client that I wasn't going to be able to meet in person, so we're going to do a video conference and I already have his site ready to run, I just need a few more things from him," he rubs his hands along the sides of my legs soothingly.

"You don't have to worry about leaving me alone." I don't want his business to suffer because of me. "I'm not going to be alone anyway. My mom is here now."

"I know that. I just..." He sighs and drops his head into my lap and brings his hands to my waist. "I don't think I can be that far away from you right now."

His words are muffled, but I have no problem hearing them. It's the first time that I realize that he's still afraid too. Our fears are different, and yet, they aren't. He's afraid that I'll be taken again, the same way I am. Maybe he's even afraid that this isn't real. That I was never found and that he'll wake up and still be waiting for someone to call him with any news. Leaning down, I kiss him on the back of his neck and just rest there for a moment. It's in moments like this that I'm not afraid. I'm home and safe and grounded in reality.

There's a knock on the door, and I move back to let Jonah get up. He kisses me before getting up from the floor and letting my aunt and my mother into the house. I am disappointed to see that they have brought my uncle and my cousin Daniel with them. I don't appreciate the way my uncle treats Jonah, especially since he found out that we were moving in together. And Daniel will never be one of my favorite people. Still, I try to be polite, especially since they're only here to check on me and make sure that I'm really okay.

My mother hugs Jonah like she's known him forever and hasn't seen him in just as long. It's almost funny. She's so tiny compared to him. My mother is an even five feet and very thin with curly black hair that I've never seen out of a ponytail. She's wearing a pair of fitted jeans, a fleece pullover, and old school Reeboks. A different variation of the same outfit that she's worn all my life, and it fills me with comfort.

"It's so good to finally meet you."

"It's good to meet you too, ma'am. I'm sorry that the circumstances aren't better." He steps back from her and takes her suitcase from my cousin after nodding a hello to everyone else. "I'm just going to run your bag to your room. Please make yourselves at home."

At that, I stand up and make my way over. Once I reach my mother, she grabs me in a hug that makes me feel like she's trying to break my ribs. When she steps back, I see that she's crying.

"No, mommy, don't cry," I hug her again. "I'm okay."

My aunt comes over and gently strokes the uninjured side of my face. Her eyes shimmer with tears as she takes in the bruising to the other side. I watch her muster that same strength that I've seen in my mother my whole life as she takes a deep breath and smiles lovingly at me. "Why don't we all sit down?"

I lead everyone over to the living room as Jonah comes back from putting my mother's bag away. My mom is holding onto my hand like she's not planning on ever letting it go and sits beside me on the couch. My aunt and uncle sit beside her, and Daniel and Jonah each take the two oversized chairs.

"Are y'all thirsty or hungry? Jonah's making manicotti that should be done soon." I'm feeling awkward with everyone staring at me.

"Got any beer? Heineken is preferable," Daniel asks, ignoring the looks that his parents are giving him.

Jonah stands from the other chair and looks around. "Does anyone else want anything? Juice or water?"

My uncle declines, but my aunt asks for a glass of water. As Jonah goes to get the drinks, Daniel stands up and turns in a slow circle, taking in the space.

"This is a really nice place. How many bedrooms are in here?" He looks at me and waits for me to answer.

While Daniel is an ass, and clearly not interested in finding out what happened to me or the person that assaulted me, his question fills me with a sense of relief. I don't want to be the subject of everyone's pitying looks and sympathetic hand pats.

Please understand that it's great to know that all of these people care about me, but their concern makes me feel like a victim, and it's abhorrent to me. Their concern is making me feel weak and needy. And just so we're clear, the waking up screaming thing and the freaking out in a parking garage thing were already doing an adequate job of that.

So, even though my cousin is a self-centered ass clown, I am grateful for that in this moment, and so I happily answer his question. "There are three bedrooms, but we're using one as an office."

"Uh huh. How many baths?"

I almost smile. "Three and a half."

He nods. "Yeah, me and Del definitely need something like this. How much did this run y'all?"

"Daniel!" My aunt sounds scandalized. "You know better than to ask something like that!"

Jonah returns with their drinks and Daniel nods a thank you and sits back down to pout. I guess he doesn't appreciate being chastised in front of everyone.

My uncle gives him a look like he wants to smack him before turning to me. "How are you feeling, baby girl?"

I try for a smile. "My face still hurts, but the doctors said that I should be fine after my surgery and that the swelling should go down in a few days."

They exchange worried looks. I know that my answer isn't what they were looking for, but I'm not about to get into the details of my deteriorating mental state with these people.

My mother rubs a hand along my back. "Jonah said that they arrested Kelvin."

I see Jonah clench his jaw at that statement. He's having a hard time with the fact that Kelvin is still above ground after everything that happened. You see all of these things on the news about unarmed people being shot and killed by police, and then you have a situation where a man kidnaps someone, beats them, and is confronted by the police with a gun in his hand, and he's taken alive. It's a hard pill for him to swallow.

"Yeah. I'm not sure what they're going to do. They've only spoken to me once, I think. The agents that I spoke to said that they were looking at charging him with kidnapping and aggravated assault." I fold my hands into the sleeves of the sweatshirt that I'm wearing to conceal the slight tremble in them.

"That guy is crazy as hell," Daniel says after taking a sip of his beer. "That why you don't deal with the brothers anymore and you're shacking up with a white boy?"

Jonah leans forward in his chair, but before he can say anything, my mother steps in.

"He isn't a *white boy*. He's a grown ass man and his mother is Samoan, and even if she wasn't, what the hell does that have to do with anything? You say it like there's something wrong with Reigney being with a man that loves her, respects her, and works hard just because he's white. For somebody that married and knocked up a stripper that got arrested for credit card fraud, you're being real judgmental about other people's relationships."

Silence descends on the entire room. Daniel is glaring at my mother and I know that there's something just waiting to springboard off his tongue that will have my mother scorching the earth with her response.

Daniel opens his mouth, and I feel my hatred for Kelvin surge inside of me. This moron is only in my house because I started shaking and threw up when we got to the parking garage. I only started shaking and threw up because Kelvin lost his fucking mind and decided to upend my life. If not for that fucking whack job, I wouldn't be suffering Daniel's presence, and neither would Jonah or my mother.

"Let's not act like everybody up in here is perfect. I mean, shit, we wouldn't even be here if *Reigney* hadn't fucked old boy's head up so bad. Trading him in for the white boy just so that you can have a nice ass condo—"

"Really, motherfucker?!" Jonah stands up from his chair, and his stance is full of aggression. Jumping up from the couch, I step in front of him and put my hands on his chest to keep him from going over to Daniel and snatching him out of his seat.

"Babe," I reach up and lay my hand on his cheek.

He looks down at me and I can see him trying to rein himself in. Taking a deep breath, he leans down and kisses me on the forehead before looking back at Daniel. "I think it's time for you to leave."

Aunt Mae stands up and smiles awkwardly. It sucks that she's in the middle of anything. "You're right. We should be going."

She comes around my mother and gives me a hug. "I'm so thankful that you made it back to us. You let me know if you need anything, and we're going to go to court with you when it's time, okay?"

I nod, and then accept a hug from my uncle. He steps back and keeps his hands on my arms. "You are so strong, and you have so many people that love you, you know that? That is a blessing."

My cousin Daniel guzzles the remainder of his beer before putting the bottle on the coffee table and walking over to the front door to wait for his parents. I really don't know why he even came.

Jonah walks them over to the door where my aunt hugs him, and my uncle shakes his hand. Daniel doesn't even look at him before he walks past him and goes out the door. I'm glad that I was able to intercede before Jonah busted his mouth open. Normally, I wouldn't worry about Jonah losing his temper over bullshit, but things are really tense right now and he's wound very tight. That being said, I don't get where the hell Daniel got the idea that I was still in a relationship with Kelvin until recently, and I don't care. It's not like Daniel's opinion matters to me.

Locking the door behind them, Jonah goes into the kitchen where the oven timer has started to beep and takes the pasta out of the oven. It smells great, but even as my hunger rears its head, bile rises in my throat at the thought of eating a single bite.

My mother squeezes my hand. "Now, how are you, really?"

I look at her and I can't lie. "I'm scared. I keep thinking that they're going to let him out and he's going to come for me again, or that I'm only dreaming that I'm safe and I'm going to wake up and still be in that truck with him."

"Have you talked to anybody?"

I sigh and drop my head into my hands. "No. Jonah wants me to, but—"

"Jonah's right. Sometimes, some things, you can't just work out on your own or push through without some help." She rubs my back soothingly.

"I don't want to sit on some couch and have somebody analyze my feelings to label my specific brand of crazy and force pills on me."

"Reigney, you're too smart to be this stupid." She squeezes my shoulder and smiles to take some of the sting out of her words. "That's not what therapy is. And whether you want to go or not, you're going."

"Mommy—"

"Smart people know that they don't know everything. You're very smart, and you're very strong, and I am proud of you every day. Be smart enough and strong enough to get help before you make things worse for yourself by trying to find unhealthy ways to cope with what happened to you." Her voice is earnest, and I know she's speaking from her own experience.

"I just don't understand why he did this—" My voice breaks and I clench my jaw in an attempt to fight back the tears. Unfortunately, the pain that explodes in the left side of my face makes the tears come faster.

My mother snorts. "Because his ass is crazy!"

I actually laugh at that. "Mommy..."

"Reigney, you can't do that. You can't try to figure out why someone else did something so far outside of anything that you could ever understand. You will drive yourself crazy trying to figure out someone else's 'whys'." She rubs my head. "It doesn't matter why he did it, because nothing—no reason could ever justify it."

I know that she's right, but that doesn't stop the questions that are circling in my mind.

"I'm glad you're here."

"So am I," she pulls me into another hug. "Your sisters wanted to come too, but they have to arrange things with their jobs. They're going to come down on Friday and stay for the weekend, but I'm going to stay until after you have your surgery."

I look over at Jonah where he's making a salad to go with the manicotti that he made. I hope he's ready for that. My sisters are a bit much. Don't get me wrong, they are both very sweet and would give you the shirts off their backs if you were cold, but they are also unfiltered at all times. Especially with family, and Jonah will be considered family by them.

"He'll be alright," my mother says as if she's reading my mind.

"I hope so."

"I know so." She stands up and pulls me to my feet. "Now come show me around and then we'll eat and talk some more about you seeing someone so that you can try to start moving on from this, and then I'm going to need to go to the store so that I can buy a few things and make you some banana pudding."

Over the course of the next hour, I show her around, try to eat some of the manicotti that Jonah made, and listen to her tell me about my uncle and my cousin and about how Angel basically hitchhiked back to Jersey after Aubrey threw her out of his dorm room when she wouldn't let him and three of his friends run a train on her. I feel like I should have done more for her. Maybe I could have spent more time with her. Taken her out to places and made her feel more welcome. I'm not sure if that would have been possible, given the fact that I work long hours and that she was determined to spend every spare minute of her time with Aubrey, but I should have tried.

Jonah ends up going to the store for my mother. She doesn't drive, and he doesn't want to take her and leave me alone in the house, so she makes a list and off he goes. When he comes back, she has him come into the kitchen so that she can teach him how to make pudding from scratch. He watches carefully and even takes notes on her banana pudding recipe. Once they finish it, she serves me up a huge helping, and I eat it all and go back for seconds. Jonah watches me eat every bite, and then he smiles at my mother like she performed a miracle and hugs her right off her feet.

Chapter Forty-Four:

I'm sitting in a police station, or maybe it's an FBI station? I don't know. I'm in a building waiting for an FBI agent to come into a room and talk to me. They called this morning and said that they needed to speak to me about Kelvin, and they asked if I could come in. On the positive side of things, I was able to make it through the parking lot of my building without having a panic attack. On the negative side of things, I'm sitting at a table in a white room with no windows, in a federal building waiting for them to tell me something that was so important that I had to come here to hear it.

Jonah and my mother are in the waiting room. He drove, and my mother didn't want to stay behind. Actually, she refused to stay behind. She made me call a therapist yesterday, and I have an appointment set up for this afternoon. I'm not looking forward to it. I don't want to talk about my fears and failings with some stranger while they 'hmmm' and 'haaww' and write down my deepest secrets in a yellow pad. Why can't I just push down what I'm feeling and ignore it until I have a nervous breakdown at some later and more convenient date? I'd be much more comfortable with that.

The door opens and the two agents that talked to me while I was in the hospital walk in. They still look like extras from *The Matrix*.

"Miss Blaire, thank you for coming in to talk to us."

The one that spoke looks a little younger than the other one, though they both have the same short, dark hair, and are wearing similar dark suits with white shirts and black ties. I think the older one is Cohen and the younger one is Chase, but I'm not sure.

"You're welcome." I'm really not sure if they are. Welcome, that is.

"We've spoken to Kelvin Williams, and after some investigating, we've just got a few things to clear up," the older agent says.

"Okay. What do you need to know?"

The older one folds his hands together on top of the table and leans forward a bit. "Were you having an affair with Mr. Williams?"

I am momentarily stunned into silence. *Are they absolutely mental?* "No, I wasn't."

"Mr. Williams—"

"Is out of his fucking mind!" I say, cutting him off and standing from my chair. "I tried to have protection orders taken out against his ass twice! I called the police when he wouldn't stop calling me and they said there was nothing that they could do unless he made a direct threat to me!"

They exchange looks and the younger agent steps toward me with his hand out in a peaceful gesture. "We're just trying to get to the truth of things. Now, Mr. Williams seems to believe that the two of you were involved. You say you tried to have protection orders put out against him?"

I nod quickly and wrap my arms around myself. "Yeah, the first time was after I came home and found him in my house. My cousin was staying with me and she let him in and left him alone. I tried to take out the order then, but I didn't have his address. I got it when he called me the next day, but when the police went to serve him, his wife told them that he had moved back to Philly, so the order was unenforceable. Then after he kept calling me and posting things online, I tried to have him served again, but no one answered their door. I was able to get an order against his wife after she started harassing me and came to my house and vandalized my car."

The older agent looks up from his writing pad. "Had he tried to contact you recently?"

"Yeah, uh—yeah, he called me at my job. He found out where I work from my LinkedIn profile. He started telling me that he wanted us to raise his son together, and I told him that I wasn't interested. I told him that I had moved on with my life and that even if I hadn't, I wouldn't want to deal with his wife and his kid and that drama. He got really angry and started cursing at me and blamed me for him losing his job in Philadelphia."

"Wait a minute. Go back a bit there. You said that he asked you to help him raise his son the last time you spoke?" The older agent jots something down and then looks at me with his eyebrows raised.

"Yeah, and I told him that I wasn't interested in playing mommy to his kid or being with him," I say again.

"Did you lead him to think that you would be interested in him if there wasn't a child coming into the picture or if his wife stopped causing problems?" The agent asks. Sitting back in the chair a bit, he folds his arms like he already knows what I'm going to say, and I feel like snatching that yellow pad off of the table in front of him and seeing if it'll fit in his mouth.

"No! I specifically told him that I didn't love him or want to be with him at all, kid or no kid!" Looking between them, I get a sinking feeling in my stomach. "Wait a minute, why...is his wife alright?"

I know that she isn't by the way they exchange glances before looking back at me.

"Miss Blaire, can you tell us exactly what Mr. Williams said to you while he had you in his truck?" The young agent asks me as he tries to get me to sit back down.

I let myself be led back to my chair and sit when I feel it behind my knees. I close my eyes and try to remember what Kelvin was saying in the truck. My memory of what happened in that truck between us and after at the gas station is really spotty. "Um...I remember him saying something about, uh, taking it back? I think he said that something was a mistake, so he took it back. I can't remember exactly what he said. He was ranting and then he was grabbing me by my hair and yelling at me. My ears were ringing, and I was dizzy..."

"Miss Blaire," the older agent moves his chair closer to mine, "we aren't trying to attack you. You've been through a lot, and we just want to make sure that there's no room for doubt in anyone's mind that you are one of the victims in this, regardless of what Mr. Williams says."

One of the victims. I don't know why, but my mind focuses on that. "Is his wife okay?"

"Mr. Williams murdered his wife and her parents the day before he took you. He says that he did it because you asked him to, and he wanted to prove his love for you."

And just like that, the contents of my stomach are on the floor. He killed them. He killed them because he thought it was what I wanted. Why would he think that? Did I tell him that? I told him that I didn't want to be a mother to his son. I told him that I didn't want to deal with his wife's drama. But I also told him that I didn't love him and that I'd moved on, so why would he do this? Do these people really think that I asked him to do this? One of them hands me a bottled water and I use it to rinse my mouth out. Paper towels are put into my hand and I press them against my face.

The agents tell me that Kelvin will be arraigned on three counts of murder and kidnapping. They tell me that a federal prosecutor will be in contact with me and that they didn't mean to make me feel like they didn't believe me. I'm not so certain.

"Why did you ask me if I was having an affair with him?" I ask.

Maybe I shouldn't be angry about that. Maybe I should understand that they're just trying to get to the bottom of things. But the hell with that. I have been beaten, kidnapped, and terrified to the point that I can't fall asleep in my own home without all of the lights being on. I am not in a space to tolerate being accused of having an on-going extra-marital, sexual relationship with the man that almost killed me.

"Autumn, we have to ask these questions," the younger agent says.

Oh, now I'm "Autumn"? Earlier, when they were accusing me of still fucking a homicidal psycho, I was "Miss Blaire"!

"Do you honestly think that if I were having an affair with Kelvin, that he would have had to chase me across a parking lot, shatter my cheekbone and rupture my eardrum with a gun, and knock me out in order to get me into a car with him?" I look at both of them like they're stupid. "This man was posting on social media about how he wanted to sodomize me and choke me unconscious and burn his name into my thigh, but I couldn't get a protection order against him because he didn't answer the fucking door!"

"You have to understand that we're not here to make things harder on you. We're on your side, but it would be negligent of us not to ask these questions when he makes this kind of claim," the older agent says.

I glare at him and keep my mouth shut. Anything that I say will be confrontational, and no one needs that right now. You may think that I'm being childish for not seeing their side of things. I would wholeheartedly disagree. Maybe I didn't take everything as seriously as I should have where Kelvin was concerned, but I did try to get orders that would keep him away from me, and I did call the police when he kept calling my house, and I did repeatedly tell him that I didn't want to have anything to do with him.

Re-Peated-Ly!

Now they make it seem like I courted this shit? Excuse me for being angry. I have been a crying and petrified mess for over a week, and I'm not about to allow myself to be made out to be the bad guy here. Fuck that with a sick dick!

"I'll escort you out." The younger agent stands up and motions to the door.

I would thank him, but why?

When we reach the waiting room, Jonah stands up, and after taking in the look on my face, frowns at me. "What happened?"

The agent clears his throat and tries to explain, "We just needed some clarification on a few of the statements made my Mr. Williams. He claimed that he and Autumn were still having a relationship when he took her."

"That man damn near killed my baby, and you made her come down here so that you could accuse her of being his girlfriend?!" My mother jumps up and pushes herself in front of the agent.

"Ma'am, I understand that this is upsetting, but we had to ask. Mr. Williams is a very disturbed man, and he is convinced that they were having a relationship."

"So, now what? You satisfied that she wasn't askin' for it?" Jonah bites out.

The agent holds up his hands in supplication. If he thinks this is something, he should be happy that my sisters aren't here.

"That isn't what we meant to imply. No matter what her relationship was with Mr. Williams, Autumn was a victim in this. But in the interest of being thorough, we had to ask."

"He killed his wife and her parents and told the police that he did it because I asked him to." The words are out of my mouth before I had even determined to speak them. It takes an effort not to throw up again.

Jonah pulls me into a hug as my mother covers her mouth with her hand and shakes her head.

"Baby, that's not your fault. Nothing that he did is your fault." Jonah speaks close to my ear and I nod, even though a part of me thinks that it is my fault. A small part, with a small voice, but it's there. It's also the reason that I'm now looking forward to speaking to a therapist.

Chapter Forty-Five:

"How did it go last week?"

I'm sitting in my therapist's office for our weekly session. I've been coming here once a week for five months. Okay, so in the beginning it was more like two and three times a week, but whatever. Her name is Helena Okur, and she is a godsend. Her office is all warm colors and comfortable furniture. There's an oversized winter green chair that I gravitated to the first time I came here, and now I think of it as mine. She doesn't sit behind a desk, but occupies a butter yellow, wing backed chair and sits with her legs crossed. Helena is somewhere in her late forties, loves side-swept ponytails, and wears lipstick that's a shade too light for her cream complexion, but I like her anyway.

"It went alright. I kept the light on in the kitchen all night, and I left the light on in the master bathroom, but it was okay. No panic attacks or freak outs," I tell her.

Jonah went out of the country for business last week and was gone for three days. It was the first time that he's been gone for more than an overnight stay in the past five months. The first month after everything happened, he wouldn't leave me by myself. He did video conferences with the clients that he needed to see, and when that couldn't happen, he made his mother or Mark stay at the condo with me. This time, I was by myself.

"I know that you installed a security system, but have you given any thought to what we talked about?" She thinks that we should get a pet. Sort of a comfort animal for me when Jonah has to go out of town, but since I once killed a cactus, I would not wish myself on any defenseless animal.

"Yes, but Jonah's allergic to cats, and we don't have the time for a dog. We both work long hours and besides that, I think that it's cruel to have a dog if you don't have a yard."

"The sentencing hearing is the day after tomorrow. Are you feeling anxious?" She watches me closely as she waits for me to answer her question.

Kelvin pled guilty to the murders in exchange for the state not pursuing the death penalty, but his lawyer argued that he wasn't mentally fit to know what he was doing at the time. Over the past few months, there have been all kinds of hearings and evaluations. They finally decided that while he is suffering from a mental illness, (first he was diagnosed with schizophrenia, then he was diagnosed with Borderline Personality Disorder, and then there were all kinds of arguments and hearings about whether or not a person could have both) he knew the difference between right and wrong at the time of the crimes, so now we're just waiting to find out how much time he'll get.

"A little," I admit. "I don't want them to say something like, he's only getting ten years, you know? I mean, realistically I know that he isn't just going to get a slap on the wrist. He killed three people."

"And beat and kidnapped someone," she adds. She never lets me avoid acknowledging the fact that Kelvin hurt me too. Helena says that you don't heal by ignoring or avoiding things.

I know that she's right, but it's still hard for me to remember being so helpless. I have a lot of pride and being in a situation where I was terrified and weak...that burns.

The kidnapping and aggravated assault charges are Federal because he crossed state lines with me. He pled not guilty to those charges and his trial date hasn't been set yet.

"Yeah, but at least I'm still here."

"It's not your fault that he killed them, Autumn. You know that," she says kindly.

This is another issue that I've had since the incident. I've gone from blaming myself for the fact that Kelvin killed his family, to feeling guilty over the fact that he didn't kill me too. Helena says that it's a condition called survivor's remorse. It's been the hardest part of this. His wife, Ta'Kendra, was two years younger than me and pregnant with her first child. The baby would have been born perfectly healthy in February. And he killed them, because in his illness, he convinced himself that it was what I wanted and needed for us to be together again. That's not easy to get over.

I read up on BPD after finding out that he'd been diagnosed with it. People with it are often suicidal. This is probably fucked up, but I keep asking myself why he couldn't just kill himself? Why did he have to kill his wife and son? Why did he have to kill her parents? Why did he have to drag me through a personalized *Law & Order: SVU* episode?

There are so many questions and nowhere near enough answers.

"Autumn?" She prompts.

"I know," I rub my forehead, "logically, I know that. It's just...this whole thing is such a mind fuck!"

She nods in understanding. "It is, but like you said, you're still here. You got through what he did to you, and you've gotten better over the past few months. You will continue to get better, and maybe things will never be the way they were before, but you'll find your new normal."

"I'm getting there." I really am, I just wish that this whole thing could be over with.

We talk a bit more about things that are happening in my life. I tell her about an opportunity that I have to advance at work and about Mark accepting a date with Christmas Party Guy. I think he should stop dating people that we work with, but Mark is Mark. Helena thinks that I use Mark's issues to distract myself from my own, which is valid. We talk about how things are going with Jonah, and I can't help but smile. Jonah is...there are no words for everything that Jonah is.

Helena looks at the clock on the wall and sits her notepad aside. "Looks like our time is up for today."

I stand from my chair and smile at her. "Tempus fugit."

"I'll see you next week?" she asks as she escorts me to the door.

"Yup. Same bat time, same bat place."

It's six in the evening. Helena is nice enough to see me after work on Tuesdays, and so I make sure to leave my office by four thirty. When I get in my car, my phone buzzes with a reminder. We're out of milk and bread. The reminder was so that I wouldn't forget to call Jonah and ask him to go to the store. I haven't been to a grocery store by myself in months. I can't avoid it forever, and I can't keep letting what happened with Kelvin affect my life.

Pulling into the parking lot of Kroger, I take a deep breath, turn off the car, grab my purse, and step out into the parking lot. So far so good, and I'm not going to lie, the fact that it's June and still light out is going a long way to helping me maintain my calm. A very long way. I doubt that I would have made this little bravery bread run if the sun had already gone down. Still, I'm going to mentally pat myself on the back for going into the store and only procrastinating a little by going down every aisle before heading to the cash register and checking out. When it's all said and done, I end up with cinnamon swirl bread, Jonah's nasty ass multi-grain bread, a bag of granny smith apples, a bottle of soy sauce, a bag of chocolate chips, a bottle of Tide laundry detergent, a bottle of Febreeze, a pack of thank-you cards, a bird feeder and a box of Milk Bone dog treats, a box of frozen waffles, a bag of frozen peas, a pack of panty liners, a twelve pack of coke, margarita mix, and a gallon of milk. I spend eighty dollars.

The real test comes when I step out of the store and make my way to my car. It's still light out, but there aren't many people in the parking lot. I manage not to run to my car and just dive in. I put my bags in the back seat, put the cart in the corral, climb into my car and hit the door locks, and turn the key in the ignition. I release the breath that I started holding right after I put the cart away and I feel an invisible weight lift off of my shoulders. The laughter that bubbles up from my stomach is freeing.

When I walk into the apartment loaded down with bags, Jonah is in the kitchen and in the process of reaching into the refrigerator. He hurries over to me when he sees everything that I'm carrying and starts taking bags out of my hands.

"You went to the store?"

"We needed milk and bread," I shrug. "There's more in my car, but I ran out of hands."

He looks at me like he thinks I've lost my mind but sits down the bags that he took from me, grabs my keys, and heads to the parking garage to get the rest of the bags. When he steps out of the apartment, I start putting away my purchases. I feel so light that it's a wonder I'm not floating right off the ground. Humming to myself, I cut an opening in the bag of chocolate chips and pour some into my hand. Jonah comes back in while I'm shoving them into my mouth.

"Can I know what's up with the bird feeder and dog treats?" He leans against the kitchen island and pulls me into him.

I swallow my mouth full of chocolate. "They were in the pet food aisle."

"I'm proud of you."

The words are simple, but they cause my heart to swell inside of my chest.

I feel my face heat up at his praise and I can't fight the smile that stretches my mouth.

Jonah studies me for a second before leaning down and kissing me. He groans when I lean into him. Reaching down, he puts his hands under my ass and lifts. I wrap my legs around his waist and hold on. Jonah takes us down the hall to our bedroom and lays me down on the bed. Leaning back, he smiles at me. I love that smile. I love that he looks at me like he never wants to stop looking at me.

He helps me out of my clothes. It takes a while because he keeps stopping to kiss me, but I'm not complaining. He reaches for the button on my slacks and I grab at his shirt, pulling it up until he reaches back, grabs the collar, and pulls it off. Have I ever told you how much I love Jonah's body? He's muscular, but not bulky. Very well defined. Before I moved in with him, I wondered how he was so in shape when he worked at a desk all the time. When he's home, he gets up at five in the morning and hits the fitness room and he boxes at a gym every Wednesday. There's also a treadmill in our bedroom and barbells under our bed. They're the things that were kept in his spare room of his apartment before we moved into the condo. Well, the workout stuff and a twin bed for the ex that wouldn't go away.

At first, I thought it was stupid to have that stuff since there's a state-of-the-art fitness room in our building, but then Kelvin went eighteen levels of batshit crazy, and I was afraid to be alone, so I was thankful that Jonah could work out without leaving the house.

I gasp when I feel his teeth nip my thigh and moan when his tongue soothes the area. Jonah has a truly wicked tongue. I look down at him where he's settled between my legs and he smiles at me before running his tongue up my slit and pulling my clit into his mouth. My eyes fall closed and he reaches up and gives my nipple a sharp pinch, only releasing it when my eyes meet his again. Jonah likes for me to watch him pleasure me. He slides one and then two fingers into me and my eyes water with the effort it takes to keep them open. When his tongue joins his fingers inside of me, I can't stop my eyes from slamming shut as my orgasm overtakes me.

He kisses his way up my body and then rolls me on top of him. I position myself over him and take him into me, and we both groan as he fills me until I feel that mix of pleasure and pain. Placing his hands on my waist, he guides me up and down along his thick length. Leaning forward, I brace my hands on his chest and pick up the pace. I watch his face as I move on him and I see his muscles start to tense. I want to see Jonah fall apart beneath me, but he cheats. Pressing his thumb to my clit, he rubs quick circles against that traitorous nub and my body succumbs to that blissful euphoria again. Reaching up, he grabs the back of my neck and pulls me down into him. His tongue slides into my mouth as he thrusts up into me and finds his own release.

I lay, gasping on top of him in the aftermath of our lovemaking and replay my day. I woke up late and rushed through my shower. When I lived alone, I would try to shower at night so that it would be one less thing for me to do in the morning. I still shower at night, but since Jonah and I typically have sex right after, I shower again in the morning. After throwing on a pair of tan slacks and a sleeveless pink blouse, I grabbed my things for work, and Jonah handed me a cup of coffee in a travel mug when I kissed him on my way out the door. I went to Panera Bread with Mark for lunch and we talked about his upcoming date with CPG and he told me that he was coming to Kelvin's sentencing hearing with me. I left work, had my session with Helena, and conquered the grocery store. Then I came home to this beautiful man that brought in the completely nonsensical things that I had purchased without pushing me to explain any of them and made love to me like he hadn't seen me in months.

"Hey," Jonah kisses my forehead and strokes his hand along my back, "what are you thinking about?"

I kiss his chest and squeeze him. "How much I love you."

"Oh yeah?" He angles his head so that he can see my face.

"Yeah." I look up at him and trace my fingers along his bottom lip.

Jonah pulls my fingers into his mouth and nibbles on them. "Do you love me enough to take off on a long weekend and go to San Francisco with me?"

I laugh, "Sure. What's in San Francisco?"

"East Brother Lighthouse. It's a bed and breakfast that's set up in a lighthouse, and I wanna take you there."

"Okay. I love you enough to do that." I smile at him. "I love you enough to do almost anything."

He tilts his head and grins at me. "Really?"

I nod. "Mm hmm."

Reaching over to the nightstand, he opens it and takes out a small black box and hands it to me. Opening it, I see a beautiful, princess cut diamond ring, surrounded by garnets, and set in a white gold band.

"Jonah..." that's the only word in my vocabulary right now, not that it matters since there's a lump in my throat that's the size of a Buick, so I wouldn't be able to say anything anyway.

"Do you love me enough to wear this? Do you love me enough to marry me?" he asks quietly.

I can't talk, so I start nodding. I can't stop either. I think I broke a spring in my neck or something. Jonah slides the ring onto my finger and I finally stop nodding when he grabs my face and kisses me.

"What if we eloped and made San Francisco our honeymoon?" he asks me.

"Mark's been planning our wedding for like eight months, so he's going to be really disappointed, but I love that idea. We can have a ceremony in a church and a reception next year." I'm going to marry him. I need to do it quick before he remembers that I can't cook, and that I steal the covers, and that I don't believe in running if nothing is chasing me so I'll probably never go to the gym with him, and that I once killed a cactus so I'll probably be a terrible mother, and that I just bought a bird feeder and no bird food, and dog treats for a dog that we don't have.

Jonah kisses me again and sighs into my mouth. I can feel his relief, but really, there was never a chance that I wouldn't say yes. A year ago, I saw him in an airport, and he was the most beautiful thing I had ever seen (rudeness aside). There have been hiccups along the way. Arguments, and exes, and cold feet, and a kidnapping, and reluctance to acknowledge what has always been true. I fell, I have fallen, and every day I am falling into this life, into this love, into Jonah.

THE END.

About the Author

Nikki Norman is a lifelong lover of books and reading. She currently resides in Georgia with her husband, three children, and ridiculously spoiled beagle/lab mix.

Read more at https://www.amazon.com/author/nikki_norman.